A Kiss

is still

A Kiss

Edited by Virginia Smith

Next Step Books
P.O. Box 70271
West Valley City, UT 84170

This is a work of fiction. All of the characters, organizations, and events portrayed in the stories are either products of the authors' imaginations or are used fictitiously.

A Kiss is Still a Kiss

Copyright © 2015 by Virginia Smith

Published by Next Step Books, P.O. Box 70271, West Valley City, Utah 84170

Scripture quotations are taken from the Holy Bible, New Living Translation, copyright ©1996, 2004, 2007, 2013 by Tyndale House Foundation. Used by permission of Tyndale House Publishers, Inc., Carol Stream, Illinois 60188. All rights reserved.

Cover design by Kim Van Meter

Library of Congress Control Number: 201590843

ISBN-13: 978-1-937671-25-9
ISBN-10: 1937671259

Critical Acclaim for *A Kiss is Still a Kiss*

Popular romance author Smith collects 22 short stories that, like a kiss, may be short and sweet or long and lingering, but nearly all are memorable. "Let's Make a Deal" is a diverting story by newcomer Crystal Barnes that conjures a headstrong young woman of the Old West. She agrees to an arranged marriage but stands her ground when it comes to consummating the union—until she actually falls in love. In "Looking for Love—and the Scissors" by romance veteran Gail Gaymer Martin, a mundane search for scissors leads to renewed love in a marriage gone sour. Kylara Silvers's "Remember This" satisfies in fewer than three pages. Scott R. Parkin drops a science fiction element into "Within Limits," and John H. Dromey's "Choosing Sides" features Civil War reenactors. This sweet assortment of smooching stories has something for just about everyone.

-*Publisher's Weekly*, Nov 2015

Contents

Introduction

This book began in a hotel room at a fiction convention in Washington D.C. After a satisfyingly full day of panel discussions, author readings, and delightful chats with book lovers over coffee in the lobby, my roommate and I settled in for the night.

"I'd like to start reading the novel I bought," she said sleepily as she turned off the lamp between our beds, "but I know I'll get involved in the story and then I'll be up all night."

"I know what you mean." I snuggled between clean-smelling sheets. "I wish I had something short to read."

"That's what you should do," she said through a yawn. "Write a book of short stories."

The more I considered the idea, the more appealing it became. Not *writing* all the stories, but reading them.

What a terrific nightstand addition—a collection of short fiction by a variety of authors, each with their own ideas and unique styles of storytelling. I've always enjoyed reading anthologies for exactly that reason, and have discovered some of my favorite authors through their contributions to those collections.

Personally, I enjoy a wide range of fiction—romance, mystery, science fiction, humor. For me the ideal short story collection should include offerings from multiple genres. But every book must have a theme, and how do you fit a contemporary romance and a fantasy story together? They'd need to share something in common.

I decided that each tale must include an element of that most basic of human needs—love. And is there any greater expression of love than a kiss? If love is the universal language, then a kiss is the alphabet by which we communicate that most basic of emotions.

Once the theme was finalized, an invitation went out to writers—send us stories of any style, any genre, but make sure they are short and include a romantic kiss. Next Step Books recruited a panel of editors to read through the submissions and narrow down the selection to a manageable number. Then we discussed each one, often agonizing over the decision to eliminate excellent stories because there simply wasn't enough page space to include them all. The resulting collection, which you hold in your hands, contains the variety we hoped for.

A Kiss is Still a Kiss offers a buffet of stories to tempt the appetites of fiction readers. Twenty authors, from beloved, familiar names to fresh new voices, present tales of love in a variety of genres. Experience the rush of first love, the excitement of unanticipated romance, and the joy of fading love restored. Within these pages you'll relish a surprising and satisfying collection of styles: sweet contemporary, romantic historical, delightful regency, laugh-out-loud humor, gripping suspense, and even a few whimsical tales of fantasy and science fiction. Why? Because regardless of genre...*A Kiss is Still a Kiss.*

Virginia Smith
Editor, Author, Reader,
and lover of stories in any length

My definition of a good story in any genre is one with a vivid setting, a compelling plot, and characters who resonate with readers so strongly we feel as though we're living the story with them. It takes a skillful writer to accomplish all three. To kick off our romance collection, I've selected a tale that exemplifies those skills. I'm a long-time admirer of Deborah Raney's books, and when you've read, "Going Once, Going Twice," you'll understand why. – VS

Going Once, Going Twice

Deborah Raney

April

The Kansas sky matched Piper Kendall's mood. Gray and stormy. For the third time in as many minutes, she checked the time on her phone. The auction wasn't set to start for another hour, but the hay wagons were circled around the driveway, piled haphazardly with all her grandfather's earthly belongings.

Already the farmyard was swarming with greedy auction-goers. A rainbow of bright umbrellas dotted the property, and underneath them, shoppers pawed at Grampa's things as if groping for the ripest peaches in the produce bin.

Piper sighed. She wasn't being fair. She understood that excitement. She and Grampa had sought out their own bargains over the years. Some of their treasures were back on these very wagons today. They'd loved getting up with the sun and setting out in Grampa's old blue Ford pickup, auction bill in hand. Grampa always wanted to be first in line to get their bidder numbers and scout out the goods.

In her excitement to get a bargain, it never once occurred to her how sad this day might be for the family of the sellers. Now she *was* the family. And except for the day they'd had to move Grampa into the nursing home, she couldn't remember being sadder.

Feeling like a traitor, she made her way to the clerk's trailer and got her number. The only thing that would make her happy again was if she could buy back everything Grampa had been forced to give up. And with only seven-hundred-twenty-seven dollars to her name—and her rent due next Friday—that wasn't going to happen. Besides, every penny this auction generated was needed to pay the astronomical cost of the nursing home. Almost two hundred dollars a *day*, according to Uncle Martin. It was highway robbery.

If she didn't need her job to survive, she'd take care of Grampa herself. Never mind at ninety-two he could never have made it up the twenty-eight steps to her third-floor apartment. Or that her degree in library science hadn't taught her the first thing about nursing care. The best she could do was to go visit Grampa each evening after she got off work.

Sometimes he knew her. Sometimes he thought she was his daughter—Piper's mother—and called her Grace. Either way, it broke her heart. Mom had been gone for a dozen years now. As many years as Piper had known her. Piper's dad had left when she was an infant, and then cancer snuffed out Grace Kendall's life when Piper was only twelve.

She'd moved in with Grampa the day of the funeral, and this farm had been home until she left for college in Missouri. Uncle Martin had warned her the next Thanksgiving that Grampa was failing. She hadn't believed him. Until she came home for Christmas, and it was clear something was wrong. Something serious.

And finally, when Grampa drove the pickup into the ditch and couldn't tell the sheriff where he lived, they could no longer ignore the truth. Piper only hoped the sale of the farm would raise enough to keep Grampa in the home as long as—

She blew out a sigh. She couldn't go there. Life without her grandfather was something she didn't want to imagine. She tucked her bidder number in her pocket and headed over to the machine shed. Might as well get this day over with.

An hour later, minivans and pickup trucks towing stock trailers were lined up for half a mile on either side of the country road. The place looked more like the Kansas State Fairgrounds than Grampa's farmyard.

The enticing aroma of cabbage bierocks and peach cobbler wafted from the open garage where the 4-H Club was serving lunch and homemade pies. But Piper was too nervous to be hungry. In her twenty-four years, this was her first auction without her grandfather, and she wasn't sure she could keep up with the bids without him at her back, nudging her elbow when she needed to hold her number high, tugging at her sleeve when she should wait out the bid.

Still, she would be crushed if she had to drive away from the farm without the clock.

She glanced through the open doors and saw the shapely grandfather clock standing proud against the corrugated steel on the back wall of the shed. Fearing rain, they'd dragged most of the furniture inside. Grampa's own grandparents had brought the clock over from England more than a hundred years ago. He would have pitched a fit now, seeing the stately clock sitting in the damp shed, unprotected from rain and dirt, and now being stroked by the grimy hands of strangers. Piper even saw one guy kick the bottom of the pedestal, as if the precious heirloom were a used car!

Grampa had once hinted that the clock would be hers someday. But now that he didn't remember things like that, she hadn't felt right saying anything to Uncle Martin, especially when Grampa needed the money so badly.

The portly auctioneer tried to get things moving, but bidding was as lethargic—and as low—as the clouds hanging overhead. If things were going to sell this slowly, maybe she had a prayer of getting the clock after all.

The auctioneer stopped mid chant and waited for the crowd to quiet. "Folks, if you knew Guy Kendall, you'd understand the value of these goods. Mr. Kendall never met a stranger, and most likely if he did meet one, it was a fella in need, and Guy Kendall found a way to meet that need. Today we have a chance to turn the tables and help out a man who had as good a heart as anyone I've ever known."

Piper teared up at the tribute, even as she wanted to correct the man for referring to Grampa in the past tense. She dried her tears, though, as things finally got rolling. And for a while she forgot to be nervous. But as they got closer and closer to selling the clock, adrenaline began to pulse through her veins.

Uncle Martin milled through the crowd, talking to those he knew, some of them friends of Grampa's she recognized from the coffee shop in town. But most of the faces in the crowd were strangers to her. As the dressers and tables from the farmhouse were sold one by one, she slipped closer to the front of the throng, edging as near to the auction block as she could get without being rude. But she didn't dare risk not being seen when bidding for the clock began.

She positioned herself in front of the platform, and the auctioneer caught her eye and winked. But as item after item sold, her hopes of getting the clock plummeted. An old oak nightstand went for over two hundred dollars, and a dressing table for four hundred. Grampa had some nice furniture—antiques he'd taken good care of. She should have been thrilled to see Grampa's stuff selling so well. He needed the money. But if run-of-the-mill furniture was going this high, what might her clock go for?

She corrected her thoughts. It wasn't *her* clock. She had no claim to it. But...tell that to her heart.

"What am I bid for this grandfather clock?"

The auctioneer's assistant motioned for his ear, and a brief whispered conversation flew between them.

The auctioneer straightened and adjusted his microphone. "Folks, I'm told this old clock is in perfect working order, circa 1910 or thereabouts. Who'll start the bid at five hundred dollars?"

Piper's heart sank. They were *starting* the bid way over her head?

But the crowd stayed silent and the auctioneer conceded. "All right then... Let everybody in," he sing-songed. "Who'll give a hundred? A hundred dollars.

9

Folks, this is a fine clock in fine condition."

Immediately the auctioneer's assistant pointed somewhere behind Piper and the auctioneer launched into his rhythmic chant. "I'm bid a hundred, now who'll give me two? Who'll give me two now, who'll give me two?"

The ring man barked a sharp "hup!" indicating they had a bid, and the auctioneer pointed again. "Two, now three, now who'll gimme three?"

Another bark from the man on the ground.

"Three now four, now who'll give me four?"

Her heart plummeted again. She hadn't even gotten her hand up and the bidding was a mile a minute and getting away from her fast. Grampa had taught her to bid dispassionately. "Don't show your hand too quickly, Pip," he'd say. He'd nicknamed her Pip—like in *Great Expectations*—and it stuck. "Be patient. Wait 'em out. Don't let 'em know how bad you want it."

But if she didn't get her hand up, she was going to be out of the running before she could even get in the game. In one smooth motion, she took her number from her breast pocket and raised it to her shoulder.

The bid-taker pointed at her and gave his signature bark.

The auctioneer acknowledged her with a bob of his head. "I have four, now who'll gimme five...four now five... Who'll gimme five?"

On an ordinary Saturday with Grampa, Piper would have loved the energy in the air, the musical cadence of the auctioneer's riff. But today there was too much at stake. And the bid was briskly approaching her limit. Two or three early bidders dropped out at four twenty-five and her hopes rose again.

"Four-fifty!" someone behind her yelled.

"Four-seventy-five," she squeaked.

"I've got four seventy-five. Who'll give me five?"

She raised her hand higher, not caring now who saw how much she wanted that clock. Maybe whoever was bidding against her would recognize she was Guy's granddaughter and have mercy on her.

"Five and a quarter?"

"Hup!"

"Five and a quarter, now five-fifty? Five-fifty?"

She raised her number again. At least the pace had slowed a little.

"Hup!"

She turned to look behind her to see who was bidding against her. A man about her age caught her eye from beneath the rim of a white Stetson. His smooth-shaven face was burnished to copper— probably a fake tan. But his eyes were kind—and blue as the chicory that grew in the ditches.

Still, she frowned and narrowed her gaze at him, turning back to raise her card again. Five hundred-seventy-five dollars.

The assistant *hupped* at the cowboy behind her, then *hupped* again to her left. *Oh no!* Had someone else gotten in on the bidding?

Her heart sank. She wasn't going to get it. She just knew it.

"Six hundred, I've got six, who'll give me six-fifty?"

"Hup!"

"Six-fifty— Hup! Six seventy-five, will ya gimme seven?" The auctioneer looked down at her with a question in his eyes. He was pulling for her, but he couldn't favor her either.

Still, she wasn't giving up yet. She held her number high, earning a smile from the auctioneer.

"This little lady has the bid at seven. Seven, now seven-fifty—

"Hup!"

"Seven-fifty, now eight, now who'll give eight, give

eight, give eight," he sing-songed. "Do I hear eight?"

"Hup!"

Piper sucked in a ragged breath and let her number slip from her hand.

She was done. It was over.

Squeezing back tears, she put her head down and slinked into the crowd. She inched her way between overalled farmers until she was behind the two remaining bidders.

The other man looked like a city boy in his trendy button-down shirt and designer sunglasses. Probably an antique dealer from Kansas City. She didn't care. She wanted to give them both a swift kick in the shins. Couldn't they see how badly she wanted that clock? Couldn't they guess it meant something special to her?

By now the bid was over a thousand dollars and the auctioneer was raising it in increments of fifty dollars. The longer the bidding went on, the more Piper started to suspect both bidders were just stubbornly trying to outdo each other.

Finally, the bids stopped, City Boy conceding to Cowboy.

"All in, all done..." The auctioneer paused dramatically, giving City Boy one last chance to show his number.

But the man shook his head.

"Sold!" The gavel came down. "To the gentleman in the cowboy hat."

A wave of chuckles went through the crowd, since fully two-thirds of the men there sported cowboy hats. The auctioneer thanked the bidders for livening up the sale, and Piper watched as the cowboy wove through the crowd—more like swaggered—toward the clerk's trailer.

She should have been grateful for the sale. She still had money to pay her rent, and the sum the clock had brought—over two thousand dollars—would keep

Grampa in his private room for another ten days. Grampa would have been triumphant the clock brought such a good price. He wouldn't have been so fond of the presence of the antique dealers, even though they'd kept the bidding lively. But Grampa was always for the little guy, and he wouldn't have liked seeing so many of his farmer friends—or *her*—shut out of the sale.

She'd intended to stay until the end of the sale, but she didn't have the heart now. There was nothing else she wanted, nothing she could afford anyway. She tossed her bidder number into a nearby trash can and headed for her car. She would come back later and help Uncle Martin clean up, but right now all she wanted was to drive out to her thinking spot and have a good cry. In fact, she just might get a head start on that cry this minute.

She quickened her steps as the tears came, fishing in her bulky bag for her car keys.

"Hey, Miss. Wait a minute... Miss?"

She took a swipe at her damp cheeks with the sleeve of her jacket before turning to see who was calling.

Figured. The cowboy. He had a lot of nerve... She took off at a trot. She had nothing to say to him.

"Miss? Hold up! You in the blue jacket..." She heard his boots on the gravel lane behind her. They sounded determined.

Stopping in her tracks and whirling to face him, she almost crashed into him. "What do you want?"

"I just wanted to say... I hope there are no hard feelings..." He hooked a thumb over his shoulder in the direction of the auctioneer's stand. "About the clock. Seemed like you wanted it pretty bad."

"Seemed like you wanted it more." She firmed her lips into a hard line and started to turn back toward the car.

"Wait! Please..."

13

She felt his hand on her arm and turned again, fury taking hold of her.

He must have sensed it, for he dropped his hand to his side. "I...I wondered if you'd like to buy the clock from me?"

Was he a total nutjob? "If I had the money to buy it, I would have bought it."

"No, I mean... I could let you make payments on it. I'd sell it to you for the price I paid."

"Sorry. That's out of the question."

"Then, how about if I drop the price to two thousand even? I wouldn't even charge you interest. You could pay me twenty dollars a month. Or whatever you could afford."

She quirked an eyebrow at him. He was talking about an eight-year commitment. "You're not real good at math, are you?"

That earned her a smile. He had a nice smile. Charmingly crooked, but showing straight white teeth and cutting a dimple in his right cheek. She decided the tan was definitely real.

He pawed at the gravel with the toe of his boot, reminding her of an impatient stallion. "I could see how much you wanted it," he said again. "I want to make it up to you. I feel bad."

"So you're going to take a two-hundred-fifty-dollar loss for a complete stranger?" That did it. He was certifiable.

Another smile. This one more subdued than before. "You're not *completely* a stranger to me, you know..."

"What?" She instinctively pulled her purse closer to her body and checked around her for an escape route.

"You're Weldon's granddaughter."

"You know my grandfather?"

A curt nod of his chin. "I do."

Most people called Grampa "Guy," but his given

name was Weldon. Still, it had said "Guy" on the sale bill for the auction, so maybe this guy really did know him.

"I'm Finn. Finn Neilson." He put out a hand.

She reluctantly shook it. His grip was firm. His hands were warm and—Grampa would have said—just rough enough to prove this guy was no stranger to hard work. But her grandfather had never mentioned any Finn. She would have remembered.

"How do you know my grandfather?"

The cowboy—Finn—screwed up one side of his face as if trying to come up with the answer to a difficult question. "It's kind of a long story. Maybe I could tell you over lunch."

"Um... No thanks. I was actually getting ready to go visit Grampa. He's in the nursing home now. But then, you probably know that."

He looked at the ground again. "I didn't know, but I'm not surprised. I was pretty sure he wouldn't sell the farm if he didn't have to."

What was this Finn Neilson's connection to her grandfather?

"Is he... How's he doing?" Those kind blue eyes looked straight into her heart.

"How long has it been since you last saw him?"

"A few years. I sort of lost touch."

"He has dementia. Pretty bad. Some days he knows me, others not so much."

"Do you think I could go with you? To see him?" He held up a hand, apparently sensing the reluctance that caused her to tense. "I'd follow you in my truck. I'm not asking to ride with you or anything. I'd like to tell him thank-you."

"Thank you?"

"I owe your grandfather my li— Well, maybe not my life, but everything that's good about it."

15

Now he really had her curious. Probably exactly his intention. He seemed harmless enough, but then so had Ted Bundy. "What if Grampa doesn't remember you?"

"I could still say thank you. It would mean a lot to me. You could introduce me."

"If he remembers *me*." She looked up at him from beneath half-mast eyelids. "Shall I also tell him you bought his grandfather clock?"

A flash of lightning made them both look up at the sky, and Piper counted off the seconds before thunder rumbled in the distance.

"I'm serious about selling the clock back to you," he said with a sense of urgency, as if he was afraid she'd make a run for it. "I'd take whatever you could afford."

"Listen...Finn Neilson. I'm a librarian, not a rancher. I'd be writing you a check every month for the rest of my life if I paid you what I could afford. That's not going to happ—"

"Make a down payment." Again he held up a hand, compelling her to listen. "However much you were going to bid today. You dropped out around seven hundred, right? Pay that now, and owe me the rest."

She grimaced sheepishly. "I was bidding my rent money. It's probably a blessing I didn't win." That was a lie. Grief over losing the grandfather clock washed over her again at the very thought, and she knew if she didn't take this man up on his—admittedly very generous—offer, she would regret it deeply a year from now.

She sighed. Grampa had taught her to make decisions that way. *When it comes to money*, he'd always said, *ask yourself if you'll regret spending it—or not spending it—a year from now. Or five. Act on that answer.*

"Okay," she said, knowing she was making a rash decision. "Here's the deal. You follow me to Grampa's. I need some time to think."

"Okay..."

"What? Now you want to back out?"

"No." That grin again. And it struck her that it was strangely familiar. "I'm just surprised you went for it."

That grin was going to be her undoing.

"Don't push your luck, buddy."

"Where are you parked?"

She pointed to the line of cars nosed in against the hedge row.

"I'm over here. I'll follow you."

"Don't lose me," she yelled over one shoulder. "I've been told I have a heavy foot."

He laughed, but at that moment the sky opened up, drenching them both.

Fishing her car keys out of her bag she took off at a trot. "I'll see you there."

Piper didn't know where Finn Neilson had been parked, but she wasn't surprised when, five miles from town, she spotted him behind her in a silver Dodge Ram. She kept an eye on her rearview mirror all the way to the city limits...half the time watching the pickup behind her, and half the time trying to fix her bedraggled hair and makeup before she got to Grampa's.

She took the lone empty parking spot in front of the nursing home, but by the time she got out of her car, Finn was somehow waiting for her at the front door. "Boy, you weren't kidding about the lead foot!"

She narrowed her eyes at him, but couldn't think of a comeback. So she ignored him, murmuring hello to the nurses chatting at the front desk, pretending she didn't see their curious stares directed at Finn.

He gave them that grin with a tip of his hat. Then,

carrying the hat in one hand, he waited for her to lead the way. She curbed a smile at the way his hair stood up in spikes without the Stetson to contain it.

He followed two steps behind her through the maze of hallways to Grampa's room.

She heard the TV blaring before she got to his room. She rapped twice on the door and pushed it open without waiting for a reply. Grampa turned from the TV, his eyes lighting up beneath bushy white eyebrows. "Well, there she is! It's about time."

She hadn't told him she was coming. Turning behind her to motion for Finn, she tripped on something—the edge of the hallway carpet?—and stumbled forward, arms flailing. She managed to stay upright, but Finn's discreet snickering behind her told her he'd seen all.

"Way to go, Grace," Grampa deadpanned from his recliner in the corner.

Oh, no. He was having one of his bad days. When he thought she was her mother.

Still, Grampa's eyes were clear and bright—and twinkling. "Have a nice trip?"

She laughed and felt herself blush. "Not that nice."

Grampa ignored her, looking past her to the doorway. "Who'd you bring with you?"

"Oh." She stepped aside to reveal Finn. "Grampa this is Finn—"

"I know who it is," Grampa said, struggling to get up. He looked happier than he ever looked to see her visit.

She hurried to his chair and locked her arm in the crook of his elbow, helping him rise. Pushing his walker in front of him, Grampa hustled to where Finn stood and reached out a hand. "It's been a long time, young man."

"Yes, sir. It has." Finn looked from Grampa to Piper

18

and back. "How are you?"

"How would you be if they moved you off your place and dumped you in a hole like this?"

Finn shrugged but kept silent.

"You know this girl?" Grampa tilted his head toward Piper.

"We just met, sir. Just a few minutes ago at your—"

"Finn is—" Piper groped for something to deflect Finn's words. She and Uncle Martin had decided it would be best not to tell Grampa the sale was going on today. They'd wait for when he was having a more lucid day, when it was all over. No need upsetting him. But she should have warned Finn. "Finn says he knows you, Grampa." She looked up at him. "How'd you two meet?"

"Well, o' course I know him." He narrowed his eyes and studied Finn. "You didn't tell her?"

"Tell her what, sir?"

"How we met, of course."

"No sir. Not yet."

Piper looked between the two of them. Grampa seemed as clear-headed as he had in many months, and she was curious about the secret these two seemed to be hinting at.

She opened her mouth to ask them what was going on, but Finn stepped between her and her grandfather, interrupting. "Sir, I'm trying to make a business deal with your granddaughter, but she doesn't seem to think she can trust me. I was hoping you might convince her."

Grampa frowned at her. "That true?"

She hesitated for a moment. "Yes, sir."

"You could sooner trust this young fella than you could trust me."

That was a lot.

"Okaaay...." She studied her grandfather. She could usually tell when he was having a confused day, but today it could have gone either way. She did not want to tell Grampa what Finn was offering to do. For starters, she didn't want to reveal that the sale had been today. For finishers, Grampa would no doubt offer to buy the clock from Finn. But he didn't have the capacity to understand that it was taking every penny they could raise from selling the farm and the property to keep him here at the home. She made a rash decision. "I'll trust him, Grampa. I know you wouldn't steer me wrong."

Even though it was kind of cute, she didn't like the smug look Finn flashed her.

Grampa lifted his walker and pivoted back toward his chair, looking wobblier than he had when she was here yesterday. She helped him sit down.

But he waved her away. "You two go on now and get your business taken care of. Make her fix you dinner, Finn. She's a mighty good cook."

"Yes, sir." He shot her a sheepish look.

"I—" Piper grasped for words to deflect Grampa's awkward order.

Finn seemed unfazed. "We'll get right on that. Good to see you again, sir. And...thank you."

"Not sure what I did, but you're welcome," Grampa said.

"Yes sir." Finn gave a little salute.

And again, Piper had that feeling of *deja vu*. Why did he seem so familiar?

An expression she couldn't read passed between the men. She didn't know what was going on between those two, but she intended to find out. She bent to kiss Grampa's crepey cheek and straighten the collar of his shirt.

"You go on now," he said. "Everything will be okay. You'll see."

"Thanks, Grampa." If she didn't know better, she'd almost think he knew exactly what was going on.

Hesitating, she finally turned to see that Finn had

left. She hurried out of the room in time to see him disappear around the corner. She caught up with him in the parking lot where the sun was attempting to peek through the clouds.

"What exactly is going on? How do you know my grandfather?"

"I don't think he'd like it if I told you. You might not either."

"What?" Was Finn Neilson bluffing? Was this some huge scam he was trying to pull off? "Why not?"

He chewed his lower lip, obviously trying to decide whether he should say anything or not.

Piper propped her hands on her hips. "If you won't tell me, I'm leaving." She wondered if he caught the absurdity of her "threat." After all, he was the one offering to help her get Grampa's grandfather clock back.

"On one condition..."

"I'm waiting."

"We talk over lunch. I'm in acute danger of starving to death."

She glanced at her phone. "It's not even noon."

"I usually eat at eleven."

She rolled her eyes. "You poor baby. Okay, fine. The cafe is open." She'd be safe there.

"We'll iron out the terms of the deal, just not on an empty stomach."

May

"How about we drive through the Dairy Barn and take our lunch to the park?"

Piper froze. They'd agreed on the going to the café like they had last month. She wasn't prepared for a change of plans. But it *was* a beautiful day and the park *was* across the street from the sheriff's office. "Okay.

21

But we sit where people can see us."

He laughed. "I'll be a perfect gentleman." He put his right hand over his heart as if he were going to spout the Pledge of Allegiance at any moment. "I promise."

Piper tipped her head, studying him. His hair was longer than it'd been just two weeks ago at the auction. His tan deeper. He was working for a rancher in the Flint Hills, he said. Had bought a little rundown house on twenty acres and hoped to have his own ranch someday.

They'd had a very pleasant lunch at the cafe. Finn was easy to talk to, and in some strange way, she felt like she'd known him all her life. And somehow by the end of that first meal together, he'd charmed her into meeting him for lunch the first of every month— payday—with a check for one hundred dollars in hand.

She still wasn't sure where she would get an extra hundred dollars a month, but she *couldn't* let the clock go. It was a piece of her history. And her connection to Grampa. She would regret it for the rest of her life if she let it get away.

Even so, she'd refused to let Finn accept less than the full price he paid for the clock. "It may take me twenty-two payments, twenty-two *months* to pay it off," she'd told him. "But I promise I'm good for it."

He'd gotten a funny look on his face—like maybe he hadn't done the math yet—but then he smiled. "I guarantee it won't take that long."

"How can you make a guarantee like that?" she'd asked.

But he only smiled that charming, crooked smile, tipped his hat, and said, "See you next month."

Now he was ordering lunch for two at the Dairy Barn drive-thru. She followed him in her car to the park where they straddled opposite benches of the picnic table closest to the sheriff's office. While the spring breeze made the cottonwood leaves whisper overhead, they sipped cherry cokes and laughed and talked over double cheese bacon burgers. Then she handed over his check, and they both went back to work.

Only then did she realize Finn never had told her how he knew Grampa.

June

"You stole money? From Grampa?" Piper couldn't make that fit with the Finn she'd gotten to know.

He looked at the ground. "I'm not proud of it. And please remember I was only thirteen at the time." He sat across from her at the cafe shaking his head, looking appropriately contrite.

"I don't care how old you were. You *stole* from my grandpa?" Grampa had never said anything to her about getting ripped off by some punk teenager. Of course, she would only have been ten years old at the time. And in the throes of Mom's illness.

Why was Finn Neilson dropping this confession on her now? Apparently he'd taken two hundred dollars from the glove compartment of her grandfather's pickup. According to Finn, his grandfather and Grampa were friends and Finn had overheard Grampa talking about the money.

"But...you gave it back, right?"

"Couldn't. I'd already spent it," he said over a bite of chili dog. "Your grandpa let me work it off."

"Yeah, and I bet he paid you twice what you were worth, too."

Finn gave her a sheepish grin. "You sound like you have reason to know."

Grampa had always been generous to a fault. If Piper was ever saving for something, Grampa would suddenly have a dozen jobs lined up for her. And a healthy check waiting at the end of the day.

"That's why I said I owe your grandpa my life. I...I was headed down a bad road, and him forgiving me like that... Well, it changed everything. That's why I wanted you to have the clock."

"You had a funny way of showing it."

"What do you mean?"

"If you wanted me to have it, why did you bid against me?"

He drew back, hands up as if he were under arrest. "I didn't start it."

"Well, I sure wasn't bidding against myself."

"It was that antique dealer. As soon as he got in on the bid, I knew you were out of luck." He studied her. "You thought it was my fault?"

"Well what was I supposed to think? When I bid my last dollar, I looked over and it was you bidding against me."

"Well, that's where you're wrong. I wasn't bidding against you. I was bidding against that city slicker behind you."

"Did...did you even *want* the clock?"

"I wanted it for you."

"You didn't even know me. Why would you spend two thousand dollars on something you don't even want, to sell it back to a girl you don't even know?"

He cocked his head, studying her. "You don't remember, do you?"

"Remember what?"

He hid a grin. "Never mind." He wadded up his napkin and lobbed it toward the trash bin near the tree. "I need to be going. See you next month."

Two down, twenty to go. She had a feeling the months were going to fly by way too fast.

Deborah Raney

July

Piper checked the rearview mirror and gave her hair one last fluff before getting out of the car.

Her third "date" with Finn Neilson. She quickly edited the thought. This wasn't a date—as much as she might wish it was. She was twenty-four-and-never-been-kissed. Well, unless you counted the time that little boy—Griff...she still remembered his name—had kissed her in the hayloft of Grampa's barn when she was five. There'd been some kind of a party at Grampa's and half a dozen kids were playing in the barn.

Griff bragged that he was eight and he hefted a seventy-pound bale of hay to prove it. He was her first crush. Especially after he leapt from a haystack in the middle of a game of hide-and-seek and kissed her on the cheek.

"Hey! You're supposed to ask!" she'd yelled, clapping one hand over the spot as if she were wounded.

He'd run off, grinning, and shimmied down the ladder to the barn below. She never saw him again, but she'd lost a little piece of her heart to that long-ago boy.

Where was that kid now? She could almost make his face come into focus, all these years later. He'd scrambled down the ladder after planting that kiss, but she could still remember how his spiky blond hair had smelled—like new-mown hay and fresh-cut grass. Over the years, she'd entertained the idea of naming her firstborn son Griff. She put a hand to her cheek now, remembering.

A knock on the passenger side window startled her and she rolled the window down to Finn's quizzical stare.

"You okay in there?"

"Sorry. I was just— Never mind. You hungry?"

"You have to ask?" He opened the door for her and put a hand at the small of her back as they went in to

25

the cafe.

Lizzie, the owner, threw her a look that asked if this guy was someone special. Piper ignored it and hurried back to their booth. *Their* booth. As if they'd been coming here forever. But hey, more than once with the same guy was some kind of record for Piper Kendall.

"What's so funny?" Finn still wore the quizzical expression from earlier.

"Oh...nothing. I'll tell you later." She waved him off, grateful when Lizzie appeared with menus.

Their hour-long lunch stretched into two and Piper handed her payment over to Finn, thinking she was getting the best end of this deal by a long shot.

August

"I found these. In your clock." Finn slid a thick envelope across the cafe table. "Figured you'd probably want them."

She lifted the unsealed flap of the manila envelope.

"It was already open," he said, looking guilty. "I didn't go through them or anything. Just long enough to realize what they were."

What they were was photographs. A thick packet of pictures of all shapes and sizes. Some of them were wrinkled and warped, as if they'd been taken out of old albums. Piper could see at a glance that most of them were of her as a little girl.

"These were in the clock?"

He nodded. "The envelope was taped to the back wall behind the pendulum."

She tucked the envelope into her purse, torn about whether she even wanted to look at them. No doubt there were photos of her mother in there. And Grampa in better days. She wasn't sure she wanted to go there.

"Where *is* my grandfather clock, by the way?"

"Well..." He winked. "It's not yours yet, but I'm taking good care of it. As of a week ago, it's out of storage and in my living room. But did you know that thing goes off every hour on the hour? That's why I opened it. To turn off the blasted gong."

She giggled. "It's called a chime. And that's sort of the purpose of a grandfather clock—to keep track of time."

"At two a.m. it's called a *gong*. Besides, I don't think I need to be reminded when it's two a.m....and three a.m....and four a.m....and five—"

"Um... I get the picture."

He grinned. "Speaking of pictures, you wouldn't want to go to a movie with me Friday night, would you? And out to dinner"—he glanced around the quaint diner—"at a *real* restaurant?"

Would she *ever*. "Let me check my calendar and get back to you."

He looked deflated, which gave her courage.

She clicked her phone on, then back off again before it barely had time to light up. "Looks like I'm free." She grinned up at him.

And was rewarded with an appearance of that dimple in his right cheek.

It struck her that she could handle looking at that infernal dimple for...well, the rest of her life.

September

Still slightly winded from climbing the twenty-eight steps to her apartment, Piper tossed her purse on the sofa and went to the refrigerator in search of supper. Grampa had thought she was "Grace" again. That made three days this week. And the nurses said he'd fallen twice wandering the halls at night.

She sighed. He'd been so good all summer she'd almost begun to hope this was as bad as it would get. But apparently that was not to be.

As September faded away, the days were getting shorter. When she'd left the library tonight the air held a distinct chill. If not for the fact that Finn Neilson had talked her into paying the rest of what she owed him in twenty-five-dollar *weekly* increments, she would have been depressed.

She let a smile come at the thought of Finn, and it pulled her out of the threatening melancholy. Tomorrow was their date night—even Finn had started calling them *dates*—and she couldn't be sad knowing he would meet her at the nursing home, help her cheer up Grampa, then take her out to dinner. The irony of her handing over twenty-five dollar checks while he paid for fifty-dollar dinners was not lost on her. Yet Finn insisted.

She looked around her apartment, wondering, not for the first time, where she would put the grandfather clock once she finally paid Finn off. She threw together a rather wilted salad and took it to the sofa to eat. As she cleared a stack of magazines and junk mail from the coffee table, the yellow corner of an envelope poked out—the photos Finn had found in the clock.

She never had mustered the courage to look at them, but tonight seemed like the right time. Her salad forgotten, she flipped through a veritable history of her childhood. Mom, in the hospital with a newborn Piper. The dad she'd never known looking on. Grandpa and two-year-old Piper fishing with Uncle Martin. Her first day of kindergarten. Instead of making her feel sad, looking at the photos made her feel blessed. In spite of everything, she'd been loved and loved well.

She flipped to the next photo and her breath caught. The color photograph had faded with age, but the image was clear and sharp. The scene was Grampa's barn with a clutch of kids peering out of the hayloft door. She remembered the day as if it had happened yesterday.

She smiled seeing the only boy she'd ever kissed. Griff. She'd have to ask Grampa if he remembered the family. Griff... That spiky hair. Those ocean blue eyes. No wonder she'd had a bit of a crush on him. And the way he was looking at her in the photo, it seemed like the feeling might have been mutual.

Something stirred in the back of her memory and she brought the picture closer, as if it had a secret to tell. *Wait a minute...* She *knew* that dimple. Knew that ornery grin.

Could it be?

October

"I have something to show you." Piper fished through her purse, realizing her hands were trembling. She hadn't quite fit together all the pieces of the puzzle, but she was pretty sure of one thing: it was Finn Neilson in the photo she'd discovered last night. It had been all she could do to wait until today to ask him about it.

Beside her, Finn straddled the picnic bench and cocked his head, curiosity sparking in those blue eyes she loved. She handed the photo to him, acutely attuned to his reaction.

Above them, the sun poured through a blaze of autumn leaves. He squinted at the photo, then his eyes widened. "Where did you get this?" He sounded...intrigued.

If she didn't love the picture so much, she might have burned it and pretended she'd never seen it.

Still, she had to know if he remembered her. From before. And if he did, why hadn't he told her? "It was in that packet of photos you found in the clock. Is that you?"

His demeanor turned wary. "Of course. But I didn't remember anyone taking a picture."

"Well someone did."

He inspected the photo, chuckling. "Yep. It looks like we posed and everything. How cool is that?" He tapped his image in the photograph. "Look at the way I'm looking at you! Man! I was smitten even then."

She held her breath. He was smitten? *Now?* "But...that kid's name...was Griff." She'd wrestled all night, so afraid his explanation would hold some secret that might make this magical thing between them unravel. But by morning, she'd decided she didn't care. She loved who Finn was now. She wasn't sure there was anything he could tell her that would change her mind about that.

He made a face. "Griffin. Always did hate my given name. I started going by Finn in seventh grade. Get it? Grif-FINN?"

Relief turned her knees to jelly. "So... You *are* Griff. But why didn't you tell me?"

Finn shrugged. "I figured if you remembered, you'd say something, and if you didn't, why would I want to remind you and get another lecture?"

"A lecture?"

"For stealing that kiss when we were kids."

She gave him a look. "Wait a minute—" She pointed at herself in the photo. "Do you remember me? From *this* day?"

"Every minute of it." That charming grin grew on his face. Guileless. "You were a little sassball even then. As I recall you informed me I didn't have permission to kiss you."

"No... What I said was, 'You're supposed to ask.'"

He grinned. "May I?"

"What?"

He scooted closer until his knees touched hers under the table. "Kiss you." He cupped a hand over her cheek, no hint of that grin now. "I've waited three lifetimes to get your permission."

"Yes," she whispered. "Yes."

His fingers knit through her hair and cradled her neck. He pulled her closer, his mouth seeking hers. She melted into the strength of him, breathing him in. He smelled of new-mown hay and fresh-cut grass. And this time he didn't shimmie down the ladder and run away. He kissed her for a good long while. Like a man with permission.

And she kissed him...like a woman who'd waited nineteen years to kiss him back.

When they came up for air, the crooked grin was back. He took her face in his hands and kissed the tip of her nose. "See? I told you it wouldn't take the full twenty-two months to pay off that clock."

Deborah Raney's first novel, *A Vow to Cherish*, inspired the World Wide Pictures film of the same title and launched Deb's writing career. Twenty years and thirty books later, she's still writing. She and her husband recently traded small-town life in Kansas—the setting of many of Deb's novels—for life in the city of Wichita. They love traveling to visit four grown children and a growing brood of grandchildren who all live much too far away. Visit Deb on the Web at www.deborahraney.com.

Ah, the old west... cattle drives... fathers who insist on choosing their daughters' husbands even from the distance of the grave. We're treated to all those elements in Crystal Barnes' debut story. One of the appealing aspects of this entertaining western is the author's use of humor. Who doesn't love a good laugh at the expense of a hunky cowboy? – VS

Let's Make a Deal

Crystal L. Barnes

May 25th, 1877 – Wichita, Kansas

"Young man, this is normally when you say 'I do.'"

Joseph Matthews shifted his focus from Sarah Asher to the silver-haired preacher who stood grinning at him. He swallowed and resisted the urge to tug at his collar. He'd sealed his fate with those two words weeks ago just before digging her father's grave, but today they threatened to crawl back down his throat and strangle him.

Allen Asher's bloody but relieved face flashed through Joe's mind. He shook away the searing image and wiped sweat from his forehead. That stampede had changed everything. That, and Allen's dying wish. His mentor knew Joe had no luck with women. Why had he made such an outlandish request? Why did marrying Allen's daughter have to be the only way to get the ranch he'd promised Joe, the ranch he'd put years of blood and sweat into?

"Son?" The old preacher shifted and placed a weathered hand on his Bible.

Twin lines formed between Sarah's dark brows.

"Uh, sorry." Joe rubbed at the tension building in his neck. "I do."

Sarah tilted her head and turned her attention to the preacher posing the same question to her. Joe let his gaze slide the length of his soon-to-be wife. Maybe marrying her might not be so bad. After all, she was a mighty handsome woman. Even bathed in trail dust. And wearing a Stetson. A smile tugged at his lips. Did she realize she still wore her hat? Doubtful. What female in her right mind got married in a cowboy hat? Then again, who would confuse Sarah for most women? If her raven locks didn't set her apart, her mouth would the minute she opened it.

"I..." Deep green eyes wide with uncertainty sought his, then shifted back toward the preacher. "Excuse us a moment, Reverend?"

"Uh, of course."

Joe looked at the minister in stunned astonishment a split second before Sarah grabbed his arm and tugged him down the aisle of the small, stuffy church to within a foot of the exit.

"What's the matter?" The words hissed through his lips. "I thought this is what we'd agreed upon?"

Sarah peeked at the preacher, then answered in the same hushed volume. "There are a few things I need to make sure of first."

"You couldn't have mentioned that a day ago? Or maybe even an hour? The preacher's waiting."

"Do you want to keep your word to my father or not?"

Joe frowned. "You know I'm a man of my word. Now what's this about?"

"First—"

"You mean there's more than one?"

It was Sarah's turn to frown.

"I'm sorry for interrupting. Go on."

"First, you must agree that our sleeping arrangements won't change. When we get back to Texas, you'll stay in your cabin with your mother like always."

He rubbed his finger around the inside of his collar. That was not something he wanted to discuss with his future wife, especially in a church house. "'Til death did them part" was an awful long time to keep his distance from such a beautiful, spirited woman. Besides, how could he protect both her and his mother by living in a cabin fifty feet away?

"Your house is much bigger and has three rooms to boot. You, my mother, and I can all have our own. I'll agree to separate rooms, not separate houses."

She chewed on her lip a moment then gave a nod. "Fine. Separate rooms. Second, you let me do my work as I please without any interference."

"What work did ya have in mind?"

"That's my business."

"This wouldn't happen to have anything to do with you sneaking off to help that quack of a doctor, now would it?"

"He's not a quack." As if realizing what she'd just given away, she scowled at him.

"Sarah, you know your pa didn't approve of you working at that clinic, and I'm not going to have you endangering yourself. I promised Allen I'd take care of you, protect you. You can't ask me to break that word to him."

"And you can't ask me to stop helping people. I'll agree to keep your safety considerations in mind, but I won't be dictated to."

"Dictated to? What makes you think that's what I'm going to do? Besides, even the Bible says the husband is the head of the wife."

Her lips pressed into a firm line, and she took a step backward...toward the door. He swallowed hard. If he didn't think of something quick, she was going to make fulfilling his word to Allen a whole lot harder.

"Look, I'll do my best to reason with you and not dictate my wishes, unless something is truly dangerous to your wellbeing. Will that satisfy you?"

"What about the clinic?"

He swallowed a groan. "One day a week."

"Three."

"Two."

"Three."

"Mr. Matthews, are you two going to be much longer? My wife is expecting me home for supper."

"We'll be right with you, Parson." Joe shifted his focus back to Sarah. "Right?"

"Fine. Two, but there's one more thing."

Of course there was. Joe resisted the urge to roll his eyes. Why did women have to be so difficult? They'd given their word to her father. Couldn't they iron out all these details later? Nevertheless, he nodded for her to continue.

"I want my share of today's profits."

"What?" He lowered his voice when Sarah's eyes widened, and she stepped backwards, her hand going to the doorknob. "I apologize. I didn't mean to shout. You're right. The money's as much yours as it is mine."

He reached into his pants pocket, pulled out the money, and counted out half of what he'd stuffed in there earlier after selling the beeves they'd brought to market. Of all the ridiculous things—paying a woman to marry him. But if that's what it took to keep his word...

Joe held out the money. "Here. Is there anything else? You want my horse too? My right arm?"

"I want it in writing."

"Writing?" Rubbing the tension knotting his neck, he turned. "Preacher, you got a piece of paper?"

Unable to feign hunger any longer, Sarah Matthews set down her fork and stared at the sandy-haired man shoveling food into his mouth as if it were any another day. Not a single cowboy in this hotel dining room seemed to realize something momentous had happened. She'd actually *married* Joseph Matthews. Despite the fact she'd never planned on marrying, on being tied down, on having to yield to any man's beck and call. If her father's final request had to be her marriage, at least he'd chosen Joe. She could talk him into almost anything. The note in her pocket bore proof of that. Not every red-blooded male would sign away his husbandly rights.

At least she'd had the preacher so flustered, he hadn't insisted upon Joe kissing her. Her focus floated to his lips. The skin around them boasted a shadow of whiskers he had yet to shave off. What would it have been like to kiss him?

Her friends back in Texas said a man was only nice until he got what he wanted, but surely Papa wouldn't have made them promise to wed before he died if he hadn't trusted Joe's character. Maybe she shouldn't have been so hard on him at the wedding, but she couldn't get Nellie's warnings out of her mind. Could being a wife really be so torturous?

"You're not eating."

Her gaze darted from his mouth. Had he noticed her scrutiny? Heat crept up her neck. "I'm not hungry."

"You barely ate dinner." Joe motioned to her plate. "Please. Eat. I promised Allen I'd—"

"That you'd take care of me. I know." Her breath caught, but Joe didn't glare at her for back talking. In fact, he actually smirked. She bit her lip and ducked her head. How had he found that humorous? Did he think she was looking forward to his tender, loving care? The heat in her neck spilled into her cheeks. She lifted a floury clod from the basket between them. "If I eat a roll, will that satisfy you?"

He nodded. "Thank you."

Sarah took a small bite and stifled a relieved sigh when he resumed eating. That was close. If she wasn't careful, her mouth was liable to get her into trouble. Would she never be able to joke with Joe again? Would tension remain between them from now on? That was a bit saddening. She'd always counted Joe as a friend. She'd hate to lose that because she'd married him. Maybe things would go back to normal once they got home.

"Hello? Sarah?" Joe waved a hand in front of her face.

She blinked and leaned back in her chair. "Sorry."

"Where were you?"

"In Texas. By the way, when are we leaving?"

He sopped a roll in the last of his gravy. "Tomorrow.

We'll get our supplies then make tracks."

"Tomorrow?" Not even one day to rest. She swallowed a sigh.

"I know Allen said something about staying longer and taking you back east, but I can't afford to leave the ranch unattended any longer than I already have. Maybe you and Ma can make the trip when we get back to Texas."

"That's fine. It doesn't matter." Seeing family back east wouldn't be the same without her father to introduce them. "Can we go back to the wagon now?"

"I thought you'd want to stay here."

"At the hotel?"

"Unless you'd rather sleep on the ground."

Sarah bit her lip. A night in a real bed? With a real pillow? The offer sounded too good to be true. He hadn't mentioned anything about staying himself, but she wasn't about to waste one penny of the money in her pocket. "Who's paying?"

"I am." With a wag of his head, Joe grabbed his hat and unfolded his long frame from the chair.

"All right then. Thank you." She set down her half-eaten roll and scooted out her chair. He cupped her elbow with his giant hand and escorted her from the dining room.

At the hotel check-in counter, the short, dumpy clerk peered at them through wire-rimmed glasses. "May I help you?"

Joe put down their bags. "A room, please."

"Yes, sir." The man opened a large book to a half-filled page and handed over a pen.

Joe scrawled ink across a line. "I'd also like a bath brought up to our room."

Our room? Sarah's knees threatened to buckle. This was not the plan. He'd said nothing about staying. Well, he could have the room. He could have the whole hotel.

She wouldn't put up with a husband in that sense of the word. She'd slept under the chuck wagon the past nine weeks. What was one more night? She'd sleep there the next month and a half anyway.

Joe grabbed her wrist, stopping her before she made a step.

How did he...? Sarah frowned. She gave a slight tug. He didn't release her or even glance her way.

The clerk nodded his balding head, the lobby lights reflecting off the hairless spot. "Yes, sir. Not a problem."

That's what he thought. How had she gotten herself into this mess? Better still, how did she get out of it? With her heart threatening to beat out of her chest, she pried at Joe's steel-like grip. His fingers wouldn't budge. Her throat constricted. She wasn't doing this. She wasn't.

Joe reached for his pocket and withdrew the payment.

How could she have misjudged him, and why did she have to be so wrong about someone so big? He towered over her like a mighty oak with arm muscles twice the size of hers and shoulders inches broader than her father's. No doubt he could inflict plenty of damage. Joe could take whatever he wanted, do whatever he pleased.

No. She couldn't afford to cower like Nellie. She refused to live like that. She'd run first. How to escape? Would Joe let go if she kicked him in the shins? Probably not. He might not even feel it through those leather chaps.

"Here is your key, sir." Baldy tucked away the money and pointed to his right. "Your room is up the stairs, last door on the left. Enjoy your stay."

Not likely.

"Much obliged." Joe released his hold and gestured for her to take the lead. The shiny brass dangling from his calloused fingers shouted at her to turn and run, but where would she go? How could she outrun a man whose single step equaled two of hers? She'd simply lock him out of her room once he opened it. Yes, that's exactly what she'd do.

With a tilt of her chin, she moved ahead of him toward the stairs, her boots clicking on the hard plank floors. Joe's footsteps echoed behind her down the long hallway as the candlelight from the wall sconces flickered across the scarred but scrubbed boards creaking beneath them. A faint breeze stirred the faded curtains at the end of the corridor.

Why didn't he say something?

"Hope they never get more than twenty-six rooms in this place." Joe stopped beside her in front of a door with a brass-covered N hanging from a nail and put their bags at his feet.

The portal opened with a loud *screech*.

He cringed then chuckled. "Apparently, the N doesn't stand for new."

Sarah tried to grin, but it probably resembled more of a grimace as she walked into a room not overly large. She turned to shut the door, but Joe was already inside. Taking a quick step back, she bumped into the simple bedstead with a log-cabin quilt. *Not the place to be, Sarah.*

She hurriedly bypassed the bed and headed for the narrow window open to the shouts of the people below. Could she fit through there? Not likely, and the distance to the ground loomed farther than she cared to risk. Was there something in the room she could use as a weapon? The mirror on the wall nearby was an option. Two oil lamps waited to be lit—one on an oak dresser opposite the bed and another on the nightstand to the left of the same. What would be best?

She swiveled at a thump, her hand going to her

throat.

Joe straightened from depositing her bag on the floor in front of a blue dressing screen. His large frame filled the room, leaving no room for any brave words she might've said. "That bath ought to be here soon. I'll head over to the bathhouse now and take my own. I'll be back in about thirty minutes to an hour, so there's no need to rush. I figure we should talk before I go to the wagon for the night. Then if you'll wait here, I'll take you to breakfast in the morning."

Talk? Wagon? He didn't intend to... The bands loosened across her chest, and air flooded her lungs until the room slanted before her.

"Sarah?"

"Hmm?"

"Is that okay with you?"

"Oh, yes, fine. I'm sure there are some things we should discuss." Like how he'd better keep his hands to himself from now on.

"That's what I figured. It's hard to talk with all those cowboys around. In case you didn't notice, I didn't feel comfortable leaving you alone with some of them."

"I noticed." Some of their looks had made her skin crawl like a host of weevils had taken up residence.

Joe paused with his hand on the latch. "I hope I didn't hurt your wrist a minute ago. I got the strangest feeling you were fixing to bolt on me." He grinned. "Guess I should've explained at dinner that I was going to keep watch over our wagon tonight with Slim and Henderson instead of getting my own room, but it's probably better if those at the hotel don't know that."

Tugging at the cuff of her sleeve, she nodded.

"See you after a while. Enjoy your bath." He tipped his Stetson with a finger then disappeared out the door, his hat scant inches below the doorframe.

Sarah melted onto the edge of the bed while his heavy footsteps receded down the hall. He never even made a move toward her. And an apology for nothing more than grabbing her wrist? Maybe Nellie had been wrong. She moved to shut the door, peeking out at Joe as he descended the stairs.

Maybe she hadn't made such a big mistake after all.

Joe strode through the hotel with determined steps, rehearsing the words he planned to share with Sarah. The sooner he got the conversation over with, the sooner he could find his bed and let sleep silence the unsolicited thoughts bombarding his mind. He'd start by apologizing for not allowing her to clean up before the wedding then ask her to keep those particulars to herself. Ma would never let him hear the end of his slip-up.

That slip of paper Sarah held would also be a topic she'd better not share. He'd be the laughing stock of Cater Springs if word got out that he'd had to pay a woman to marry him. Part of him still couldn't believe it. Still couldn't believe they were hitched either. But if he had to be tied to someone at least that someone was Sarah. After years of working around each other on the ranch, she understood his quirks even if she didn't always agree with them.

Swiping the disturbing notions from his mind and some stray hair trimmings from his fresh shirt, Joe stopped at room N. He knocked on the door with three sharp taps. The response—a frightened yelp, a loud splash, and a dull thump. Seconds ticked by. Silence resonated from the opposite side of the wood. Had Sarah fallen and hit her head?

"Sarah?"

The belted tune of "Jeanie with the Light Brown

Hair" jerked Joe's attention to the top of the stairs. Two men, arms slung across each others' shoulders, staggered into the wall, tottered backward to the stair's ledge with a laugh, and then lurched forward with a renewed burst of zealous singing.

With a frown, Joe turned back to Sarah's door. Water seeped through the crevice at the bottom. Not good. He pressed his ear to the wood, straining for a rustle, a screech, anything to hint she didn't need his help. The busy diners downstairs, the raucous laughter from the saloon down the street, and the idiots behind him littered the air with noise. He couldn't hear a thing.

Leaving her drowning in a tub because he'd startled her wasn't an option. At the risk of embarrassing them both, he turned the key. *Allen, where are you when I need you?* Shutting his eyes, he inched the door open and stuck in his head.

"Sarah?"

Another off-tune blast from the drunks in the hall jerked Joe's eye open. A dressing screen nearly touched his nose. The spreading puddle inching his way tugged him inside.

"Sarah, you better answer me." He shut the squeaky door behind him. Looking to his right, he caught a reflection in the mirror over the washstand. In an instant, his mouth went dry as he beheld Sarah digging in the satchel on the bed, her curvy figure hidden only by the bag, a thin chemise, and the waist-length, midnight strands falling from her head in thick, wavy masses.

"I did ans—" Sarah's gaze collided with his in the mirror. With a squeal, she yanked a large shirt from the bag and pivoted.

Joe hastened to avert his eyes. A quick turn and the world slowed down. His booted feet slid beneath him on the slick floorboards. A balancing hand flailed about and latched onto the dressing screen, making the flimsy

43

partition collapse inward and fall toward the tub. Oh, no. Not good. The screen carried him along for the journey. A shout, a splash, and a split second later he found himself on his back in a pool of sudsy water.

Spitting and sputtering, he dragged his soaked self above the water's surface. The flower-scented liquid poured off his fresh clothes into the tub and onto the floor. He'd done it now. More than a little uncomfortable, he made himself turn and face the gorgeous woman standing not two feet away.

His new wife clutched a man's gray shirt to her front, water cascading off her to gather at her feet, her emerald eyes the size of saucers. "Joseph Collin Matthews! I told you to wait. What do you think you're doing?"

A sheepish grin curved his mouth. "Uh...taking another bath?"

Her glare could've curdled cream.

He looked away and eased onto the edge of the tub. Heat crawled up his neck and seeped into his face. Unable to help himself, his attention gravitated to the yard of creamy white peeking below the shirt that hovered above her knees.

"Ah-hemm!"

Joe's straying gaze shot upward. The heat in his cheeks burst into an inferno.

"Would you get out of my room?"

"Oh, right. Sorry." He emptied his boots of water and hurried to stand, trying to explain all the while. "I-I heard a yell, then I couldn't hear anything over those dolts singing in the hall. I thought you'd slipped and knocked yourself out. I'm glad to see you're undressed— *unharmed*! I'm glad to see you're unharmed. I'll leave you to get dressed. We'll talk tomorrow. At breakfast."

He took a step toward the door, slid, and fell to his back with a thud. Stifling a groan, he reached for the back of his head and sat up. He gripped the edge of the tub and moved to rise. The tub tipped. His hand slipped, and he pitched forward with a splat.

"Why don't you set up that screen before you knock yourself out and I'm stuck with you all night?"

The idea of being with her all night held way too much appeal. Joe snapped the flimsy apparatus upright, grabbed his saddlebags, and all but ran out the door.

☙

Approximately three weeks later – The Chisholm Trail

How could a man's back be appealing? For weeks, Sarah had driven the chuck wagon behind her very distant husband and had yet to grow weary of the sight. In fact, at times she questioned why he remained so far removed. Sure, that scene in her hotel room had been embarrassing, but it wasn't something that had to ruin their friendship. After all, he'd left. Just like a gentleman. Despite the interested gleam in his eye. He'd kept his word. Separate rooms. No dictating of his wishes.

Why did that bother her so much? Why did she thrill at every one of his smiles, wish for another moment alone with him, welcome his assistance each morning with the fire? The more time she spent around Joe the more his deep baritone drowned out her fears.

"Hold up."

At Joe's command, Sarah sat a little straighter and hauled back on the reins. Something was wrong. She could hear it in his voice. But what? Her gaze went to the Red River and widened. That river looked a lot deeper than it had on the way up. Sticks swirled in multiple little eddies. Dirt kicked from the bottom turned the water a rusty red. The current moved even medium-sized branches at a hurried pace.

She wanted to get home quickly, but this didn't look at all safe. "J—"

"Let's keep moving." Joe prodded his black-and-white pinto onto the well-trod path, heading to the river's edge.

Sarah swallowed her suggestions and slapped the reins over the pair of mules. She sure hoped he knew what he was doing.

"Lord, please keep us safe." The prayer became a mantra while her speed decreased and the wheels pushed into the angry waters. The wagon lurched from side to side as it ran along the rutted bottom. Sarah held the reins in a stranglehold, both for control of the mules and to maintain her jarring seat. Debris sped by, occasionally bumping into the wagon or team. Counting the seconds, she held her breath and coaxed the animals forward. If the waters got much higher, the mules would have to swim.

Reaching the halfway point, she dared to breathe again. As air entered her lungs, the wheels caught in the sands beneath. The jerking stop propelled her forward. The reins slipped from her fingers. She landed with a splash between the mules.

"Help!"

Fighting panic, she grappled for anything to prevent a hasty trip downriver. The animals shifted farther apart with loud brays. She clutched at a leather harness. The strong current pulled at her fumbling grasp. *God, save me!*

Joe whirled at Sarah's scream. Pure terror coursed through his veins when he spotted her in the rusty waters between the mules. He kicked the sides of his horse and shot a plea heavenward as he angled against the angry current.

The mules sloshed forward. Sarah shrieked as one hand slipped.

Joe urged Whiplash to go faster.

He had to rescue her.

He had to protect her.

He couldn't lose her.

His ranch hands worked to circumvent the wagon while his horse splashed closer. Movement to the left caught his eye. A log crashed into the water and ran with the current toward them.

O God, no.

Joe reached for his lasso. "Slim, grab those reins! Henderson, control that team."

The wagon lurched.

Sarah screamed and disappeared from view.

Joe's heart slammed against his chest then fell to his toes while he scanned the churning waters. *Please, God.*

She resurfaced yards from the wagon. Her arms flailed about, splashing against the strong current pushing her farther and farther away.

Joe charged forward, swirling his lariat above him. The rope flew through his grip the same instant Whiplash stumbled. Joe tumbled into the water, the horse rolling on top of him, pressing him into the muddy bottom. He found himself dragged, his boot caught in the stirrup. His lungs burned by the time his foot slid from the boot. Surfacing, he gasped for air and searched for his wife.

Some forty yards downstream, she fought the current, doing a far better job at staying afloat than he expected.

He swam her direction, the waters propelling him forward. A branch smacked into his shoulder. Ignoring the searing pain, he pulled her to him. "I've got you."

Sarah's fingers dug into his arm as she nodded. Kicking as hard as possible, he swam toward the bank. The current fought them, threatening to carry them away, making the short distance to shore longer. His muscles burned. Water splashed into his face, blurring his vision. His foot brushed the bottom, but the current refused to let him stand.

A shout traveled from shore. Henderson rode on the bank, his lasso already in motion. The circle flew through the air, landing a foot in front of them. Joe snatched it and immediately felt it tighten around his wrist. He turned his head away to keep the water out of his face while they were towed toward shore. When he could finally stand, he lifted Sarah in his arms, water pouring from them both, and trudged through the deep sucking mud. Coughs wracked her body as she clung to his neck. He lowered her to the ground and all but collapsed beside her.

Henderson vaulted from the saddle. "You okay, Boss?"

"Fine. Just let me catch my breath." Joe swiped the water from his face and turned to Sarah, placing a hand on her back. "You all right?"

She nodded while she continued to cough, her attention fixated on the swirling red monster they'd narrowly escaped. Damp ringlets curled around her face, her ever-present braid nonexistent.

His gaze roved over the rest of her, looking for injury. "You didn't hit anything, did you?"

Curls swung when she shook her head. A tremor shuddered through her body.

He needed to get her into some dry clothes. Wait. The branch! A bend in the river blocked his view upstream. He turned to Henderson. "The wagon? Did y'all get it unstuck?"

"Just barely. That floatin' log purt near clipped us

'fore we did. I headed y'all's way soon as we got it movin'. Good thing I did, what with that horse of yours comin' outta the water without you."

"Thanks, Henderson. I owe you one."

"Think nothin' of it. Why don't I let the men know y'all're good and bring yer things from the wagon?"

Joe started to answer, but Sarah spoke up.

"Henderson?"

"Yes, ma'am?"

"Will you bring my doctoring bag from under the wagon seat? Joe's bleeding."

"I am?" Joe shifted to look where she stared at the back of his left shoulder. All he could see was a rip in his favorite work shirt and dark red staining the blue material.

"I'll be back in a jiffy." Henderson hurried to his horse and soon galloped up the riverbank, flinging wet sand in his wake.

"Take off your shirt."

Joe's head whipped around at Sarah's instruction. She inspected his shoulder, all business. She sure had forgotten about that river mighty quick, but she was highly mistaken if she thought he'd be removing his shirt anytime soon. He hadn't taken his shirt off in the presence of a woman since the war, and this woman looked ready to take a needle to him.

"No."

"Don't be such a ninny. Take your shirt off, so I can see how bad it is."

"It ain't that bad." He winced when she peeled the torn fabric from his skin.

"That cut is at least three inches long. I need to see how deep it is. Now, it's either you take the shirt off or I'll cut it off when Henderson gets back with my bag."

Joe gritted his teeth. The set look in her green eyes confirmed she'd carry out her threat. "Can the shirt be salvaged?"

"What?"

"The stain and the rip. Can you fix them?"

"I-I think so. Why?"

Joe started unbuttoning his shirt, the growing pain in his shoulder forcing him to work one-handed. "Because it's my favorite."

He unfastened the last button as Henderson appeared around the bend. He stopped his horse inches from them.

"Here's the stuff y'all asked for. You need any help patchin' him up, Boss Lady?"

"I think I can handle it. Although, I can't be for certain considering he's taking his precious time letting me get a good look at it."

Henderson grinned. "Well, that ain't too surprisin'. The boss hates needles."

Joe glowered at the older man, but Henderson only chuckled.

"Yell if ya need me to come hold him down for ya. I'm gonna go help the boys fix supper. We're makin' camp around the bend a good stone's throw from the river. Y'all shouldn't have any trouble findin' us."

Sarah opened her nursing bag. "Thank you, Henderson."

The weathered ranch hand tipped his hat, rotated his mount, and trotted out of sight.

"Joe? The shirt?"

Begrudgingly, Joe turned and did as she requested, letting her help slide the material from his back. He expected it to hurt more, but she kept the fabric from brushing his wound. More than a little self-conscious, he swiped at the red dirt clinging to the jagged scar on his stomach and watched from the corner of his eye as she rummaged in the bag by his hip. He closed his eyes rather than see what came next.

The light touch of her fingers against his skin surprised him, and their warmth surely distracted him. That was until she started wiping his cut with a rag that burned like a bullet.

"Ouch!"

"Sorry." She dabbed softer. "I think this needs stitches. It's too deep. What hit you?"

"Half a tree." His stomach did an odd flop when she lifted a needle from her bag. He clenched his eyes shut again and waited for the torture to commence.

Air hissed through his teeth at the first jab. What a wonderful reward for rescuing her.

"Thank you for saving me out there."

"Had to," Joe grunted as she struck again ... and again ... and again. He had to get his mind off the pain. "I think I'm going to have to forbid you from going near water from now on."

"What?"

He gasped at her sharp yank. Maybe teasing wasn't the best choice, but he'd already started. "If you haven't noticed, things don't go so well for me when you get near the stuff."

"That's supposed to be my fault?"

"I don't know about it being all your fault, but you're at least a contributor." A grin touched his lips until the next needle jab. "You know how to swim, don't you?"

Her rhythm faltered. "Yes."

"Who taught you?"

"Pa. We used to go swimming after we'd catch fish for supper."

He hated the sadness in her voice. "Maybe we can do that together sometime."

Her fingers stilled.

Uh-oh. He should've kept that comment to himself. Men and women didn't swim in mixed company. Would she get the wrong idea by that comment? Did he already have the wrong idea by just making the comment? Sarah was his wife, though. Sort of. It was his job to see to her happiness. If only she would say something. Let him know if he'd made a huge mistake, if he'd crossed a line. The way his heart had reacted to her scream earlier said it'd crossed the line a long time ago.

The silence ate at him until he couldn't take it anymore. "Sarah?"

She jerked.

He grimaced at the tug on his flesh. Yep, he'd messed up. A sigh seeped from him as she resumed her sewing.

His nurse gave a small tug then tucked her scissors into the bag. "All done. Let me put something on this to help prevent an infection. Then I'll wrap it, and you can put on a clean shirt."

Joe nodded.

The cloth gleamed white against his skin as Sarah wrapped the pale strip around his shoulder and across his chest to keep the bandage in place. She worked so close he could see a water droplet roll from her hairline all the way to her collar. Her long black curls poured over her shoulders, the raven locks glistening as they fell to her hips and brushed the sand. He clenched his fingers, forcing them to stay in his lap rather than reach out and test the silken strands.

At his chest, the length of bandage ran out. She tied off the end, her bottom lip caught between her teeth in concentration. Poor lip. If only he could rescue it. But he didn't want to steal a kiss. He wanted it freely given.

Her clover-green eyes met his. Their gazes held.

Did she know what traipsed across his mind? Could she sense how his heart had stopped when she'd disappeared under the current? *God, what do I do?* He needed distance. With Sarah's wet clothes clinging to her curves and playing havoc with his imagination, he needed to retreat before he did something stupid, something he couldn't undo. Joe reached for his saddlebags. Thankfully, he'd started keeping his things in the wagon, and they weren't soaked. He withdrew a dry shirt.

"Joe." Her hand settled on his, but it was the tone of her voice that got his attention.

He looked up. Confusion, not anger, not grief, deepened the depths of her lovely green eyes.

"You wanted to kiss me just now, didn't you?"

His lungs forgot to function. *Oh, God, don't let me ruin our marriage so shortly after it's started.*

Her fingers worked around his, pulling the shirt from his grasp, sending tingles of awareness up his arms, straight to his heart, which now beat with a fury she had to hear.

"Please answer the question."

His head fell forward with a despondent nod.

"But you didn't. Why?"

He scratched at his chin. "Because that's not what you want."

"What if it is?"

His gaze collided with hers. A small smile touched her lips. He was afraid to speculate on what that meant. "What are you saying?"

Sarah bit her lip. Did she have to spell it out for the man? She avoided his intense stare and fiddled with the tie on his bandage. "I'm saying that perhaps I messed up."

His shoulders drooped. Her fingers touched one of them, marveling at the strength of the man who'd saved her life but enforced such great restraint on himself. He hadn't changed when he'd put a ring on her finger. He was still the sweet, considerate man she'd known for years.

She was the one who'd changed, who'd allowed her fears to dictate her actions. Life held too much unpredictability for that. Her fingers dropped from his shoulder and searched out the soggy slip of paper in her buttoned pocket.

"What if I wanted to make a new deal?" Sarah offered him the list of promises that were nigh unto illegible.

"New deal?"

"Yes, you see... I find myself falling in love with my husband."

His Adam's apple bobbed. Blue fire blazed in his eyes, trapping her gaze as surely as a fire would trap her inside a burning building. "That's good. 'Cause I've done gone and fallen in love with my wife."

He leaned forward but hesitated, his mouth a fraction from hers.

The man could take being a gentleman just a bit too far. She closed the gap.

Every ounce of his hesitation fled. The fire that had burned in his eyes flowed through his lips and straight through her. With a zeal she didn't know she possessed, she returned his kiss. How could Nellie find this torturous? The only torture would be if he stopped, which he didn't seem inclined to do in the least. That suited her just fine. Her fingers slipped into his hair. He must've taken that for another cue, for he drew his arms around her and deepened the kiss. Like butter in a hot skillet, she melted against him.

He smiled against her lips. "Do I need to apologize?"

With an answering smile, she traced a finger along his scruffy jaw. "Only if you don't do that every day for the rest of our lives."

"I like the sound of that deal."

They sealed it with another kiss.

Crystal L Barnes is an award-winning author, who also happens to be a born-n-raised Texan. She is an active member of American Christian Fiction Writers (ACFW), her local ACFW chapter, 19th Century Writers, and her local church. In 2012, she was a semifinalist in the ACFW Genesis contest. When she's not writing or reading, Crystal enjoys knitting, sewing, or crocheting while watching old movies/sitcoms. Find out more about Crystal at booksbybarnes.com or connect with her on Facebook, Goodreads, Google+, or Pinterest.

Some stories are difficult to fit into a particular genre. I'd call this one contemporary romance, and yet there's a dreamy element that defies categorization. It's not fantasy. It's not science fiction. Perhaps it's best described as whimsical. Regardless, the story is captivating, and I'm confident you'll enjoy it as much as I did. – VS

A Kiss in Time

Amy Barkman

"Come here!"

The voice called from far away, over a distance of at least twenty years. Hand trembling, Susan set the coffee mug on the kitchen table and pushed away the plate containing her half-eaten muffin. She listened with every cell in her body, but after several minutes only managed to hear one more faint word.

"Hurry."

Without a doubt, the voice was her own future self. She knew it with a certainty that astounded her. Nor was there any doubt of the urgency.

She shook her head but the voice would not be dismissed. Surely it was one of those silly things that sprang from the imagination after watching a sci-fi movie or reading a book about time travel. Nothing applicable to her life. Nothing real.

But whatever their origin, the words resounded throughout her body.

"Come here!" and "Hurry!"

Something in her yearned to comply. But how?

She pushed her chair away from the table. Gathering the dishes, she deposited them in the sink, thoughts whirling. Books and movies about the fourth dimension had always fascinated her but if time machines existed, she didn't have one. And there was no fairy godmother to send her into the future with the wave of a wand.

A scene from her favorite movie rose in her mind. A man dressed himself in clothes of an earlier era and, concentrating on a picture and a year, settled himself on a bed. When he awoke, he had traveled backward in time. Fiction, certainly. But was it possible?

Sweeping the last crumbs of her muffin from the table, she dismissed the idea. That was all very well for him but she had no clothing from the future. No way to obtain a picture on which to focus. Nothing but the vague feeling that her own voice was calling from sometime beyond today.

But she did have a bed. Maybe the call resonating in her soul would be enough.

She'd made her bed up for the day less than thirty minutes earlier, but now she tore away the comforter and settled back on the pillows. What to think about? The urgency of the call, perhaps. And what would she look like in the future? Two decades from now, for instance. What would her body be like at the age of forty-three? Would she have a different job? Would she be married?

Ah, that was the question that occupied her in this time period to the point of obsession. Who would be her husband?

Her thoughts served only to stir her wakefulness. She glanced at the clock. Eight forty-five. Already late for work. With a sigh she gave up the experiment. It was a foolish fancy anyway. Better call her boss to let him know she'd be there shortly.

The rest of the week passed with no more experiences of a supernatural type. And while she didn't actually forget the incident, she refused to think about something over which she had no control. Well, maybe that wasn't true. She certainly spent a lot of time thinking about her romantic life and she appeared to have no control over that either.

Michael had been crazy about her from the time they met three years earlier. Two years ago there was only a little doubt in her mind about their eventual future, but then she'd bumped into David in the lobby of her office building. His sparkling blue eyes and mischievous grin drove all thoughts of Michael out of her mind for the rest of the day.

Since then, she'd seen Michael on Friday nights and David on Saturdays. Almost every Friday, Michael proposed. He professed love, and their mutual physical attraction could not be denied. But did he love her, or did he merely consider her a "trophy wife"?

David was completely different in pursuing her–he didn't. Sometimes she thought he'd just as soon continue meeting every Saturday the rest of their lives with no commitment to anything more permanent. She was very aware that Michael considered her a "trophy wife" but was David even cognizant of her virtues? Frustrating creature!

Tonight - Friday - Michael would be there as usual right at 7:30 with reservations somewhere nice at 8.

But tonight he wasn't in his usual hurry to leave for the restaurant. "Can we talk a minute?"

Uh oh. She knew what was coming. What would she do?

He looked so handsome and so, so very in love with her as he guided her to sit on the couch and then slid to his knees. He pulled the ring box from his suit pocket.

"Will you marry me?" He'd asked so many times, but this time he had the ring and she knew she owed him an answer.

Surely this was the right thing to do. Surely this was the man she was meant to spend her future with. But before he could open the box, she bent forward and put her hand on his shoulder. Looking into her eyes, Michael set the ring box down and then enfolded her in his arms.

There was nothing wrong with the kiss. It was gentle and loving and even comfortably familiar after three years of being together.

But it wasn't David's kiss. It wasn't the kiss that made her feel complete, as though she'd found her home and would never ever be lonely again.

"Well?" Michael said as he released her.

She hated to hurt him but she just wasn't sure. "Can I sleep on it?"

He looked both hurt and surprised. "Of course, my love." He replaced the ring in his pocket and they went to dinner. Gentleman that he was he never mentioned marriage again, not even when he brought her home.

After turning the deadbolt, she looked around at her

living room. Whoever she married, they'd have to move in here. She loved this house. The inheritance from her parents made the down payment, and every cent toward the mortgage and remodeling were her own contribution. All hers and she was proud of it. Settled in her warm bed, she thought about the two men she loved. What did the future hold? Her experience earlier in the week surfaced in her mind, but she dismissed it. That call from the future was nothing but a frustrating distraction. If her future self wanted to send her a message, she'd have to be clearer. She fell asleep thinking how nice it would be to be married to someone who truly desired and appreciated her. That would be Michael.

"Come here!"

Susan awoke with a start. She lay on her bed, and she was not alone. A glance at the sleeping figure next to her gave her a start. She was, literally, beside herself. How had she managed it? Was she in the future? But her future self was wearing flannel pajamas, very unlike her present taste in nightwear. She climbed out of bed and looked around the room.

This was her bedroom, but it looked different. Heavy draperies hung in place of her white ruffled curtains. Burgundy replaced the light green paint on her walls. Everything was heavy, masculine, not her personality at all. She walked from the bedroom to the den. Same house, different furniture, different decor.

Picture frames filled the place where her demitasse cup collection once rested. Her gaze fell on a wedding picture. Her younger self gazed at Michael, love shining in her eyes, while he smiled at the camera. The next frame held a picture of Michael's parents, another of him and his sisters. She looked over at the fireplace. Her china cat no longer sat on the hearth. In its place was a basket filled with sports magazines.

In the kitchen she saw with horror that the daisy yellow walls were now a claustrophobic dark green. And her white enamel appliances had been replaced by black. Very slick and modern, no doubt. But ugly.

Back in the bedroom, she examined her older self more closely. The pajamas were wrinkled and her hair matted. Even in sleep, her face showed the ravages of worry. She caressed the cheek of the sleeping woman. "It's okay. I'll fix it." She'd never realized before that "trophy wife" could mean ownership. Lying back down, she arranged herself for sleep.

"Come here!"

She jerked to consciousness. Remembered. Looked over at the place on the bed next to her. She was still beside herself.

But something was different. The white ruffle curtains were back in place. No, these were different but just as pretty. The walls were still green, but a different shade. Just as pretty as her current bedroom. She decided she liked it even better.

The figure sleeping beside her looked the same...wait. The first other self had worn pajamas but this one slept in a pretty gown. A matching negligee hung on one of the posters at the foot of the bed. Her curls, though tousled, were shiny and smooth.

Susan got out of bed and hurried into the den. A laugh of relief burst forth when she saw that the demitasse collection had grown. On the wall was a wedding picture and she approached it with caution. She and David smiled at each other with adoring looks.

When she walked through the kitchen door, she breathed a sigh of relief. A warm yellow glow enfolded her.

Back in the bedroom, Susan crawled into bed. She patted the sleeping figure. "Smart girl."

She snuggled into a pillow and breathed in the lingering scent of David's cologne. When she got home to the past, she knew what to do.

Amy Barkman is in her 18th year as pastor of a small rural church, Mortonsville United Methodist, and has been Director of Voice of Joy Ministries since 1979. Amy is married with children, grandchildren, and great-grandchildren. She has written one non-fiction "Everyday Spiritual Warfare" and several Christian fiction books, along with some e-book fiction.

While not a licensed counselor, Amy does a lot of pastoral prayer counseling with individuals and rehab groups. She speaks for churches and other groups as well as holding retreats, workshops, and conferences through Voice of Joy.

As I read through the many stories submitted for this collection, I was struck by a couple of common themes. One was struggling marriages, which makes sense when you think about it. Every relationship experiences rough spots, and that doesn't end when the couple says, "I do." In her fiction debut, Sarah Monzon crafts a sweet story of love's triumph over the difficulties that every romantic relationship encounters. – VS

Carousel Kisses

Sarah Monzon

"Michael would kill us if he knew we were here."

Eric sidestepped a half-eaten corndog lying in the dirt. The bright lights of the fair splashed a rainbow of color on the darkening sky behind his wife. His lungs filled with the aroma of giant turkey legs and hot oil from the we'll-fry-anything-you-can-imagine concession stand. If his plans turned out tonight, maybe he'd be able to get himself out of the frying pan and back in his wife's good graces.

"Our five-year-old will not kill us," he reassured her. Lily's eyebrows rose, her arms crossed over her chest.

"Okay, you're right." He lifted his hands in surrender. "He'd turn into a Nerf gun sniper and scatter a LEGO minefield on the floor." He chuckled. "Although that's likely to happen even if he doesn't find out we're here."

The line moved, and they stepped in front of the ticket booth. "Ten please." He handed over his debit card in exchange for a long train of beige tickets.

"Look over there." Lily pointed to a giant slide where kids flew down on burlap sacks. "Michael would love-"

"Sweetheart, this is our first date night in over two months. Michael is having the time of his life with your mother." He wrapped an arm around her shoulder and squeezed, ignoring the stiffness of her body against his. "Do you think we can *not* spend the whole evening talking about our son?"

Her shoulders rose and fell with a shrug, and his heart plummeted. Was she even going to give tonight a chance? Finally, her gaze met his, and his hopes rose. Concealed excitement radiated from her eyes. "Where should we start?"

"That's my girl." He scanned the fairgrounds.

The spinning cars on the Tilt-a-Whirl circled on their tracks to the left and the spaceship-like Gravitron spiraled in the air to the right. Just beyond, shrieks filled the air from the nausea-inducing, ever-rotating Zipper.

"No," he said before she could ask.

Throwing up on her wasn't part of his romantic plans for the evening.

He looked over the heads of a group of teenagers

milling about and spied the lemonade stand. Perfect. He indicated with his head. "How about some sustenance before I try my hand at winning that panda bear I promised you eight years ago?"

Her eyes lit. "Is funnel cake on the menu?"

"Definitely."

"What are we standing around here for then?"

Eric grinned and let her tug him across the promenade. Music drifted over peals of laughter and pulled his attention to the right. There it was.

"Lily, wait up."

She turned, her brows knit. "What is it?"

"Look." He thrust his chin toward the ride.

A question appeared in her blue eyes. "The carousel?"

In answer, he put a hand to her elbow and propelled her forward. The woman operating the ride accepted his tickets, and they climbed onto the circular platform.

Everyone riding was looking for the perfect mount, and he was no exception. But where was it? Twin boys squealed as they rushed past, one climbing atop a lion and the other a bear.

Lily put her foot in the stirrup of a pink unicorn. With a hand on her arm, he shook his head. "Not that one."

An are-you-feeling-okay look crossed her face, but she stepped down. Hand in hand they wove in and out of carousel creatures before stopping in front of a white horse. "Your trusty steed, M'lady."

"I married a lunatic." Despite her words, her lips curved in a smile.

Eric mounted the tiger beside her.

Children rushed around them, and he leaned toward her. "I know things have been hectic and strained lately, and I haven't given you the attention you deserve, but I want you to know that I'll always remember who's most important in my life." With one hand braced around the pole in front of him, he lifted his other hand and cupped her cheek. "Eight years ago the most beautiful girl in Grant County sat astride a white horse just like this one." His gaze shifted to her mouth. "Do you remember what happened?"

Her cheek pressed into his palm as liquid joy shone from her eyes. "How could I forget? My handsome knight sealed his undying love with a kiss."

Time and space vanished as their lips met. Memories mingled with the there-and-now, creating an intoxicating concoction. The ride started with a jolt and Lily's horse rose, pulling her away and severing their connection. She smiled, and Eric extended his hand palm up. She slid her hand into his, their fingers intertwined. Their mounts rose and fell, up and down.

He never realized how much life was like a carousel—sometimes up, sometimes down. He gazed at his beautiful princess on her white stallion.

Thankfully, he'd found someone's hand to hold through the ride.

Sarah Monzon is a pastor's wife and stay at home mother of two young children. When not changing diapers or singing the ABC song, she escapes into other worlds created by the written word. Sarah is an active member of ACFW.

One element of an enjoyable story is the reader's ability to identify with the characters. Not only have I experienced the same laundry dilemma as the heroine in our next story, I've suffered similar mortifying situations—in church, of all places! I'm confident you'll enjoy "Static" as much as I did. – VS

Static

Mary Laufer

Every Sunday at church, I sat behind the man of my dreams. His broad shoulders blocked my view of the altar, but I honestly didn't mind. I gazed at the back of his suit jacket and imagined running my fingers through his wavy, blond hair.

After the service, my dream man would wait patiently as those ahead of him exited. Behind him, I'd wait for the people in my row to move out, too. During those few minutes while we inched along, he always glanced my way. I'd try to think of something to say to him, but then lose my nerve and just smile. He smiled back, his blue eyes sparkling.

One Sunday I arrived a little late, and my usual seat was taken. Mr. and Mrs. Jackson and their two children had claimed the place directly behind my guy, but there was an empty chair right beside him. "Excuse me," I whispered, and he looked up. I pointed to the chair. "Are you saving that seat for someone?"

"Not at all." He shifted his feet, and I brushed by him.

My heart beat wildly as I sat down. I wondered if he would talk to me. While we waited for the service to begin, Reverend McCarthy, a tall middle-aged man with glasses, approached us. "Rick, would you pass the collection plate today?"

What a nice name. I wonder what his last name is.

"I'd be happy to," Rick said in a deep voice that resonated within the wooden walls of the church and within my heart.

We kept our distance until it was time for The Lord's Prayer. Reverend McCarthy instructed us to join hands, and an elderly woman on my left stuck her cold, bony fingers in mine. My right hand hung limp, unable to move. Rick's big warm hand reached down and clasped it.

"Our Father, who art in heaven," Reverend McCarthy began.

With Rick's hand in mine, I was the one in heaven. "Hallowed be Thy name," I said reverently and lowered my eyes.

That's when I noticed a little bump above my left knee. Was something bunched up inside my slacks? Probably a sock. My socks always clung to my pants when I took them out of the dryer.

I gently jiggled my leg to dislodge the sock, and it

fell down inside my slacks. A bright red, satiny cloth peeked out of the end of my pant leg. *That's not a sock. That's my thong!*

A few days ago, the thong had mysteriously disappeared. When it wasn't at the bottom of the washing machine, I thought it had been sucked up the drainage tube. Now my indecent underwear pooled at my feet, and against the hardwood floor it stood out like rose petals.

"And lead us not into temptation," the congregation continued.

Maybe I could cover it with my shoe. I stepped on the thong, but that didn't help. Part of the red satin stuck out in plain view.

"But deliver us from evil..." I could wait until the end of the prayer when my hands were free, pick up the thong and nonchalantly stuff it into my pocket. Yet that might draw Rick's attention to it.

"Amen," Rick said. He let go of my hand and bent to sit down. I had to do something quickly! In desperation, I kicked the thong backward with one swift motion of my heel.

Almost immediately, a child behind me shouted, "What's this, Mommy?" and a feminine voice answered, "Where in the world did you find that?"

Oh, Jesus have mercy! The Jacksons merely had to look at who was sitting in the chair ahead of them to figure out the owner. Would Mrs. Jackson tap me on the shoulder and ask with a disapproving frown, "Is this *yours,* Holly?" Would she hold up the shocking underwear for everyone to see?

My cheeks burned. They must have been the same scarlet as the thong. There was only one thing to do. I excused myself, squeezed by the old woman, and rushed down the aisle toward the door.

Unable to face Rick the following Sunday, I sat in

the back of the church. To my surprise, he sought me out after the service. "You ran out so fast last week," he said.

He was finally talking to me, and all I could manage to say was, "I had to leave."

His lips quivered as if he were suppressing a laugh. He reached into his pants pocket and pulled out something red. "Does this belong to you?"

I sucked in my breath. *My thong!* I snatched it from him, pushed it into my purse, and looked around to make sure no one else had seen. "It clung to the inside of my slacks when I did laundry, and then fell out at the worst possible moment. How did you–?"

"After you left, someone put it on your seat."

I clapped my hand over my mouth, not knowing whether I was going to giggle or cry. He stood there grinning, waiting for me to recover.

"I was afraid you'd think the wayward panties belonged to a wayward woman."

He chuckled. "Let's start over, okay? I'm Richard Wright. And you are?"

"Holly Anderson." I shook his outstretched hand. *Mr. Right? 'Right' was actually his last name?*

By the following summer, it was mine. Reverend McCarthy married us on a beautiful July day, not far from where my embarrassing incident occurred. When it came time in the ceremony for Rick to kiss me, I ran my fingers through his wavy hair and thought about the silly thong that had ultimately brought us together. No one could see it through the layers of my wedding dress, but I knew it was there, red and satiny and full of static for our wedding night.

Mary Laufer has a degree in English from The State University of New York at Albany. Her stories and poems have been published in *The Christian Communicator, Love is a Verb Devotional* and in several volumes of *Chicken Soup for the Soul, A Cup of Comfort,* and *Whispering Angel Books.* She works as a substitute teacher in Central Florida.

Who doesn't love a strong lady cop? Introduce her to a street preacher with chocolate brown eyes and a heart for wayward kids, and you've got romance ready to happen. Now throw a police investigation into the mix. Is there a better premise for a gripping story? If you're like me, you won't be able to stop reading this romantic mystery until the last, satisfying word. – VS

Common Ground

Laura Ware

My partner Jim Madison and I pulled up to the Elaine Collier Center for Disadvantaged Youth. We'd never been here before, even though the building was in the neighborhood we were assigned to. Small, rundown homes lined the nearby streets and a good number of the businesses were boarded up.

Jim cocked his head. "Looks like it used to be a store

of some kind," he observed. "What do you think, Rachel? Maybe a dress shop?"

I ignored my partner's stupid questions, got out of my department-issued sedan, and studied the one-story concrete building. Two large windows in front sported black security bars, necessary in this part of Whitaker, Florida. Unlike the buildings on either side of it, the front walls were relatively clean and free of graffiti. Someone had painted the building a burnt orange – not what I would've picked, but I suppose it had seemed a good idea at the time.

Bicycles jammed the racks underneath the windows. I heard a faint bass beat coming from the building and assumed someone had their radio on full blast.

I turned towards the sound of an opening door. The smell of frying onions and peppers from the Cuban restaurant across the street tickled my nose before the door shut. A stooped, elderly Hispanic man briefly met my eyes, then dropped his eyes and shuffled down the street towards the residential area. I guessed he'd seen the badge dangling from a blue lanyard around my neck.

Jim smirked at me. "Cat got your tongue, partner? Or would a dress shop be too girly for you?"

I frowned at him. Jim was a temporary replacement for my regular partner, who was home recovering from emergency gall bladder surgery. Unlike Dave, Jim seemed to have an issue partnering with a woman and expressed it in little digs and jabs that I tried to ignore.

But sometimes I tired of it. "Come on, rookie, let's do our job." I moved towards the carved oak door that led into the youth center.

Jim's smirk turned into a scowl, but he fell in step behind me without another word. Hopefully, reminding him that I was senior detective would make him behave professionally once we got inside.

When I pushed open the door, I heard a screech of guitars and a wailing voice that a generous person might have called singing. I walked up to a waist-high counter that extended across the large open area. A white chain provided access to behind the counter where I saw rows of long tables set up.

A large number of teenagers clustered in groups at the tables. Several glanced up as we approached the counter and then stared at us with wary eyes. I scanned the young faces, seeing if anyone matched the description of our suspect.

Just as I spotted the kid, a man stepped into the room from a door to the left. He followed the teens' gaze to us and concern flickered across his tanned face. He quickly stepped to the counter and grabbed a computer mouse. Seconds later the awful noise ended in mid-note.

I studied the man. He had dark brown hair cut short and chocolate brown eyes. He appeared to be around my age and wore a pair of faded jeans and a t-shirt that displayed characters from the latest *Avengers* movie.

"I'm Eric Farmer, director of the center," he said in a voice that was cautiously pleasant. "Can I help you?"

I pulled my blue notepad out of my navy pants pocket. "I'm Detective Rachel Harmon and this is my partner Jim Madison. We're looking for a Carlos Perez and were told we might find him here."

As I said the name, I saw the kid I'd first noticed stiffen and pale. He was short and wiry, and his black hair tumbled over his forehead. He wore denim shorts and a plain white t-shirt. A couple of the bigger boys stepped between us and the boy, as if trying to protect him from us.

"May I ask why you're looking for him, Detective Harmon?" Farmer asked.

"It's part of an investigation I'm conducting," I said. "Nothing to concern yourself about."

"These boys are very much my concern." Farmer stood his ground, not moving to let us past the counter. "If you intend to question him, I'm going to insist that I be present as his advocate."

I stared at the man. Jim took his hands out of his pockets and scowled. "That's not your call."

"Then you're intending to interrogate him without his parents or a child advocate?" Farmer asked, looking from Jim to me.

"We'd like him to answer a few questions," I said. "We'll contact his parents or an advocate if he requests it, or we have to arrest him."

A low rumble sounded from the teens in the room. I realized there were a dozen of them there, all stiff with anger. Was anyone armed? I wondered.

Farmer turned towards the boys. "Enough of that!" he snapped. "Carlos, come here."

The wiry kid didn't move. "Aw, Preacher Eric, I didn't do nothin'."

My eyebrows shot up. "Preacher?"

Farmer glanced back at me. "Long story." Turning back to the boys, he began to speak to Carlos in rapid Spanish. The kid fired back, and they went at it for a few minutes while Jim and I listened. I knew a little Spanish but not enough to follow the conversation, and my partner knew less, so I wasn't sure what was being said.

Finally, Carlos heaved a huge sigh and dragged himself over to the counter. My source said he was fifteen, but up close, he appeared younger. He glared at me and Jim. "What you want?"

I worked to keep my patience. "Carlos, we have a few questions for you. If you'd just step outside- "

He shook his head. "I ain't goin' with you. I don't

have to talk to you. I know my rights!"

Jim frowned. "You want us to read you your rights and arrest you, kid?"

"On what charge?" Farmer demanded.

"Jim, stop," I said. "Look, Carlos, if you'd like us to call your parents and have them meet us here..."

"*Mi mama* is at work. And good luck finding my dad– he's been gone for years." Carlos glanced up at Farmer. "If I talk to you, I talk to you with Preacher Eric with me. Or else forget it."

Farmer laid a hand on Carlos' shoulder. "Look, let's take this to my office, all right? Better to talk there then out here."

"Are you a child advocate?" I demanded.

"As a matter of fact, I am," he replied. "My certificate's in my office if you want to take a look. And unless I'm mistaken, if Carlos wants me present, my certification is irrelevant."

That stopped me. Jim's mouth dropped open. "No freaking way."

Carlos bristled. "Preacher Eric don't tell lies."

"Okay," I said. I figured it might be better to take this somewhere private, away from the other kids. "Let's see this office of yours."

Farmer removed a stack of files from a folding chair, shrugging an apology for his small, crowded office. My eyes swept the cream colored walls and I saw his child advocate certificate, framed and hung to the left of the door.

Farmer placed the files he'd moved in front of a dark green filing cabinet with a dent near the bottom. He waved towards his battered metal desk. "Make yourself at home."

The desk had more files piled on it and a black

leather Bible with Farmer's name in gold letters on the cover. I glanced at a picture of Farmer with his arm around a slender woman with long blond hair and a huge smile. They were leaning against a wooden rail and the background of the picture was thick with greenery. Farmer guided Carlos to the padded armless office chair behind the desk. I decided to take the offered seat, leaving Jim no choice but to lean against the wall next to me. He crossed his arms, looking unhappy.

Carlos looked down at the Bible, not meeting my eyes. I decided to get this whole thing over with. Consulting my notes, I asked him, "Carlos, do you know a family by the name of Pemberton?"

His head jerked up at the name. "I know their boy Roger. He don't like me."

I raised an eyebrow. "I get the impression you don't like him very much, either. In fact, you guys got into a fight last week on the final day of school, correct?"

Carlos chewed his lip and didn't answer. Farmer put a hand on his back. "You didn't mention this, Carlos, but the others told me. Tell the detective what happened."

"He started it!" Carlos burst out. He looked at Farmer pleadingly. "Did they tell you that? I didn't start nothin', he did."

"What happened?" I asked.

"Roger, he starts talkin' s-stuff about *mi familia*," Carlos said with another glance at the director. I got the impression "stuff" wasn't the word he first had in mind but he was controlling his language for Farmer's sake. "Then he pushed me. I hadda push back, or I'd lose...lose..."

"Status?" I guessed.

Carlos nodded. "We both got into trouble, but it was his fault."

Farmer squeezed the kid's shoulder. "You shouldn't

let him provoke you like that."

"He started it." Carlos repeated.

"And you told him you'd get even, right?" I said. "That's what witnesses said they heard."

Carlos' cheeks flushed. "He talked trash about my mama. He can't do that."

"So you decided to get back at him," Jim said, trying but failing to look sympathetic. "Right?"

Farmer frowned. Carlos shifted in his seat. "What do you mean?"

I flipped back to my notes. "He means that someone broke into the Pembertons' house this morning while everyone was gone. Trashed Roger's room and took some things."

The kid went pale. "No! I didn't do that." He started to get up but Farmer had a firm grip on his shoulder. "Who says I did that?"

"Where were you this morning between eight forty-five and ten AM?" I asked.

Carlos cut his gaze towards the door. "I was sleepin'."

"Not according to one of the neighbors." Jim flipped through his green notepad. "They saw someone who looked like you on a bike across the street from the Pemberton house this morning."

Farmer's shoulders slumped. He looked down at Carlos. "You need to tell us the truth. You know how I feel about lying, Carlos."

To my surprise, tears filled the kid's eyes. "Okay. I was there. I was lookin' for Roger. But I didn't see him, so I left. I didn't go into the house, Preacher Eric. I swear I didn't."

Farmer gazed into Carlos' face a long moment. Then he turned to me. "Do you have any evidence that he was in the house?"

"No direct evidence," I admitted. "But he was in the

area. He has a grudge against Roger Pemberton. And it wouldn't be the first time he stole something."

"I know about his record," Farmer said. "But I believe he's telling the truth now. So unless you have a reason to detain him or have further questions..."

"Think carefully, kid," Jim said, straightening up. "We got your fingerprints from the shoplifting incident. If you were in the house, better to come clean now."

Scrubbing his face with the hem of his t-shirt, Carlos glared at Jim. "I wasn't there. I went from there to here and I ain't left here today."

I looked at Farmer. "Can you verify that?"

Farmer narrowed his eyes as he thought. "He got here sometime this morning–I'm not sure when. But he's pretty much been here since. I remember he was here for lunch."

"You serve lunch?" Jim asked.

"Some of the boys pitched in and we got pizza for everyone." Farmer's gaze slid to me. "Anything else?"

I scribbled a few notes onto my pad. "Carlos, how can I contact your mother? We might want to search your house."

Carlos stiffened. "You gotta talk to her?"

Jim snorted. I worked to stay patient. "I would like her permission to look through your house. So, yes, I have to talk to her."

The kid shifted in his seat. "You can't call her at work. She's a waitress and she has to keep her phone off while she's working."

"I understand," I said. "Just give me the number."

He muttered a phone number that I took down. I then pulled out a business card with my name and contact information on it. "I want you to call me if you can think of anything that will help us find out what happened."

Carlos made no move to take the card. Farmer

reached over and plucked it from my hand. "Thank you. Carlos, I think you can go now."

At my nod, the kid scrambled out of his seat and all but ran out of the room. When the door slammed shut, Jim shook his head. "Bet he's got the stuff stashed somewhere. We should take him to the station and talk to him some more."

"I thought in this country someone was innocent until proven guilty," Farmer said with an edge to his voice. "Or are poor, troubled kids the exception to the rule?"

"'Troubled kids,'" Jim snorted. "Yeah, they're trouble all right."

"Jim, stop." I stood and held my hand out to Farmer. "Thank you for your help. Please don't hesitate to contact me if you learn anything."

Farmer shook my hand. "No problem, Detective Harmon. I hope you find out who robbed that family."

He led us out of the office. As we headed to the door, I could see Carlos was surrounded by the other kids, who followed our movements with hostile eyes. I kept my head up and my step sure as we walked outside.

"What a jerk," Jim said once we were in the car. He mopped his face–the car had become pretty hot after sitting in the afternoon sun.

"He's sticking up for the kids," I said, starting the car. "And he's right –we don't have enough evidence to take the kid to the station. You know that as well as I do."

"That's a matter of opinion," Jim said. "I think you chickened out there, Rachel. You let those kids and that guy intimidate you."

I clenched my jaw, fighting to keep my temper. "I'm not going to start an incident with a group of kids on the evidence we have. We'll get permission to search his house and dig some more. You know, do detective work."

"Whatever," he groused.

I bit back a harsh response and we thankfully travelled the rest of the way back to the station in silence.

"Detective Harmon?"

I glanced away from my computer screen. To my surprise, Eric Farmer stood next to my desk. "Mr. Farmer? What can I do for you?"

He shifted his weight from foot to foot. "Well, I know this will seem strange. I was wondering if we could go somewhere and talk."

"We could talk here, if you like." I waved my hand to encompass the squad room. About half the desks crammed into the room were empty, including my partner's. The murmur of half a dozen conversations took place around the room, occasionally punctuated by the ringing of a phone. Despite the fact the building had central air conditioning, the room was always warm during the summer months. Most of us shed our jackets while working in here and occasionally curse the dress code.

Farmer shook his head. "I was hoping we could go to the diner where Carlos Perez' mother works." With a small smile, he added, "The coffee is some of the best in Whitaker and their Dutch apple pie is superb."

I stared at him while my thoughts raced. What I was currently drinking was coffee in name only, certainly not the best anywhere. All I was looking forward to was whatever I could scrounge out of my nearly bare fridge and a lonely evening.

I remembered the picture on his desk and tried to see if he wore a ring. "What about Mrs. Farmer?"

A shadow crossed his face. "There is no Mrs.

81

Farmer." He dropped his gaze to his shoes. "Maybe this wasn't a good idea. I'm sorry."

"No, wait," I said as he turned away. "Just give me two minutes and I'll go." I grabbed the folder I had been reviewing and began stuffing papers into it.

He looked at me with a mixture of hope and trepidation. "I don't want to be a bother, Detective Harmon."

"First," I said, stacking my paperwork into neat piles, "this isn't a bother. And second, if we're going to go out together, my name is Rachel."

The smile came back. It looked good on him. "Then please, call me Eric."

I stood up and grabbed my navy dress jacket from the back of my rickety office chair. "Well then, let's go, Eric, before someone finds something for me to do."

⚬⚬⚬

The Blue Moon Diner, located a few blocks west of the youth center, had a black and white checkerboard floor, blue leather topped bar stools along the long clean counter, and booths done in dark blue padding. We took seats at one of the booths in front of the large window that had the diner's name etched on it with a picture of a steaming cup of coffee.

Eric insisted on one check and got himself a Philly cheesesteak sandwich to go with his coffee and pie. I decided on a bacon cheeseburger and fries. The waitress who took our order wasn't Carlos' mom, but she promised to send her over when the dinnertime crowd slowed down a bit.

While we waited for our food, Eric asked me about myself. Had I always wanted to be a detective? Was it hard being a woman in the job? What did I enjoy doing in my off time?

I paused to sip some of my coffee, which was as good

as he said it was. "You'd make a good interrogator, Eric."

He grinned. "I'm sorry. I'm just curious, that's all."

I cocked my head. "My turn. How long were you a preacher?"

The grin fell away from his face. He busied himself with unwrapping his silverware from his paper napkin. "What makes you say I was a preacher?"

I ticked off my points on my fingers. "One, Carlos called you Preacher Eric. Two, there's a Bible on your desk. Third, Carlos didn't want to swear in front of you. So you're either very religious, or a preacher. Which is it?"

He sighed. "I was a preacher. But that was over a year and a half ago. Now I work with the boys."

The waitress brought our food. I waited until she was gone and squirted some ketchup on my plate. "What happened?"

He didn't answer for a long moment, just stared at his food. Finally he sighed. "I suppose I should 'fess up' like I tell the kids to."

I paused, a French fry halfway to my mouth. "What, did you steal from the collection plate?"

My feeble attempt at humor fell flat. He shook his head. "I thought I was ready for this," he muttered. When he raised his head to look at me, I could see he was fighting tears. "My wife...she died. At the church building where I served."

My fry fell back on my plate. Whatever I'd been thinking had been nothing like that. "What happened?"

He swallowed. "Well, our auditorium has very high ceilings. Some of the light bulbs in the chandeliers needed to be changed. I said I'd do it but I forgot...Monica, she got the ladder and climbed up to do it for me. They say she lost her balance and...well, the ladder was twelve feet tall and she hit the top edge of a pew...her neck broke."

"Eric, I'm so sorry," I breathed.

"I can still hear her scream." His hands clenched together in front of his face. "I was in my office...when I got to the auditorium, she was laying there..."

"Stop," I said. "You don't have to tell me anything else."

"Don't you see?" It was as if he couldn't hear me. "I couldn't stand at the podium and look out there again...all I'd see is her...and how can I preach God's word when I failed Him so badly?"

I blinked. "How did you fail God? Seems to me He failed you."

"No," he shook his head. "I know it was an accident, He didn't cause it...I did. Because I couldn't be bothered to do what I was supposed to do. I didn't look after Monica and protect her like she deserved."

I reached over and pulled his hands down so they lay between us. Grasping them, I said, "Listen to me, Eric Farmer. I don't know you that well, but I know you well enough that I can say you would *never* have done anything to hurt your wife. It was, as you said, an *accident*. Stop punishing yourself and start giving yourself the forgiveness you'd give someone else in your situation."

He stared at me, his mouth slightly open. Then he pulled one of his hands away and wiped his eyes. "You sound like a more blunt version of my counselor."

I smiled. "Well, they're right, okay? And so am I."

"I suppose you are." He gestured to the food in front of us. "Your food's getting cold. You should eat...and thank you. For understanding."

"It's fine," I said, picking up my burger. "I bet you've done it for others."

We'd just finished up our Dutch apple pie with whipped cream and were nursing final cups of coffee when Yolanda Perez came to talk with us. She wore her black hair in a bun and looked tired. "Preacher Eric?" she asked, her English heavily accented. "You wished to speak with me?"

Eric waved a hand towards me. "This is Detective Rachel Harmon. Someone has accused Carlos of a crime, and she's investigating it."

The woman's worried dark eyes shifted to me. "My Carlos...he is a good boy."

I placed my white coffee mug on the table. "I still need to check out the accusation. Carlos is accused of breaking into a house and taking things. I would like permission to search your home."

The woman's hands twisted her white apron. "I cannot leave yet. Today I work a double shift. Tomorrow I work too."

"If you give me permission, I can go and check things out." I said. "Is Carlos home?"

"He should be," she said. "But he won't let you in. I tell him, no strangers in the house."

"He met me today," I said. "I'm not a stranger."

She still looked doubtful. Eric spoke up, "Yolanda, what if I went with the detective? I promise you, she is good at her job. Carlos is in no danger from her."

"The *policia*...they always think bad of my boy." Carlos' mother gave me a look that was half fearful, half defiant.

"She will give him a fair hearing," Eric said. "She was fair with him today. Not all police are prejudiced, Yolanda. You know that."

"I am sorry, Preacher Eric," she said, lowering her eyes. "If you go with her, I will say yes."

"Thank you." I turned to Eric, I said, "When do you

want to go?"

He shrugged. "No time like the present. You up for looking around tonight?"

I thought about it a minute. If Carlos was our thief, the longer we waited, the more time he had to get rid of evidence. "All right. Let's finish up and go."

❧

I followed Eric to a street not too far from the youth center. Clearly the neighborhood had seen better days. Despite the lateness of the day, there was enough sunlight to note the broken sidewalk and patchy lawns.

Carlos' home was a small gray frame house with dirty white trim. A flower box sat under a front window on the left which held bright red and yellow blooms that I couldn't name off the top of my head.

Eric got out of his black Jeep Patriot and waited for me at the steps that led to the door. Someone had swept the walkway free of dirt and I wondered if it had been Carlos. There was a green bike leaning against the house near the door.

We climbed the two concrete steps and Eric knocked. "Carlos? It's Preacher Eric."

Nothing. I heard voices, glanced to my left, and realized that the window I saw was open. The voices came from the television. I looked at Eric, who shrugged and knocked again, louder this time. "Carlos! Your mom said I could come over. Open the door!"

I went around to the window and peeked through the screen. The TV set, an older boxy model, gave faint light in the darkened room. I saw the shape of a lumpy couch and a low coffee table.

I stepped further to the left to see if I could see any more. That's when I heard the crash, followed by a cry of pain. It came from somewhere in the back of the house.

I dashed around the house. Eric called out a question to me but I didn't catch his words as I circled the place. A small backyard held a rusting swing set and more blooming flowers that I barely noticed. A window screen leaned against the house. I peered into the open window and looked at a small breakfast nook with a round black table and three matching chairs. There were scuff marks on the sill, as if someone had climbed in.

I could hear the fight more clearly back here – wordless yells and banging. I levered myself through the window. Though I was probably messing up evidence, my gut screamed at me to get in the house *now*.

Once I straightened, I raced towards the source of the sounds, catching a glimpse of the small but tidy kitchen to my left. I could hear Eric pounding on the front door but instead of letting him in, I turned down a narrow hallway and into a bedroom.

Carlos was there, struggling with someone. Someone bigger than him and blond, whose back was to me. Just as I shot through the doorway, I saw the blond raise a knife.

I yanked my gun out. "Drop it!" I screamed, just as he brought it down, burying it in Carlos's chest.

The smaller boy groaned and fell. Yanking the knife out of his victim, the blond turned. I stood face to face with the Pembertons' son, Roger. He was breathing hard, his eyes bright and dilated. "Go away," he said.

Great. He was high. "Drop the knife, Roger," I said. He bent down to pick up a large green trash bag. "I'm not kidding, drop it!"

"I was gonna leave some of the stuff here," he slurred. "So you'd find it. Didn't expect the little wetback to be here. You're ruining everything."

"Drop the knife," I repeated. My thoughts raced. Carlos was on the floor, bleeding badly. I could still hear

87

pounding in the background. Roger wasn't in his right mind. And I didn't want to shoot a drugged up kid.

I holstered my gun and slowly reached for my Taser. "Put down the knife, and let's talk."

A loud crash came from the front of the house, startling both of us. Fortunately, I recovered first. Yanking my Taser from my belt, I leapt towards Roger and hit him with the voltage.

He jerked, the knife falling from his nerveless hand. I kicked it away and shoved him to the floor. Dropping on top of him, I yanked out my handcuffs and secured him.

Eric appeared in the doorway, holding his right shoulder. He took in the sight before him at a glance before seeing Carlos. "No!"

I got there first, my hands pressing down on the bloody wound in his chest. "Carlos, stay with me, okay?" To Eric I snapped, "Call 911."

The kid shuddered under my hands. "Hurts," he gasped.

"I know it does, but I've got to stop the bleeding." Blood seeped through my fingers and I pressed harder, trying to ignore his groan of pain.

Eric knelt beside me, taking one of Carlos' hands. "Yes, operator, I'm still here..." he said into the phone. "I think he was stabbed. Please hurry."

Carlos gasped again. "Can't breathe."

Had the knife nicked a lung? I prayed not. "Help is coming. Just hang in there, okay?"

"Carlos, you're going to be fine," Eric said, squeezing his hand. "Talk to me. What happened?"

I felt Carlos' chest rise as he struggled to take a breath. "Roger...found him in my room...dunno how he got in...heard a noise and went to check an' there he was..."

I heard the welcome wail of sirens. "Hear that?

88

Help's almost here, Carlos, you're doing great, just a few more minutes."

"Dear God, please help Carlos," I heard Eric pray next to me.

As I listened for the arrival of the EMTs, I added my prayer to his. *Please help Carlos.*

∽෩∾

"Thank you," I said to Eric as he handed me a Styrofoam cup of coffee.

Yolanda Perez sat next to me on the brown vinyl couch in the Whitaker Memorial Hospital's Surgical Waiting Room. She murmured "*Gracias*" as Eric handed her a cup. He went back to the coffee machine by the door and fixed one for himself before coming to sit next to Carlos' mother.

I sighed and looked down at my hands. While answering questions and helping to secure the scene, an EMT had given me some wet wipes to clean the blood off my hands. I'd done my best but now I could still see some red under my nails. I hoped no one else had noticed.

Yolanda Perez had already been in the waiting room when we arrived. She told us that Carlos had been taken to surgery. Now we just had to wait.

I got up and paced the small room. It helped that we were the only ones in here. Eric watched me, his eyes dark with worry.

Carlos' mother finally asked, "Can you tell me what happened, Preacher Eric? Who hurt my son?"

I half-listened as Eric filled her in. We'd been lucky. Lucky that Eric suggested we visit the house that night. Lucky we got there when we did.

Eric was still talking when a woman with light brown hair, dressed in stained green surgical scrubs, came into the room. "Family of Carlos Perez? I'm Doctor

Stevens."

Yolanda Perez stood up. Eric put an arm around her. I stopped pacing and held my breath.

The doctor smiled. "Your boy is going to be fine. We repaired the damage to his lung and he'll need respiratory therapy, but I expect him to make a full recovery."

Carlos' mother sagged against Eric's arm. I hurried to help him lower her to the couch. She began to cry. "He's going to be all right. Praise God."

"Yes." Eric looked at me, his eyes shining. "He's going to be all right."

And before I knew it, he grabbed me by the shoulders and kissed me.

I was surprised–but I have to admit I was pleased too. The kiss was sweet, and I found myself kissing him back.

Then I remembered where I was. Eric must have realized it too, because we both broke the kiss at the same time, each taking a step back.

Dr. Stevens watched, smirking. My cheeks blazed.

Yolanda Perez stood up, smiling at both of us. "Doctor, can I see my son?"

"Of course," the doctor said. She held the door open for her and they left the waiting room.

Eric's face was as red as mine felt. "I – I'm sorry," he stammered. "It was just I was so relieved, and you – I feel a connection to you, Rachel, and –"

"No, it's okay," I said. "It was the heat of the moment. But maybe." I swallowed. "Maybe we could get to know each other better before you kiss me again?"

He smiled. "I'd like that. I'd like that very much."

"So would I." I couldn't help but return his smile. I knew that the memory of this kiss would carry me through the days and weeks of getting to know this man better. And I was looking forward to the whole thing.

Laura Ware's column, "Laura's Look," appears weekly in the *News Sun* (Highlands County) and covers news items or ideas she can talk about for 600 words. She is the author of a number of short stories and several novels. Her latest novel, *Two Weeks in Guyana*, the story of a sixteen-year-old's reluctant first mission trip, is scheduled to come out the summer of 2015. She is currently working on a sequel to her novel, *Dead Hypocrites*. Laura lives in Central Florida. You can find out more about her as well as news about her current and upcoming titles at www.laurahware.com.

In today's world we're hard pressed to find someone who has not been touched by the wounds of war. Maybe that's why this story resonated so deeply with me. Or maybe the symbolism of the fountain struck a chord. Regardless, I hope Ms. Iacuzzi's debut story is the first of many from this talented author. – VS

The Fountain

Patricia Iacuzzi

"What's under here?" The gardener nudged the heavy tarp with the toe of his boot. They were the first words the taciturn man had spoken since he'd arrived, exited his truck, and followed Rachel into the backyard.

Memories. The thought was like a fist squeezing her heart.

"It's equipment for the fountain and reflecting pool. I was going to do it myself, but after I looked at the plans the project was a bit more than I could handle. That's why I called you." She lifted her chin indicating a spot near the patio. "I'd like it installed over there, near those violets." She moved toward the area were the tiny flowers grew thick in the shade. "It reminds me of a forest glen." When he made no comment, she folded her arms and scuffed a spot in the grass with her sandal. "I mean, if you do that sort of work. Landscaping, that is. Your newspaper ad said you're a gardener."

He hunkered down, grabbed the edge of the heavy plastic covering and peeled it back to reveal a large stack of building materials; natural stones, pool parts, sacks of concrete. "I do some."

Rachel sucked in a breath, let it out, and pasted a smile on her face. "By the way, my name is Rachel Marshak." She extended her hand.

He stood and took her hand without looking at her. "Mark Cameron." Instead, he continued to study the site where she wanted the fountain. Did he think it was a pathetic idea? He nodded slowly. "It's a good spot."

Shielding her eyes in the bright morning sun, she watched him walk over to the place she'd pointed out. Highlights glinted off his thick sandy hair. *Almost like Steve's.*

When he returned to her side, she withdrew some photos and a small sketch from her jeans pocket. "Here's what I had in mind. The fountain is a memorial." She swallowed. "For my husband." It felt as if a lump had taken over the air space in her throat and her voice fell to a whisper. "He was killed in Afghanistan in '09."

Squinting, Mark examined the faded photos she'd handed him. The first of two pictures showed Rachel leaning into her husband's shoulder, their arms around each other. A high waterfall provided a gorgeous backdrop. Rachel tapped the picture with a glossy pink fingernail. "That was on our honeymoon at Watkins Glen. We both loved the outdoors and camping. He was the photographer in the family, and I like to draw. The other one is Steve in his Marine uniform just before he went overseas."

Her gaze fell to the Semper Fi symbol tattooed on Mark's steely-looking right forearm. She recalled the same image in his gardening ad, and noticed his limp while he'd walked around silently scrutinizing the area.

His expression slammed shut as he shoved the photo back at her. Rachel felt a sting of remorse and hesitated before she handed him the drawing. Had she stirred bitter memories for him?

"This is what I'd like the fountain to look like. Kind of a miniature version of Watkins Glen with rocks and a pool beneath it, so it has a natural look. Oh—and some pink roses planted near the patio. I love roses and had them for my wedding bouquet."

He gave an ill-concealed groan. "I can do the fountain. But you'll have to plant the roses yourself." Mark grabbed a spade and started to turn over the earth.

What an odd thing for a gardener to say. Or maybe he had another job lined up and wouldn't have the time? She shrugged inwardly, folded the drawing and slid it back in her pocket. She'd need to make sure she wasn't charged for any work he couldn't finish.

Rachel crossed her arms and, shifting from one foot to the other, watched as her dream finally began taking shape. When she riddled Mark with detailed questions about each step of the project though, he gave terse answers, and eventually fell silent when the digging became more strenuous. Reduced to hovering silently nearby, she studied his features, her brows puckered. *Mark Cameron...* Both his name and face seemed familiar, somehow. Where had she seen him before?

❧

Mark clamped his hands around the steering wheel of his Dodge truck to keep them from shaking as he headed toward the nearest Home Center to exchange the fountain's water pump. How had he gotten into this mess? His eyes left the road for an instant to glance at the address book on the seat next to him. Dad had answered Rachel's call, and Mark hadn't seen the name and address until this morning when he'd started out for work. Until it was too late. He certainly couldn't refuse to do the work now. That would be unprofessional—and just plain dishonorable.

But he never thought he'd have to create a memorial for a fellow Marine, let alone one for Steve Marshak. His throat constricted from the sting welling in his eyes. Swallowing hard, he clenched his jaw and slammed his fist against the steering wheel. Sometime before he finished the memorial he'd need to explain to Rachel what had happened to her husband.

As soon as he'd sped off in the truck, Rachel dashed for the bedroom, yanked open a large bureau drawer and rummaged beneath the bed linens stored there. She seized the photo album of pictures Steve had sent back from Afghanistan and began leafing through the plastic-sheathed pages. About half-way through she froze. Sure enough. There was Mark Cameron, a member of Steve's rifle squad.

A smiling Steve with two men on either side of him hunkered down in the front row, while a stalwart Mark stood behind them with four other soldiers. Rachel stared at the picture. How well had they known each other? If they served as brothers-in-arms, wouldn't they have been close? *What did they say—once a Marine, always a Marine?* And why didn't he say something when she showed him Steve's picture?

The memory of Mark's halting gait jarred her thoughts. Should she ask him, especially if he seemed to have such a difficult time talking about much of anything? Rachel sank onto her bed's floral print comforter, the open album resting on her lap. She brushed her fingertips over the picture of the small, seemingly tight-knit group of men beneath the plastic cover.

When she heard Mark's truck return she replaced the album in the drawer and headed back into the kitchen. Did Mark know how Steve died? She itched to question him, but did she really want to know?

"Would you like to take a break and have some refreshment? I just made up a pitcher of iced tea." Rachel stepped up on the patio and set the tray on the umbrella-covered table.

Mark turned, his camo-green t-shirt dark with sweat. Setting his spade aside, he removed his sunglasses and swept a bronzed, muscular arm across his forehead. He closed the distance between them in a few long strides. "Sounds good, but you didn't need to go to all that trouble."

He looked up from the tray, and a tiny jolt shot through her at the intensity of his blue eyes. Unmistakable, now that she'd seen his picture.

Startled by her reaction she tore her gaze away. She told herself it was merely the first opportunity she'd gotten to notice the unusual color of his eyes. What a unique shade of blue, like the canopy of clear summertime sky that covered them. A smile tugged at the corner of her mouth. She had a winter sweater exactly that shade. But at the moment, there was nothing warm or sweater-like about those cold, remote eyes.

"It's no trouble." She picked up the pitcher and poured a glass of tea. "Steve enjoyed a cold beverage when he did yard work too." Why did she need to mention Steve so often? It was as if everyone had to know she'd not abandoned her husband's memory after two years. Or had she hoped for a response?

Handing him a glass, she poured another for herself and scanned the gaping hole where the fountain would eventually rest. Rachel couldn't wait to see it completed, and how its beauty would enhance the property. She held her glass to her lips and watched over the rim as Mark closed his eyes and took a few deep swallows.

"You should sit down and rest a minute. You've been really going at that spot all morning."

The broad area, revealing overturned clumps of dark, damp earth, reminded her of a burial spot. She immediately shook the thought. Settling back in her chair, she crossed her legs and rested a hand on her knee. Maybe if she relaxed, he'd take the hint.

He took the chair across from her and his shoulders seemed to ease from the tension of a labor-intensive morning.

"Could you tell me something?" She held her glass close, ready to tilt it to her mouth.

"If I can." His gaze roamed the yard as though measuring the distance to the chain link fence in the likelihood he needed an escape.

"Why did you say I'd have to plant my own roses? I mean—I just thought since you're a gardener you must do that sort of thing." An easy question, at least to start. The real ones she struggled with would come later, questions he might not want to answer.

"Yeah. But I'm allergic to them."

"Then why are you in this line of business? If you're allergic to plants—"

He tossed back another swallow of tea. "No. Just roses."

She shrugged and nodded as if she understood. But she didn't, really. Her gaze shuttered, she studied his face—straight nose, strong chin and a firm jaw. For a moment, a bittersweet memory of Steve's hazel eyes crinkling with laughter filtered through her. She shifted in her chair as that annoying lump surfaced in her throat again and she tried to swallow it down. When she looked back at Mark's very blue, but very troubled eyes, she reminded herself again there were things she might not want to know.

Rachel straightened at the buzz of her cell phone in her pocket. She set her glass down and checked caller I.D. Her mother-in-law's number. "I'll be right back, Mark. Help yourself to more tea."

❦

"Hello, dear."

"Hi, Marge." Rachel grabbed a kitchen chair and sat down.

"Just wanted to ask if our Danny-boy could stay for supper tonight and spend some time with his grandma." Her mother-in-law's voice came across strong and clear. A sign not only of the same vibrant personality she'd shared with her son, but Rachel suspected she'd begun to lose her hearing as well.

Rachel hesitated on an intake of breath then slowly released it. "That would be fine, Marge. But you need to make sure he gets his homework done, too."

"No problem. So how did your project go today?" She sounded eager to hear the details. The suggestion to build a memorial of some sort had been Marge's, and Rachel, warming to the idea, worked out the specifics. Her and Steve's honeymoon spot—the image she'd try to capture in her drawing of a bubbling stream, rocks and flowers—came to mind. It would look perfect in the yard.

"Pretty well. I never realized there was so much to it. Digging out an area for the reflecting pool, mixing concrete for the stones, planting flowers. The guy I hired is doing a great job. And he served in the Marines about the same time Steve did." She braced an elbow on the kitchen table. "I think I might have Mark put in a small shade tree next to it, too."

Hesitation on the other end. "Mark? Anyone I know?"

Rachel smoothed a hand over the denim fabric of her jeans. After all, just because Mark was in Steve's photo didn't necessarily mean he'd been a close friend. There were eight men in the squad and over forty in the platoon.

She clipped her answer short. "I don't think so. My sister gave me the local paper with his ad and there was a twenty dollar discount. It had a Marine symbol in it, and I wanted to support vets, so I called him."

"I'm so glad you took my advice on this, Rachel."

"I am too. I think it will be beautiful."

"It will help keep Steve's memory alive, and that's especially important for Danny. Every time he goes out in the back yard to play, Steve will be there."

Oh, Marge. Please don't do this to us.

Unable to speak, Rachel closed her eyes and swallowed against the ache lodged in her throat. At first, shared moments of grief with her mother-in-law had drawn them closer together. Now Marge seemed shackled to those memories, unable to take pleasure in anything that didn't involve him, including their conversations. Rachel loved the woman dearly, knowing she'd feel the same if she lost Danny, but the thought she'd become like Marge, wallowing in bitterness, gnawed at her.

Rachel straightened, took a deep breath and glanced over at the paper with Mark's ad resting on the table. *Until today.* Her mood lightened as Mark's blue eyes swam before her. Had she begun to surface from a pool of memories once too deep to rise above?

"You'll always have Steve, Marge. Danny is the image of his father."

"For which I'm thankful every day."

When Marge's voice wavered, tenderness welled in Rachel's heart and compassion blossomed for the woman. She couldn't imagine losing Danny, and Rachel was grateful he was such a blessing to them both. She had her son, and Steve would live through him. She might have some difficulties with Marge, but she'd never be so cruel as to withhold her grandson from her. "Do you want to pick up Danny at school?"

"Sure. We'll make a stop at the library too."

"Sounds good, Marge. I'll be over to get him around eight. See you later."

Rachel disconnected the call and stared at her phone a few seconds, glad the conversation had ended so well. She glanced down at Mark's ad again. Thank goodness she hadn't said anything inadvertently hurtful.

At her stomach's rumbling complaint, Rachel checked her watch. Past noon. She'd actually not thought about lunch.

Rachel opened the refrigerator door. The thought struck her as brightly as the interior light that she hadn't tried too hard to make healthy lunches for herself anymore. As a mother she used her energy to make decent meals for her son. A few months ago she baked a cake from scratch for Steve's birthday. She'd gone to great lengths to prepare his favorite dishes so

Danny would not forget his father. But after Danny had eaten, he'd run off to play with friends leaving more of a gaping hole in her heart than if she'd not gone to the trouble. Had this been one of the signs she'd begun to live in shadows of the past as Marge had?

As she closed the refrigerator door, she looked toward the kitchen window and caught sight of Mark carrying a bag of concrete mix over his shoulder. A sudden spark leapt in her mind and she quickly moved over to the window. Should she invite him to lunch? She'd eaten lunch by herself every day for two years, unless Danny was off from school or her mother-in-law popped in. A cloud of butterflies rose in the pit of her stomach. The tea she'd offered his first day of work was a quick refreshment done out of courtesy, but the thought of preparing a good meal for a guest ramped up the tension. Especially a man—and a virtual stranger. Could she... *should* she offer?

She crossed her arms and leaned on the sill. "Mark, I'm going to throw together a chicken sandwich for lunch. Want one?"

He looked up at her, his sunglasses shielding his blue eyes and gave a curt nod. "Sounds good."

Used to his short responses now, Rachel grinned as she moved around the kitchen with a lighter step. Mark had immediately agreed. He hadn't made excuses. She opened a drawer to gather utensils she'd need to put together sandwiches and a salad. He said he'd be finished with the project by the end of tomorrow, so it would be nice to make a new friend, get to know him in the brief time they had before he left. Nor would she press him to say anything about Steve, or the war.

Or maybe he was just hungry? Another broad smile tugged at the corners of her mouth. Either way, she wouldn't be eating alone today. How had she gotten into such a rut? Her sister constantly reminded her that it wasn't healthy to be so withdrawn and alone. Chris, an extrovert "by design" as she always reminded her, would shake her head and call Rachel a typical ivory tower artist. Rachel had been fine with that...until now.

But like a moth emerging from a cocoon to try its wings, Rachel wanted to talk to someone, preferably someone she'd just met. There was something to be said about meeting new people and learning their story. No preconceived notions either way. It might offer some fresh insights into their lives. A few robins chirped wildly at the feeder outside, and Rachel's spirits lifted further.

And now that she thought about it, Mark seemed as private a person as she was.

In fact, maybe she'd be able to cheer him up. He certainly looked like he needed a mood lift. She recalled the limp and the tattoo and his picture in the album. He had to have a story as well. She grabbed the jar of mayo from the fridge and began spreading it on the crusty bread, ready to layer with lettuce and tomato. Rachel set the table with another fresh pitcher of iced tea, salad and chicken filet sandwiches. She'd even put fancy toothpicks in the bread to hold them together.

Rachel chewed the corner of her lip, surveying her table setting. Had she forgotten anything? There was an empty spot in the center of the table, just waiting to be filled. She snapped her fingers. In the living room a vase of lilacs sat on the coffee table. Inhaling the flowers' heady scent she loved so much, she set it in the center of the kitchen table.

Pausing at the window in the kitchen again, she called to Mark. "Time for lunch."

He sought her out, acknowledging her with a brief smile as he set aside his tools.

She heard him come through the breezeway and turned to see his tall frame fill the space of the open kitchen door. He certainly was good-looking and had a great build. But why wouldn't he, with all the physical labor he'd done for his business? Her hand shook slightly as she gestured with the salad tongs.

"If you want to wash up, the bathroom's the first door on your right."

He nodded and left her standing there watching him, a hint of the limp in his right leg still visible. Did he have pain with it, considering the work he did? When he returned, they sat opposite each other, the lilacs' fresh fragrance wafting between them. They reminded her of fresh-washed linen hanging out in the sun.

"Hope you like leftovers."

"Looks good." He braced his hands on his thighs and scanned the meal she'd laid out before him. "Can we say grace?"

"Of course." When had she left off saying grace before meals?

She would have to get in the habit again for Danny's sake.

Mark folded his tanned hands and bowed his head. His words, short and to the point, were nevertheless reverent and sounded sincere. Touched, Rachel added her silent thanks. Straightening, she handed him the bowl of salad greens and tongs. He added the mix to his plate then reached for the pitcher of iced tea.

A tiny prickle of concern nudged at her. Would it be a struggle to engage him in conversation after all? "I've been thinking about your allergy to roses. My son has allergies and the spring is a bad time for him." She smoothed her hand over the napkin spread on her lap. "Doesn't it bother you, being in the gardening business this time of year?"

He held up his sandwich ready to take a bite. "I'm in a partnership with my dad and I enjoy the work." He took a bite of his sandwich, chewed and swallowed.

"And I'm not really allergic to roses. Just don't like being around them. They were my wife's favorite flower." Picking up his fork, he stabbed at a mouthful of salad.

'Were' her favorite flower? Rachel's brows lifted. Everyone had a story, and it sounded like he'd been through some difficult times. Would he be interested in sharing if she questioned him further? After all, she probably wouldn't see him after he finished the memorial. Talking also might lighten a burden he seemed to be carrying.

Shifting in her seat, she cleared her throat. "You spoke about your wife in past tense. I'm sorry. When did she pass away?"

"She didn't." Mark sat back, his damaged leg sprawled out while he stared into the glass of golden-brown fluid his fingers were wrapped around. He twisted it a couple of times and the ice clinked. "A couple of years ago I was recuperating in Germany after I'd been wounded in Afghanistan. Sent her some roses for her birthday." He looked up at Rachel. "She liked red ones, though."

Rachel leaned forward, supporting her chin on folded hands. Painful memories seemed to be something they had in common.

"I eventually got a thank-you note, and she'd hoped I was feeling better." He took another sip of tea. "Hoped I felt better so she could break some news to me—that she'd filed for divorce and would I sign the papers that accompanied the note."

Rachel gasped. No wonder he'd been turned off by the mere thought of roses. What kind of woman would abandon him when he was so vulnerable?

"To be fair, she felt it took two to be married. I'd finished one hitch, and signed up for a second. By that time we were virtual strangers and the marriage, to her thinking anyway, was broken beyond repair."

"It seems to me, though..." Rachel smoothed out the folds out of her napkin again, choosing her words carefully. Should she venture an opinion on Mark's personal life? She looked up to see his eyes search hers, a hopeful look in their depths, and a feeling she wanted to ease his burden took hold in her. "I'm sorry you didn't get the support you needed while you were gone—especially considering the dangerous situation you guys were in." Rachel toyed with the emerald birthstone at her throat Steve had given her. "Perhaps she should have considered parting ways when you were in the states and on equal footing to discuss it."

He shrugged. "No. It was my fault entirely. I went ahead with my plans and signed up for that second time around." Mark stood, set his hand on the table to steady himself and gave a wry smile. "Anyway, it's all water under the bridge now."

Surely he deserved better than such selfish woman. Rachel rose. "I'm sorry things didn't work out."

"Well, thanks for the great meal. Really enjoyed it. Now I'd better get back to work."

As he headed for the door she caught a hint of his aftershave. It smelled a little like sandalwood mixed with the light film of sweat still clinging to his shirt. But it was not altogether unpleasant. Nudged by another memory, she was surprised how much she'd missed a man's scent around the house.

"Um... before you go, I wanted to ask... where did you serve?" *Tread lightly, Rachel.*

"Helmand Province, northern Afghanistan." Looking like he'd just side-stepped a trap, he moved quickly toward the door. "That fountain isn't going to get built by itself." He paused, his hand resting on the door knob as he seized her with his azure gaze.

In that brief instant, she felt immersed in that deep blue pool again, cool and bottomless. A surge of heat flooded her cheeks, and her lips parted to take in air and steady her rapid pulse. With a trembling hand, Rachel grasped the stone at her throat. *Helmand Province. Where Steve died.*

He gave a lop-sided smile. "I guess I'll pick up a couple of those rose bushes for you and plant them tomorrow."

Mark stepped into Rachel's kitchen to receive his check for the work he'd completed, a payment he'd decline before he said good-bye. This would be the last day he'd spend with her, and he already missed her hospitality—missed her. The thought created an emptiness inside that would take a long time to overcome.

Looking back, he examined the finished fountain and reflecting pool beyond the patio. Flowers surrounded it, a "Peace" rose bush, just now beginning to bloom, and a small Japanese maple planted nearby. He'd done his best, and Rachel had come out several times to watch its progress and tell him how much she liked it. They'd chatted about a lot of things; and whether he truly liked working as a gardener. He closed his eyes for a few seconds, the feelings her question had stirred washing over him again. It was great to be a gardener, to encourage new growth. Certainly a far cry from where he'd been.

He watched her move around the kitchen, graceful as a dancer in the simple task of setting the table. Dark hair flowed over her shoulders with every turn, her jeans hugged her figure and the soft green lace top she wore shadowed her curves.

"Sit down. I tried a coffee cake recipe my sister gave me. Hope you like it." She gave a throaty laugh.

What a beautiful laugh. She needed to do more of it.

But after what he had to tell her, she might not laugh again for a long time. He slipped his hand in his pocket to withdraw his wallet. She deserved to know. "First I have something to show you."

Still holding the pot of coffee, Rachel turned, her brown eyes puzzled.

"I knew your husband." From one of the wallet's photo sleeves he slipped out a picture and handed it to her.

Her hand trembling, Rachel took the photo and stared down at it. It was a copy of the honeymoon shot she'd shared with him the first day Mark had begun work on the memorial. The picture Steve always carried for good luck. With one tiny difference—a rust-colored stain in the top left corner. Steve's blood.

When she nearly dropped the coffeepot, Mark steadied her hand to set it on the table. She covered her crumpling mouth, closed her eyes tight and turned away. At a loss for words, he chafed a thumb across his forehead, wanting to gather her in his arms and comfort her. It was the least he could do.

He made a move to touch her and his hand fell to his side, the gesture fruitless.

The pain he'd just inflicted turned on him like a knife, searing through his gut. And after she'd tried so hard to reach out to him.

She looked down at the picture again, touching the corner almost reverently. He'd expected her to throw it back at him, throw him out. Maybe even wanted her to. But she'd never do something like that.

Finally she exhaled a shaky breath. "How well did you know him?"

"He took a bullet for me."

Mark couldn't meet Rachel's gaze. He'd finally said the words, but his stomach churned as badly as if he'd made his first kill. His hands curled into fists as he fought the urge to hold her, to protect her from his words and the knowledge of who he was. *That he was the reason her husband was dead.* He'd added to the burden of her grief as surely as the stones he'd piled up for the memorial she'd asked him to build.

"He was a hero." The words sounded so useless now. He needed to sit down. "He always talked about you and Danny. Gave me that picture just before he passed. "

Rachel finally relinquished the photo. He took it, his hands fumbling as he slipped it back into his wallet. Silent tears trickled down her cheeks and she gave a wobbly smile.

"Steve always liked to share," she said, her voice cracking.

He reached up to take her hands. When she surrendered and moved closer, his hands went to her waist and drew her closer still. She was warm to the touch, and he eased her down to settle on his lap. Supporting her with one arm across her back, he cupped her chin and turned her face to his. Her brown eyes melting and sweet, Rachel buried her tear-streaked face in his shoulder.

He cradled her head gently, and began rocking her. Her weeping ripped out another piece of his heart.

Rachel hung up the phone and lifted her face toward a ray of autumn sunshine filtering through the kitchen window. A noise behind her alerted her to the arrival of someone entering the room. She turned with a smile.

"Marge called. Her car is down and she wondered if she could catch a ride with us to church."

Mark took Rachel in his arms and planted a kiss on her forehead. She slipped her arms through his open jacket and around his waist, enjoying his strength as he tightened his embrace and pulled her close. She leaned back, and he tilted her chin up to gaze into his eyes. That distant look, once clouded with painful memories, had lifted. With gentle hands he cupped her face, and anticipation welled through her like a fountain. His lips feathered her mouth, teasing lightly across them before he pressed deeper to claim them.

As if she'd awakened from a trance, she opened her eyes, her breath sighing like a light breeze. Taking a step back, Mark made a visible effort to curb the desire etched in his eyes. They'd both be hard-pressed to wait until the wedding in December.

She offered him an impish grin. "We'll never get there if we keep wasting time like this."

"You call this a waste of time?" Mark grazed her forehead with his lips again before he released her. "Why, I'm just showing my gratitude, Ma'am." He winked. "Thanks to you, I no longer have an allergy to roses."

Rachel laughed, her hand lingering in his warm grasp as she spoke to her son coming down the hall, carrying his suit jacket. "Danny, get moving kiddo. We're leaving in a few minutes."

"Are we gonna chop wood after lunch, Mark? It's getting cold and you said we needed to store up more for winter."

"Yeah, and we'll pick up Grandpa Cameron too." Mark kneeled on one knee to button Danny's jacket and straighten his lapels before the boy bolted out the door.

"I'll be right along. I need to get something first," Rachel called as she went through the side door and grabbed a pair of garden shears on her way out to the backyard.

She paused before the fountain, its waters tumbling in lively abandon over the random piles of rocks. Bright shards of sunshine glanced through the branches and leaves of a miniature forest glen, and bounced off the waterfall to the pool beneath.

Soon she'd need to turn off the pump to stop its flow during the winter. But it would bubble to life again in the spring, like good memories flooding back. Rachel bowed her head. "Thank you, Father, for the gift of memories, and others to share them." She inhaled a deep breath of crisp autumn air. With her eyes once more fixed upon Jesus—the Source of Living Water— she no longer lived in the shadows.

Rachel cut a last vibrant rose still clinging to its bush for Marge, and headed for the car.

For you are the fountain of life, the light by which we see. Psalm 36:9 NLT

Patricia Iacuzzi ~ Retired art teacher from upstate New York. Enjoys writing, painting and making historical figures for museums. She is thankful the Lord has given her a purpose where she can witness to His love and glorify His Name through her work. She hopes her first published short story "The Fountain" blesses you, and dedicates it her son Anthony; to Bev, Jay, and Beth, and all American service men and women.

Jan Davis Warren is one of two authors who have multiple stories in this collection. When I read "Factor X," I was intrigued not only by Jan's ability to tell a captivating tale, but the premise of experimental drugs that could cure some of our most devastating illnesses...yet at what cost? – VS

Factor X

Jan Davis Warren

Taking great gulps of air, Elaine Singleton sat straight up, exhausted as if having fought her way out of a deep sleep.

O-oh, stupid move. She pinched her eyes shut to ward off an orchestrated burst of colored neon, which danced a silent but rhythmic beat through the bare windows. She grabbed her head to try and stop the loud pounding going on within her skull in sync with each flash.

The move evicted another groan. Pain radiated around her forehead, down her neck and arms. The room swirled. She eased back onto the pillow, clutching the sheet to anchor her.

Where am I? Certainly not home in Tulsa. The brief glimpse of the garish surroundings, before clamping her eyes shut, confirmed that much. Could it be another hallucination from the drugs?

A strong odor of roses invaded her thoughts and magnified her growing nausea. Once an avid gardener, since the accident she could no longer tolerate the smell of her favorite flowers.

She inched her head away from the light then chanced another peek. Through the dim haze of blurred vision, she noticed a note pad on the nightstand. Easing a hand toward the paper, she brought it closer. As her eyes fought to focus on the logo, her heart skipped a beat. *Las Vegas Hilton.* What was she doing in Las Vegas?

Had she been kidnapped? Her panic only increased the intensity of her pain. She knew the drill. Relax. Breathe. Her heartbeat slowed.

A door knob rattle nearby. China clinked, as if a cart had been pushed into the room.

Panic spiked her adrenaline into full alert. She had no weapon and no energy to escape.

Please Lord, protect me. Tugging the bedcovers over her head, she lay still as a corpse.

"Hey, E, where are you, babe? Did you get a nap?" The man came closer. "I brought dinner. What? Still in bed? Missed me that much?"

Except for the playfulness in his tone, and the fact he hadn't called her babe in years, the voice sounded suspiciously like her husband.

"John?" She peeked out from beneath the feather comforter as the person turned on the bedside lamp.

Piercing hot pokers stabbed into her cranium. "Turn out the light!" Her plea cost her plenty, but he did as she commanded. An undulating glow still intruded from outside. If only there were black-out curtains like at home.

"Elaine, I see you're back. The doc said this might happen." His cheerful cajoling of a moment before was replaced by a familiar hardness in his tone.

"What's going on?" She whispered as loud as she dared.

Garlic, green peppers and onions assaulted her senses as he move closer.

"Put that food into another room, and those, too." She pointed to a vase full of red roses on the night stand, before motioning him away. "You know I can't stand strong odors." As he complied, she slowly shifted to a sitting position. It was then she noticed she wore a skimpy nightie of black lace, something she would have never bought.

"Oh, my." She tugged the sheet up higher to cover the offending garment.

"Better?" He pulled a club chair up to the bed. "I'd almost forgotten how bad it used to be." Compassion softened his words. His eyes searched her face as he leaned forward, resting his elbows on his knees. "What is the last thing you remember?"

She rubbed her temple hoping for some measure of relief. Finding none, she searched her memory for the last entry.

"I was in the hospital." She glanced up for confirmation and was rewarded with a nod. Encouraged, she sought for more. Only snippets of disjointed images surfaced, then nothing. "I can't remember. Tell me...please."

He straightened and rubbed his hand through his hair.

When had he started to gray around the temples? The dusting of silver gave a distinguished air to his rugged contractor's tanned features.

"Do you remember the car wreck that caused the headaches?" He waited. She nodded and he continued. "Five years ago today, to be exact, you were hospitalized with unmanageable migraines. As a last-ditch effort for relief, you were admitted into an experimental program called Factor X." He stood, but then sat again, his posture stiff. "The research doctors had come up with a drug that was ready for human testing, which had the potential to do away with incessant migraines forever."

She sighed with the promise of relief. No more suffering? Such a medical breakthrough would be an answer to prayer.

"Wait! Five years ago? Didn't it work? Have I been in a coma?"

"Yeah, it worked, actually better than could be expected...until now." He looked grim.

"Great. Give me the meds, and we'll finish talking when they kick in. I don't know how much longer I can stand this pain." Sweat beaded her forehead. Her hand trembled as she reached out, palm up.

"Wait. There's something important you should know first." He pressed back into his chair and closed his eyes, as if saying a silent prayer. After a few moments, he leaned forward and took her hand within his work-calloused fingers.

Fear again thumped against her ribcage. She'd known, and loved, this man since they were in junior high. Only when things were really bad did his gunmetal-gray eyes darken to the color of soot. Like now, when he met her gaze.

"The medication had an unexpected side-effect." He paused, as if searching for the right words. "The drug took away the pain, but it also suppressed . . . the old you." He must have noticed her confusion for his voice softened. "A different version of you took dominance." His grip on her hand tightened. "The doctors started reducing the dosage over a month ago, as an experiment to see if the old and new personalities could merge without the pain coming back." He stared down at her fingers intertwined with his. "Apparently it didn't work."

"A different me? I don't believe it." She pulled loose from his grasp and clutched the sheet. "I have no memory of the last five years, how can that be?" Surely this was all a nightmare. If she could just wake up. One move of her head set the thumping in her skull up a notch. No. The pain was excruciatingly real. Definitely not a dream.

John stood and went to the other room. Moments later he returned with a newspaper and laid it on her lap.

She read the date. Lightheaded with disbelief, she struggled to breathe. How was it possible? Five years gone? Tears gathered and blurred her vision. She crushed the paper. Why couldn't she remember?

"The doctors pre-recorded a DVD to explain everything in case this happened. I'll go get it."

"John, just tell me in your own words...please." At her plea he hesitated then settled back into the chair.

"Reducing her meds even more this last week was E's way of helping with medical expenses. Our insurance has maxed out and they denied payment for the last two prescription refills. Eight thousand a month is worth every penny to keep her well." He closed his eyes. A tick pulsed at his jaw with the effort to control his emotion. "I didn't know what she'd planned until she'd already skipped every other day for a week."

"Who is E?" Jealousy squeezed her chest.

"E is you. Or rather a version of you. The part of you who emerged after the second dose of Factor X. She's everything you used to be...and more." He got up and paced to the window. "Getting rid of the pain allowed her to purge her system of the narcotics, but the withdrawal was heart-wrenching to watch." His words wavered. "She never complained." He cleared his throat and faced the bed.

"Afterward she convinced me to get healthy. We started taking ballroom dance lessons as a way to exercise together. The reason we're in Vegas is to compete in the National Ballroom Dancing Competition." He grinned. "E's really good." With a heated glance, he swept her length. "In case you haven't noticed, you've lost over forty pounds and are in great shape."

As he waxed on about the many virtues of "E", a growing outrage burned within Elaine for the injustice of it all. Irreplaceably gone were the last five years of her life. According to him, she'd become the vivacious person she'd always longed to be. It wasn't fair.

Before her car wreck, she couldn't get John to go to a movie that had singing or dancing in it. Now he was dancing in front of people? This imposter he called E had saved their marriage, successfully raised her two children, helped him grow his business by designing a new website, volunteered in the community, and even managed to take better care of her body than she ever could.

The pounding in her head intensified with the effort of wrapping her mind around all she'd been told.

"John, cut to the part where you give me the medicine." She could no longer sit up and shifted down into the covers. "The pain is getting worse by the minute," her voice lowered to a desperate whisper.

"I have the pill right here." He showed her a shiny white pill, about the size of an aspirin, with a large purple X in the middle.

Jan Davis Warren

She reached for it.

"Wait." He pulled his hand back, a flush staining his cheeks. "I love E and can't stand the thought of losing her, but she would want me to tell you the whole truth." His voice hardened with determination. "If you take this pill part of you will disappear again, most likely forever. The doctor said the medicine is no longer merely blocking the pain receptors and personality pathways from one region of your brain to the other. The drug is beginning to seal off those areas permanently." He hesitated then took a deep breath and plunged on. "The researchers have come up with a few newer drugs in the last five years that *might* lessen your type of headaches, but there is still too much unknown about your condition."

"If I try the new medicine and it doesn't work can I still take Factor X?" Anger crept into her tone. "Then you could have your precious E back." The jackhammer pounding away in her skull grew relentless.

"No. According to the doctors, there are too many variables involved. Once the meds are eliminated for a time, there is no guarantee E will ever surface again." Worry furrowed his brow. "Since you've reappeared, it could already be too late." He rubbed a hand across his face.

"So, I'm left with one of two options? Pain-free oblivion or killing little miss-perfect-alter-ego by my very existence." She instantly regretted the cruel tone of her words when John paled.

"I have to call the doctor and let him know what's happened." He placed the medication on the nightstand within her reach. "Tell me what you've decided when I get back." After a slight hesitation, he bent down and kissed her. His lips pressed against hers with intent, evoking a once familiar response with his gentle passion.

117

"No matter what, know this." He brushed away a tear that had slipped down her cheek. "I love you . . . all of you. Now and forever." His voice was husky with emotion and truth shone in his eyes.

He walked into the other room. She heard him pick up the phone, press some numbers and then ask to speak with a Doctor William Brante before he closed the connecting door.

Her eyes were drawn to the pill. *I've heard of dying to one's self, but this gives the saying a whole new meaning.*

Images of her previous existence filtered into her mind. The pain had reduced her home to cave-like environment shrouded with loneliness. The narcotics produced a "me" mentality that had forced her family to walk on egg shells if they wanted peace. Her condition had taken a toll on everyone.

Hadn't she cried out to God for her healing or her death so her family could return to normal? Who was she to complain about how God chose to answer her prayer? Factor X had produced both. Now was the time to ask the really hard question. What would love choose to do?

John hung up the phone. The conversation had taken longer than anticipated and confirmed his worse fears. It may already be too late.

He dreaded going back into the bedroom knowing he might have to face losing E, the woman he loved. That sounded insane. Elaine and E were the same person.

E was the adventure-loving version of Elaine that he'd married twenty years ago. That woman had disappeared after the car accident. She had survived being pinned in the mangled wreckage for several hours. Her extensive injuries resulted in severe nerve damage that caused the horrible migraines, which changed her...changed them all.

After the first treatment of Factor X, the transformation had been nothing less than miraculous. Pain-free for the first time in eight years, she radiated joy from every pore. She had gaps in her memory, but with determination and a healthy lifestyle she had overcome those obstacles. Every aspect of their marriage improved. Just thinking about her left him weak-kneed.

Finally freed from the need to think up excuses for delaying his return home to a darkened house of hushed conversations, he'd spent the last five years looking forward to his retirement and spending the rest of his life with her.

He didn't know if he could stand by and watch Elaine go through such suffering again. Maybe the doctors could regulate the new meds to set her free once and for all from her prison of pain. If so, then E might again emerge.

E had a thirst for life that continued to thrill and amaze him. She was the answer to his prayers.

He should probably call down and drop out of the dance competition. Disappointment weighed on his chest at not ever dancing with E again.

High heels tapping against the hardwood floor behind him made him jerk around. What he saw sucked the air from his lungs.

"Why aren't you ready, Johnny? Didn't you say we needed to check in with the contest coordinator by nine?" E stood in the doorway, breathtakingly beautiful, covered from neck to floor in a gown of royal blue satin. The color highlighted her short fiery locks, which she'd arranged to fluff around her smiling face.

"E!" In three strides he lifted her into his arms and whirled her around before he captured her lips with his.

119

The kiss deepened until he was ready to forego the contest and pursue more personal interests. Oh, how he loved this woman.

"Johnny, let me go, or you'll mess my makeup." She pushed away then patted his rear. "Scoot, cowboy, or we're going to be late." E turned to the table in the corner. "I'm starving. Is this our meal?"

"Sure, Babe. Enjoy, I won't be long." Words he could barely get out with the emotions clogging his throat. Funny, she never liked to eat this close to a performance.

He threw off his clothes and pulled on his tux. As he walked by the rumpled bed on his way out, he noticed a sheet of the hotel stationery on his pillow. Dread pounded like an iron fist in his chest when he recognized Elaine's handwriting.

Dear John,

I don't know how long before this miracle drug takes effect, but I want to free you of any guilt. This was my decision. Actually it is an answer to my prayers. I died in the car wreck. The doctors may have saved my body, but the years of pain trapped me inside a prison I couldn't escape, that you and the children couldn't escape either. Hug them for me and know I'm fine. I would have loved to see them one more time but not this way.

My head feels fuzzy. It's strange to finally be free of the migraine and the fear. Enjoy your life. Until we meet again. El...

Her stiff handwriting relaxed until it scrolled off the page.

The knot of regret clogged his throat and stole his breath, eased only the slightest with the knowledge that Elaine was still with him. A sudden feeling of relief washed over him. She was no longer in pain. A shadow of sadness mixed with gratitude squeezed his chest for her sacrifice.

He shoved the note into his pocket and went to find E. She was wiping her lips with a napkin.

"Hey, did you save any of the pineapple for me?"

She turned, dabbed the corner of her mouth then grinned.

"You can have the pineapples. I ate all of those huge strawberries. Yum." She stood, sent him a flirty wink over her shoulder and headed toward the bathroom. "Let me touch up my lipstick, and I'll be ready to go."

John watched her walk away. A shiver of dread sped down his spine. E loved pineapples and detested strawberries. Who was this woman?

An avid reader and story teller since childhood, **Jan Davis Warren** didn't start writing seriously until 2004. She would like to dedicate this adventure to her children and grandchildren, Shelley, Paul, Whitney, Kent, Kayla and Cole. And to her late husband, David whose love, support and encouragement still remain a source of strength in her life. And especially to the Lord Jesus whose blessings and creativity are a never-ending fountain of fun characters, fresh plots and exciting adventures, both real and imagined.

What would a romance collection be without a story featuring handsome cowboys and honorable marshals and maybe a horse thief or two? In our next tale, Angela K. Couch takes us back to a time without the conveniences of telephones and Internet, a time when the nearest town took days to reach, and when a woman sometimes had to rely on her own resources if crisis struck. – VS

Shackled

Angela K. Couch

Arizona Territory, 1883

The pounding of rifle fire reverberated off the mountain ridge and deepened into the rumble of thunder. Lydia O'Conner glanced at the cabin and barn cradled in the open meadow. Too far. Better to hole up in the timberline. She let the kindling fall as she dropped to her knees on a cushion of spruce needles and aspen leaves, her gaze never straying from the valley and the wisps of smoke rising from the foliage. A man on horseback broke through the green, dust churning under the animal's hooves as he veered toward the cabin, a second horse and rider only paces behind. Strange how this rider wavered, his hands...behind his back?

Lydia rocked forward. Surely she didn't see right. But no. The second man had no control of his horse's reins. His hands were bound. No wonder his horse clung to the heels of the first. More shots rang out. The riders hunched lower in the saddles as they bolted across the open terrain toward the back side of her home. Just before reaching cover, the first jerked to the side, almost pulling his horse over as he fought to stay upright. Then they passed beyond her view.

As the gunfire subsided, Lydia gripped a low branch and heaved herself to her feet. Mid-motion, her abdomen clenched, stealing her breath and making it hard to proceed. She paused for the weight of her unborn child to settle. Deep breath.

A horse nickered as she approached from the back of the farm, past the small wagon tangled in weeds. A large bay eyed her from where he'd been tethered to one of the wheels. Beside him, a coal-colored mare rubbed her white blaze against the wagon's seat. Lydia crept between them, her fingers smoothing over the sleek black summer coat and the all too familiar pale strip of hair marking a thin scar across the muscular shoulder. Her mind seized and her head spun. Bile seared the back of her throat as she twisted to the bay and tugged a rifle free from its saddle holster. The pack held ample ammunition, and she shoved a cartridge into the chamber before clicking it into place.

Nielson Bennett dropped into the chair as ordered, but winced as his hands scraped the roughhewn back. Sleek leg irons clanked as they met the hard packed dirt floor. "Are those really necessary, Marshal?"

"Kick your boots off."

He caught the heel of one boot with the toe of the other and pushed it loose. "With the lynch mob out there, I wasn't planning to go anywhere. Besides, the least I can do to thank you for saving me from that rope is to take a look at that hole before you bleed to death."

"First of all, you can save your thanks until after you've been tried, and second..." The US marshal grunted as he stooped to clamp Nielson's ankle in iron. "I'd rather bleed to death then trust a two-cent horse thief."

"If you really believed I stole that horse, why did you risk getting shot to save my worthless skin?"

Marshal Winters looped the two-foot length of chain around the leg of the chair and up through the crossbeam before securing it to Nielson's other ankle. "I risked my life for law and order, not for you. If you get any smart ideas about trying to run, don't think I won't kill you myself."

Nielson tweaked a smile as he formulated a response, but before he could open his mouth, the door to the cabin swung open to reveal a very pregnant woman glowering down the barrel of a Winchester. Fire lit her eyes as they flitted to Winters, to the star on his chest, and then back to Nielson. Her lip curled with indignation.

"I think she might beat you to it, Marshal."

Winters staggered to a chair and placed his revolver on the table. He clutched his wound. "You can lower that rifle, ma'am. I'm US Marshal Peter Winters and this is my prisoner. We apologize for barging in, but we don't plan on causing you any trouble."

She didn't move.

"I don't think she believes you, Marshal."

"Shut up, Bennett."

"And let *you* talk her into putting a bullet in me?" Nielson squinted against the brilliant sun streaming from behind the woman—younger than he'd first supposed. "Look at her finger over that trigger." He shifted in the chair, his wrists pinching from the ropes."

"If anything is going to get you shot, it'll be that mouth." Winters groaned as he yanked free his handkerchief and pressed it to the side of his torso. His face had lost all color but the tan. "Now ma'am, if you wouldn't mind putting down that gun and boiling some water. I could use some help."

The loathing in her gaze faltered as she stole a glance at Winters. Then her finger again tightened over the trigger. "But this man murdered my husband."

Winters scooted his chair back an inch so he could see his prisoner without twisting. The form of his eyes started to resemble the woman's.

Perspiration traced escape routes down Nielson's back. "Marshal, I've never killed a man in my life. I've never even seen this woman before now." With those large brown eyes and defined features, he would have remembered.

Winters gave his head somewhat of a shake. He was wearing down quick. "I have no reason to believe anything you say, Bennett."

"But..." How could things spiral out of his control so fast? This morning he'd been a free man without a care in the world. Wait. That was it. "Timing."

"What do you mean?"

Nielson looked up at the young widow past the Winchester's long barrel. "When was your husband killed?"

Her expression didn't change. "You know the answer as well as I."

"Believe me, I don't." He lifted his shoulders a fraction. "Humor me."

"Six—no..." Her gaze dropped to her extended middle. "Seven and a half months ago."

Nielson took in the proof of her approaching maternity before looking into her youthful face. "How far along are you?"

Vulnerability flickered in her eyes. Fear. "Stop talking." She set her jaw and waved the barrel of the rifle at him.

"I can't. And before you decide to shut me up permanently, you need to know I couldn't have been responsible for your tragedy." He looked to Winters who wavered and braced himself against the table. If anything, Nielson had to convince them of his innocence before the man passed out and left him without any protection from the widow's wrath. "I left St. Louis only two months ago. I'm sure there are plenty of people who would recognize me and vouch for my story all along the Santa Fe Trail. You could even wire Hartford and Sons Carpentry Works in St. Louis where I was employed before that."

The rifle lowered an inch.

Winters cleared his voice. "Did you see him kill your husband?"

Her head twitched with a shake. "No. But the black mare he rode here was my husband's. The man who shot him stole her."

Winters gritted his teeth. His forehead gleamed with sweat. "The horse you stole from the McCants's ranch."

"The horse I bought," Nielson corrected. Surely the marshal could be reasoned with. "Isn't it clear? The McCantses are the rotten ones. They probably stole the

Angela K. Couch

horse to begin with, then sold it to me. If they already killed one man for it, why not lynch a second?"

◌◌◌

The rifle slipped in Lydia's grasp and she lowered it, allowing herself to fill her lungs. She'd never come so close to killing a man. Would she really have pulled the trigger? And what if everything he said was true...if he was innocent? His pale blue eyes pleaded his case loudly enough. Strange how greatly they contrasted the darkness of his shaggy locks and expressive brows.

Lydia yanked her gaze away and slid the rifle onto the table. Now wasn't the time to decide what the man deserved. Not while a US marshal bled out. She moved to him and braced his shoulder. "Let's get you to the bed so we can look after that wound."

He mumbled something about his prisoner, but the words slurred as his head bobbed. She needed to hurry while he still had the strength to lift himself. No way she'd move him if he hit the floor. "Come on, Marshal Winters."

Thankfully the small cabin required only several steps to cross to the thick straw mattress. She didn't bother removing or covering the quilt. It was old anyway. As soon as Winters's head hit the pillow, his eyes rolled back, and then closed. Lydia set her hand over his chest. At least he was still breathing.

A deep voice rumbled behind her. "Untie me so I can help you with him. I think he's still carrying the shell."

She didn't turn—didn't like what his eyes did to her insides. "I can manage on my own." Couldn't she? What did she know about tending bullet wounds? Her husband had already been dead when she'd found his body, the shell lodged in his chest.

"Be reasonable. At least untie my hands. You have no idea how this rope digs in."

127

"Much less than a bullet would." She hurried to fetch the kettle from the stove. The water was now tepid, but would have to suffice. But what else did she need? Bandaging. Something to extract the shell with.

Lord, help me.

She glanced at the man in the chair. Perhaps she should take him up on his offer. No. The marshal had reason to shackle him. Even if he told the truth about not killing William, who knew what other crimes wore his name.

Grabbing several of the cloths she'd been sewing into diapers, and a thin bladed hunting knife, Lydia set them on the edge of the bed.

"You'll want to make sure it's plenty clean."

"I know that," she snapped at him.

"Best light the fire and hold the blade in the flames."

Lydia pressed her eyes closed and took a breath. She couldn't let her pride be the cause of the marshal's death. As she stirred the morning coals and added kindling, the scraping of chair legs against the packed dirt brought her head around. Bennett was halfway to the marshal, his hands loose. She ignored the firmness of her huge stomach as she sprung toward the table and the revolver. "How did you get free?"

His shoulders sagged as his elbows leaned into his knees. He motioned to his feet. "I'm hardly free."

"But your hands were tied."

His lip turned upwards. "Been working on that one for a while now. Why don't you finish preparing that knife, Mrs....?"

She didn't move as the mild contraction eased. "Lydia O'Conner."

"Nielson Bennett." Light twinkled in his eyes and his countenance softened. "Pleasure to make your acquaintance. I'll see what I can do for Marshal Winters."

She lowered the gun, but shoved both it and the rifle to the far side of the table—farther from the criminal. If that's what he was. Never had a man been so hard to read. When he directed his attention completely to the wound, shuffling his chair to the side of the bed, Lydia returned to the fireplace. Flames already licked at the kindling and she added several spindly branches. She'd given up on splitting logs weeks ago. Thankfully the weather did not require it.

She looked back at Nielson as his hand stole into the marshal's vest pocket.

Nielson suppressed his smile as his fingers hooked the key and drew it out. He kept his palm down to conceal his find.

The revolver clicked in his ear. "Tut-tut-tut. What have you there?"

He picked up the key and opened his hand. "The ability to stretch my legs would make this a lot easier. It's not as though I'm going anywhere."

She snatched the key away. "No, it's not as though you are." Collecting the Winchester from the table, she disappeared from the cabin for a minute, returning with only the revolver. With his luck she'd dropped the keys down the latrine and he'd be stuck in these vises forever.

"Is that knife ready, yet?" he grumbled as he bared the marshal's seeping wound. "We might as well get on with this."

Water dripped from Nielson's fingers as he reached for the cloth Lydia held out to him. He nodded his thanks as he took it and wiped his hands. His breath seeped from him like a sigh. "That's all we can do for now."

"He lost a lot of blood." Her voice cracked.

Nielson returned the cloth to her and pulled the blanket over Winters's bandaged torso. "It's not as bad as it looks. The important thing is the location of the damage."

He leaned back in the hard chair. His knees cramped. There had to be a way to convince her to give him back the key. Unfortunately, only one idea came to mind. "Can I use your latrine?" Not exactly a permanent fix, but it would let him stretch his legs.

Though she hesitated, a nod was granted and she slipped out of the door to fetch the key from its hiding place. With the revolver in one hand and the key in the other, Lydia lowered herself to access the shackles, but only released one side. She staggered as she tried to lift herself, and Nielson caught her arm. "Careful."

She jerked away. "Don't touch me."

Holding his hands so she could see them, he pulled his ankle free and dragged the chain from its entanglement. Her chest heaved as she looked on. He peered back at her. "Are you out of breath?"

She glowered at him. "I have significantly less room for breathing than I did a few months ago."

"I don't doubt it."

Her lips tightened and her eyes became narrow slits. "Enough talk. Move."

After two steps, he paused and glanced at her with a motion to his socks. "What about my boots?"

"What about them?"

"May I put them on?"

Her eyes gleamed. "No. We don't have far to go."

Nielson feigned a cringe. "Still..."

All mirth fled her face as one of her hands dropped to her abdomen. Her breath slowed.

"Are you all right?"

"Fine." She straightened her back, but still seemed uncomfortable. "Keep moving."

The latrine proved to be a good twenty yards from the back of the cabin and the ground was less than friendly in the fading light. Still, his legs appreciated the time to stretch tight muscles, and the evening air wafted over him like a fresh breath.

The tension between them relaxed a little during the walk back to the cabin, which like the latrine, seemed to beg for a few straight boards and some nails. It was hard to mind the slow pace Lydia set, her gait betraying a slight waddle. His chest tightened. Concern? Is that what he felt? Completely reasonable. The woman faced childbirth without husband or kin to see to her needs. From what he could tell, she'd been fending for herself for seven months. Young, fiery, but utterly alone.

"Why are you still here?"

Lydia's steps faltered. "What do you mean?"

He stopped and faced her fully. "Out here in the middle of the wilderness. It can't be safe. Especially for someone in your condition."

Her chin began to rise, but then tipped away. "Where else would I go? Any family I have is back in Illinois. I don't know a single soul in town, and even if I did, it's a distance. Between feeling inexplicably ill, and...everything else..."

"You don't have another horse, do you?"

She didn't even look at him now. "William traded him when we first arrived for a milk cow and chickens and such."

At least she had a source of food. "I'm sure Marshal Winters will see you are taken care of when he recovers."

"If he recovers."

"He looks to be a resilient sort of man, and now that the bullet's out and the bleeding's stopped, he'll pull through. You'll see." Nielson lifted his hand to touch her shoulder, but froze mid-motion. That was not his place. And she'd probably shoot him if he did. "Besides, when the marshal first confronted my volunteer judge and executors, he sent his deputy back to town for more men. It's only a matter of time before someone finds us."

And then? Another judge would decide his fate based on the testimony of McCants and his son who were well known in the area. In all likelihood, Nielson would soon be facing another noose. If he was smart, he'd take his freedom now. It would be easy enough to overpower the woman—especially in her condition.

If only his conscience would allow it.

In the cabin Lydia waved him toward his chair, again fettering him to the legs. "You expect me to sit here all night?"

She answered with a nod.

He raked his fingers through his hair. "Why don't you just hide my boots or something?"

"Because I am exhausted and want to be able to sleep. The marshal seemed to think this is a good place for you—the least I can do is keep you around 'til that posse gets here."

Served him right for trying to argue with a pregnant lady. "Can I at least have a pillow or something so I can lean against the table?"

Nielson stretched his neck from one side to the other in an attempt to ease the kinks and knots burning in his spine and every adjacent muscle. His rear hurt just as bad. He glanced to Winters, still inert across the bed. Even with the bullet hole, the position was enviable.

Rubbing knuckles over his grit-filled eyes, he rotated his chair to Lydia as she set a steaming mug in front of him on the table. He mumbled a thanks. Strong coffee was just what he needed.

The mug only made it halfway to his mouth. The mild aroma rising with the steam had no relation to coffee. "What is this?"

"Wild mint." She settled into the chair opposite him. The fullness of her lips hinted a smug smile. "Is there a problem?"

"Don't you have any coffee? You made me spend the night in a chair—don't I deserve that much?"

"The marshal and those men who tried to hang you would probably disagree as to your meriting any courtesies."

Leave it to a woman to put a man in his place. Nielson waved at Winters's sleeping form. "I did save his life."

A smile slid across her face. "That's true. But also is the fact that I used the last of my coffee near three months ago. This is all I have to offer." She shrugged and raised her own mug to her mouth. "It has a pleasant flavor if you give it a try."

Nielson cocked an eyebrow before taking a swig. Not awful, but a far cry from coffee. "There should be some ground beans in my saddle bags. Some other food, too. Help yourself to whatever you find."

"Thank you." She took another sip.

"I suppose you're entitled to the animal as well, if what you say is true."

Lydia cradled the mug with both hands as she lowered it to the table. "You doubt my word—that my husband was murdered, or our horse stolen?"

"No, I don't doubt that for a moment." How could he? It'd almost cost him his life.

"I still have the bill of sale to prove it."

Nielson pressed his lips together. At least someone did.

❀

Lydia stared into the tawny liquid and breathed deeply of its refreshing scent. If she focused hard enough on the drink in her hands, she could hopefully avoid those sky-blue irises of his. She'd been alone for too long. Why else would she be so hungry for the resonance of his voice, or his nearness? It's not like she was a wide-eyed schoolgirl any longer. She'd experienced traveling hundreds of miles to be with the man she'd loved. She'd worked by his side for over a full year in this valley only to bury him with her own hands. Yet all of that seemed nothing to what still approached.

Her abdomen tightened—an ever clearer reminder that her time neared. How much longer? A day? No more than a week, surely. But how would she know? All she had was guesses.

Lydia glanced across the table. Guesses, an unconscious US marshal and a possible criminal. "How did you really get that mare?"

"I bought her, like I said." Nielson's expression seemed detached from his words. His eyes peered into her soul. What did he see? He cleared his voice. "My horse fell lame, so when I came to the McCants's ranch, I made the best trade I could. Still felt like I was being robbed blind. He took my horse—a fine animal who only needed a rest—as well as a fair amount of cash."

"Why didn't you just wait until your horse's leg mended?"

"Didn't feel like sitting in one place for too long. I came west because I was tired of being bound down, working for another man's gain and living another man's life. I wanted to set my own pace and to make my own decisions."

"Freedom?"

He nodded.

She leaned out from the table to glance at his dirty socks and the iron that hugged them. "How's that been for you?"

A laugh rumbled from the back of his throat. "It's not working out quite the way I'd envisioned."

"Life usually doesn't." She took a long drink—anything to escape the downward turn of thoughts. "Abraham McCants and his son are quite shrewd. My husband never did care for them. Who did you do business with?"

"Depends which business you mean. The older one sold me the mare. Two hours later junior and some of his friends tried to string me up."

"Did Abraham deny the sell?"

"According to that boy of his. Of course, Burton McCants held a match to my bill of sale as he said it. What do you wager McCants Senior goes along with what his son says when the judge comes through town?"

"I'm sure..." What reassurance she'd thought to give clogged up her throat. Of course the old rancher would lie in court. If what Nielson said was true, either Abraham or his son, Burton, was guilty of murder. Why not let a stranger hang for it?

Nielson covered a yawn and stretched his spine, which crackled and popped as it realigned itself. Why did she treat him like a common criminal if she believed his story? If he remained there another night, the least she could do was shackle him so he could lie down to sleep.

Lydia leaned into the wall, bracing herself against another wave of pressure, the pain growing with each. Was this what it was supposed to feel like? Was it time? It must be. Over the past couple days the tightenings had become more frequent and intense, but nothing like this.

As the contraction subsided, Lydia straightened her back and caught her breath. She needed to rest. It would only be a matter of minutes before the pain returned. Maybe if she went outside, she could keep moving without interrupting Nielson or Winters. She'd stay close and return when it became too difficult to walk.

The next contraction struck before expected. Not quite to the door, Lydia grabbed for the nearest chair, jostling it against the table.

Lord, help me. Let my baby come without harm. Let me live through this.

"Mrs. O'Conner? Are you all right?"

The gentle concern in Nielson's voice tore her. If only she could ask him for help. If only she didn't have to do this alone.

The pain ebbed and she gathered herself up. "I'm fine. I just need some air." She staggered the last few paces to the door and pulled it open, then leaned into the frame and stared into blackness. Only a sliver of a moon hung above her head. Why did it have to be so dark tonight? She pressed her temple into the solid frame as another wave weakened her knees and evoked a cry from the back of her throat.

"Lydia?"

The contraction remained strong, stealing her ability to reply. A sharp crack erupted from behind her, followed by the snapping of wood and the clatter of a chain. Moments later strong hands braced her shoulders and she sunk into his chest.

Nielson's breath brushed her ear. "You need to lie down."

"All right."

His hands shifted their hold to her arms as he led

her across the room. The chain between his feet rattled with each step.

"Did you break my chair?"

"Don't worry, I can fix it. I didn't have the key. You don't have it with you by any chance?"

"No..." She gripped his arms, pushing into him. "I hid it...outside...again."

"It doesn't matter. I've got you. Try to relax."

Pain embraced her center. *Relax?* This man was insane.

After another minute or so, they crossed the last few feet to the makeshift bed she'd made for herself with several quilts and he guided her down onto her back. "Can I get you anything?"

Lydia let her eyes close, but didn't release his arm. "Don't go anywhere."

The warmth of his fingers embraced hers. "I won't."

The next wave spiked down her spine and she rolled onto her side. Then to her hands and knees.

"You should lie down."

"I can't," she gasped. "It hurts too much." She rocked back on her knees as he slid nearer. Her arms encircled his neck and she pressed her forehead into his chest. His heart thundered in her ear. Was he as nervous as she?

"Tell me what I can do for you."

Unable to answer, she swayed side to side and moaned. Much more bearable. Perhaps he was right. She needed to relax and let her body work. To not think about anything but this moment, the subsiding pain, the feel of his arms so securely around her.

Nielson let his finger trace down the length of Lydia's arm to her elbow. Her eyes were closed, but the corners of her mouth tipped upward. She wasn't asleep after all.

Shackled

His spine pinched from his angle against the wall, and
the quilt under them did little to pad the firm floor, but
he had no interest in moving her head from his
shoulder. This felt too good. Too right. He fought the
urge to lay a kiss on her temple. His reserves had worn
away during the long hours of watching her labor and
then deliver that tiny miracle, leaving him exposed and
vulnerable. And in awe.

The morning light glowed from the small window
above them, illuminating tones of red in her hair as he
brushed the waves away from Lydia's face. Each breath
was slow but deliberate, each saturated with her and
this moment as he stared down at the small but perfect
human in her arms, snuggled against her chest.

"What will you name her?"

She stirred against him as her eyes flickered open
to peer down at the infant. "I'm not sure. I thought I
might call her Hannah after my mother, but I have no
memory of her." Lydia sank deeper into him. "She died
in childbirth."

He drew his arms around her as memories of the
night returned with potency. No wonder she had clung
to him as though he could keep her from slipping away
forever. No wonder the fear. He pressed his lips to her
hairline.

"Did you know your mother?" she asked.

"Yes."

"Tell me about her."

He tried to swallow. "You should rest."

"I am resting." Lydia shifted positions slightly. "Why
don't you want to talk about her? Are the memories so
unpleasant?"

"No." *Not at all.* Which was why they singed the back
of his eyes. Strange. He'd wanted to leave so badly.
Homesickness was the last thing he expected, and yet
it seeped through the fibers of his soul. "My mother was

138

as kind and good as they come. She worked hard but knew how to make farm chores feel like play. She sang a lot. When she washed dishes. When she hung laundry. There were seven of us kids, and I'm pretty sure we each felt like her favorite."

"What was her name?"

"Her name's Louise. Before she married my pa, she was Louise Nielson."

Lydia rotated in his arms, her eyes finding his. "She gave you her name."

He glanced away, blinking. Nielson managed a nod, grateful when she settled back against him. He forced a chuckle. "You remind me of her. She used to get pretty sassy with my Pa."

"I'm not sassy."

The laugh came easier now. "My mistake."

"I was only dealing with the situation at hand. You were a criminal."

"Were? Does that mean you'll tell me where the key is?"

"Nope."

"What did I say about sass?"

She sighed. "I just don't want you to leave yet."

A groan from the opposite side of the room brought their heads up. Nielson began to shift out from behind her. "I'm not going anywhere until I have to. But I should check on the marshal, and you should sleep."

He lowered her head to the pillow and tucked a quilt over her and the baby. Then smoothed his thumb across her brow. Why couldn't he turn away? He leaned lower, his fingers entwining in her tangled locks as his mouth brushed hers. Then sank into a kiss. Slow. Gentle. Wrapping a rope around his heart and binding it securely.

Lydia sank back into the pillow as Nielson withdrew. Why did every breath feel animated? Why did her lips tingle as though they'd never been kissed before? She closed her eyes to hide confusion. She needed to sleep. She'd just given birth, for goodness sake! How could she expect to think clearly?

The jingling of chains marked Nielson's stinted walk across the room. She still needed to tell him where she'd hidden the key. Maybe it was best he took his freedom before Winters recovered or the posse arrived. Nielson was innocent—she could not doubt that—but who could guess what the law would do to him if it couldn't be proven?

She opened her mouth, but another voice spoke first. The marshal. "Don't get too comfortable here."

"You're the one who's been sleeping the past twenty-four hours." Nielson sounded as weary as she felt.

"Not near as much as you think." He grunted, probably shifting positions.

"Then I'm sure you could use some more. Do you need anything before I go?"

"If you leave, I'll send that posse after you. You won't get out of the territory."

"Well, if they arrive in the next hour, you can tell them I'm in the barn seeing to the animals."

Lydia smothered her chuckle but couldn't keep her lips from their simple curve. He wasn't leaving her. Not yet. He'd still be here when she woke.

Nielson set the pail of milk on the ground, crouching down as the first riders breached the edge of the woods. He glanced to the cabin, ten yards away, and then back. Had the lynch mob returned for a second try, or had the posse finally followed their tracks? Seven—no, eight

Angela K. Couch

men. Well-armed. The sun glinted off the metal pinned to the leader's chest. The deputy marshal.

Standing, Nielson folded his arms across his chest, his hands visible. A shout rang out, and they veered toward him. Abraham McCants held his place beside Winter's deputy and heat rose in Nielson's chest. How had he gotten the mare from Lydia's husband? Had it been murder?

"That's the horse thief," McCants said as they neared. "Burton may have stepped out of line trying to hang him, but he had just cause."

Nielson raised his hands to his head as guns leveled at him. "Not much cause to try killing a US marshal."

"My son has a bit of a temper and that horse you took was a favorite of his. Paid a lot of money for that mare."

He gritted his teeth against the urge to drag the man from his horse and remodel his face, but the last thing Nielson needed was to join Lydia's husband. He pressed his words between tight lips. "So did I."

Before he could say anything more, the deputy swung from his saddle. "You can argue that before the judge. Where's Marshal Winters?"

"In the cabin laid up with a hole in his side thanks to Mr. McCants's boy."

"Show me."

"You have a key that will fit these?" Nielson motioned to his feet. No use hobbling across the yard again if he didn't have to. A minute later he dropped the shackles into the deputy's hands. "Thanks."

The deputy just motioned to his hands. "Don't thank me yet."

With the iron biting his wrist, Nielson picked up the pail of milk and led the way to the cabin. He stopped with his hand on the door. "Just you, Deputy. The woman of the house gave birth last night. She needs

141

rest, not a mob storming into her home."

"Fine." He waved the others back then pushed Nielson through the door.

❧

Lydia jerked awake as the door flew open and Nielson staggered inside. "What...?"

Her question answered itself as a large man powered in after him, his hard gaze taking in the full room. She instinctively cuddled her newborn closer and drew the quilt a little higher.

"Winters?" The deputy marshal moved to the bed. "Dare I ask what happened?"

"Like I figured, Burton McCants and his friends didn't like their fun being interrupted. They were probably gunning for Bennett here, but their aim was wide. They lit out pretty quick after they hit me."

"At least they were smart enough to draw the line there. Burton's pa insisted on joining us. He's pretty bent on making sure your prisoner feels the full weight of justice."

Lydia glanced from Nielson's silent stance near the door to the marshals. "Is it justice he wants, or to cover his own sins?"

Winters waved her to silence. "Don't worry. I'll get to the bottom of all this. Your husband's bill of sale for the mare will be useful, though."

With a nod, she motioned to the deputy. "There's a tin box in that chest by the bed."

He dug out the box, turning through the papers until he found the right one, then handed the bill of sale to Winters, who tucked it inside his breast pocket. "Thank you, Mrs. O'Conner, I'll make sure the judge sees this."

The deputy helped him into a sitting position. "Are you sure you should go anywhere?"

"If Mrs. O'Conner will lend us her wagon, I'll manage all right." He looked to her. "I hope you understand, ma'am, I'll need to take the mare with me as well, but I'll see that everything is returned to you."

She managed a nod. "Of course. Thank you."

Winters dragged the pillow behind him and slumped into the wall as his deputy headed out to have the wagon hitched. "I feel bad leaving you here alone, but I'll send a rider for the midwife so she'll be here by nightfall. When you're back on your feet, give some long hard thought to moving to town. It isn't safe for a lone woman and child this far out."

Nielson's eyes bore into her until she met his gaze. Then he looked to the chains at his hands. Not much more was said. Two men assisted Winters to the wagon and the deputy came for the prisoner. Nielson allowed himself to be led three paces before he pulled to a stop.

"Can I say goodbye?"

"Does the lady want you to?"

Lydia pushed herself up a little more. "Yes."

The deputy stepped out of the way, but instead of coming to her, Nielson moved to the bed, throwing aside the soiled blankets and clearing the floor. The broken chair ended up under the table. Only then did he find his way to her side. "Let's get you to the bed."

Even with his movements restricted, his touch was tender as he assisted her across the room and tucked her into the cleanest quilts.

"I'll be all right. Don't worry about me." Lydia squeezed his fingers. "Louise and I are stronger than we look. And you heard Marshal Winters. He'll send someone."

Nielson blinked as his gaze dropped to his mother's namesake. His Adam's apple dipped low. "I wish it were me."

Lydia smiled despite the churning in her stomach.

"Then come back...someday...if you can."

"I will." His thumb brushed over her lips, and then across Louise's cheek. The infant's large blue eyes stared up at him. He stood and backed away. Then turned.

"Goodbye." The words fell from Lydia's lips as the door closed. Her eyes burned, then filled. Tears spilled down her face. As though sharing her fears, Louise bawled, her newborn cry tearing through any resolve to be strong.

"I don't expect to see him again, Lord, but that doesn't matter. Prove his innocence. Keep him safe. Give him that freedom he so desires."

With the prayer repeating over and over in her heart, Lydia pulled her child to her breast. How gracious the Lord had been to give her help when she needed it most. But with Nielson Bennett gone, she needed to continue on.

An hour or so later, Louise drifted to sleep and Lydia laid her in the depression in the mattress. The pail of milk still sat near the door. Moving slowly, she rose, took it to the table, and gathered what she would need for straining. Then she melted into the nearest chair. With her elbows planted on the table, she leaned her face into her palms. So tired. And sore. How was she supposed to do this on her own? The mountains of blankets, towels and clothes that required washing. Nielson obviously hadn't found any of the eggs. Were all the animals even fed? How long could she keep the farm producing enough to support their needs? How would she raise a child by herself? Her shoulders shook as sobs wracked her body.

Lord, I can't.

The door creaked behind her, and she twisted in the chair, her hands attempting to wipe the moisture on her cheeks. "Nielson?" She tried for her feet, but her legs remained paralyzed. "What are you doing here? Won't they come for you?"

A grin split his face, and his eyes shone like the sky at the breaking of a storm. He shook his head. "I'm a free man."

"How?" Not enough time had passed to get halfway to town, never mind acquit a man of a crime.

"Seems Marshal Winters is quite practiced at interrogation—especially when he's got most of the puzzle pieces sorted. Guess he *was* doing more than just sleeping."

"But..." That still didn't explain what happened. "Were the McCants responsible then?"

"Let's just say that when Marshal Winters showed Abraham McCants's your bill of sale for the mare and asked to see his..." Nielson gave his head a shake. "I've never seen a man's face drain of color so fast. Winter's told him that until he can produce the document, there is no proof that I stole the horse, but there is some suggestion his son may be guilty of murder."

Lydia sank back in the chair. "And then they let you go?"

He shrugged. "I've been asked to testify in court."

But at least he wasn't the one being tried. "And you think Burton McCants is the one responsible for my husband's death?"

Nielson rubbed his hand across his throat. "He seems the type...a lot more than his father. I reckon Abraham was only trying to protect his son."

The mystery dissolved along with all the questions that had tormented her the past seven months. Closure embraced her like a warm quilt. "And you rode into the middle of all this."

"Seems that way."

"What now?"

He walked to the table, pulled the pail in front of him

and placed the cheesecloth over the pitcher. "I should strain this milk before it spoils, and you should crawl back in that bed and get more sleep. Maybe tomorrow I'll go into town for some supplies. With a little work, this place could start to look like something. You deserve better than a dirt floor. I'll need some nails and—"

"You're staying?" She stared at him.

Nielson crouched beside the chair and cupped his hands over hers. "For as long as you need me."

And if I never stop needing you? Her vision blurred. "What about not being stuck in one place for too long? What about that freedom you came west to find?"

Nielson's mouth stretched into a smile. "Nothing like being shackled to a chair for a day to change a man's perspective on what freedom really means."

Fascinated by history and in love with creating fiction, **Angela K Couch** has been lost in writing most of her life. As a passionate believer in Christ, she can't help her faith from permeating the stories she tells. Often her martial arts training, love of horses, and appreciation for good romance sneak in there as well. She lives in Canada with her "hero" and three munchkins.

Our next tale comes from a veteran author who literally wrote the book on how to tell a captivating and clean romance story. In "Looking For Love—and the Scissors," Gail immerses us in a fictional situation that may be all too familiar to readers who've been married long enough to experience love on the rocks. But a writing pro like Gail wouldn't leave her readers without hope, would she? – VS

Looking for Love—and the Scissors

Gail Gaymer Martin

Jill Brady darted forward to catch the cantaloupe as it rolled from the kitchen counter. It hardly seemed worth grocery shopping anymore. Being alone felt horrible. She grabbed the carton of eggs and shoved them into the refrigerator. The eggs reminded her of her marriage to Kevin—fragile and breakable. They had been walking past each other on egg shells, their feelings enclosed behind flimsy casings until they made the decision to separate.

Separate? Unbelievable. What happened to the "better or worse....until death us do part?" The promise had splattered on the floor like a dropped egg.

Eggs had become the theme of her life—walking on egg shells, living on scrambled eggs, and killing herself with an overload of cholesterol. Tears escaped the rim of her eyes and rolled down her cheek. "Stop feeling sorry for yourself." Though she heard the command, the pain and pity stayed lodged against her heart.

Now pride and stubbornness kept her from admitting she wanted to make amends. Pride was a negative. Though she prayed for help, why couldn't she allow wisdom to work in her life?

The telephone's strident jangle jarred her thoughts, and the canned goods in her arms toppled from her grasp. Like a juggler, she caught three of them before they hit the ground. She set the cans on the kitchen counter, dodged those on the floor, and caught the phone on the fourth ring.

"Jill, this is Kevin."

When she heard his voice, a chill rolled down her spine. "Kevin." She choked on his name.

"Is something wrong, Jill?"

His concern surprised her. "I'm fine." She pictured his soft green eyes and familiar full lips—kissable lips.

"I thought you weren't home. You usually grab the phone on the first ring."

"I have so much going on these days I barely have time to sit down, much less rush to the phone." She cringed at her blatant fabrication. Her life had been dreadful without him.

"Oh." His response sounded like a deflated balloon.

If her foot could reach, she would have kicked herself. Why play games when she wanted to forget their problems and tell him to come home? "Why are you calling, Kevin?" The tone of her voice hit her ear like a brick. Why had she spoken to him as if he were a stranger instead of the man who'd been her husband for eight years?

"I...I wanted to come by and talk. We have some things to discuss."

Her throat slammed closed, and her response clogged like the drain in her bathtub. "Discuss? I suppose we do." But what? Discuss a... Her thoughts sank into a black mire. A divorce?

"Is this afternoon okay? I could be there within the hour."

She closed her eyes, imagining his face and the way his eyebrows raised when he asked a question. "I guess." Her response sneaked past the knot in her throat. "An hour's fine."

She replaced the receiver and swallowed back her emotions, tumbling and knotting like clothes in the dryer. Closing her eyes, she grasped for control, and with a ragged sigh, she returned to the groceries and stored them in their proper places. Each item had a spot on the shelf. After eight years, Kevin still hadn't learned how to put away the groceries. She'd find the canned green beans mixed with canned peaches. Tomato sauce with the salad dressing. The procedure seemed so simple.

When she finished, she folded the grocery bag and jammed it into the canvas holder in the closet, decorated with large blue letters—*Old Bags*. Today, she felt like one. In two days she would turn thirty. Friday. February 14. Valentine's Day. Two horrible occasions to be alone and unloved. She'd messed up her life royally.

Staring at the kitchen cabinets, her thoughts

skidded to a stop. Had she been the problem? Her mind flew over the issues they'd faced. Why was it so important that the jam be on the jam shelf? She remembered being in a tizzy one day because she couldn't find the scissors in the scissor drawer. Kevin found them with the utensils where he'd put them. "Here." His shout had shocked her. "Run them through my chest. Maybe then I'll learn where they belong."

They'd laughed that day when it was over, but now, it wasn't funny. Why had she allowed scissors to become that important? Wasn't their love worth more than scissors?

She plopped onto a chair and stared at the clock. With each noise, her heart plummeted to her toes. She walked to the door. She paced. Finally, the doorbell chimed, and she froze.

The image struck her heart. Kevin....standing on the porch and ringing the bell at his own home. Before their problems, he would open the door and call, "I'm home." Then she would greet him. "Hi. I'm in the kitchen." Or wherever she was. Always, she rushed into embrace him, wrapping her arms around his neck and placing her eager lips on his.

But today he stood on the porch and rang the bell like a stranger.

Heavy with guilt, she opened the door.

Kevin faltered, peering at his shoes before looking at her. His muttered "Hi" touched her ears.

Aching inside, she pushed open the storm door. "Come in."

He stepped into the foyer and she motioned him into the living room. After closing the door, she followed him, avoiding his eyes where she'd witnessed his apprehension...the same as her own.

"Have a seat, Kevin, please."

He sank into an occasional chair, his hands

knotting in his lap.

"Would you like a soft drink or something?"

"Sure. A cola would be nice."

"I'll be right back." Dashing into the kitchen, she stopped inside the doorway and took a deep breath before pouring the drink into a glass. Her hands trembled, and her chest ached.

When she returned to the living room with his soda, he'd shifted to "his" chair. Her heart warmed at the familiar picture.

After a moment of nervous silence, he leaned forward. "I told Rod when I moved in with him almost two months ago that it was only temporary. Only until I found my own place."

She held her breath. "Have you found a place?" Her heart spiraled downward.

"No." His eyes searched hers. "No, I haven't looked."

Her chin shot upward. "You haven't?"

"I don't want to look, Jill. I want to make our marriage work." He lowered his elbows to his knees, his hands folding and unfolding in front of him. "I can learn where to put the canned goods and the scissors. I will do anything to make our marriage work. I promise."

She lowered her head. *The scissors.* Trivial things had grown out of proportion, and she'd been the center of the problem. She rose and stepped toward him, ready to fall on her knees, ready to take the chance. But the doorbell's summons stopped her in mid-step.

She eyed him, but he only shrugged.

Jill looked through the front window. "It looks like a delivery truck."

She opened the door to find a young man holding a large package in his arms. Printed on the paper wrapping and on his jacket pocket was the name of a local florist.

"Someone is pretty lucky." The man grinned and

handed her the immense box.

She nodded, bewildered, and closed the door. "What in the world is this?"

Kevin gaped at the box as if surprised at its size.

And no wonder. The thing was huge. Jill carried it to the coffee table. As she tore the paper from the arrangement, a small card fell from the wrapping. She lifted it from the floor without taking her eyes from the flowers, a lavish spray of red roses.

"I don't think these flowers were meant for me, do you?" She gestured toward the gorgeous display of roses and baby's breath that resembled a casket spray. "I think they should have been delivered to a funeral home."

"They're meant for you." Kevin's lips curved into a smile. "I wanted something special for your birthday. It's your thirtieth, and I told them I wanted a unique table top arrangement of red roses—one for each year. Then I decided you're worth twice that much, so I told them to make it two for each year. "

"You sent me sixty roses?" She gaped at the lovely, though very large, display.

He grinned at the arrangement. "I wanted something special. I didn't know it would look like a casket spray."

The situation settled over her like a balm, and a warm feeling rolled through her. "Are you sure this isn't meant to be a final goodbye?" She'd found her sense of humor after a long dearth of finding anything to smile about.

Kevin gave her a blank look.

"I thought maybe you were telling me we should bury our relationship."

His cheeks heightened in color as he rose and moved toward her. "Not by a long shot. I'm praying for a rebirth."

"Me, too, Kevin. Me, too." Tears of happiness flooded

her eyes, and she opened her arms.

He met her halfway and pressed her close to his chest. He was her Kevin. For better or worse, she cherished him. In his arms, she felt loved and needed. For the past months, she had been longing for the love they had lost. Today it filled her heart and glowed in his misty green eyes.

His tender lips sought hers, and her heart swelled. The kiss deepened as Jill clung to him, trembling in his arms. Her prayer had been answered and finally she had faced the truth about herself. Drawers and shelves weren't important. What was, was Kevin. Now he was here, and she wasn't going to lose him again. They could work it out. Wrapped in the amazing feeling of love she'd missed for too long, she didn't care if she ever found the scissors again.

Multi-award-winning novelist, **Gail Gaymer Martin**, is the author of contemporary Christian fiction, romance, romantic suspense and women's fiction, with 57 published novels and four million books sold. She is author of Writer Digest's *Writing the Christian Romance*. CBS local news listed Gail among the four best writers in the Detroit area. She is a cofounder of American Christian Fiction Writers and serves on their Executive Board. Gail is a keynote speaker at churches and women's event and a workshop presenter at conferences across the U.S. She lives in Michigan with her husband. Contact her at www.gailgaymermartin.com

Until a few years ago I was unaware of the existence of an entire subculture surrounding Civil War reenactments. For days or even weeks on end, people leave their modern lifestyles behind to dress in period clothing, participate in mock-battles, and generally experience life in the mid-1800's. John Dromey has written a story in which those events are portrayed so engagingly I almost feel like I've participated in a reenactment myself, but with the convenience of air conditioning. – VS

Choosing Sides

John H. Dromey

"I do declare there's something irresistible about a man in uniform." Miss Daisy's practiced drawl resounded among the onlookers gathered alongside the battlefield. Peeking over the top of her handheld fan, she fluttered her eyelids. Her dangling flaxen curls—those not concealed by her stylish bonnet—brushed her cheek in response to the breeze.

"Which one?" Miss Scarlett scanned the busy meadow. "The drummer boy who looks like he's still in grammar school? Or the potbellied sergeant? I assume he's a sergeant, but it looks to me like he sewed his stripes on upside down." She leaned closer and continued in a lower voice. "I don't know about you, but baggy trousers in that icky shade of butternut don't exactly set my heart aflutter."

Miss Daisy dismissed both observations with a flutter of her fan. "None of the above. I have my eyes, and my heart, set on the colonel."

"The man with the sword and the colorful sash?" Her friend rolled her eyes toward the wispy clouds that hovered overhead. "I'll admit he cuts a dashing figure, but in case you hadn't noticed, the gray appears to have migrated from his uniform to his sideburns. He looks old enough to be your grandfather."

"Not him. The other colonel." Miss Daisy gave a coy toss of her head to indicate a young man in an officer's uniform. Miss Scarlett looked in the direction indicated.

Her spine went rigid. "But he's wearing blue!"

"Who cares?"

"I do!" Turning completely away from the battle, the brunette planted her hands on generous hips. "We could have come to this Civil War reenactment as spectators, but no! You insisted we get all dressed up in authentic costumes and pretend to be Southern belles." She tugged at the lace on her high collar. "If ever I'm offered a free ride in a time machine to return to this period of history for real, remind me to say no."

"Don't you like channeling Miss Scarlett?"

"Not in the least. I'm wearing enough petticoats to make curtains for an office building. This corset is squeezing the breath out of me. Oh, and did I mention, I'm about to melt?"

Janice, alias Miss Daisy, delivered a reprimand with

a rap of her fan. "Quit complaining, Marcy. This is the only way we can participate fully in the event. I'm especially looking forward to the formal dance."

"And you think you can get close to your colonel there? Are we allowed to mingle with the other side?"

"I hope so." She grinned. "If not, I'm going to break the rules."

Marcy studied the gentleman in question. "He is rather handsome. Do you suppose that mustache is real, or fake?"

"I'll let you know." Jan stopped fanning herself long enough to wink and cross her fingers. Then, resuming her antebellum persona, she lifted her nose high into the air. "I can scarcely wait for this war to be over."

During the mock battle, the two young women observed from the edge of the field. From where they stood, onlookers dressed in period costumes clearly outnumbered the spectators wearing shorts and tee-shirts.

Marcy flinched every time an artillery piece discharged, the sound jangling along her nerves. "I had no idea it would be this noisy."

Jan tilted her head slightly. "What did you say? I couldn't hear you over the sound of the cannon." She concentrated her gaze on only one part of the battlefield as her eyes followed every move of the Union cavalry officer they'd discussed earlier.

Marcy raised her voice. "I said..." Her words were drowned out by another boom. "Never mind," she muttered to herself.

There was almost no wind. Smoke from black powder lingered over the field like an immature cloud afraid of heights.

The noisy engagement continued with the firing of

revolvers and a wide variety of rifles and shotguns, mostly muzzleloaders. First one side seemed to dominate, then the other.

"Why aren't they using a wooden stick like they do on TV?" Marcy asked.

Jan ignored the question, but a nearby spectator spoke up. "You mean a ramrod. For safety reasons. If accidentally left in the barrel after reloading with a blank charge, the ramrod itself could become a lethal projectile."

A few heartbeats later, the Union colonel swayed in the saddle. He reined his horse to a complete halt as a couple of foot soldiers ran forward and helped the officer to dismount. The colonel took one hop then fell forward and lay stretched out full-length on the ground.

"He's hurt!" Janice cried out. She directed her fanning efforts toward the cloud of smoke that obscured her view.

"It's only a show," a veteran observer assured her. "They decide in advance who's going to win the battle and who's going to make believe they've been shot. It's a lot like a professional wrestling exhibition."

"Then why do I feel like I'm going to faint?"

"I think you're supposed to say 'swoon.'" Marcy giggled. "Perhaps you've been smitten by Cupid's arrow, but I'd vote for the early stages of heat exhaustion. Let's move into the shade." Marcy took Jan's arm and led her toward a clump of trees. On the way Jan swiveled her neck so she could watch the spot where the man in blue had fallen.

When the spectacle was over and the spectators' applause had died away, the fallen soldiers on both sides got to their feet.

Jan insisted on Marcy going with her to meet the colonel. They had no trouble catching up with him. He was walking beside his horse, holding onto the saddle.

Reprising her Miss Daisy accent, Jan inquired of the Union gentleman, "That appears to be a fine horse, Colonel. Why aren't you riding?"

"In order to climb into the saddle, I'd have to put my full weight on my left foot."

"Does that mean you're one of the walking wounded?" Marcy asked.

The horseman answered Marcy's question but kept his gaze fixed on Jan. "Not by design. Dismounting, I hit the ground harder than I'd intended and may have done something to my ankle."

"Maybe I can help," Jan said.

The Union reenactor looked closely at her costume. "I'm no expert on feminine attire, ma'am, but I doubt Clara Barton put on a dress fit for a cotillion when she went to field hospitals to tend the wounded."

"I don't pretend to be someone of her stature, sir, but in your hour of need I'll do my best to emulate her example."

The object of her sympathy responded with a mildly puzzled look.

Marcy assumed the role of interpreter. "What Janice is trying to tell you without breaking character is she's a nurse. An RN."

"You may have a look then." He sat down on the grass. Jan examined his ankle.

"I don't have X-ray vision," she said, "so it's possible you have a hairline fracture, but I don't think so."

Her impromptu patient pretended to twirl the corner of his mustache, which failed to conceal a rakish grin, and mimicked Miss Daisy's drawl. "Are you going to tear strips of cloth from your petticoat and wrap my ankle?"

A blush rode high on Jan's cheeks. "I can do a better job by getting an Ace bandage out of the first-aid kit. Your boot will conceal the evidence anyway, unless you want to avoid using anything from the twenty-first century in the interest of authenticity."

"I'm not that much of a fanatic. In fact, I'm glad to be wearing contact lenses. This way I don't go around the bivouac area tripping over tent pegs."

When she'd finished applying the bandage, Jan said, "That and a couple of aspirin should keep you going until you have a chance to see a doctor."

"Thanks. My name is David, by the way. I'll not be in any condition for dancing this evening, but I'd be honored if you ladies would join me on the veranda. There's a big porch swing there."

"Not me," Marcy said. "After perspiring like a pig all day, I'm going to stay inside where it's cool. The ballroom is air-conditioned."

"I'd be delighted," Jan said, and curtsied.

After the banquet, David strode across the hall and offered his arm to Janice. His limp became more noticeable as they walked slowly out onto the veranda, but neither one mentioned his injury. As he'd predicted, he was in no shape for dancing. With their arms still linked, they looked over the railing at a broad expanse of neatly trimmed lawn that was enclosed by a stand of timber.

There were no power lines in sight. They could have been living in a different century entirely. Back in simpler times with no electronic distractions. No traffic sounds.

After a while, they sat side by side on the porch swing.

Following a picturesque sunset, the skies slowly darkened, but their faces were bathed in the warm glow of light that came through the curtains covering the floor-to-ceiling windows of the ballroom. The unamplified sound of acoustic musical instruments floated through those same tall windows.

David cleared his throat. "The first shot was fired on Fort Sumter in April of eighteen-sixty-one." He paused. "The battle we commemorated today took place in March of eighteen-hundred-sixty-two."

"How interesting," Janice said. "Is that important?"

"Yes it is. Doubly so." David lowered his voice to a whisper. "Considering the times we live in and your being a fine Southern belle, I didn't think it proper to kiss you on the *first* date I mentioned."

The sound of Jan's girlish laughter was music to his ears. He'd got the response he wanted. When she stopped giggling, he moved his face closer to hers, and she met him halfway.

Their lips touched. A perfect end to a nearly perfect evening.

❧

During dinner, Marcy and Janice were seated at separate tables. They didn't have another chance for a private conversation until they were on their way back to the city.

"Nobody swept me off my feet at the dance." Marcy heaved a sigh. "My costume was too heavy for that. I had fun though. How was your evening with the colonel?"

"He was charming, and a perfect gentleman." Janice kept her hands on the steering wheel.

Marcy sensed a juicy secret hovering behind her friend's secretive smile. "He didn't try to pull rank on you?"

"Not even once. For the most part he managed to stay true to the character of the officer he represented. I'd say he treated me very much like a lady from the eighteen-sixties, except for one major anachronism."

"What was that?"

"Rather than asking where he could send me a letter, David gave me his cell phone number." A giggle filled the car. "And I gave him mine."

Marcy zeroed in on her friend's close-mouthed attitude. She could sense information being withheld like she had radar. "Otherwise, you just spent the evening holding hands and talking?"

"Well, I don't like to kiss and tell, but there was a kiss."

"I knew it!" Marcy pounced on the announcement. "What was it like kissing a colonel? Give me details!"

"I think I was temporarily transported back in time." A grin broke free on Janice's face. "One thing holds true no matter the generation. Even a chaste kiss can tickle the kissee when the kisser has a mustache. David's is real, but he told me he's willing to shave it off if I decide I don't like it."

John H. Dromey was born in northeast Missouri. He's had short fiction published in *Alfred Hitchcock's Mystery Magazine*, *Stupefying Stories Showcase*, *Woman's World* and elsewhere, as well as in a number of anthologies.

You've already read one of Jan Davis Warren's stories. This tale is told in a completely different vein, but is every bit as engaging as "Factor X." What a delight to discover a new author with a creative imagination and many stories to tell, and who's developed enough skill to tell them well. – VS

Zoo Day Mystery

Jan Davis Warren

"This could be downright dangerous. What was I thinking?" Amy Etheridge muttered to herself after she paid her admission and walked through the gate of the city zoo. Her fascination with solving mysteries might have gotten her into real trouble this time.

It wasn't too late to go back home. Indecision slowed her pace, but curiosity kept her walking to her destination. "If John finds out and is upset, I'll just blame it on hormones." She gave her stomach a soft touch and smiled. Maybe she could distract her husband with other news.

The squawk of exotic birds in the distance drew her attention back to the matter at hand.

Finding the location from the note, she stopped and waited, shifting from one sandaled foot to another. A quick check of her watch confirmed the same time as the large cast iron clock standing in the flower bed. Ten minutes until ten. She'd made it with minutes to spare.

Was it the ninety-eight-degree July weather or excitement that flushed her skin and left her breathless?

She pulled the crumpled Post-It Note from the pocket of her shorts. It wasn't signed and she didn't recognize the handwriting. The bold script could have been written by a man or woman.

A glance around the area confirmed there were no other people nearby. Maybe she should have been more cautious. For a busy public place, there was a noticeable lack of people wandering around.

The African elephants in the nearby enclosure stood like statues, their eyes fixated on her. It gave her the creeps.

With determination to ignore the uneasiness that crept up her spine, she turned completely around to check the other paths, which fanned out like spokes of a wheel, from this central hub.

No one. Not even the snow cone vendor manned his cart.

If she was kidnapped and sold into slavery it would be John's fault. He had arrived home late every night this last week with the excuse that he'd taken another shift at the mill because of layoffs. A sob squeaked out. He was a hardworking man who provided for their family. Exhaustion had sent her to bed early every night feeling guilty and neglectful, too weary to stay up and greet him as she used to do.

Still he'd forgotten her birthday. And in his hurry to leave this morning, he'd left without even a peck on her cheek.

Her emotions swung from hurt to angry then back again. She fanned her face against the heat that burned at the thought of being completely taken for granted.

He'd also left the front door open in his haste to get out before she could say more than "Good morning" to him. That's when she saw the mysterious pink note stuck on the glass pane on her front door. It sounded vague yet urgent. Or maybe it was simply the hint of a little mystery that made her actually drive across town to see who would show up.

Meet me today at the city zoo in front of the elephant statue. Ten sharp. Come alone and don't tell anyone. Don't be late. Please. It's a matter of life and death.

Even after she dropped off her seven-year-old son, Joey, at his elementary school she'd wrestled with her curiosity. What should she do about the note's ambiguous contents? Perhaps if she had not faced a long, lonely day stretching before her she might have chosen differently. But who wouldn't want a little excitement on her thirtieth birthday?

Still, now that she was here, second thoughts filled her typically-logical mind. She should call John. A quick search of her purse for her cell phone came up empty. She groaned. In the chaos of getting her darling, but doddling son and his school bag into to the minivan she'd left it at home.

Maybe she should look for a pay phone. There would be one near the zoo's entrance.

The large bull elephant that had stood motionless staring at her all this time suddenly shook his head and trumpeted. She jumped with a squeak of alarm. Was he telling her 'no'? Okay, she would stayed here for a few more minutes.

"You better be right big guy." She shifted again.

As the note instructed, she stood beside the life-size bronze elephant sculpture. Its bulk, at least, shaded her from the hot summer rays.

She read the plaque. "Donated in memory of Dandelion, the last dancing elephant of Boyd's Circus. She died doing what she loved best." The image of an elephant draped in a feather boa was also etched in bronze. For an elephant, she did look happy.

Well, I'd like to solve this mystery. If I died here and now, would John put on my headstone—"She died doing what she loved best"?

"Ha!" A laugh escaped in a heavy tone of sarcasm. She loved a lot of things better than mysteries. Her mind counted off several until she came to her husband.

John had been downright secretive lately, as well as vague and unapproachable. They needed to talk. If she went on line could she find any books on how-to-tell-your-husband-you're-pregnant-after-five-years-of-trying, when he's never around?

Her chest ached with disappointment, and tears blurred her vision.

No! Today of all days she wasn't going to think about the negative. Okay, turning thirty could be considered a negative when no one bothered to remember. Not even her best friend nor her mother had called to wish her happy birthday. A dreaded milestone and no one cared enough to remember.

A tear rolled down her cheek and dropped onto the sidewalk. She tugged a tissue out of her purse and dabbed her eyes. She needed some privacy and the lady's room was the closest place to release her sorrows. Against the advice of the mammoth beast, which again shook his head, thankfully without the loud trumpeting.

What did he know anyway?

The iron clock chimed, mocking her silly adventure. When she turned to go, she ran into a solid wall of muscle. A sob escaped from her. Embarrassed, she glanced up to apologize and saw her husband's cheesy grin before he swept her into his arms and kissed her like a man in love. A kiss that left her weak in the knees and about to swoon from the sheer glory of it. Her grief melted instantly into a puddle of relief surrounded by his strong arms, secured in his love.

Voices erupted all around her in a loud chorus.

"Surprise!"

"Happy Birthday, Amy!"

With a squeal of surprise, she felt John's arms tighten around her with support until she could acknowledge those surrounding them. His kiss still tingling on her lips, she gave them all her best smile. One glance at her grinning husband told her he was as weak-kneed from that epic kiss as she. The sparkle in his eyes and the wink he gave her promised more such kisses once they were alone.

The good-natured cheering continued for several minutes as John led her to the boat dock at the zoo's manmade lake. A cloud of helium balloons filled the area and tables of food and brightly wrapped gifts lined the outer edges. Even the snow cone vendor had appeared with his cart and was handing out the icy treat.

A lot of effort had gone into keeping this party secret from her. A feat she hadn't thought possible before today.

"John thought of everything. He barely let us help." Her mother hugged her. "He even had his boss write the note so you wouldn't guess who sent it. Although the whole life and death part was a bit over the top. I was sure you'd discard the thing because of it." She put on her stern this-is-serious look. "I was sure I'd taught you better." Then she chuckled and headed for Amy's father who was greeting some late arrivals.

Getting everyone's attention for a moment of silence took the experience of their pastor. He blessed Amy on her birthday, the food and festivities, and then waved to John to take over.

Amy grinned as John pointed everyone to the buffet of his famous smoked brisket and turkey legs. Judging the amount, it must have taken him days to prepare so much. No wonder he smelled of smoke when he came home. She should have missed the huge smoker usually parked beside the house. How had she overlooked such clues? A clear sign perhaps she should give up on further sleuthing.

As the crowd headed toward the food, John insisted she sit in the rattan chair with the high back, which had a sign that read, "Reserved for the Birthday Queen".

He brought a plate full of her favorite foods, set it down, and pulled up a bench beside her.

"Are you really surprised?" John's earnest expression lit her heart with joy. "I almost told you this morning. You looked so sad."

Before she could answer, her son ran up to them.

"Mommy, did we surprise you? I got to get out of school, too." Joey hugged her then danced from foot to foot, waiting only for her nod before he shot away to explore the bounty on the tables.

"You both surprised me." She reached up and ran her fingers down her handsome husband's face. He captured her hand and kissed her palm.

She had a surprise for them, too. After the party when they were alone, the mystery of her rollercoaster emotions, exhaustion and tears would be solved when she shared her wonderful news. She could hardly wait.

Widowed after 39 ½ years of a happily-ever-after kind of marriage, **Jan Davis Warren** has been blest to have known romance and many perfect kisses. She would like to dedicate this short story to her wonderful children, grandchildren and especially to the Lord, whose sacrificial love will remain humanity's best example.

Writing a good romantic suspense story is kind of like juggling. The writer must introduce an intriguing mystery, maintain an atmosphere of tension and danger throughout, and develop a romantic relationship that is as appealing to readers as the other plot components. In our next story, versatile writer Anna Zogg manages to do all those things while delicately blending in the faith element that is her trademark.—VS

A Weekend Blast

Anna Zogg

"Lee-ah."

The eerie cry pulled Leah Bennett from the depths of sleep. She sat up. What was that? With her bed positioned beside the open window, she squinted from the second story to the moon-splashed landscape below.

I've been home a week and Vic is already pranking me? The night before she heard her brother in the garage. At midnight. Though nearly twenty-one, he sometimes acted twelve.

"Vic?" She kept her voice low, even though their father probably couldn't hear. His first-floor bedroom was on other side.

A noise, like a throaty chuckle, wafted up. Her breath caught as shadows flickered. Was that her brother? Or someone else? In seconds, Leah yanked on a robe and stumbled down the stairs. She flipped on outside lights. Illumination flooded the driveway and the area by the detached garage. From the safety of the dark house, she peered out.

Nothing.

Had it been Vic? Though charming, he often indulged his mischievous side. More than once, Dad had bailed him out of jail for some silly reason or another. Vic's recent acquisition of illegal fireworks would probably land him there again.

Leah checked another window and still saw no one. Now that she was more fully awake, doubts pounded her. From down the hallway, the snores of her brother and father dueled. So the voice couldn't have been Vic's.

After turning off the outside lights, she crept up the stairs. Must have been a dream.

Even so, she locked the sash and pulled the curtains before crawling under her covers.

❦

"July fourth is only a few weeks away." Leah pointed to the large crate that sat with their camping gear. "Why're you bringing fireworks?"

"Because I don't feel like waiting until then." Her brother tossed their sleeping bags into his pickup's bed. "Geez, when did you turn into such a spoilsport?"

She clamped her mouth shut. *Everything changed when God got hold of my heart.* Vic had already mocked her beliefs several times since her return home. To prove that she was still the same ol' Leah, she'd agreed to go on this big camping trip he'd organized. More than a dozen friends—people they'd known since grade school—were going. In the morning they planned to witness some big detonation event at a nearby quarry.

Everything in me says stay home.

She knew what would happen once they reached the campsite. The outing would morph into a drunken bash. Been there, done that. But no more.

Vic planted a fist at his hip. "You and your religion are really starting to bug me."

She bristled. "That's not fair."

"You used to be fun. Now you're..." Disgust flashed across his face.

She bit her lip, tempted to tell him to forget it. That she was staying home. Besides, she didn't trust Bram Edwards, the blaster who would initiate the morning's shot. Too much bad blood existed between their families.

Refusal poised on her lips when the blare of horns made them both swivel. Several cars and pickups pulled alongside their driveway.

Amid the excited shouts to her brother came welcome-homes to her. Above the hubbub, her brother yelled, "Ready for some fun?"

Everyone whooped.

"We'll go as soon as some last-minute additions show up." When pressed for names, Vic merely shook his head.

Not much later, a brand-new red pickup appeared in the distance, two people inside. Some of Vic's friends whistled in appreciation, others groaned.

"Alan Gohlke? Why's *he* coming?" Derision laced one guy's tone. The comment prompted snickers.

Poor Alan had been the brunt of teasing all through

high school. Apparently attitudes hadn't changed while Leah was away at college. Not even a high-paying job had elevated his status.

"Relax everyone," her brother responded. "I invited him because he's bringing a case of beer. And Gavin Wheeler. Remember him?"

Gavin?

Leah's world screeched to a standstill. *That's* who the dark-haired passenger was? Her heart began to thump out of sync.

"Hey, everyone." Alan leaned out the cab's window. "Look who's back."

"Gavin!" Several girls squealed.

How well Leah recalled his dazzling smile and dimpled cheek. Apparently everyone else did too. He stepped out of the truck and into the animated group. Feet glued to the driveway, she stood apart, watching the hugs and backslapping.

Nearly eight years ago, Gavin had moved in the middle of his senior year. He'd been class president and the Homecoming King. Occasionally he, along with half the guys in high school, dated her older sister. After he left, Leah tried to keep in touch, but her crazy work and school schedules never allowed for a deeper friendship. Not that he indicated he wanted one.

I never expected to see him again.

Alan shuffled up and touched her shoulder. "Hey, Leah. Welcome home." He seemed even taller and more gangly than in high school.

"Hi." Though dying to rush to Gavin, she focused on Alan.

"Heard you were back from college." Cool blue eyes raked her.

"Yeah, finally graduated. What's up with you?" Last she heard he was working out of state.

"Oilfield job didn't pan out. They wouldn't pay me

what I'm worth."

She made a sound of sympathy. "Sorry to hear that."

"Yeah, well." He glanced around. "You going camping?"

"Of course. Can't say no to Vic."

Alan chuckled. "Who you riding with?"

"Not sure." After their little spat, she doubted her brother would want her along. Definitely not with his new girlfriend. The petite redhead stared at Vic with adoring eyes.

Alan pinned her with his gaze. "Wanna check out my new pickup?"

And sit beside Gavin? Heat flooded her face. "Got room?"

"Sure."

"Okay, thanks." She climbed in the cab to wait.

Alan helped load the heavy crate of fireworks into the back of Vic's pickup, then secured it. Everyone dispersed to find their rides.

Leah's heart sank when Marti-the-life-of-the-party grabbed Gavin's arm and dragged him to her car. He threw Alan an apologetic grin. Four other giggly females crowded in the vehicle.

Leah wasn't sure what was worse—riding alone with Alan or Gavin's ignoring her.

Definitely Gavin's slight.

What am I doing here?

Leah asked herself that repeatedly as midnight neared. Instead of winding down for the night, the revelry ramped up exponentially. Because of all the alcohol?

As she sat alone by the bonfire, she tried not to notice everyone pairing off. Gavin had long disappeared with Ms. Party. Even Alan abandoned her when his girlfriend showed up.

I don't mind being alone, Lord. Really.

It merely confirmed she was different. Permanently. While she'd been away at college, God changed her.

"This seat taken?" Gavin's deep voice made her jump.

After scooting over on the smooth log, she found her tongue. "Help yourself."

"Sorry I didn't get a chance to say hello earlier." The fire's reflection danced in his deep brown eyes.

The sting from earlier vanished. "You had to keep your fan club happy."

He pulled on his ear. "If I'd known I was that popular, I would have returned sooner."

She laughed.

"Beanpole Blondie," he said under his breath.

Her cheeks grew hot at the nickname he'd given her so long ago. "Ack, you remembered."

"Of course. Although, you're not so much a beanpole anymore." The glance he threw her was nothing but respectful. "Glad you're still blond."

"Every time you called me that, I wanted to punch you."

"You should've." He tilted his head. "You cut your hair?"

"A few weeks ago. For graduation." She fingered the ends. "How'd you know?"

He grinned rather sheepishly. "Social media. I'm addicted."

"We can get you help for that." She spoke with mock seriousness. "I know a great counselor."

He threw back his head and laughed. Something squeezed in her chest at the unselfconscious way he gave into humor. *Wow.* Some things never changed.

Like my feelings for him? They flamed to the same degree as when she was a teen.

"Nice to see you developed a sense of humor." He studied her. "You used to hate when I teased you."

"Forgiven and forgotten."

His eyes seemed to smolder. "I'm glad."

"Smoothed over by all those holiday cards you faithfully sent us. Dad really appreciated them."

One corner of his mouth curved and that single dimple deepened. "Every Christmas I was reminded how much I missed your family."

She was about to respond when several campers staggered closer to the bonfire, yelling for marshmallows.

Gavin leaned closer. "Let's go someplace where we can talk."

"Sounds great."

They walked along a well-marked trail until they came to a fenced cliff.

He looked around. "I remember this spot. I conned my parents into coming here once or twice for a picnic."

The full moon painted the rocky landscape in silver. Leah drank in crisp air, a fresh love for the Utah mountains rushing through her. "This is gorgeous."

"Certainly is." Only Gavin wasn't looking at the panorama, but at her.

Gripping the handrail, she steadied herself. *Careful. He's probably downed a few beers.*

"Have a seat." He indicated the lone picnic table.

After settling on the metal top, she wrapped arms around her knees. Now that she was away from the bonfire, the chill of the air became more pronounced.

He sat beside her, resting elbows on his legs.

"I heard your parents bought a house in Spencerton," she said after a few minutes. "Your dad get a job here?"

"Yes. With ATF."

"That's the Bureau of Alcohol and...?" She couldn't

remember what the letters stood for.

"Tobacco, Explosives and Firearms," he finished.

"Nice. How long are you visiting?"

"Not visiting. Moved. As of three days ago."

"Really?" She tilted her head. "I just returned home last week."

"I heard. Been keeping tabs on people. My social media addiction again."

Smiling, she bumped him with her shoulder. "Then I suppose you know about my sister." In case he didn't, she added, "She's happily married. With three kids. In Denver."

Again he laughed. "I know. That's why I moved *here.*"

She chuckled, then sobered at the implication. "So, why Spencerton?"

His mouth pursed. "I love this town. Couldn't get it out of my head. And I loved," he threw a glance at her, "your family."

She tightened the grip around her knees. "Yeah, lots of guys were gaga over my sister."

"That's not what I meant." His gaze fastened on her. "While I was in high school, both my parents worked a lot. And traveled. Your family was amazing, particularly your mom. Dating your sister may have been my excuse, but I loved spending time with all of you. I always felt I belonged."

"I never knew."

He grinned. "You probably also didn't know that I threatened to run away when my parents told me we were moving."

"I bawled when I heard the news." She bit her lip at the confession. "I had such a huge crush on you."

"I know. But your dad would've killed me if as a senior, I asked you—a mere freshmen—to Homecoming."

She giggled. "Yeah, he would've."

They both fell silent as they looked at the star-speckled night.

Leah took a slow, deep breath. "Were you really going to ask me? Or is that the beer talking right now?"

"I haven't had any." He crossed his heart. "And I know you haven't either."

"How?"

"Your brother's comment."

"Oh." She chewed her lip, imagining what Vic said.

"I'm glad you didn't drink, Leah."

The look in his eyes made her shiver. In a good way.

"Cold?" he asked.

"A little."

After pulling off his jacket, he draped it over her shoulders. Warmth enveloped her, not merely from the garment.

Gavin cleared his throat. "I have a confession. About my return."

"Oh?" She waited with bated breath.

"I came back because of—"

She shrieked when the picnic table suddenly heaved. A massive boom instantly followed.

Sitting in the hospital's lobby with her father, Leah waited for news. Last night was a blur. All she remembered was Gavin shouting at her to head to camp as he plunged down the trail. She'd not seen him since.

Crowds lingered in the waiting rooms. Ambulances kept arriving with victims—others who'd been at the campout. Rumors abounded about what caused the blast. Most were saying Vic's fireworks somehow ignited. Could the M-80s he favored really cause that huge explosion? Or had he brought the kind reserved for licensed pyrotechnicians?

Unable to meet the semi-hostile glances, Leah kept her head lowered. As she released a frightened sigh, her father squeezed her arm.

"Mr. Bennett?" A hospital volunteer paused before them. "You and your daughter can see Vic now."

They leaped up and followed the woman to a private room on the second floor.

Leah didn't know what to expect, certainly not the battered and bandaged young man on the hospital bed. She hardly recognized him. Burns and abrasions covered his exposed skin. A splint engulfed one arm.

"Vic?" Her voice squeaked.

His expression was one of infinite sadness. "So glad," he rasped. "So glad you weren't with us. I don't know what I would've done if you'd..." A tear rolled down one cheek.

"Oh, Vic." She gently touched his uninjured hand.

"Dad," he croaked. "Dad, I'm so sorry."

Knees giving out, their father slumped on a chair. In moments he appeared to have aged a dozen years.

Hospital staff came and went. Time crawled. Leah tried to ignore the never-ending sounds of grief from the hallway.

After an hour, she slipped away to grab Dad a drink from the cafeteria. On the way down, she avoided the family members of the other victims. Somehow she ended up in the tiny hospital chapel.

Head bowed, guilt pounded her. *Why didn't I try harder to dissuade Vic from bringing those fireworks? Or at least alert Dad?*

But would he have done anything? Since Mom's death five years before, he seemed unable to restrain the willful and ever-charming Vic.

When Leah felt a hand on her shoulder, she looked up to see Gavin. Shooting to her feet, she crumpled against him and melted into tears. He held her until her weeping subsided.

"Heard you were here somewhere." His voice came low, sympathetic.

"I'm sorry." She pulled away. "I didn't mean to rain all over you."

Then she noticed his bleary eyes and dust-covered clothing. Was that dried blood on his shirt? "You okay?"

"Minor injury." He held up one bandaged hand. "Burned myself trying to put out flames. Stupid of me."

"*Brave* of you," she corrected.

"I'm glad you stayed at camp. You didn't need to see..." He shook his head as though trying to banish the haunting scene.

Her stomach clenched. "How many were hurt?"

"Eight." A muscle in his cheek spasmed. "One dead."

"Oh, no." She pressed fingers to her mouth.

"I don't think it was anyone you knew."

Tears swelled again. "I'm so sorry."

"Where's Vic?"

"Moved to a room." She pointed upward. "They want to keep him a few days."

"Can I see him?"

"I'll take you there right now."

Upstairs, Dad's friends crowded the small room, including Alan who stood in one corner. He too had apparently escaped the explosion, but unlike Gavin, had showered and donned clean clothing.

Since her brother was recounting events, she went to her dad as he sat beside the bed. In a halting voice, Vic shared that he and some buddies left early to scope out an optimal spot to watch the quarry blast. He and his girlfriend rode in the backseat of a second vehicle, while someone else took his truck.

The explosion killed the driver of the car Vic rode in. Everyone else was injured to varying degrees, several seriously.

179

As her brother told the story, Dad wept, silently, painfully. Leah bent to caress his shoulder. Everyone in the room seemed to be crying. The only one who wasn't was Gavin as he stood by the door. Brow drawn and mouth hard, his face was turned toward someone out of sight.

She didn't have time to wonder as police officers entered the room.

"Victor Bennett?" One man spoke in a cool, professional tone.

Leah gulped. *They're holding him responsible!*

Her knees buckled.

"Was Vic really arrested?" In the warm evening air, Alan stood by the kitchen door. "I came as soon as I could."

Leah glanced behind, keeping her voice low. "Can we not talk about that right now? Dad's taking it hard."

"Of course."

She leaned her hand on the doorframe, not wanting to be rude but unable to entertain yet another guest. For two days they'd been inundated with calls and visitors. Leah's sister had left only that morning. "We appreciate your stopping by."

"That's not the only reason I came. Be right back." He trotted over to his truck and pulled out yellow roses wrapped in cellophane. "Something to cheer you and your father up."

She stared at the extravagant gift. "They're lovely."

How could she turn him away now?

"Come in." After propping open the door, she put her finger to her lips. She didn't want to disturb Dad in the living room. That worry vanished when the TV snapped on and he started channel surfing.

"Sorry, I didn't bring a vase." Alan spoke quietly.

"I'm sure we have one. Somewhere." She began searching cupboards.

"Make sure to cut the ends. There's a packet with instructions."

She smirked. "How do you know so much about roses?"

"Mom loved 'em."

Hand resting on the counter, Leah faced him. "I was so sorry to hear about her death. How long has it been?"

"Seven weeks." Alan's face grew tight.

A flash of sympathy shot through her. "I know how hard that is. My mom died when I was eighteen."

"At least you have your father." Bitterness flashed across his face.

Leah didn't respond. When they were younger, most kids teased the fatherless boy. As far as she knew, no man had ever claimed Alan as his son. Did his mother tell him before she died?

"Mind if I use your restroom?"

"No, go ahead. First door down the hall." Leah finally located a vase. By the time she positioned the arrangement on the table, Alan rejoined her in the kitchen.

"Perfect." He nodded. "The leaves match your eyes."

Was he flirting? She shifted her weight. "Uh, my eyes aren't that dark."

"Close enough." He scrutinized her.

"I'm sorry to rush you out," Leah said in an apologetic voice, "but Dad's really tired. Do you mind?"

"No problem." Alan backed toward the door.

"Thanks again for the roses."

"My pleasure." Before he reached his truck, he swiveled on his heel. "Everything's going to work out. You'll see."

Leah gulped thin air as she jogged up a steep slope. *You can do it.*

The exercise felt great—a needed break from being cooped up in the house. With Dad back at work, she didn't think she could field one more phone call about Vic.

She reached the top and paused. As she panted, hands resting on knees, a distant sound caught her ear. *There it is again.*

She slowed her breathing. Several times already she thought she heard a car. A soft purr replaced the whine. From an idling engine?

"Hello?" she called.

No response. Shielding her eyes, she peered down the road. Nothing. Mountains and trees were all she could see.

Despite the late June sun, she shivered. Was someone trailing her? Every time she proceeded, the vehicle seemed to move with her.

She walked on, attuned to that elusive noise. After a few moments, the drone resumed, keeping pace.

Suddenly aware of the lonely road and steep cliffs, Leah's mouth went dry.

Is someone after me because of Vic?

Ahead lay a sheer drop as well as a turnout. Fear crashed over her. *What if someone is waiting there for me?*

She decided not to find out. Wasn't there a trail before the waypoint? That seemed the safest route to take. Adrenaline coursed through her as the engine gunned.

Go. Now!

She sped up, hoping whoever followed wouldn't immediately notice her increased pace. By the time she found the path, she was flat-out running. After many yards, she cut off the track and vaulted over rocks. Stones tumbled as she skidded, regained her balance, then leaped down the steep hill.

Would they ditch the car and pursue her?

She kept up the impossible speed until she reached their property. Catching sight of the house, she pushed harder. Sweat-soaked and out of breath, she slammed open the door, then shut and locked it. She secured every door and window before slumping against a wall. Hard panting turned into sobs of relief.

Flexing her hand, Leah studied the scratches on her palm. Had she only imagined her followers? She chided her overactive imagination, conjuring up many reasons why someone might have been driving slowly along the road. The panoramic view and fresh air enticed many travelers. Seemed a plausible explanation now.

However, the visit by police overrode everything else in her mind. After Dad arrived home from work, they had searched the house and garage, not even bothering to replace the screen they'd apparently knocked out of Vic's bedroom window. They'd given her a list of what they'd confiscated. Part of a model airplane? When she asked about the item's significance, they didn't answer. Leah couldn't help but think it boded ill for her brother. A nameless worry gnawed her.

Wandering into the living room, she watched her dad pretend to read the newspaper. His eyes didn't move as he stared at the printed page. When he glanced up, she flashed a smile. "Tired?"

Normally he didn't retire for another hour, but tonight he seemed especially weary. "Yep. Think I'll hit the hay."

"Love you." Before he rose, she kissed the top of his head. Every day, more of his blond hair blanched into silver. He shuffled down the hallway. Soon the house settled into an unnatural quiet.

After half an hour, her pacing wore her out. As she shut off kitchen lights, a vehicle pulled into the driveway. She glimpsed broad shoulders and curling, dark hair. Gavin? She'd not seen him since the hospital. Was it almost a week ago already?

He tapped on the screen door.

"What's going on?" She kept her voice low. "It's after ten."

"Can I come in?" Tension emanated from him.

She gulped as she opened the door.

"Your dad still up?" he whispered.

Leah shook her head. Without explanation, Gavin brushed past her and headed into the well-lit living room. He took a deep breath as he perched on a chair's edge. "Sorry I haven't stopped by earlier."

"Understandable."

"I don't want to give you false hope," he finally said. "Or scare you."

She slowly sank to the loveseat. "What is it?"

"The explosion wasn't an accident." His brown eyes bore into hers. "It was a set up."

Ice flooded her veins. "What?"

"I don't have proof. Yet. But I need to ask you some questions."

She spread her hands. "Anything."

"Does Vic have enemies? Anyone who'd want to hurt him?"

"Not that I know of. Everyone loves him."

"Anyone angry with you or your dad?"

Pressing her lips together, she hesitated to mention one name that repeatedly popped up in her family's life. "Only Bram Edwards, the blaster at the rock quarry. He wasn't happy when Dad bought this property. They almost ended up in court." She shrugged. "But that's ancient history."

Gavin's mouth settled into grim lines.

"What're you—?" She rubbed her arm. "What are you *not* saying?"

Abruptly he rose and sat beside her. "I want you to stay close to home. Don't go anywhere without letting a couple people know where you are. At all times. And make sure you have your cell with you."

"Gavin, you're scaring me."

"I'm sorry." His mouth tightened. "I think what happened with Vic is the tip of the iceberg. Someone's been planning this awhile. And the target isn't just your brother."

A chill ran down her back as she recalled her unease while she'd been running.

He took her hand. "I'm probably blowing this out of proportion." His attempted smile didn't reassure her. "My education makes me paranoid."

"What education?"

"I have a master's degree in criminal psychology."

"I didn't know." They'd not had time to talk since the camping trip.

"Not glamorous, believe me. Makes me see shadows in brightly lit rooms."

She grinned, then glanced at his hand, still holding hers. He too looked down but didn't seem in a hurry to pull away.

"At the campout..." He jaw flexed. "I know we haven't seen each other in years, but that night I felt like we connected."

Heat slowly crept up her cheeks.

"I meant what I said. About Homecoming." His grip tightened. "When my dad accepted the job with ATF and moved here, I couldn't wait to graduate so I could have a reason to come back." The look in his eyes spoke volumes.

She slowly withdrew her hand. "You know so little about me."

"I know more than you think." Gavin's dark eyes gleamed. "You had a habit of blowing up social media with your beliefs. About loving God, loving others."

"Yeah." She trailed her fingers along the cushion's piping. "I was pretty vocal on my blog."

"I've been reading it for the last two years."

"Really?"

Gavin nodded. "It reveals your heart. And faith. I wanted to find out if you were for real."

She lifted her chin. "And did you?"

"Yes. I made the right decision. To come back for you."

Leah caught her breath.

"I have so much more to say," he spoke softly. "But until your family is safe, and this mystery's solved, I need to stay focused on this investigation. But believe me, I intend to finish this conversation. Soon." He touched her arm, then rose.

Heart full, she followed him through the dark kitchen to the backdoor.

"Please don't say anything about my suspicions, especially to your dad."

She nodded.

When she reached to flip on the porch light, Gavin blocked her hand. "It's best no one sees my car here. Just in case."

Was someone watching? Her stomach tightened.

"Leah." His voice barely breached a whisper. "Watch out for yourself. 'K?" His fingers, lightly brushing her cheek, created a warm trail that seared all the way to her heart.

Second-degree murder? Leah clutched her father's

arm during Vic's hearing. What had the prosecutor said? Although the explosion appeared accidental, her brother was responsible. Vic had a depraved indifference for life. Not only that, but his previous arrests caused the judge to cast a jaundiced eye on him. But those were misdemeanors. Silly, childish acts.

Vic's charm and youth couldn't outweigh the incriminating evidence police had discovered in his room and the garage. They found blasting materials stolen from the rock quarry and the remains of a radio-control model. Obviously the transmitter was used for the detonation.

Someone planted them. The truth screamed in Leah's mind. *Can't you see what Gavin sees?*

People left and entered the courtroom. Seats filled with those awaiting upcoming cases. Leah remained chained to her seat as one memory replayed in her mind's eye—Vic's horror-stricken face as officials escorted him from the courtroom.

I didn't get to hug him goodbye.

She didn't know how she managed to help her father stand. Didn't know how they got through the building to the parking lot.

When they got home, the July air from the closed-up house hit her like a furnace blast. The roses on the table drooped, mocking the hope for Vic's release. For a long time she leaned against the sink, longing for her sister. But two of her kids suffered with the flu, forcing the family to remain in Denver.

Leah tossed the flowers into the trash and wandered into the living room where Dad stood by the window.

Snuggling against him, she sighed. "I'm so sad it hurts."

He rubbed her shoulder. "Grab a nap, sweetheart. That'll help."

"Want me to make you something to eat?"

"No." Worried eyes scrutinized her. "Go rest."

She squeezed his waist before trudging up the stairs. Despite swirling thoughts, she eventually dozed. Sometime later, she started awake from a tap at her door.

"Yes?" She sat up groggily.

Dad's voice came from the hallway. "Someone downstairs to see you."

Before she could ask who waited, his footsteps moved away. Was it Gavin? He had arrived late at court and hurried away afterwards before she could talk to him.

She yearned for his arms again, like at the hospital. All his texts and calls indicated he wanted their relationship to progress to the next sweet step. However, his investigation kept them apart. Despite his warning to be careful, nothing weird had happened to her or Dad.

Had Gavin's worries been unfounded?

Leah changed her shirt and brushed her hair. However, nothing could be done about her gaunt cheeks or weary eyes.

As she slowly descended, her heart pounded in anticipation.

Gavin wasn't waiting, though.

"Oh. Alan." She smiled politely.

"Hey." He looked extra spiffy tonight. Was he going on a date?

When he moved closer, she stepped behind a chair. *I can't take one more of his hugs.* Over the last week, he'd dropped by so often she could almost accuse him of stalking.

"You don't sound very happy to see me."

"It's not been a very happy day." She indicated his outfit. "What's the occasion?"

"I came to see how you're holding up. Thought we

might go catch a bite to eat."

"I'm not hungry."

"Then how about a walk?" He spread his hands. "We won't go far."

"No, really, Alan. I'm sorry, but I—"

"Why not go?" Dad interrupted as he peered around the corner of the living room.

Glancing between them, Leah sought for a graceful way to decline. She vividly recalled the uncomfortable ride with Alan up the mountains, especially the awkward pauses in conversation.

Dad stepped closer. "You've been cooped up too much in the house lately. Fresh air will do you good."

She chewed her lip. "I suppose."

"Great." Alan's smile grew brilliant.

"Let me put on shoes." As she slowly slipped on sneakers and grabbed a loose-knit sweater, she tried to come up with an excuse. Nothing came to mind. Besides, she didn't like to disappoint Dad. He stood watching her, a concerned frown etching his face.

Alan opened the kitchen door as though to hurry her along. With one last desperate look toward Dad, she headed outside.

She clasped her hands behind her back. "Which way? Toward the pond or the bluffs?"

"Definitely the bluffs." Without waiting, Alan struck off toward the southwest.

After a couple minutes, she called, "Hey, hold up."

"Sunset won't wait." He threw the comment over his shoulder.

Risking rudeness, Leah stopped. Finally, he turned, frowning as he backtracked.

"Can we please not jog? I'd enjoy this more."

Impatience seized his expression, but quickly vanished. "Sure."

What was on his mind? Alan seemed gripped by a

growing tension. She walked even more slowly. "Something bothering you?"

"No, no." His gaze flicked to her, then down the path. After a moment, he amended, "Other than the tragedy in court. Again, sorry."

Despite the sympathetic words, his tone rang hollowly. They walked on.

The further they got from the house, the edgier he grew. He continually adjusted his ever-quickening pace to her slower one. Several times he sighed.

Why is he in such a hurry?

The intolerable silence pressed her. "Have you been out here before?"

"Yeah. Lots."

"Really?" When he didn't elaborate, she asked, "When?"

"After you left for college." He threw her a glance. "Your father didn't mind. As a matter of fact, he invited me to come anytime I wanted."

Funny, Dad never mentioned that.

She again stopped. "He doesn't usually allow people to prowl around." She pointed to a nearby "No Trespassing" sign.

Again, Alan faced her. "Well, things changed."

"I thought you were out of state. Working in an oilfield."

"Actually, several. Oilfields." He jerked a hand across the back of his neck. "Up north. And Colorado."

When he acted like he wanted to move on, she held her ground. He may have coerced her into taking a walk, but that didn't mean she was going to race to the property line and back. "Why didn't you stick with one of them? You could've saved up money, gone to school. Or moved somewhere with more opportunities."

"Yeah, right." Contempt scorched his tone. His eyes blazed in the fading evening light.

Why is he so touchy?

She pulled the corners of her sweater together. "Maybe something better will pop up. Something you'd really like." She hoped to ease the storm between his clashing eyebrows.

His mouth settled into a slash of anger. "What do you know about me or my life? Everything's been handed to you on a silver platter."

"That's not true." Leah took a slow breath. "While going to school, I slaved at a terrible waitressing job. I paid out-of-state tuition and lived in a basement apartment."

"You still don't have a clue."

Discomfort stirred in her chest. Not only at his unwarranted anger, but at a new realization. *I left my cell phone on the nightstand.* "You're right, of course. I'm sure no one can truly understand what someone else's been through."

"You don't know the half of it."

She lowered her voice. "Then tell me. I want to be your friend."

"Too late." He spoke through clenched teeth. "If it wasn't for your father, this would've been my land."

"Your...?" She blinked. "What are you talking about?"

Jaw jutting, Alan remained silent. He wouldn't even look at her.

Dear Lord, what should I say? What can I say?

"I'd better get back to the house." She softened her tone even more. "It's getting late."

He straightened as though coming out of a dream. "I'm sorry. I guess this whole day has gotten to me."

"It's okay." She remained wary.

"Let's catch that sunset. Before it's gone." He smiled, but the gesture never reached his eyes.

Something's wrong.

The full import of their destination hit her. The bluffs. At the end of the trail awaited a forty-foot drop. Her heart hammered.

"Come on, Leah. We're not done with our walk."

She shivered at his words, delivered in a monotone. When he moved as though to put his arm about her shoulders, she ducked. Cold fury etched his face as she evaded him.

Alan's eyes narrowed. "I said come on."

Run. Now. The urging seemed to come from outside herself.

When he swiped at her, he got only a handful of sweater as she bolted. His breath rasped behind her as he gave chase.

Though he yelled for her to stop, she didn't slow. Again she heard her name. From behind? Or ahead?

"Leah!" The sound came again.

Gavin!

"Here," she shrieked. "I'm here."

She stumbled, righted herself and ran on.

Alan's thumping footsteps followed for a few more moments, then suddenly evaporated. Had he given up?

"Leah." The calls multiplied. Several beams bobbed in the dusky woods. Flashlights?

She ran toward the beckoning rays. The space between her and the approaching party closed with torturous slowness. Finally, she spotted Gavin.

As she fell into his arms, he gasped thanks to God for her safety. Around him streamed uniformed men. One officer stopped beside them, hand resting on his weapon as his eyes darted about.

When she caught her breath, all she could say was, "I'm sorry, Gavin. I should have listened to you."

In the warmth of Gavin's embrace, Leah sighed.

Anna Zogg

They sat on the loveseat, her head resting against his shoulder.

"How're you doing?" his gentle voice prodded.

"Better now that the police arrested Alan."

Though it was nearly three in the morning and her father had long since retired, she wouldn't let Gavin leave.

He squeezed her shoulder. "Ready to talk about it?"

She tensed.

"It'd help." He brushed her bangs to one side. "I promise."

Needing to see his face, she straightened. "I'm ready."

"Alan Gohlke is the son of Bram Edwards."

"But Mr. Edwards is married. He—"

"Had an affair." Gavin made a face. "According to my dad, rumors flew, but Edwards never acknowledged the baby."

Leah recalled her earlier conversation with Alan. "His comment makes sense now."

"Alan? What'd he say?"

"That our property would've been his if it weren't for Dad."

"Alan must've figured out who his father was. Or his mom told him before she died." Gavin's mouth pursed. "I'm speculating, but I bet Alan grew up hearing stories of how your dad stole this land from Edwards."

"So he blamed Dad—all of us—for how his life turned out." She lowered her head. "Sad."

"Alan stole Edwards' keys to the magazine where explosives were stored. Edwards didn't report anything because he thought he'd misplaced them. When some materials went missing, he called ATF and other agencies."

Her heart thudded as she contemplated the pieces to the puzzle. "So Alan planted something in the back

193

of Vic's truck and blamed the fireworks."

Gavin nodded. "Remember after the explosion when I ran ahead of you? I surprised Alan and his girlfriend at the campsite. I didn't think anything of it at first. When I went back later I found the transmitter he'd used to set off the blast, tossed into the bushes. His mistake was not retrieving it."

"What tipped you off about him?"

"That day in the hospital. When your brother recounted what happened, everyone appeared grieved. *Except* Alan."

She recalled Gavin's face as he'd stared at someone out of her line of vision.

"He *smiled*. It was so fleeting, I thought I imagined it." Gavin shook his head. "Even in high school, he was always like a simmering pot ready to blow his lid off. When he found out the identity of his father, that gave him a target for his pent-up anger—your family."

"And he didn't care how many others he hurt."

"Exactly."

Leah stared into a memory. "He came over right after Vic's arrest. That had to be when he planted evidence in my brother's room." She straightened as a thought occurred to her. "The screen in Vic's room was pushed out. I thought the police had done it, but it must have been Alan."

"Would be pretty easy to put a bag of stuff outside the window, and then pull it inside while no one was looking."

Leah nodded. The day he brought roses. *He played me.* In retrospect, she had no doubt he was the prowler in the middle of the night. And her follower when she'd been running?

"At court today, I videoed Alan," Gavin continued. "He smiled again. After the hearing, I got a chance to corner his girlfriend—told her I knew everything and that she should cut a deal with the police while she could. My bluff worked. With her testimony, I was able to convince authorities they had the wrong guy."

Leah remained silent for a moment, afraid to ask. "What was tonight all about?"

His gaze flickered away. "While you were napping, Alan told your dad how worried he was about you, how stress makes people do crazy things. I think he was going to claim you committed suicide."

Suicide? She sucked in a sharp breath. No wonder Dad insisted she get some fresh air. Eyes burning anew, she met Gavin's gaze. "I'm glad you arrived in time."

"I called to see how you were doing. When you didn't answer, I almost gave up. But for some reason, I felt uneasy, so I tried the house number. After a dozen rings, your dad finally picked up. When he mentioned Alan, I called the police and drove like a wild man."

Squeezing her eyes shut, she shuddered.

"You don't need to be afraid anymore." Gavin caressed her hand. "Alan's going to be locked up for a long time. Best of all, Vic will be released. I've no doubt a judge is signing the papers right now."

"In the middle of the night?"

"Absolutely." His smile filled her with reassurance.

She again settled into his embrace. After awhile, a deep sigh banished any lingering fear. However, exhaustion conquered her relief.

Gavin stroked her shoulder, voice husky. "I think it's time we finished our original conversation."

"I'm sorry." She shook her head. "Right now I'm totally talked out."

"Fine, because this part doesn't involve talking." With a gentle finger, he lifted her chin.

After one kiss, she forgot all about her exhaustion. He kissed her a second time—so thoroughly that she thought she might faint from happiness.

As the sky gradually heralded a new day, Leah realized the fourth of July had arrived. But fireworks couldn't compare with the explosion of joy in her heart.

Anna Zogg is a romantic who believes in happy endings. (After all, isn't the greatest love story about God's love for humankind?) Author of many articles and two books, she finds herself drawn to love stories again and again. Ms. Zogg and her husband, John (of 35 years) currently live in Utah. www.annazogg.com

Since the mid-1700's, the Scottish village of Gretna Green has been a favorite location for eloping couples. I'm sure the town has seen many cold-footed brides back out at the last minute, but perhaps not for the same reason as our heroine in this next story. Grab a cup of tea, settle yourself in a cozy chair, and travel back to the eighteenth century with your tour guide, author Eva Maria Hamilton. – VS

Disinherited Love

Eva Maria Hamilton

Spring, 1795
Northern England, near the border of Scotland

"I can't marry you," Lily whispered. Her eyes stung with unshed tears.

Gavin leaned in closer and took hold of her shoulders. "I beg your pardon?"

Lily knew she shouldn't, but she couldn't stop

herself. She raised her head and looked past his cravat, directly into deep brown eyes that reflected a love that could never be.

"Lily?" His hand caressed her cheek before tucking a ringlet of hair behind her ear. "Why will you not join me in the carriage?"

She shut her eyes to summon all her mettle, but a tear escaped and Gavin's gentle touch as he wiped the wetness away weakened her resolve. Nevertheless, the words of the letter clasped behind her back burned a hole through her skin and singed a path straight to her heart. She had to do this.

"I can't marry you," she repeated.

"I fail to understand." His fingers squeezed into her flesh. "You must explain. We are mere hours from Gretna Green. You are to be my wife. Just as we planned. Just as we dreamed."

She squirmed out of his hold and turned her back to him. How could she say goodbye to the only man she'd ever loved—the only man she would ever love? She pressed the letter firmly into the calico fabric that covered her midriff, but nothing could cease the agony that raged inside her.

"Please do not turn away from me." He spun himself in front of her so fast she didn't have time to avoid his pained gaze and her stomach heaved more violently. "You must know I love you." He bent down so close she could feel his warm breath in her face.

She swallowed the lump in her throat. Aye, she knew he loved her. And she loved him more than she ever thought possible. But it wasn't enough. Not in his world. And certainly not to his uncle, who expected a marriage to bring wealth and alliances.

"I found this." She thrust the letter into his firm chest. "It fell from your coat as you exited the carriage."

With a glance at the paper, recognition swept across

his features. "Forget what you read." He snatched the letter and ripped it to shreds. "It is of no consequence."

"I disagree." She watched the bits scatter into the late afternoon breeze. "I won't condemn you to a life of misery."

"*A life of misery?*" He stepped closer. "Those are not your words, and I implore you not to repeat my uncle. I am a grown man of four and twenty, and I do not need permission to marry."

"Your uncle disapproves of our marriage." She could barely force the words past her lips. "He thinks me unsuitable."

"He does not know you."

"And he never will." She stepped back.

"Do not utter such a threat." He closed the distance between them again. "In time he will amend his misconceptions. How could he not, once he bears witness to our happiness?" Gavin lowered his voice and almost lulled her into believing him.

She shook her head. "That line of thinking is fraught with error. Our marriage will only anger him more. Right now he despises me. However, the moment you give me your name, he'll be sickened by the sight of you as well."

"What would you have me do?" He raked his fingers through his wavy brown hair. "Comply with his whims?"

Even though the exertion was excruciating, she forced herself to nod.

"Ask anything of me, but not that." His hands, tender and soothing, cupped her face. "I could never part with you, my flower. And I believe God wants us to be together."

Lily swatted his hands away. "Then why would He place such insurmountable obstacles in our path?"

"I do not see impediments."

Exasperated, she stared at him. He did nothing but

thwart her arguments. But she had to convince him—for his own good. She glanced around the main street of this small, remote village, as if it held the key she needed to unlock some persuasive fact.

But the stone buildings rose around them like barriers set to imprison her in this narrow cobble stone road. And her ears were inundated with the thunderous noise of horses' hooves, wagon wheels, conversations, and a multitude of other contraptions and people milling about. Her nose wrinkled at the rancid smell that eddied about in these close quarters. And yet, the assault on her senses paled in comparison to the pounding in her head. An ache put there by Gavin.

She turned her glare upon him as the reason for this elopement became clear. "Why didn't you confide in me about your uncle's displeasure?"

"And begin our marriage under such unpleasantness?"

"Did you intend to hide me?"

"Never." He grabbed her wrist. "I love you. Please, profess your love for me as well."

She stared at her hand nestled between his large masculine fingers. A long silence stretched between them. "Gavin." She pulled her hand out of his.

"Do *not* do this." A rumbling growl infected his plea. Her heart clenched. He knew her too well.

"I must." The need to touch him one last time outweighed the misery that strangled her heart and she traced the hard line of his set jaw.

But to help him she needed to extinguish her emotions. "Goodbye." She snatched her hand back and the loss of contact with him stung like she'd pulled her hand from a fire. She clenched her seared palms into her skirts, lifted the layers, and ran toward a stagecoach about to embark on its journey south to London.

"Lily!" His shout pierced her soul. But she didn't

turn. Tears streamed down her cheeks, and the driver gawked as he helped her up into her seat.

She knew she looked dreadful, but her pitiable outward appearance was nothing compared to the devastation being plundered within her. *God help, me.* She buried her face in her hands. *I do not know what Your plans are for my future.*

"Lily! What're ye doing here?" Her paternal aunt, Vera, dropped her sewing. "'Tis morning shouldn't ye be working?"

"Nay, I can never return there." She trembled as she choked back a sob.

Her aunt rushed across the threadbare mat. "Hush." She took her into her arms and led her to the settee. "Are ye certain 'tis that grave?"

"Aye." She collapsed onto the thin cushion with a long sigh. "I behaved with the utmost of foolishness."

"Ye relinquished yer post?" Aunt Vera shrank into the hard seat beside her.

"In a manner of speaking." Her throat closed tight. She couldn't admit the truth, and her fingers clawed up her neck.

"Don't fret." Her aunt pulled her hands away. "Ye always have a home here with me."

With appreciation, her lips tipped up at the corners before she looked about the barren room. The walls were unadorned, the wood floorboards discolored and splintered, and black smoke stained the hearth. Two wobbly wooden chairs flanked the fire and the only decorations were serviceable candlesticks.

Her aunt followed her gaze. "I know 'tisn't much and 'tis outside the more genteel districts of London, but it has been my refuge these past twenty years."

"I do thank you." She patted her bony hands.

"Without you, I'd have succumbed to a treacherous life as a destitute orphan."

"Come, come. 'Tis the least I could do for my only living relation." Her aunt adjusted a ruffle on Lily's gown. "But I must insist ye unburden yerself."

She took another deep breath as shame cursed through her. "I failed to heed your counsel."

"Ye will have to be a wee bit more specific." Aunt Vera laughed quietly.

"I fell in love with my employer."

"Nay!" A hand flew to cover her mouth.

Lily's gaze sank to the floor. "You asserted that nothing good could ever come of such feelings and you were correct."

Her aunt stood, one hand crushed to her forehead and the other fisted on her hip as she paced the room in silence. But the floor planks creaked and moaned, as if to vocalize her displeasure.

"Please, don't scowl at me. I never intended to disappoint you," Lily pleaded. "And I can assure you I conducted myself with only the utmost of propriety."

Blue eyes widened before they fixed on her. "It would be most hypocritical of me if I reproached ye for behaving as I did at yer age."

Lily jumped forward in her seat. "You never once alluded to such a past."

"Nay. Only God's heard my confession." Her shoulders sagged as she dragged herself to a chair beside the hearth. "But 'tis long enough. I should like to divulge my secret, and ye are one and twenty." She glanced at her and then her gaze penetrated the hearth as if she could see into the past.

"He was set to inherit a large fortune, and even though we fell in love, he ultimately chose his duty over me. He wouldn't go against his father's wishes and marry below his rank. I was naught more than a maid in his household, so I left. I told him I'd leave England. I couldn't watch him court another, let alone marry and have someone else bear his children."

Her aunt ripped her eyes from her memories and gave her a weak grin. "He was kind enough though, made sure I received a good letter of recommendation, and secretly gave me some funds, which I used to purchase this cottage. But 'twasn't enough..."

"Your heart was tattered." Lily hugged herself and pondered how different her aunt's life would've been devoid of the loneliness, drudgery, and childlessness— how different her own life would now be without Gavin. "You have my deepest sympathy."

Aunt Vera dipped her chin. "Did ye encounter the same heartache?"

She nodded. "Very nearly. His parents are deceased though, it's his uncle who rues the day I commenced work in his nephew's home." Her mind travelled to Northern England. "I stumbled upon a letter his uncle had penned."

"While ye were cleaning?"

"Nay. We were en route to Gretna Green."

Her aunt sprang from her chair with more agility than a cat. "Ye were on yer way to marry?"

"We were a few miles short of Scotland."

"Lily," her aunt cried. "He asked ye to marry him, even though he knew of yer situation?" She nodded. "Then why didn't ye marry him? Do ye not love him?"

"It's because I love him." She wrung her hands. "His uncle vowed that if he married me he'd forfeit his inheritance. I couldn't be the cause of such misfortune. Gavin may say it's of no consequence, but after years of degeneration, toil and poverty he'd come to resent me. Possibly even detest me. I couldn't endure that."

"Ye don't have to succumb to a life akin to mine." Aunt Vera enveloped her hands. "This man loves ye enough to relinquish all he has. The man I loved never offered." Tears appeared in her kind eyes, and were blotted with a plain cotton handkerchief. "Although I can't fault him."

Lily's chest ached. "I haven't failed to understand the enormity of the sacrifice Gavin was willing to endure. It's precisely why I could never be the cause of him disinheriting."

"But if he truly loves ye..."

"It's immaterial now." She strode across the quaint room to the lone window. "I could never marry him with the knowledge that I caused him to be stripped of the only life he's ever known."

"Oh, how I prayed yer life wouldn't parallel mine." Her aunt knotted her handkerchief. "I've failed ye."

"Nay." She marched back to the settee. "You always loved me as a mother." Aunt Vera smiled, but with a noticeable effort that stuck Lily like a thorn. "I apologize for my unexpected visit at this early hour. Have you eaten your morning meal?"

Her aunt shook her head of chestnut brown hair. "I doubt I have the appetite."

"Nonsense. You must. Come, I'll cook." She reached out to help her aunt up.

"Only if ye partake."

"Fine. And there shall be no more talk of former beaus." Guilt wrenched her gut for having roused such sorrowful memories. "Let us not forget that you've done well for yourself and I've made my decision."

She jutted her chin as they strolled from the drawing room toward the kitchen. What choice had she but to renounce Gavin? To dwell on her loss would only prolong the hurt. She would keep herself busy, so as not to have enough time to think about *him*. Aye, she would even cease to use his name. Surely, that would help.

... but her heart was another matter. But it would learn!

She cringed. Her head could be sensible and practical, but her heart was another matter.

But it would learn!

She bumped into the entryway table and the newspaper she'd purchased, to stave off an anticipated night of sleeplessness, fell to the floor. She bent to retrieve it, but it scorched her fingers more ruthlessly than Gavin's uncle's letter.

"That can't be!"

Her eyes latched onto the black print.

LORD MACKENZIE, MARRIES HIS MAID, LILY CHRISSON.

As he exited his carriage, Gavin tipped his hat toward his servants. With a raised brow he ignored his butler's peek inside the carriage as if he sought to aid another passenger.

"I'll be in my study." He hauled himself into his estate house. It had been a long, arduous journey and every ounce of him screamed with exhaustion.

The entire trip he had trailed Lily's stagecoach, much like a tormented dog commanded not to devour a piece of savoury meat placed on his muzzle. Sure, he could take comfort in the knowledge of her safe return, but not being with her... was torture. She should have been at his side, as his wife. Instead she had rid herself of him. How was he to live out his days without her?

Simple.

He would not.

He whirled and walked straight back out the door. "I need a horse," he called to the nearest servant and a lad was sent to the stable immediately.

Moments later his head groom greeted him with two of his finest horses. "My lord, we didn't expect ye home, but these two geldings are fit to ride."

Strange. Gavin cocked an eyebrow. Whatever was the matter with his servants? Why would he need two horses? Ah, well. Perhaps the groom supposed he preferred a choice.

"I thank you." He mounted the black thoroughbred.

In a swift canter he reached his uncle's estate home with a mind to articulate precisely his thoughts on the letter that gentleman had hidden in his coat.

"I must apologize on behalf of yer uncle," the butler informed him. "He isn't to be found at home. Would ye care to wait?"

"Aye." He dipped his chin and followed the neatly dressed servant to the parlor.

"I'll send up some congratulatory tea." The butler bowed.

"I thank you." He scratched his head at the butler's meaning. "But that is not necessary," he turned to say, but the butler had already left. With a sigh to the elegant room, he conceded his inability to sit and began to pace.

Past the family portraits, damask paper hangings, tapestry and wainscot, the words he wished to tell his maternal uncle took form.

"Yer tea." A footman laid the tray on an ornate side table.

"Please do not bother yourself to pour it." He preferred to be alone with his thoughts.

"As ye wish." The footman retreated.

Gavin eyed the silver tea service in all its expensive splendor. A luxury he would most willingly relinquish. He loved Lily, and no amount of worldly possessions would keep him from her. He clenched his fists. He should never have to choose between his inheritance and her.

When would his uncle return? He plodded toward the wooden inlaid table. Maybe tea would calm him. He

206

reached for the teapot, but his eyes tumbled on the newspaper beside it.

LORD MACKENZIE, MARRIES HIS MAID, LILY CHRISSON.

He grabbed the paper and devoured the article. They had been recognized on the toll road to Gretna Green. That explained all the oddities he had confronted this morning. But those were trivial compared to what she might encounter. An elopement with her employer. She would be rumored about ad nauseam.

He slammed the paper down. Society's newsmongers would destroy her reputation, and that was under the belief that they had married. What would be said, and done, when the truth was unearthed?

He knew the answer only too well. She would be cast out as a fallen woman.

Anger seared through him. He would not let her be dishonored. Only one thing would uphold her reputation. A sly smile spread across his face. He must convince her to marry him.

༼ ༽

"Whatever shall I do?" Lily's hands shook so violently they strangled the newspaper.

Aunt Vera stood stunned. "Who sold yer whereabouts to that rag?"

"I. Don't. Know." She stared back, the gravity of the situation declared between them without the need for words.

"Do ye suppose *he* did this? To force ye to marry him?" Her aunt spat venom.

If Gavin was responsible—she glanced down at the mangled newspaper in her hands—he wouldn't fare much better than this paper.

"I can't inquire after him." Her voice grew feverish.
"I must think of what I'm to do. We're not married."

"I know." One weathered hand pressed into her
forehead, whilst the other hounded her hip.

She winced. How much agony would she beget her
aunt? "I can't tell a falsehood and proclaim myself
married. But neither can I deny my presence on that toll
road preceding Gretna Green."

"I know," her aunt repeated.

"I'm ruined." The words escaped her in a rush of
defeat. "I must quit London. Perhaps even England."
Her eyes darted around the bleak entryway.

"Come." Warm arms hugged her. "Let's not act with
haste. We must think."

Lily nodded, and her gaze settled on her aunt's kind
face, until a knock sounded on the front door.

"Who can that be?" she whispered. "Would any of
your acquaintances call in light of this?" She shook the
newspaper.

"I'm not expecting anyone." Aunt Vera pulled her
toward the kitchen, but the incessant knocking grew
louder.

"Whomever it is won't go away," Lily hissed.

"Take yerself into the kitchen and I'll rid us of this
intrusion."

She frowned, but conceded after her aunt gave her
a tender squeeze and a little push.

"May I help ye?" Aunt Vera asked. Her voice calm
as if nothing were awry.

"Aye, I'm looking for Miss Lily Chrisson."

Her hands stilled on the kitchen door she hovered
behind.

"And why would ye ask for her here?" Her aunt's
tone indicated she wasn't acquainted with the man
before her, nor was she about to surrender the secrets
of her household. Lily's heart swelled for her protector.

But she knew that voice only too well and couldn't remain hidden any longer. "Gavin, why have you come?" He strode past her staunch defender, whose expression turned from shock to stone. "You read the article." He glanced down at the contorted pulp in her hands. "Aye." She waved the paper at him. "Is this your doing? Did you intend to force my hand?"

He shook his head. "I am pleased you think me so clever, but nay, I must concede it surprised me as much as it has you." His head jerked down to her aunt, who stood with crossed arms and a menacing expression. "Lord Gavin Mackenzie, Ma'am." He dipped his chin in introduction.

The suspicious eyes narrowed. "I don't know yet if I appreciate yer using that term with me. Do ye love my niece?"

"Aunt Vera," she gasped.

But he laughed. "Aye. I most certainly do love her."

"Then what're yer plans to mop up this mess?" Her aunt didn't cower as she berated a man so high above her in rank there was no accounting for it.

A slow grin crept up his cheeks. "What I have long planned for and hoped to do. Marry her."

"Stop this nonsense." Lily stormed closer. "This published falsehood doesn't alter the fact that if we did indeed wed you'd lose your inheritance."

"Why must you compel me to repeat myself?" His easy manner perturbed her. "I am well aware of all that I stand to lose, and have determined that it is naught compared to what I would gain."

Her aunt's hand flew to her heart. "If that's not the dearest sentiment I've ever heard."

Lily rolled her eyes. Gavin's charm was no secret, and coupled with his appearance, he was a man who commanded notice. But this was sheer gibberish.

She opened her mouth to tell him so, but was interrupted by a knock on the door. "Now, who can that be?"

"Back into the kitchen with ye." Her aunt shooed her, then turned to Gavin. "Ye, as well." With a dip of his chin and a smile, he complied.

He took no offence to her aunt's impertinent demands and Lily fought the ache it caused in her chest. "I apologize on behalf of my aunt," she whispered, as they situated themselves near the door to listen in on who'd called.

"No need. My fondness for your aunt continues to mount. Especially now that she has ordered me to be alone with you in such close quarters." His eyes dropped to her lips. "She is currently my most favorite person."

His nearness rendered her mouth dry. But she tore her eyes from him, and without a comment, or even a hint to her true feelings, she cracked open the kitchen door and peeked out.

"May I help ye?"

"Aye, I've a message for Lord Mackenzie."

"And why're ye asking for him here?" Lily grinned at her aunt's ability to ward off strangers.

"'Tis the address I followed him to."

"Oh, no," Lily moaned.

"Not to fret." Gavin threw open the door and strode through.

"Lord Mackenzie, I've news that may be of interest to ye."

"I thank you, Sam." He motioned for him to enter, and immediately she recognized his most loyal driver, who'd accompanied them on their journey to Gretna Green, and hence knew they'd never reached their destination. "Please, divulge your news." When Sam looked bashful, he nodded. "You can speak before them."

Sam cleared his throat. "I was just informed that yer uncle has gone to Gretna Green to find ye."

"I beg your pardon?" He ran a hand through his hair and then rubbed his chin. "If he inquires after us, he will surely ascertain that we never set foot in Scotland."

"Good." She stepped forward. "Then he'll know we never married and you won't lose your inheritance."

He glared at her. "Have you considered the ramifications to your reputation if he speaks of this?"

"Aye." She rose her chin. "But that *is* the truth."

"A truth I intend to hide." He turned back to his driver. "Please, bring my carriage. We must set off for Gretna Green posthaste."

"As ye wish." Sam withdrew himself with such speed, Gavin was barely able to utter his gratitude.

"Must you lead this wild goose chase?" She charged at him. "Even if you locate your uncle, I fail to see how your presence will aid matters."

"I cannot sit idly by."

"So you propose to disclose the truth in the hope he'll conceal the fact that we have not married?" She spoke as if there was a bitter taste in her mouth. "But to what end?"

"I shall confide in him and implore him to conceal his knowledge. But only temporarily. Because, as I will inform him, I still have every intention of marrying you."

"Do you suffer from delirium?" She threw up her arms.

"My sole affliction is love." His gentle, yet earnest, voice wiggled its way into the center of her being. "And since your reputation is ruined unless we wed, I will also inform him that should you refuse me, I shall be forced to leave London to follow my heart. That is, go wherever you must to establish yourself anew."

She froze. He was correct about her having to leave.

But her future was far from mapped out. She hadn't the faintest notion of where she'd go or what she'd do. Although she could clearly see it was impossible for her to hide in her aunt's house forever.

"Then I shall accompany you," she blurted.

Hope gleamed across his face. "Will you aid me in my effort to convince my uncle?"

Aunt Vera stepped forward. "I will."

Lily's scowl slid between them as a dark cloud threatens a sunny day. "When he won't be persuaded, I shall request that he station me in a remote position where you'll never find me. I won't be the cause of your demise."

The light left his features. "Why do you continue to distress yourself on that concern?"

"I've good reason." She paused, not wanting to have this conversation in the presence of her aunt. And yet, he needed to know her family's history. She wouldn't let there be a recurrence. "Have you never wondered why my speech is akin to your own, or why I'm literate?" His brows knitted together, but he didn't utter an answer. "I grew up witness to the consequences of what happens when people marry for love. My mother was a lady who married without her parents' blessings."

Aunt Vera's gaze fell to her well-worn shoes. "I do apologize for speaking of this, but you know how bitter my mother became even though she dearly loved your brother." The sight of her aunt's pain nearly stopped her, but she had to proceed. Time was of the essence.

"My mother was of your mind, certain her parents would recant. Sadly they did not. The servants, fancy house, exquisite finery, balls and society she was accustomed to vanished as she laboured to survive in a wee, shabby, old house. It... altered her and I won't watch you fall as she did."

He stared at her. "Let us not quarrel about this

now."

Her eyebrows slammed together. Did he just insinuate he had every intention of arguing with her later? Hadn't he heard a word she spoke?

"Our carriage will arrive shortly, and although I see your belongings have not yet been unpacked, your aunt's things need to be collected and I believe she will desire your help."

"Indeed I do." Aunt Vera rushed to the stairs.

She shot him a scornful look. "Don't delude yourself. We're not finished." She ascended the stairs, pretending not to notice how his lips curved into a smile at her provocation.

"Nay, we most certainly are not finished, my flower. Not by any means."

Gavin leaned over, and through her sandy hair he spoke in hushed tones so as not to rouse her slumbering aunt. "I dare say we are nearly at Gretna Green and you have yet to speak a word to me."

Lily huffed. "What more is there to say if you won't heed my warning?"

"Plenty." He chuckled, but she did not respond and kept her head positioned to gaze out the window at the early evening sun. "Is there much of interest to behold?" He persisted, because at long last she had acknowledged his existence and he craved her conversation.

She shrugged, apparently determined to do her utmost to ignore him. But her taciturn aloofness was marred when the carriage hit a bump and she jostled into him. He admired the sweet blush that rose to her cheeks, and could not bear another moment of silence. He would goad her to speak. "In a thousand words, I could not begin to express my gratitude to your father for ripping your mother out of the comforts of her parents' home."

"Excuse me?"

He bit back a smirk. "I am most thankful for all your mother suffered, and I dare presume your father was tormented with, as well."

"Gavin." She spoke his name reminiscent of how his governess scolded him as a lad. "How can you take pleasure in other people's misfortune?"

"Because..." He brushed his hand along the soft skin of her face and pushed her silky hair aside. "Their union brought you to me."

She stared at him, her green eyes like a forest that demanded to be immortalized on canvas. And although their shamrock density appeared impermeable, she had not only conversed with him, but had not recoiled from his touch. Hope rose within him.

"I love you, my flower, and I will never retract my ardent affection." Her eyes fell to his mouth as if she needed to watch the words come from him to believe he had spoken them. He took her hand and brought it to his lips. "Unlike our last journey, today we will reach Gretna Green. Please affirm that upon our arrival you will become my wife?"

"I can't." She snatched her hand away. "You must understand that at present my sole purpose is to ensure you keep your inheritance. I do care for you."

"You *care* for me?"

"Aye." She scrutinized her hands as they brushed her blue skirt. "You always displayed the most generous and considerate of gentlemanly behavior and I will never fail to remember all we've shared. Hence why I can't consent to allow you to be hurt."

"Then I beseech *you* not to hurt me."

Her eyes flew to his and he thought he saw them soften. "I apologize, but it is not for me to decide."

"Then upon whom does this decision rest? My uncle?" He sneered. "Please do not put the fate of our lives in his hands."

"I don't. I believe the decision belongs to God."

"Good, then we are in agreement." He paused, amused his comment begot a shocked expression. However, he knew her countenance would fade when he finished. "Because I have complete faith, that the same way God led me to you, He will lead me to you again and again if need be."

She grimaced. "The carriage stopped."

Leaning back, he took a deep breath. He would not pursue the matter. At least not now. But he would pray with fervor for God's intervention.

Gavin inched to the seat's edge. "I will inquire after my uncle."

Lily dipped her chin, and unable to look at him, she tapped her aunt.

"Was I asleep?" Aunt Vera fussed with her appearance.

"We've arrived in Gretna Green." An ache wrenched in her chest as Gavin exited the carriage with a piece of her heart. It would all be over soon. Too soon.

"I'm glad for a moment alone with ye." Her aunt leaned forward and took her hands. "How do ye fare?"

Lily shook. "I apologize for my foolish question. I should've supposed as much."

"I'm petrified." She squeezed her confidante's hands to stop the tremble in her own. "I've pondered the entire journey and have yet to conceive of an alternate outcome. Gavin's uncle *will* disinherit him if we wed. Hence, I'm obliged to plead for employment from his uncle because that man will relish the prospect of stationing me far from London—away from Gavin."

She blinked back tears, fighting to continue. "Although I'll be grateful for the opportunity, considering what remains for me here is a ruined reputation, I never conceived of a day I'd leave London, let alone board a ship set for the Americas, which is where I believe he'll send me given the nature of his business."

Tears welled in her aunt's eyes. "Take heart, my dear. I hope 'tis a comfort to ye that I aim to follow ye wherever ye should go."

Lily's jaw dropped. "But you've made a comfortable life for yourself in London. What would become of your cottage? All your possessions?"

"I'll find a buyer." Her aunt reassured her with a smile. "There is naught that means more to me in this world than ye. Ye are the only reason I stayed in London."

The world blurred as tears streamed down her cheeks. "You're more than simply my aunt. You're my dearest friend, and I thank God for you daily." She hugged her.

"As do I." Her aunt laughed through their tears. "Perhaps the good Lord knows this is precisely the change I need. 'Tis time I cease thoughts of past hurts and begin to live once more. I'm scarcely forty. That's hardly decrepit."

"Aye." Lily giggled. "You're more than capable of starting anew."

She, however, was not. Her own heart would certainly not mend, because her love for Gavin would never cease. But she would leave, for him, and be content with the remembrance that he'd loved her...once.

"Lily." Gavin knocked on the carriage door. "My uncle's been found at that inn yonder." He pointed, after he'd helped them disembark.

Her entire body quaked. However much she didn't want to do this, she had to. The words from John 13:34 dashed into her thoughts...*Love one another; as I have loved you...* Aye, she would sacrifice herself for him.

"I wish to speak first with my uncle unaccompanied." His jaw clenched, and she nodded. She already knew the outcome. He wouldn't sway his uncle. Nevertheless, in the years to come, perhaps he'd take comfort in the knowledge he'd done his utmost. She'd pray he'd find peace, because she didn't want him to mourn her and live a sorrowful existence.

"We'll partake of refreshments." She took her aunt's arm, and walked in complete silence, as if the inn were a courthouse and they were to be put on trial.

"After you." Gavin held the door open to the crowded, dimly lit room. Smoke from the hearth added to the oppressiveness as all eyes turned toward them.

"This way." He led them across a rickety wooden floor, to a recently vacated table, by a four-paned window.

"Nephew." A gruff voice behind them stilled their movement.

"Jack Lockswood?" Aunt Vera planted her feet a shoulder's width apart and crossed her arms. Her body steeled into a shield more formidable than the stone walls that surrounded them.

Lord Lockswood mimicked her and they glared at each other.

She'd seen Gavin's forty-two year old uncle on numerous occasions when he'd visited the estate house, but they'd never been introduced. How was her aunt acquainted with him enough to use his Christian name?

"Vera Cinders? I presumed you'd emigrated."

Lily exchanged a glance with Gavin, who appeared as bewildered as she was.

"What's your business in Gretna Green?" Gavin's

uncle demanded.

"Likewise, might I not inquire after ye?" her aunt retorted.

"Are you to be wed?" His eyes narrowed.

"If I am, 'tis no longer yer concern." Aunt Vera sneered, and understanding flooded Lily. Gavin's uncle must be the man who'd jilted her aunt.

"Are you well-acquainted with one another?" Gavin searched their faces.

"Aye," his uncle answered.

"Nay," she said simultaneously. "Our paths haven't crossed in twenty years."

In want of her fan, Lily put the back of her hand over her mouth as Lord Lockswood and her aunt frowned at each other.

"Perhaps it would be best to continue this conversation out of doors." Gavin tilted his head toward the attention they'd attracted.

His uncle jerked a nod. "Aye."

"Nay." Her aunt didn't move.

Gavin's baffled expression flew to Lily for help.

"Please, Aunt Vera." She placed a hand on her elder's arm. "Some air might benefit us."

Her aunt stormed past Lord Lockswood, who stomped out in pursuit. They stared after them.

"Are you as perplexed as I am?" Gavin asked.

"I believe my aunt and your uncle used to court."

"Goodness!" He couldn't contain his shock and spoke louder than propriety dictated. Eyebrows rose around the room. Embarrassed, he offered her his arm and they scampered out.

Angry voices led them around a corner to a lush garden.

"You never married?" Lord Lockswood interrogated her aunt.

She shook her head. "And ye?"

"Nay," he answered.

"For what reason?"

Lily grinned at her aunt's boldness, but held Gavin's arm tight to restrain him. Neither his uncle nor her aunt had seen them and she didn't want to intrude. At long last, her aunt might lay her heartbreak to rest.

"Surely, you can surmise the reason I never married," Lord Lockswood muttered.

"Never have I witnessed my uncle behave in such a fashion," Gavin whispered with a bemused expression. "Can it be that he still loves my aunt?"

He shrugged, but his intense gaze sought hers. "No amount of time would ever quench my love for you."

She yearned to agree, but bit her lip. Neither of them would benefit from her affirmation of love. The thought of their imminent separation roiled her insides. She wrenched her eyes from his and hugged herself, but it did little to suppress the despair.

"If what I surmise is true..." Her aunt thrust her finger in the direction of the inn. "Then how can ye forbid their love?"

"Whose love?" Lord Lockswood demanded.

"Yer nephew and my niece." Fury saturated her voice.

"Your niece?" Lord Lockswood laughed. "Surely this proves God is the greatest of all humorists."

"Don't distract from the question."

"I never forbade their love."

"Don't stoop to a falsehood." Her aunt's brows furrowed. "Did ye not tell Gavin that if he wed Lily he'd lose his inheritance?"

"Aye, but 'tis not akin to forbidding their love. True love would cast aside such ramifications. And he's proven himself to be most fervently in love."

"But ye weren't?"

"On the contrary." Lord Lockswood stepped toward

her. "But I was a foolish youth." Lily's hand flew to conceal her slack jaw as her aunt sobbed. "Not a day passes that I don't regret my mistake. Please, forgive me."

Aunt Vera's head bobbed as she dabbed her eyes with her handkerchief.

"You subjected me to a test?" Gavin surged forward, momentarily silencing his uncle.

"Aye, and you rendered me most proud. You achieved that which made me falter. My father's disinheritance threats unnerved me." His head drooped. "I was unable to perceive a life devoid of wealth and nobility. Unable to foresee obtaining a lucrative occupation or dwelling, let alone caring for a wife, and if God blessed us with children..." He emitted a low whistle.

"Oh, Jack." Her aunt swatted her handkerchief at him.

"Are you bestowing your blessing upon us then?" Gavin stood rigid.

"Aye!" He gripped Gavin's shoulder. "I apologize, but unfortunately it fell upon me to ascertain your readiness to enter into matrimony. I only wish I'd conducted myself in the same manner." He looked at Aunt Vera. "I hope to rectify my wrong." A blush rose into her smooth cheeks at the kiss he placed on her hand.

"Lily!" Gavin ran back and swept her in his arms. "There is naught to hinder you from becoming my wife."

Tears streamed down her cheeks as she hugged him and he spun her around.

"Halt," Lord Lockswood shouted. "You did not yet enter into matrimony?"

"Lily refused to wed yer nephew if it eradicated his inheritance," her aunt explained.

Lord Lockswood's mouth gaped open. "Once more, I

apologize. It appears our bizarre family tradition has put this fine twosome through a terrible ordeal."

"Fortunately, their turmoil was *short-lived.*" Aunt Vera poked him.

"Aye." He winked. "But then they'll never know the happiness that awaits the rekindling of a long lost love."

Their laughter faded as Gavin set Lily down and cupped her face. "I love you, Lily Chrisson, and I pray you will do me the honor of becoming my wife?"

With glee that flowed from her heart, she nodded. God had answered her prayers. His design had always been for them to be together. He'd merely postponed their union to reunite another couple.

She wrapped her arms around her intended's neck, then slid her hands up into his thick, brown hair. He pulled her closer. "I have longed for this, my flower." His lips touched hers and thrills shot down her spine.

"I never stopped loving you," she breathed. He smiled, and the depth of his kiss exposed his steadfast belief in her declaration.

"Shouldn't such affection be deferred until after the nuptials?" Lord Lockswood bellowed.

"A mere formality." Gavin laughed. "Since society already believes us to be married."

"And we have lost time to recoup." She rose up on her toes and they melded into one.

Award winning author, **Eva Maria Hamilton**, spent years studying people across all different areas of academia and brings that understanding of the human condition into each of her written pieces. She is the author of *Highland Hearts*, a Love Inspired Historical novel published by Harlequin, which won 2nd Place in

the Historical Romance, as well as the Traditional/Inspirational Romance Categories in the 2013 Heart of Excellence Readers Choice Awards, and was an Inspirational Series Finalist in the 2013 Gayle Wilson Award of Excellence. To connect with her, please visit her website at
www.EvaMariaHamilton.com

In this coming-of-age story, author Deb Wuethrich tells the beautiful nostalgic tale of two young people from very different backgrounds who form a special bond. Adolescence is not easy, and is harder for some than others. Though not a romance in the strictest definition of the genre, I was drawn to the characters and captivated by their realistic struggles and emotions. – VS

Not My Boyfriend

Deb Wuethrich

September 1963

Let's be clear. Reginald Black was not the sort of boy a girl wanted to be seen with, according to my new classmates at Perry Junior High. He was not my boyfriend.

"He and his delinquent friends are troublemakers," said Wanda Jackson, who befriended me in homeroom after learning my family had just moved to Carver Creek Road in the small upstate New York community. "Stay away from that bunch."

As it went, I had little choice in the matter. The first afternoon of my seventh grade year, Sam Driscoll, one of the delinquents that had been pointed out, plunked himself in my school bus seat on the way home, sandwiching me in.

"Hi ya, four eyes," Sam said, as his friend, Woody Jones, sat sideways in the opposite seat, snickering.

Like a cornered bird, I moved as close to the window as I could get, keeping my head low.

"Aw, c'mon, I don't mean nothin' by it." Sam edged closer. "You're actually kinda cute, blondie."

The nearness of his leg to mine made my skin itchy. I looked out the window, not wishing to engage in this conversation. It was then I caught movement out of the corner of my eye and felt the seat shift as Reginald Black picked Sam up by the collar and physically walked him two seats forward.

"What?" Sam protested. "I didn't do anything." But he soon quieted. My seat squawked as the larger boy folded his stocky form next to me, the worn knees of his corduroys touching the back of the next seat as he fit his long legs up against it.

"Don't let 'em scare ya." He settled in and reached out a hand. "I'm Reggie."

I stared for a moment. God had peppered this one with more freckles than there were stars in the sky. I'll never know why I responded, but I shook his hand.

"Caroline." I was now wedged in the seat like tuna packed in a can by an even bigger person than before— a freckle-faced, red-haired boy with startling blue eyes.

"Does anyone call you Caro?" he asked.

I looked into the penetrating blue pools. Aquamarine, I thought. Like the pale blue of the birthstone for March.

"No." Most people used my full name.

"Caro it is." Reggie seemed to suddenly become aware of my unease. "Look, don't mind my rowdy friends. They haven't yet learned the SOCIAL GRACES." He aimed the last words loudly in Sam and Woody's direction.

"You're such a jerk!" Sam returned before he and Woody then turned their attention elsewhere.

During the bus ride, Reggie just talked. I learned he lived in an old two-story house about a mile from the ranch house we moved into in August when my father's manufacturing company transferred him to Perry. Our property included an old barn, which would be a good place for my dad to tinker with cars. It also had a stall that would someday shelter a horse, if I could talk my parents into getting me one. There were two other buildings, one teetering a little, set off toward the back near the woods. They hadn't been used in years but looked like they'd once been machine sheds. One had an old abandoned car inside. Someone had taken the seats out of the rusty sedan and set them against the wall. I quickly claimed this building for privacy to read and daydream.

Reggie had lived on Carver Creek Road all his life. His eyes sparkled when he said his big brother, Wayne, was a junior on the football team, but I saw his expression change when he mentioned his mother, Linda, and father, Buck. He called them by their first names. What was that about?

"We have a little sister," Reggie added. "Her name is Margaret, but we call her Sissy. She's eight."

As the school bus approached his stop, just before we'd go around the big bend toward mine, Reggie appeared to realize I wasn't volunteering much information. He rose to exit, and then turned back.

"Look, Caro. If those guys bother you again, just let me know, okay?"

☙

From that day on, Reggie sat on the aisle of whatever seat I claimed, fielding the occasional snide comments tossed over the shoulder by his buddies, who apparently had no interest in challenging him for his now-designated spot.

On a warm April day in the spring of 1964 when the birds were chirping and the sun warm on my face, I was eager to get to the solitude of my hideaway. Book, sack lunch and a Pepsi in my hands, I used my shoulder to open the creaky door, but came to a halt when a form moved on the car's bench seat.

"It's okay, Caro, it's just me, Reg." He sat upright. A sunbeam fell across his features. "Close the door, please," he added, shielding his eyes, but not before I saw the purple bruises.

"Were you in a fight?" My friends often said that's what Reggie and his pals were good at, though I'd never seen them in action.

He shrugged. "You could say that."

After several months on the bus, I was no longer afraid of him. While we rarely talked at school, Reggie insisting being around him would only tarnish my reputation, we had talked about stuff on the morning and after-school bus trips. He could be moody, but I found him to be sensitive and a good listener. Sometimes there were no words between us, just a comfortable companionship. When President John F. Kennedy was assassinated in November, we'd shared a somber silence, except for the commentary coming from my transistor radio. I cried some and Reggie's eyes were a little wet in the corners.

When the Beatles headed to America in February,

then appeared on Ed Sullivan, Reggie at first feigned indifference, saying he preferred new music coming from California to the British invasion. Then one day he remarked, "So what's the appeal of the one with the big nose and the jewelry? Ringo? What kind of name is that? He's kind of homely, ain't he?"

"So you did watch the show," I countered. When classmates began wearing long hair that looked like it was cut with a bowl over the head, Reggie remained his familiar freckle-faced self. But I knew he had a dark side — a side augmented by a poor choice of friends. Once, someone placed a cherry bomb in a row of mailboxes in front of a trailer park on Carver Creek Road, rending them all unusable until residents could replace them. There was little doubt as to who did it, but no one could prove it. Reggie would neither confirm nor deny involvement, even to me. He was loyal to his friends, even if their characters were questionable.

Now in my secret hideaway, he deftly touched his split lip and winced. I sat next to him. I'd never seen a black eye up close before.

"Did you win at least?"

He didn't answer the question, but looked down, then finally back at me. "What do you think of me, Caro?"

"Well, I'm fond of you. Despite what others say, you're easy to talk to. I worry about your fighting, though."

"Are you afraid of me? Because I'd hate that. I'd never hurt you, I hope you know that."

"I know," I said. "I knew the day you plucked annoying Sam right out of my seat. You kind of made me bully-proof — at least on the bus."

"I wish *I* was bully proof," he said quietly. "Sometimes the worst bullies are the ones who are supposed to protect you."

"What do you mean?"

"It wasn't other guys, Caro. It was Buck." He nearly choked out the last part as tears filled those pale blue eyes like waves surging onto a seashore. "He drinks and he's a mean drunk."

I was shocked.

"And the other times?" I'd seen some yellowing bruises on his arms before, but told myself it was just from rough-housing with his friends.

"I've been in a few fist fights — but mostly Buck." He stared past me, as if the movie of his life were playing out on a screen back there, revealing scenes no young person should have to deal with. "Especially lately. They've cut his hours at work. I think drinking is how he copes. He thinks he's powerful when he drinks, but it really makes him weak and pathetic."

"Haven't you ever told anybody? What about your mom?"

"He pushes Linda into drinking with him so he won't have to drink alone, then when he gets out of hand she just cries and cowers in the corner." His eyes were now fixed on the dusty plank floor. I could almost see him processing his disappointment at that. Then, he looked at me. "I tried telling my shop teacher once, but he just avoided me after that. I don't think other people know what to do and it scares them so they avoid the whole issue and hope it goes away. You're the first person I've ever told since. He's slapped Wayne, too. He says he's enlisting as soon as he turns 18. Wish I could."

"Oh, Reg." What could I say? I touched his shoulder. He sniffed then straightened.

"So what's the word from Robert?" he asked, changing the subject and snatching half my sandwich. I'd only heard from my former crush twice since moving.

"I think Robert has moved on." I caught his eye and smiled to let him know I was past the devastation stage.

Reggie's eyebrows lifted when he smiled back. He looked pleased. "His loss." Then his brow wrinkled and his voice took on a more serious note. "If you were my girlfriend, I'd write you every day."

We saw each other at school, but at Reggie's request we didn't socialize unless a class project threw us together, which sometimes happened throughout eighth grade. Our real friendship was kind of our secret. We were pals in the shed where Reg made fun of my fan magazines—16 and Tiger Beat especially. We waded in Carver Creek and sometimes explored the woods behind my house. Once, he showed me the camp he and his friends had built further down the creek. It used to be his hideaway until his privacy was constantly compromised by other boys, including his older brother and his friends, whom, Reggie said, sometimes brought girls there.

He stopped suddenly, and turned me to face him. "If you were my girlfriend, I'd never treat you the way they treat some of the girls they bring here. I'd treat you like a queen."

I didn't want to know any more than that, and we walked on.

One evening early in the summer of 1965 before we were to enter high school as freshmen, we were on our backs on the grass, looking for shooting stars.

"Do you ever wonder what comes after?" I always felt a little dizzy viewing such an expanse of sky and contemplating how puny we seem by comparison. Could God really zero in on the needs of each person when there were billions who had lived and walked the Earth? Reggie looked comfortable with his arms up underneath his head.

"Have you forgotten Sunday School?" he said.

I'd been surprised when my family entered Carver Creek Road Baptist Church and encountered Reggie and his family there. They looked so normal. Reggie said they were normal—until they drank. Alcohol changed them, igniting and spreading the flames of personal problems to out-of-control proportions.

"Didn't you go under for the Lord, as they say?" Reggie asked.

I had, at my old church, when I was nine years old, and told him as much. His next comment took me a little off guard.

"I did, too," he said. "When I was 11."

"Huh?"

"What?" He grinned sideways. "You think it's strange a rascal like me could be a believer? I believe there has to be something better, someplace where people don't go hungry, or get sick. Someplace where people don't judge you for who they *think* you are. Someplace where there are no wars—and where fathers don't smack their kids."

His voice trailed off and he was silent for a time.

"I know, let's make a pact." He reached for my hand, which he held just for a moment, tracing a little cross on my palm with his index finger as if to seal the deal. "Whoever goes first, we'll wait, right up there at the end of the Milky Way. Up there in heaven we won't care who sees us together."

"Deal," I said.

⚈⚈⚈

It was mid-August when Reggie stopped coming to the shed. I scoured the woods and couldn't find him. Wanda said she'd heard a rumor that Reggie had finally lost it this time and because of his fighting, he'd been sent away. Sam and Woody just smirked when I saw them in town one day and asked about him, and I didn't know his family well enough to walk down the road and around the big curve to inquire.

Reggie had not returned by the time school started that fall. Even without him, the boys on the bus didn't bother me anymore. I think they knew there would be payback when Reggie returned if they did.

One day, my mother handed me an envelope addressed to me and I ran to the shed to read it.

Dear Caro: You probably wondered what happened to me. Don't believe everything you hear. They call this a work farm for wayward boys. I am fine and it isn't too bad here, except I don't get to see you. They make everyone learn to milk the cows and bale hay. They work us hard, but we get three squares a day and some time in the evening to study, watch TV or write letters. You're the only one I care to write to. I don't know when I will be home, but don't worry about me. I believe I needed a break from home as much as they needed a break from me. I think of you daily. I know you're not my girlfriend, but will you write to me? I would like that. I also understand if you don't. Your Friend, Reg.

I wrote him back, sharing the first heady days of high school and he, in turn, wrote me.

Dear Caro: It was so good to hear from you. Mark is a fool not to see how much you like him. If you were my girlfriend, I wouldn't ignore you. I'd give you 100 percent of my attention!!!!! Are you still listening to those longhairs? I mean, come on, what's with the names. Hermits? Turtles? Really? And what a lame song, Henry the VIII. I still dig the surfer guys. American made, you know? Hope to see you soon, but don't know when. Reg.

By mid-September, I'd had my heart set on

attending my first high school dance, but the boy I wanted to go with let me down. I wrote Reg all about my heartbreak.

Dear Caro: So it's Larry now. How dare he hurt your feelings by asking another girl to the Harvest Dance. If you were my girlfriend, I'd jump at the chance to take you. But then, we wouldn't want to ruin your reputation with the likes of me! I'm incorrigible, remember? Did I spell that right? Seriously, I'm sorry you won't be going. Thinking of you, Reg.

It was like Indian summer the night of the Harvest Dance—a warm breeze carrying over from a sunny day, rustling leaves dancing in the wind and that distinct scent only fall can summon. My friend, Wanda, who had a date, wanted me to tag along anyway, but I declined, choosing instead to sulk in my room.

"Caro-o-o. Can you come out to play?"

It was around nine o'clock when I heard the voice outside my open window.

"What are you doing here?" I said, half-scared my parents would hear, half-excited to see him.

"Nice specs," he said of my Granny glasses like all the kids were wearing. "C'mon. I want to show you something."

When I got outside, he took my hand. "Don't read anything into it. Just close your eyes." He then led me to our shed. "Okay, open."

The dusty room bad been transformed. Crepe paper streamers decorated the walls, and three camp lanterns covered with colorful rayon scarves dangled from the ceiling. A transistor radio set on WKBW out of Buffalo was playing Sonny and Cher's, "I Got You, Babe."

Reggie released my hand and faced me. "If you were

my girlfriend, you wouldn't be sitting home alone tonight. So I thought I'd bring the Harvest Dance to you."

The comfortable familiarity I had missed settled between us. He'd covered the car bench with an afghan and led me to it. There were cider and donuts on a TV tray next to it.

"And for you M'lady." He stuck a golden chrysanthemum in my hair then draped a filmy orange and black scarf around my neck.

I splayed my arms, feeling suitably dressed for the occasion. "You thought of everything."

"House of the Rising Sun" played as we sat to sip some cider.

"Animals? Really?" Reggie couldn't help saying.

We listened for a while, just enjoying the moment.

After draining my cider, I turned to him on the bench. "Time for truth. Why did they send you away, really?"

He was quiet, considering.

"He went for Sissy," he finally said. "Linda just took her place in the corner. She'd been drinking, too. With Wayne in the army now, it falls to me. I threw myself in front of Sissy. Buck lashed out—I pushed back. Knocked him on his bony behind. I think it scared him. I don't think up 'til now he's noticed that I'm bigger than he is. I couldn't let him hit a little girl. I had to do something. When he started to sober up, he turned it around—used that word. Incorrigible. Linda backed him up and they made up a story and came up with the work farm idea."

"But they let you come back home?"

"We're all guarded with each other, but I think Buck realizes now that I can take him, plus he knows he shouldn't have gone for Sissy." Reggie leaned back, splaying his arms across the back of the seat. I was facing him, one leg tucked under me. He looked past me again, fixing his eyes on that movie I could only glimpse through his words. It made me sad to watch the hurt in his eyes, even as the muted light from the lanterns glowed within them. "He says he's not drinking anymore, but I think he's just not drinking as much." From the sound of his voice, I don't think Reggie believed his father. "Linda's all apologetic, says they've changed."

Suddenly, Reggie came back to the present and touched my shoulder. "But I don't want to talk about all that right now."

"Thank you for this," I said after a time. "It was sweet."

"That's me. Sweet as sugar." He reached out and tucked a strand of my hair behind my ear and smoothed the scarf. The gesture felt incredibly intimate and my heart did a strange little skip. Before I could react, Reggie backed up a little. "I would've taken you to the dance, but you know, I don't want to pull you into my drama. And I'm not your boyfriend. But if you were my girlfriend..."

"Shut up," I said. When Peter and Gordon began crooning "True Love Ways," I hopped up and pulled him to his feet. "Dance with me."

We stood together, a little awkward at first. He took my specs off and placed them on the tray, then we managed to put our arms in the right places and started to rock together to the song. Dancing with Reggie felt like the most natural thing in the world. On impulse, I leaned closer, looking up into those pale blue gems that glimmered even more on his tanned-from-the-farm, freckled face. His return gaze registered a second of surprise, then he closed the distance and our lips met. It was a soft, sweet kiss that lasted a few seconds before I rested my head on his broad chest, feeling his breath on my hair as he tightened his bear hug and we swayed to the music. Safe, I realized. That's how I felt with Reggie. Safe and a little cherished, even in friendship. When "Louie, Louie" came on, we belted it out along with the Kingsmen. A little before midnight, Reggie walked me to the edge of the lawn, staying in the shadows where the porch light met the tall weeds.

"G'night, Caro." His lips brushed my forehead. "That was fun. We'll have to do it again sometime."

"For sure," I said, feeling emotions I couldn't identify, something like butterflies fluttering in a net. Then he walked away, whistling into the night.

It was the last time I would ever see him.

Tragedy struck on Sunday night that same weekend. Reggie was struck by a car while walking after dark on the wet, slick curve of Carver Creek Road. They said he died on impact. Purely an accident. The driver was not charged. I'll never know if he was headed to our secret place in hopes of seeing me again, or to nurse fresh bruises and broken promises after another run-in at home.

I didn't go to the funeral. I wanted to. I was all dressed to go, but a sudden onset of flu that weekend made the decision for me. I couldn't very well take a bucket to a funeral home. In retrospect, I think it was a mixed blessing. I didn't have to see Reggie's weeping and remorseful parents and wonder if he'd been trying to get away from them again, or watch people who disliked him suddenly feel sorry for Reggie. Hypocrites. He would've hated that.

Wanda said half the school was there, all puffy-eyed and sad-faced. I don't know if they were crying for Reggie or, more likely, for themselves in the transition from the invincible attitude of youth to a stark recognition of their own mortality. Though I would wonder years later if things would have been different had I experienced the closure of a funeral ritual, I tell myself it's better that I remember the Reggie of a warm autumn night when we held our own Harvest Dance.

One day Sam sat in my seat. He stared straight ahead and didn't say anything until just before his stop.

"He was a good guy." He spoke quietly, without looking at me. "People shouldn't judge by what they think they know about a person. Reggie deserved better."

I respected Sam for that. Maybe what he said was true for others as well. Maybe it was true for Sam and Reggie's friends. Everybody has baggage of some sort. It doesn't have to define them.

The other day I took out the orange and black scarf, laid it against my cheek, and remembered our kiss—an almost chaste but incredibly sweet meeting of lips. Was I the only one who knew the real Reggie Black? The sensitive, thoughtful boy who promised to treat me right, if I had been his girlfriend? I gazed up at the stars and focused on the twinkling Milky Way. Reggie would not want me to feel sorry for him. He was safe. Home, A rascal, but a Believer. No one would hurt him there. And someday he'd meet me at the designated spot.

Would God somehow allow Reggie to hear my thoughts? I whispered to the dark night sky. "Maybe in that moment, the night you made me feel cherished and special, I really *was* your girlfriend."

Deb Wuethrich is a retired newspaper journalist who has also published work in anthologies such as *Miracles and Moments of Grace: Inspiring Stories of Survival, Cup of Comfort for Parents of Children with Special Needs*, among others, and several magazines. She has received one national and several Michigan press awards and was the recipient of a 2003 Amy Award of Outstanding Merit. Deb is co-founder of Southern Tier Christian Writers that meets in the First Baptist Church in Olean, NY, and serves as president. She writes extensively on love, loss and healing.

By now you've no doubt realized that I enjoy humor in fiction, and I also admire characters whose voice is so unique that they stand out long after I've read the end of a story. Both are true in the case of "Within Limits." One thing I admire about this story is Scott's ability to weave a science fiction element into a perfectly normal, everyday setting without overpowering the compelling romance plot. Besides, I just love his sense of humor. – VS

Within Limits

Scott R. Parkin

A life without romance is an empty thing. But a life without romances is utterly unthinkable.

So I make a weekly pilgrimage into town to trade in one pile of romance novels for another. I go to the giant Sam Weller's in downtown Salt Lake City—best collection of used books in six states. Sixty-five miles each way, but I've tapped out all the local bookstores, so it's really my only choice. It's worth it.

I know, what's a thirty-something guy doing reading romance novels? Aren't those for bedraggled housewives and silly teenage girls? Don't I have anything better to do with my time and money? Well, we've all got our vices, and it's better than hanging out on street corners. Besides, it's not like I believe they're real. I mean that stuff just doesn't happen in real life. No love at first sight. No saving the girl from the raging flood or the corrupt landlord or the enemy invasion. No tender thanks or passionate embraces or heaving breasts.

Still, one can hope—within reasonable limits—and this is as good as any other day for the impossible to happen.

The radio's blaring from the tiny in-dash speaker. A serious voice drones on about space aliens from the planet Fisbane, how they're transporting stolen goods across national boundaries, and how they've sparked an international diplomatic crisis. I wish for a moment that I could meet a Fisbanian, or any alien for that matter, but nothing that cool ever happens to people like me.

The drive's an easy one—at least until you get out of Utah County. Brown in more shades than you thought possible, from the deep coffee brown of the western hills to a dull grey-yellow the color of old wheat at the point of Traverse Mountain that separates Utah County from Salt Lake County.

The promontory really does come to a point there. Not just a peak that slopes down on each side, but a finger of land that juts out into the valley and separates one world from another.

Now I don't know anyone in the world who can drive the speed limit coming down off Traverse Mountain. I mean, it's a straight road that drops directly into outer

Salt Lake City suburbia. You have to actively brake to keep from accelerating, and who's got time to brake when there're romances to be had? Especially after forty miles, with twenty-five still to go?

No one. That's who. At least no one less than three hundred years old who can actually see over the steering wheel and isn't wearing a hat. But that's a different problem.

So I let my speed creep up a bit on the way down the other side, and I don't work very hard to slow down.

Okay, I don't work at all to slow down.

Fine. So I keep my foot on the gas and take advantage of the hill to get my speed up to eighty-five. Or so.

Now don't get me wrong. I'm not a speed demon—or at least not ordinarily so. But when you drive a little three-cylinder fuel economy special, you have to take advantage of every downhill you get. The poor little beast grinds to barely over fifty on the way up the hill; it just seems like justice that I should be able to make up the difference coming back down the other side.

Which is why it's so unfair that a cop is waiting for me at the bottom of the hill.

On any other day there would've been at least a dozen other speeders all clustered together, and the cop would've had to pick one and let the others go. Usually, they didn't bother.

But today the road is empty, and the cop pulls right out after me, lights a-flashing.

I suppose the general emptiness of the road should have been a sign, a warning that all was not right and I needed to pay more attention. But up until now I was just so happy to have clear sailing that it never occurred to me to wonder about the downside of my good fortune.

So I pull over and fish my wallet out of my back pocket and wait. And seethe. And wait. And mutter. And wait.

I think they do that on purpose. They wait in their cars, talking on the radio to some old hag in Dispatch about their bunions or elbow warts or some such thing, just to see how long they can stretch you out. They watch through tinted windshields and wait until you're as taut as you can get, then they saunter up and say, "Do you realize how fast you were going?"

Of course I realize how fast I was going—I was going it, wasn't I? Do they really think it's possible to go twenty miles over the limit and not know you're doing it?

They know you're in a hurry—that's why you were speeding in the first place. They do it to tick you off, because all cops are just little dictators waiting to exercise their power over the common man. What made it really annoying was that this time the would-be tyrant was right.

And they wonder where road rage comes from.

I've been sitting there for at least three hours waiting for the cop to get off the phone with his bookie when my eye catches on the pile of romance novels in the passenger seat.

It would be wrong to say that I'm embarrassed by my habit, but it is something I try not to advertise. People just don't understand how a six-two, three hundred pound man with a full beard and a genetically sour expression can read such things. Their eyebrows raise and they suppress giggles and they smirk like you're wearing a pink tutu or something.

I wasn't in the mood for that just now.

So I grab bundles of books and shove them in the glove compartment and under the seat. I run out of space after the third bundle and I'm just turning to look in the back seat for a bag to stuff the rest into when I hear a tap on the window.

"Doggone it," I say much louder than I mean to and turn to face the fascist pig cop with the domination complex and a whole lotta nerve for pulling over a generally law abiding citizen who may have pushed the limit a little bit but who deserves a break because everyone makes a mistake and it's a Saturday and all I want to do trade in a few paperbacks so I can find something in my life that isn't empty and depressing but there aren't any decent bookstores in Santaquin so I have to drive to Salt Lake and it's a nice drive but even Eden gets boring after you've seen it a couple hundred times and I just wish you'd go away and arrest some real evil-doer and—

And looking at me through the window is the most beautiful fascist pig cop I've ever seen in my life.

She smiles and her teeth...well...*sparkle* in the bright noonday sun. She has three dimples on one side of her smile and two on the other, a delightful imbalance that makes her face that much more interesting. Her little nose tips up just a bit at the end, and a wisp of mouse-brown hair pokes out from under her dark blue hat. Her name tag says Harbaugh. I roll the window down and she's speaking in a lilting, musical voice like the sound of Spring. Then she stops and raises an eyebrow, and I have no idea what she's just said.

"What?" I ask.

"May I see your driver's license, please?" she says in that sweet, lyric voice.

"Oh. Yeah." I hand her my license.

"And your registration, please."

I open the glove compartment and a pile of pink-covered romances falls out. I gather them up and flip them over, but the back covers are no less lurid than the fronts. I toss them between the passenger seat and the door.

I turn back and hand her my registration. She's

smiling. "Into romances, huh?"

"I...they're just..." I sigh. There's no dignity left to save. "Yes, ma'am. Very much so."

She takes off her Ray Bans to reveal sparkling hazel eyes. "So am I." She grins and takes my registration card. "Back in a second," she says and heads to her car.

I watch her in my side mirror and can't help but admire the slender, athletic figure that her plain blue uniform can't hide. Her movements are fluid, powerful, revealing an understated femininity so much more entrancing than the overt sexuality so many women go for.

Then she gets into her car and closes the door, and the trance breaks. I'm about to get a speeding ticket from this lady. This woman. This icon of confident feminine power. This astounding creature of surpassing strength and beauty. This...this...

Cop.

She's a cop, just like every other surly, overbearing jerk I've ever met at the side of the road. And she is going to give me one whopping ticket, too. I'll have to go through traffic school or pay a huge fine. Or both. My insurance rates were going to skyrocket. This thing could well ripple through the next five years of my life. And for what? A couple of romance novels.

At least it's for a good cause.

I'm still pondering the potential for personal ruin and the slim outside chance of asking Officer Harbaugh on a date when she appears at my window.

"Do you realize how fast you were going?" she asks.

All the pithy retorts I've spent the last ten years preparing flee my mind as I gaze into her sweet face. "Yes."

"If I let you go with a warning, will you promise to slow down in the future?"

Now I *should* nod and tell her that I'm very sorry and

that I will never intentionally abuse the speed limit again, that I am a reformed man and her mercy will be rewarded with temperate roadway behavior for all the days of my life.

But I can't lie. Not to her.

"I don't even think about the speed limit. So I can't promise that the next time I want to get somewhere, I won't speed again."

I look down at the steering wheel. That's it. Now she'll give me a ticket. I just hope she'll be the one teaching traffic school so I can meet her again.

When I look up, she gazes at me with those penetrating eyes. "Thank you for your honesty, Mr. Hantz." She looks at her ticket book, then closes it and shakes her head. "I'm going to let you go. But I strongly advise that you slow down in the future."

I blink at her. "What?"

"You can go." She hands me my registration.

I should shut up and accept my good fortune. But that means she will go away and I'll likely never see her again. It's silly of me, but I feel that if I keep her here—with me—for long enough, something good will happen.

"Why?" I stammer.

"I've been patrolling this stretch of road for over a year," she says. "In all that time, I've never seen you go less than eighty through here—not if conditions would allow."

She looks up and down the road, then leans in toward the window. "And in all that time, I've never seen you make a dangerous lane change or run up on another driver. You never shave or read the paper or talk on a cell phone while you're driving. You're fast, but you're safe. I appreciate that."

She smiles that sparkly smile again and I melt.

"Be well, Mr. Hantz."

She turns to go and I feel my heart go cold. I let my

head droop forward until the seat belt stops me. I should have said something else, maybe asked her out, or at least found out what days she patrolled the road so I could plan to be pulled over again. I smack myself on the forehead. "Jerk," I mutter.

"Excuse me?" she says.

I sit up and she's there at my window, bent down and looking in at me, my driver's license in her hand. "I was uh...I said, 'jerk' but I wasn't talking to you. I was talking *about* you, but I was saying it to myself. I mean...oh brother."

She laughs, a fun sound like children at play. I smile and blush.

She hands me my license and a white business card. "If you have any more questions you can give me a call. Drive safely."

Then she's gone and I'm staring at the card. It's a Utah Highway Patrol card with her name listed as Officer Harbaugh. I flip it over and see flowing script on the back in blue ink. It says, "Suzanne. 555-9160. After 4:00."

I look up and see her pulling out onto the road. She waves and speeds away.

It may be true that I spend a lot of time in the world of romance novels. It may be true that I prefer warm fantasy to the hard realities of daily life. It may even be true that I actually own several billow-sleeved peasant shirts and occasionally put one on and act out the torrid scene where me and my love finally clutch each other in passionate embrace after the cruel struggle that's kept us apart.

But I never in my life expected to experience real, honest-to-goodness love at first sight.

I put my car in gear, check over my shoulder and pull out onto the empty road. For once, driving a mere sixty-five doesn't seem like a hardship, and I find that

I'm totally relaxed as I approach the speed trap at the South Towne mall. It's the first time I can remember that I don't care if a cop is there or not. Kind of refreshing in an odd sort of way.

I'm contemplating the joys of feminine companionship and the virtues of driving the speed limit when a black Porsche blows by me so fast that the wind of his passing pushes me hard to the side of the road, and I have to use two hands to keep control of my little Geo. I figure he must be pushing a hundred—way too fast, even for me.

"Go get him, Officer Harbaugh" I mutter.

Officer Harbaugh. Suzanne. Sue? Susie? No. Not that she's stiff or formal or anything, but she's got herself together in a way that suggests completeness. Order. Definitely Suzanne.

Sigh...

I see her pull onto the highway from the median ahead of me and I wave at her as she speeds away. I'm sure she can't see me, but for just a moment I think I see her wave back.

I'm considering all the bad things that can happen at high speeds and trying to figure out what she'll do if the Porsche decides not to pull over and the fact that there's construction about three miles ahead and the road narrows to a scant two lanes but you don't have time to react in such tight quarters if something goes wrong and I wonder how many highway patrolman are injured in car accidents every year so maybe I ought to try to catch up to them and help herd the Porsche to the side of the road so Suzanne doesn't get injured because I don't know what I'd do if she got hurt or killed and I wonder if a Geo Metro can go a hundred even on a downhill with a tailwind and—

And ahead of me, a giant black cube descends from the sky and blots out the world.

Okay, maybe not the whole world, but enough of it that I swerve and skid and almost lose control of my car because I can't see anything ahead of me but a short length of road, then black. It must be five miles wide and just as high, because I can only barely see its edges, and I can't see the top at all. It's centered on the highway, and just before it hits the ground the black Porsche darts beneath it and vanishes.

Suzanne's white Camaro noses down and swerves as she hits the brakes, and my heart stutters as I realize that she's not going to stop in time.

The cube hits ground with a rumble more felt than heard, and her car careens toward it. The Camaro's back end breaks loose, then straightens out. It hits the black wall, disappears part-way into it, then stops suddenly.

I stop thirty feet away and leap out, run to her car— or at least the half-car sticking out of the shimmering black wall. The airbag has deployed, and dingy yellow-white cloth spills out as I yank the door handle. The hinges have vanished behind the black wall, and the door pulls away and drops to the ground, sheered neatly off at the wall line.

Suzanne pushes the airbag away. Her face is red, like it's been sunburned, and her eyes are glassy. Then she gasps and pulls back from the steering wheel, jerks her feet away from the pedals.

"Are you okay?" I ask.

She nods slowly. "It's cold," she says and points down at the floorboard. I look and see the strange black wall inside the car. It's sliced down through the firewall and its oily, coruscating surface covers the space where the pedals should be.

It radiates an icy chill, a menacing bite that promises instant freezer burn if touched. Suzanne shifts in her seat and I look over at her feet. The fronts of both shoes are gone, cut cleanly off. Her toes are curled back, and I realize that the toes of her socks are gone, as well.

I grab a foot and she starts, then relaxes. The ends of her toes are bright red and starting to swell. I look closer and see that the nail of her big toe is absolutely flat right to the edge of her flesh. As though cut with a wide blade. Or a laser.

"Get out of the car," I say in as calm a voice as I can muster. "But stay away from that black wall."

I stand up as she unbuckles her seat belt, then help her turn in the seat so that her feet are outside the car. I take her hand and pull her out, and I'm thinking how soft and warm her hand is and how this is actually the first time I've touched her even though I feel like I know her very well and I think I like it and I hope there are other opportunities which there might be because she isn't pulling away at all even though I'm essentially a stranger who she just met and—

And a semi-truck appears at the top of a gentle rise in the road, blasts its horn, and careens toward us too fast to stop.

Like I said before, I'm a relatively big man at over six feet and further over three hundred pounds than I like to admit. When you're that heavy, you automatically develop a certain amount of strength just to carry your own body around. Which is not to say that I'm in any way athletic—far from it, I'm a dedicated couch potato and member of the Loafer's Guild. But when you carry three hundred pounds around with you every day, an extra one-ten is hardly noticeable.

So I grab Suzanne around the waist, pull her out of her car, and trundle as fast as I can toward the median, trying to ignore the warbling screech of tortured rubber and the ever louder blare of the semi's horn.

Maybe that was unnecessary. Maybe she could have

gotten out on her own and would've made it to the center median with a little less jostling and flopping of limbs. But she'd just been in a head-on collision with that weird black wall, she'd been blasted in the face by a hot airbag, and the fronts of her shoes were missing. It seemed like the right thing to do at the time.

The semi jack-knifes and comes in sideways. It hits the Camaro and knocks it through the wall, then starts through as well. It stops half-way. The driver jumps out of the cab and stares at the shimmering black wall. He shakes his head as he comes toward us.

"Lousy Fisbanians," he mutters. "They ought to warn people before they drop those stupid transport cubes." He shakes his head.

Suzanne and I stare at the trucker for a moment, then turn and face each other.

"Sorry if that was a little rough." I look down at my hands.

When I look up, she's smiling at me. She takes my hand without saying anything, then reaches up and kisses me lightly on the lips. "Thank you," she says, then hugs me. I hug her back and everything in the world is perfect, if only for that moment.

Maybe it wasn't your standard romance-novel ending. Then again, it was awfully close. There was the electricity when we first met, the disaster of unnatural proportions, and the heroic rescue from the madman about to cause her grave bodily harm. There was the kiss and the tender thanks and the embrace that was about as passionate as I could have tolerated at the moment. At least in front of witnesses.

Good enough for me. In fact, more than good enough.

Because in the instant after the kiss and before the hug, her eyes sparkled and her face glowed. And while I can't be completely certain, I'm pretty sure that her...or rather that I thought I saw...which is to say, that she...

That her breasts actually heaved.

Scott R. Parkin is an award-winning science fiction and fantasy author whose short fiction has appeared in *Marion Zimmer Bradley's Fantasy Magazine*, *Writers of the Future Volume 31*, and the *Fiction River Valor* anthology, among others.

One of the challenges issued to authors who desired to submit a story for consideration in this collection was to write a flash fiction piece—an extremely short story that includes all the elements of a full length tale. An author must hook the reader, describe a compelling dilemma, and resolve that dilemma with a satisfying ending—all within a couple of pages. The task is far more difficult than it looks. I think you'll agree that Kylara Silvers succeeded in, "Remember This." – VS

Remember This

Kylara Silvers

"'Cmon, Jen. Try to remember. Think of our table at Maguire's. The funny waiter with the hairpiece that makes us laugh."

The man standing in front of her—Patrick, he said his name was—peered at her through eyes that held enough hurt to stir guilt in the pit of her stomach. She ought to remember him. She wanted to! But where the memories should be inside her aching head lay nothing but a fuzzy gray mist.

Perched on the edge of the hospital bed, Jennifer clenched the sterile white sheets and swallowed against a medicinally dry mouth. A waiter with a hairpiece? Maybe if she focused...

"I think—"

Hope surged into his features, and he took an eager step toward her. "Yes?"

The elusive image receded into the mist. She shook her head, tears burning her eyes. "I can't."

Patrick's shoulders slumped, disappointment etched in the lines on either side of his mouth. "It's okay, sweetheart. The doctor says your memory will return eventually. In the meantime, let's focus on our blessings. You're lucky to be alive after that car wreck. The Toyota is a total loss."

Jennifer half-heard his words, but her attention was drawn to the lips that spoke them. Generous lips that tightened with pain, but softened to speak words of comfort. Something about his lips sent the fog in her brain swirling enough to glimpse a shadowy memory. She rose from the hospital bed and wavered in a sudden wave of dizziness.

Patrick rushed forward to support her. "Maybe you shouldn't try to stand. You've been in bed for a week."

She raised her hand and brushed a fingertip across his mouth. "Would you kiss me? I—I think it might help."

Doubt and longing battled in the dark eyes that searched her face, but he hesitated only a moment. His head descended toward hers, and she tilted her face to meet his kiss. Tentative at first, barely a brush of soft skin against her mouth. She inhaled the scent of him, a fragrant blend of cologne and soap, and the cloud in her brain churned.

A word surfaced. Eternity. She'd given him a bottle of the expensive cologne for Christmas.

Encouraged, she pressed into the kiss. Memories surged. Hanging pictures in their apartment, and Patrick's kiss when they stood back to admire their work. The candlelight dinner she burned on their first anniversary and his kiss before he picked up the phone to order pizza. The agony of yet another negative pregnancy test, which even his kisses couldn't soothe.

"Albert," she whispered against his lips.

He pulled back, alarm coloring his face. "Sweetheart, I'm Patrick."

She smiled. "The waiter with the hairpiece. His name is Albert. I remember."

She wrapped her arms around his neck and pulled him back into their kiss.

Kylara Silvers is the author of two short stories and multiple novels-in-progress. She loves stories with adventure, strong women, and handsome heroes. Though she enjoys writing fantasy and adventure, she's learning to follow the whims of her muse. "Remember This" is her first attempt at flash fiction, and she enjoyed it so much she might try it again. Visit Kylara on the web at www.KylaraSilvers.com.

Human beings are prone to insecurity, especially when it comes to believing we're worthy of love. We can't fathom that the one we love could actually love us back. Though unpleasant to experience, those feelings lead to the misunderstandings that make romance stories so satisfying to read. In our next story, Bethany Rae blends that classic romance element with a situation that has become all too familiar these days, a soldier's return from war. – VS

His Sister's Keeper

Bethany Rae

He leaned back against the head rest, closing his eyes in an effort to block out thought. It didn't work, as all the images he saw underneath his eyelids were worse even than his thoughts. Blood and death and pain were imprinted in his memory, the first thing he saw in the morning and the last thing he saw at night, sometimes haunting him even in sleep. He was tired, so tired. His limbs felt heavy, disconnected from his body. With that thought, he tried to control the morbid snort of laughter as he realized that he had been very close to that statement being true. Except it had been Johnny instead of him.

He grunted in pain, his eyes popping open as someone walking down the aisle stumbled and fell against his arm. Even strapped to his chest it seemed to be a target, a flag drawing all attention to it and to him. It didn't help that he had to wear his uniform until he arrived home. He might as well hold a sign declaring that he welcomed all pity and false admiration. Wounded in duty, a hero. Everyone seemed to connect the two as inevitable. If one was wounded, one was a hero. Even the doctors and nurses seemed convinced of this, no matter how often he told them it wasn't like that. No matter how often he told them he didn't want the label. They just smiled and shook their heads and tucked him in reverently. It made him sick.

The bus slowed, and he looked out the window to find that they were approaching a stop light. They were in town. Soon he would be home. He had thought for so long that going home was all he wanted. Now he dreaded it, the knowledge that he was almost there sitting like a hard ball in the pit of his stomach. His mother would fuss over him, his father would, possibly, clap him on the back and proclaim his pride, his sister would tease and mock him just to keep from crying, and his younger brother would look up at him with that stare of awe that used to make him feel like he could conquer the world. But he didn't deserve it, and he had to tell *her* that. He had to see her, and it would just about kill him.

Humming along with the radio, her hands immersed

in soapy water as she did the breakfast dishes, Gemma paused when she heard the sound of a car pulling up to the front of the house. She tilted her head, listening to see if the vehicle would pull past or turn around. The engine shut off, and she rinsed the last dish, stacking it carefully in the drying rack. She dried her hands, then flipped off the light in the tiny kitchen and moved into the even tinier laundry room. It was indeed a small house, all that her parents had been able to afford. When they died, they'd left it to her brother – the house and everything in it. There had been no question about where Gemma would go. She stayed with her brother, and neither of them would have had it any other way. The two of them had been happy there. Everything she needed was right there in that house, familiar and safe. At least it had been.

As she pulled the clothes down from where they'd been hung to drip dry on a line Johnny had installed for her, footsteps sounded on the front porch. Heavy, quick steps. Then came the rap on the door, decisive and determined.

In the front room she stopped at the mirror over the fireplace to fix her hair back into place with the hair comb Johnny had sent to her. Then she opened the knob.

Her heart nearly stopped when she saw the uniform. No, wait. Johnny wouldn't knock. If he had been alive. She looked up from the broad, solid chest in front of her at eye level to a familiar face. Eyes as green as a Christmas tree peered down at her. The last time she looked into those emerald depths, she thought she'd never see them again. An unknown emotion flashed through those eyes, so quickly she didn't have time to even wonder what it meant before the hood was drawn back down. But something lingered there, something she instinctively knew he was unaware of.

"Gemma?" The deep, expressionless voice brought her attention back to the matter at hand.

"Liam?" Her voice came out faint and breathless, and then she felt the odd sensation of the room around her starting to tilt. With a firm grasp on her arm, he guided her into her own front room and gently pushed her into the chair beside the fireplace. For several moments she tried to calm her mind and her racing pulse.

She opened her eyes again, and he was still there, kneeling in front of her, looking anxiously up into her face.

He took off his cap and ran a hand over his hair, then looked back up into the face that stared at him with a mixture of hope and confusion. It was a startling face, the delicate line of her jaw as fine as china, her mouth wide and full and strong. He looked into the luminous, large blue eyes, such a deep blue that they appeared almost purple, the color deepened by the dark lashes that framed them. She was even more beautiful than he remembered.

"I'm all right now. Sorry. I was just...very surprised. They told me you were dead, that you died with Johnny."

Her voice shook, and it was with difficulty that he resisted the impulse to take both of her slim hands in his. To take all of her in his arms. "Well, I'm not sure how that happened, but you can see that I didn't."

His voice was gruffer than he intended, and something flickered in her eyes.

"Yes, I see that now. Please, sit down."

She gestured to the sofa beside her, and he realized that he was still kneeling at her feet like some kind of supplicant. He stood, averted his face so she couldn't see the wince of pain, and perched uncomfortably on the edge of the sofa.

"You were injured though." She stated it matter-of-factly, with none of the fuss his mother and sister had spilled out over him. He was grateful, though a part of him, deep inside, regretted that there wasn't a bit more concern in her tone.

He nodded and offered no more explanation. Anything he had to say would surely give her pain. But he underestimated her.

"Was it—was it the night Johnny...?" A silent appeal flashed in her eyes, and she blinked back tears.

"Yes," he finally said. He owed her this much. "I was injured the same night Johnny died."

He waited for her to ask the next question. *How did he die?* He forced himself to not look away, to look into the eyes he could feel searching his soul. *How much could she see?* But then, to his surprise, she simply nodded and looked down at the hands clasped tightly in her lap. A comb held up her dark hair, silver, with bright purple blue stones. He had bought it for her, but lost his nerve and made Johnny send it to her as a gift from him instead. It was enough that she had it, she didn't need the awkwardness of receiving it from her brother's friend.

"I'm sorry," he said suddenly, standing to his feet. "I didn't mean to stay long, I just wanted to stop in and see how you're getting along."

She stood as well, but made no move to go to the door. "Are you sure you wouldn't like a cup of coffee?"

"No, thank you. I told my mother I'd be home in time for lunch."

She walked to the door then and held it for him as he passed back out onto the porch. He was cursing himself vehemently for the way the entire visit had gone when she called his name. He turned to face her again.

She stood in the doorway, one hand against the doorjamb, the other in her skirt pocket.

"You said you stopped to see how I'm getting along, but you never asked." There was a curious lilt to her voice as she spoke, a look in her eye that he couldn't identify.

"You're right, I apologize. How are you, Gemma?"

"I'm doing much better now, thank you." She gave him a small, sparkling smile just before she stepped back and shut the door.

He stood for several seconds like a block of stone before he remembered to keep moving out to his car. Now what on earth did that mean? He silenced all thoughts before he could answer his own question.

Gemma leaned against the door, hoping her heart would at some point return to its normal rhythm. She resisted the urge to look out the front window and watch his car pull away from the curb. He was alive, and he was back. Wounded, and deeper than just the arm strapped to his chest. But he was alive and whole, and he'd come to see her. Johnny's death still cut like a knife at her soul, but Liam...he made her feel as though the pain might actually diminish. His presence reassured and comforted, and at the same time made her pulse erratic and her world topsy-turvy, just like it always had.

She made herself finish her laundry and do her household cleaning chores, carrying on her normal routine for her day off work at the café. The telephone rang twice, both times with invitations to see a movie that night with friends. She declined, feeling no desire to laugh and be jolly when her entire world had just shifted.

The third time she heard the ringing, she almost

ignored the call but reluctantly took off her cleaning gloves and went to answer.

"Hello?"

"Gemma?" The sound of her closest friend's voice made her smile, even as it made her heart skip a beat. Her friend and Liam's younger sister.

"Desiree! How are you?" Her voice was a bit higher pitched than it should have been. *Tone it down Gemma.*

"Right as rain, I got back the day before yesterday, just in time to greet Liam at the bus station. He told me you had been informed that he was KIA, and I wanted to let you know how sorry I am. You've been left having lost both of them for weeks, and I could just kill myself for not checking up on you sooner. Truth is, I didn't know about Johnny either." Her voice lost its usual strident cheeriness. "I'm truly sorry, Gem. I know he was...everything to you. I wish I'd been here."

"Oh, Des, don't be silly. You've been off helping the cause. You've done all those wounded soldiers more good than should've been wasted on me. I'm fine, really." She put confidence into her voice. She was glad, very glad, that this conversation was taking place over the phone.

"Yes, of course you are." Desiree's tone was dry. She knew Gemma only too well. "Listen, Gem, Mom's having a huge dinner tonight to celebrate Liam's homecoming. Please say you'll come."

Gemma twisted the telephone cord around her finger. "Oh, I don't know..."

"Come on, it'll be good for you. No point in sitting at home by yourself. Oh, rats, that wasn't very sensitive, was it? Try again. I'm begging you for my sake. If you don't come, I'll be stuck entertaining cousin Peggy all by myself."

"But I'm sure your mother has it all coordinated, another mouth to feed, another place at the table..."

"My mother, in fact, is deeply chagrined that she never called you after Johnny...you know. She practically begged me to convince you to come. Say you will?"

Gemma sighed. "Yes, all right."

A squeal of delight met her ears. "Yay! Thank you, you're a Gem. On a side note...what did you think of Liam today?"

Gemma stammered, "What do you mean?"

"He's just...different. He's trying to be pleasant, but it's as though all the fun's gone out of him. I keep catching him staring off, as though he's miles away."

Hearing the concern in her friend's voice, Gemma hesitated. "You have to remember what he's been through, perhaps what he's had to do. Besides losing Johnny."

A pause. "I suppose you're right. I'm sure he'll be back to normal soon enough. Well, I'll see you at six, come a bit earlier if you can. Toodles!"

She rang off, and Gemma slowly put the phone back in its receiver. What on earth had she committed to?

Liam had his back to the door when the bell rang. It was a quarter to six, fifteen minutes before guests were supposed to arrive. Except, of course, Mrs. Nelson, their next door neighbor. She was a widow with no children who had taken it upon herself to invest her interest in the lives of everyone around her, whether they wanted the attention or not. She was harmless, but his head ached as she pried, with the innocence of ignorance, into the intriguing life of a U.S. soldier. He tried to smile and nod and not think about her questions, when she stopped in mid-flow, her eyes growing wide and her mouth forming a tiny flower of bright pink lipstick.

"Oh my goodness, I haven't seen that poor young

thing in months. They say she's taken her brother's death pretty hard. Perfectly understandable, as he was her only living relative, God rest his soul. You wouldn't know it to look at her, she's such a lovely thing, though come to think of it, she does look a bit pale. Wouldn't you say, young man?"

His shoulders had stiffened as soon as Mrs. Nelson mentioned the poor young thing's brother dying. He heard his sister's squeal of pleasure, and pictured her throwing her arms enthusiastically around her best friend, who would, of course, endure it with every appearance of enjoyment. He remembered his companion, and realized suddenly that she had a look of determination in her eye, and was facing Gemma with obvious intent.

"Mrs. Nelson, I think I remember my mother saying something about needing help with the punch. I wondered if you might be willing to help. Your recipe is, after all, the most sought after."

She responded instantly, her rouge-covered cheeks pinking with pleasure. "Oh, goodness, of course!"

He accompanied her into the kitchen to sacrifice his mother to her. When he turned to the side to let the older woman precede him, he caught Gemma's eye for a split second. She wore a lilac-colored dress that accentuated her slender neck. Her hair was pulled up, one tendril of curl escaped to rest along the creamy slope of skin.

Desi hadn't said anything about Gemma coming. Not that she would, of course. She delighted in catching him off guard, and she probably figured she was doing him a favor, hearkening back to a pre-war admission he had foolishly made to her just before he shipped off. She couldn't possibly know how vastly things had changed since then, how she had just thrust a knife into a festering wound.

He deposited Mrs. Nelson in the kitchen, smiling over her head at his mother's pained expression and staunch refusal to look him in the eye. Instead of going back into the front room, where more guests were arriving every minute, he slipped out the back door and sat on the steps to look out over the yard. These days he sometimes got lost in memories, forgot, in a sense, where he was and what was happening around him.

With the swish of the door opening behind him the fog lifted and he saw again the green grass in front of him, the old play set in the corner of the yard, the football at his feet.

"Oh, I'm sorry," a gentle voice said.

He turned to see her draw back, a mixture of alarm and sadness spreading over her finely etched features.

"You don't have to go," he said, glad to have changed the phrase to something non-committal, instead of the plea that had first crossed his mind.

"I didn't mean to interrupt." She hesitated. "I just, haven't been around so many people for...a while. I needed some air."

"Plenty of it out here." He managed a smile and scooted over on the step. After a moment, the edge of her skirt brushed his shoulder and she sat beside him. A quiet settled over them, as soft and pleasant as the brush of a downy feather.

After a bit, Gemma said, with humor in her tone, "You're causing quite the ruckus in there." She gestured over her shoulder at the door with her chin.

"Oh?" He barely took notice of her comment, instead fascinated by the corner of her mouth. He dragged his eyes up to hers with some difficulty. They smiled, laughing at him gently.

"Are you still on military time? It's been forty-five minutes you've been MIA."

He looked down at his watch. Twenty five minutes

past six. He let out a whistle. "Mom's gonna kill me."

"Don't worry, I'll protect you," she said, laughing now. His heart caught in his throat, and all he could do was smile back at her. "What are you hiding from out here anyway?"

He looked away. "Myself," he muttered under his breath.

"Sorry?"

He turned back to her, a gruff, off-putting reply on his lips. The response died as he found her looking at him, her eyes wide and deep as though they read his very heart. That little tilt in the left corner of her mouth bewitched him. As though indeed under a spell, he reached out to touch the dark curl caressing her neck, then slipped his fingers under it, lightly brushing the soft skin. His hand cupped the back of her neck as though it had found its home, his thumb resting on her jaw, sliding over to touch her ear lobe. She shivered, and his gaze moved from his hand up to her face, to her eyes. They watched him, wide, but not startled. She didn't pull away. Her lips parted as though she was about to say something, but no sound came. His fingers tightened around the nape of her neck and he bowed his head to hers, covered her lips with his own.

He hadn't known what to expect, had been, in fact, expecting nothing. But her mouth, soft and sweet under his, responded to his kiss immediately, though gentle and hesitant, as if she was holding back. He deepened the kiss, asking more of her. She responded again with an immediacy that sent fire running up his spine, and he curled his fingers into her hair, heedless of the delicacy with which it had been pinned.

When he drew back for breath, his pulse stumbled over itself. He gazed into her face, still just inches from his, and she looked as disconcerted and taken aback as he felt. He was contemplating the idea of kissing her again when the door opened behind them. He pulled his hand away as though burned, and turned away from her, trying to breathe less raggedly.

"There you two are. You're an awful traitor, Gemma. You found him and didn't even report."

He couldn't risk a glance back at his sister, couldn't even begin to speak. After a half second's pause, Gemma answered in a light voice that only shook slightly. "You know what a sucker I am for the underdog. I promised I'd protect him." She stood, and her foot slipped, but she caught herself on the railing, careful not to touch him.

"Oh, don't worry, I know all his tricks. You coming Li?"

"In a minute." He sounded almost normal.

"Uh-huh. Well, we know where you are now, so if you're not inside in five, we'll come after you in force."

Gemma moved up the steps away from him to join Desiree.

"What's happened to your hair?" Desiree asked.

"Oh, I think I've lost a bobby pin or two. I'll just go to the ladies' and fix it."

The door shut and he didn't hear anything else. He dropped his head into his hand, his one good hand, and used every epithet he could possibly think of to describe himself. He'd had no right to do that. Though to be sure, he'd never have thought she'd respond like she had. Why did he let it happen before he told her? Now he would have the memory of that kiss imprinted on his brain for the rest of his life, never to be repeated.

Gemma tried to concentrate on what the girl in front of her was saying. She unconsciously reached back to check her hurriedly-fixed hair, and felt again the memory of his fingertips brushing her skin, his fingers curling into her hair. She shivered, and laughed with a little too much enthusiasm to cover it up. Now that dinner was over she could escape with grace. If she wanted to, which she hadn't quite made up her mind about. She was still trying to understand what had happened, to believe that it had happened. When he looked at her as though he saw the world in her eyes, she knew she was never getting over him. She had told herself when he shipped out with Johnny that it was just a crush, that she would forget him in his absence and move on. But she thought of him every day, no matter how hard she tried not to, and she had prayed for his safe return with equal fervency to her request of the same for Johnny. She told herself then that she loved him like a brother. Clearly he thought of her as a sister. But when merely his touch could completely undo her, she knew, beyond a doubt, that she had never thought of him as a brother.

Why was she staying? She couldn't focus on a single thing anyone said to her. Liam avoided even looking in her direction. Time to leave. Gemma made her excuses and went into the guest bedroom off the hall to collect her jacket.

She slipped her arms into the sleeves and slid the buttons into the correct holes, then picked up her purse and turned around.

"Oh!" She stepped back when she saw Liam standing in the doorway.

"Gemma." His voice was serious, distant. He still wouldn't look at her. Her heart sank. "Gemma, I just wanted to apologize...for earlier. I was way out of line. That should never have happened."

She said nothing, willing herself to think of a response, willing him to look her in the eye so that she could read there what he wasn't saying.

"It won't ever happen again," he said.

For a moment she couldn't reply. "If that's what you want," she forced out finally. She couldn't let him see the agony in her heart. If only she hadn't come. She had revealed far too much in that kiss, and now she had lost them both. Things would never be the same between them.

She could scarcely breathe for the pain. Keeping a tight rein on the tears that pricked her eyes, she walked past him, then stopped in the doorway.

"I just want you to know that Johnny's death is not your fault." She did not look back at him as she spoke. "No matter how it happened, I don't blame you. You should also know—" Her voice broke. Moistening her lips, she began again. "You should know that before he left, Johnny made me promise to not be mad at him if he died. He told me–he said that he would do everything he could to keep you alive." She held up a hand to stop him before he could interrupt. "He did it for me, Liam. He knew that I–I love you, and no matter what I told him—" She broke off, laughing apologetically and brushing at the tears that slid down her cheeks. "No matter how I tried to make him believe that you didn't feel the same, he wouldn't listen. So, I just wanted you to know, in case...in case you hold yourself to blame. He wouldn't want that. Goodbye Liam."

Liam stood in the guest room, watching after her, unseeing. Everything that happened that night just over a month ago suddenly fell into place with a clarity he had been searching for ever since. They weren't even supposed to be there, but Liam had agreed to change shifts with another PFC, and Johnny stubbornly persisted in changing his shift as well. When the bomb hit the bunker, Liam reacted without thinking. There were soldiers in there, and he had to get them out. He ran in and started shoving the burning rubble off the men the roof had collapsed on. He grabbed one man, and half carried, half dragged him out. Behind him Johnny did the same. No one else had responded yet, and both of them went back four times. They were each lowering an injured man to safe ground when Johnny asked, his usually laughing face smeared with ash and soot, "That was everyone, right?"

"No, there's one more," Liam responded, already turning to jog back to the bunker. Johnny ran in front of him and pushed him to a stop with his palm hard on Liam's chest.

"I'll go. You're already hit. Stay here and cover them." Before Liam could argue he whirled and ran, dodging flaming debris and then disappearing into the rubble of the bunker. He was gone longer than it had taken them with any of the others, and Liam started to feel uneasy. Leaving the injured in the care of the medics who'd arrived, he walked toward the bunker. "Johnny!" he yelled. "What are you doin', roasting hot dogs? Hurry it up, man!"

With relief, he saw Johnny's face appear in the broken doorway. He paused, and though Liam still couldn't decide if it had been dream or reality, he could swear Johnny smiled at him. Then he disappeared in the flash of a roaring explosion that threw Liam backward, rendered mercifully unconscious.

Now it was Gemma's face that hovered in his mind, haunting him. Hope had flooded her eyes when she'd first caught sight of him. Love had replaced hope when she'd told him she didn't blame him for her brother's death. Then love was swept aside by pain when he let her believe that he didn't love her. The tears and her forced laugh cut his heart when she admitted that she loved him. There had been forever in her tone when she said goodbye.

The thoughts swirling in his head gradually slowed, melding into one single purpose. He had to find her. In his haste he nearly knocked over a man and woman coming in to collect their coats. In the main room a woman spoke to him. He ignored her, searching instead for one face. She was not there.

Desiree appeared at his elbow. "Who exactly are you looking for, and what did they do to you?"

"Where is she?"

Her eyebrow raised. "If you mean Gemma, she's long gone. I didn't stop her because she looked like she might burst into tears. What did you say to her?" Her hands were on her narrow hips now, and she glared at him with pointed accusation.

"How long ago did she leave?" He gripped her arm.

"Five, ten minutes? Why, are you going after her?"

He was already heading to the front door. "Yes."

"About time," she called after him.

Out in the driveway, his car was blocked in by at least five other vehicles. He didn't waste time considering his options, but started running flat out the moment his feet hit the pavement. She wasn't going to get away, even if he had to run all the way across town. He slowed when he saw her straight, slender form in front of him, her chin lifted high. A second dark curl escaped at the back of her head where his fingers had clutched the soft masses.

"Gemma!"

Her shoulders stiffened, and she stopped abruptly. After a backward glance, she quickened her pace. He ran to catch up, ignoring the pain from the wound in his leg. He reached her side and took her arm to stop her. She still didn't meet his eyes, so he let go of her arm and with his fingers on her chin, gently nudged her face towards him. Tears spilled over from red rimmed eyes and slipped down her cheeks.

She was quiet, then said softly, "I'm not sure what there can possibly be left to say. Why did you come after me?"

"I'm sorry, I didn't mean to hurt you. I–I didn't know any of, of what you said...Johnny's death...it's been eating at me. I thought that you..." He couldn't get the words out, still couldn't believe that she might actually want him. "I'm sorry," he said again lamely.

"You have nothing to be sorry for, you owe me nothing. Just let me alone for a bit, all right?" The smile on her lips seemed to hurt her as much as it did him. She turned to walk away.

"Gemma, I love you." He'd said it, and there was no going back.

She stopped again, but this time whirled around so fast he took a step back. Her hands clenched into fists at her sides. "Don't, Liam. Don't you dare! You don't have to pretend to love me. And you don't have to make yourself love Johnny's lonely, orphaned sister in order to honor him." Her eyes flashed like he'd never seen before, brilliant sparks of sapphire against the large black pupils. A flush rode high on her cheeks, and she looked angry enough to square off against an entire army. But then her lower lip trembled, ever so slightly, and another tear slipped down her smooth cheek.

He stepped toward her and wiped the tear away with his thumb, two fingers under her chin. Placing a hand on the small of her back to keep her close, he kissed her forehead, her nose, the corner of her mouth. He paused and looked into her eyes, willing her to see what he felt.

"I love you, Gemma." He brushed her lips lightly with his, then again met her gaze. Surprise and hope mixed with disbelief in her look. He kissed her again, firmly. She gradually melted into him, and her hand came up to the back of his neck. When he started to pull away, her hand brought his head back down to hers. He smiled against her lips and pulled her closer, his arm wrapped tightly around her slim waist.

At last she pulled away and leaned back against his arm to look up at him. Her hand rose to caress the side of his face. He closed his eyes and pressed his cheek into her palm.

"Why did you push me away?" Her soft voice broke the silence.

"I thought you would hate me, because Johnny died and I lived. It should have been me who died in that explosion. I didn't know how you could ever forgive me." He wound the smooth hair at the back of her neck around his finger.

"You forgot that I know Johnny even better than you. You forgot who Johnny was."

"No, I never did...I just never knew there might be a reason he'd put himself in danger when he had you to take care of. He never told me that you...care for me..." Even still, he couldn't say it, couldn't believe it, couldn't even hint at her loving him without wonder in his voice.

Gemma's finger traced his hair line, his ear, trailed down his jaw to his chin. "He never told me about you either." She grinned, in spite of another tear filling her eye. "That's just like him, leaving us both to figure it out on our own. Leaving it up to chance."

His breath caught in his throat when she looked up at him. "Johnny never left anything to chance. He knew I couldn't stay away from you any more than I could stop my heart from beating."

He held her gaze, and knew that his assurance was true. Even had she not told him that she loved him, he would have found himself by her side again. He was drawn to her as though an unbreakable string bound their hearts together, bringing them back to each other time and again.

With the prick of tears in his eyes, Liam remembered Johnny's face, smiling against the backdrop of burning rubble. Johnny didn't take chances. Liam smiled down at Johnny's sister and pulled her close. He looked up at the sky. *I've got her, Johnny.*

Bethany Rae was born and raised in central California, but currently resides in the mountains of Idaho with her husband and their Malamute. She is a writer of adventure stories with a hint of romance, including a short fantasy tale, The Willow Fairies.

Set in the aftermath of one of America's most violent periods of history, this story captures the injury and pain of those who suffered horribly, both on and off the front lines of the Civil War. As terrible as the price was, that bloody war delivered a time of healing and reconciliation—for a nation, and for its individual citizens. From great suffering can come even greater victory, as Jan Brand demonstrates in "Always and Forever." – VS

Always and Forever

Jan Brand

The parson's parlor was sparsely furnished. Cora Lee Sullivan stood next to Jubal Wakefield in the near-empty room, her hands sweating even though big snowflakes plopped against the window. Her heartbeat pounded in her ears more loudly than the tick of the wall clock. The old man who stood in front of them held a well-worn Bible. His words were solemn and full of admonitions concerning God's sacred trust about the marriage vow. Cora Lee wanted to cry. She wanted to run. She didn't want the baby that was forced on her in pain and degradation by a rebel deserter, and she didn't want to marry this Reb who stood beside her and who thought he was doing a noble deed by marrying her and giving her and the baby his name.

"Miss Cora Lee, do you?"

"What?"

The parson's voice pushed through the fear that wrapped around her mind like icy fog. "Do you take Jubal for your husband?"

There was nothing to do but go through with this charade. All of her dreams of white lace and candlelight died the day she was attacked in the barn by three grimy, lice-infested deserters. Without the farm she had no place to go. The fields had to be planted; the buildings were falling down in disrepair because the men in the family had died fighting this terrible war. This was too much work for an old black man and a pregnant woman. The day Jubal walked into her life, she thought the farm was saved. Jubal knew that too. By marrying her he would own his own land—her land, her family's land—and she would be joined forever to a man who didn't love her. There was no place to run and no justice to be had.

"Yes," she said, none too graciously. They could force her to go through with this outrage for the sake of decency, but they couldn't make her like it.

She stood silently while Jubal signed the wedding certificate and paid the parson. Outside, she allowed him to help her up onto the seat of the buggy. They drove back to the farm in silence. There would be no wedding supper. Well, what did that matter? This wasn't a real marriage anyway. It was two people using each other. Without this farce of a marriage, the small town of Johnson's Corners would shut its doors on a

Jan Brand

soiled woman and her bastard child. Even though she didn't want the child, she didn't want it to suffer.

Jubal pulled up to the hitching post by the back door and hopped down. When he lifted her out of the buggy, his gaze looked remote and cool. Did he think marriage was too a high a price to pay for a hundred and two acres?

"You've had a long day. You should get some rest." His eyes were hard as flint, and he looked surreal with the snow circling his gray slouch hat.

"I can manage." The newly fallen snow crunched under her feet as she made her way up the back steps and into the cold kitchen. The temperature matched the frigid desolation in her heart.

Jubal unhitched Buckley from the buggy and walked him into his stall. Cora Lee looked beautiful today, even if she was madder than a settin' hen protecting her eggs. She hated all Rebs for what happened to her, and now she hated him in particular. All of his dreams to woo her and make her see what a wonderful life they could have together were just that— pipedreams. Dreams weren't real. Any hopes he had she would want the baby and let him be the father died today.

He saw how precious life was when men in blue and men in gray shot and killed each other across a peaceful, green meadow. Both were Americans, but on that day in Franklin, Tennessee, it was impossible to tell. Men he cared about were blown into the next life. Their screams for help still awakened him in the night with sweat beading his forehead and his breath coming in ragged gasps.

If he could survive the awfulness of the war, he could survive a loveless marriage. A man could dream about love and a family all he wanted, but not everyone got lucky. He'd made the most of his bargain. Even if he slept alone for the rest of his life, he would never do anything to shame her. She had been shamed enough already.

"Mistah Jubal, you here?" Moses stuck his head in the barn. The old black man was the only person on the place that Cora Lee seemed genuinely fond of except her granny, who sat and mumbled unintelligibly ever since she lost her husband and two sons to the war. Moses was a good man. Jubal was glad to have him here.

"I'm here. What is it?"

"The missus say it's time to eat and for me to fetch you. She just put out some cold meat and stuff for sandwiches."

"I'll be in later, Moses. Thanks all the same."

"Hmm, well, now, Mistah Jubal, ain't none of my business, but I don't think she'll be likin' that much. Maybe you just need to come on in and eat with her." Moses thread the brim of his old battered, sweat-stained felt hat around and around in his big brown hands.

"Moses, have you ever been married?" He stopped brushing Buckley and looked into the time-worn, wrinkled brown face topped with short, curly white hair.

"Well, sir, I don't know iffin' you'd call it a marriage, but me and a woman named Clarissa done jumped the broom together some thirty years back, but the boss he done sold her, and the little baby boy we had together." Moses stopped twirling his hat brim and stared at the dirt floor of the barn. "I never did know who he sold 'em to. I just come back from the fields one day and they be gone. The boy'd be twenty-somethin' now. I didn't want me another woman after that. It was a hard thing."

"I know what you mean," Jubal muttered under his breath.

He scrubbed his hand across his eyes. There were

worse things than marrying a woman who didn't love you. You could marry one you loved who loved you back, and have her taken from you with no say in the matter. At least he had the farm. He would be content with having a place to call home, and see if he could make it up to the baby. He would make certain the baby felt loved, like he never had.

An hour later, Cora Lee still sat at the kitchen table when he came in to wash up and make a sandwich. A plate with a few crumbs and an empty milk-stained glass sat in front of her on the table.

"I thought you'd be in bed by now. You've had a long day." Jubal washed his hands in the pan and dried them on a towel that hung on a nail. Breakfast had been a long time ago, and his stomach had been letting him know for the past few hours. He sliced off hunks of bread and ham and poured buttermilk into a glass.

"You got what you wanted. The land. Don't pretend this farce is anything other than what it is." Her voice was weak and wispy.

After she said it, she bowed her head as if the fight had gone out of her. He didn't want her submission, he wanted her fire. He looked at her bent head and watched tears fall on her old blue work dress. Sadness settled over him like death. His last hope died on the kitchen floor.

"As you say, Mrs. Wakefield." He rose from the table and walked out the back door. Snow swirled around him, tossed by icy wind. "And I will always and forever want to love you, Cora Lee Wakefield," he said softly to the gathering night.

A noise awakened him and he waited for the sweat to gather on his forehead. It must have been the nightmare. Then he heard it. A soft moan. He sat up and listened, and it came again. As he pulled on his work pants, the moan sounded louder. The noise came from Cora Lee's room.

When he opened her door, he could see by the pale moonlight that had broken through the snow clouds. She was doubled over on her side, thrashing her head from side to side.

"Cora Lee, is it time?"

"Go away." Pain filled her voice.

He walked over and sat down on the side of the bed. "I'm going to help you. Everything's ready. I just need to get Moses so he can do a few things while I take care of you. I'll be right back."

After he awakened Moses and asked him to build up the fire and boil water, Jubal helped Cora Lee sit up. He put a folded quilt under her hips, then retrieved the basket of clean rags on the dresser. Her normally smooth, placid face twisted with pain, and a loud wail escaped through her dry lips. He wet a rag and dragged it across her mouth, and then wiped the perspiration from her face.

Jubal took her hand, and she squeezed it as the groan became a cry. Each time a pain gripped her belly, she clenched his hand harder. He pushed the wet, tangled hair off her face and she grimaced as a scream escaped through cracked lips.

"It's coming. I can feel it." Cora Lee gasped out the words and crushed his fingers. He tried to free his hand, but she wouldn't let go. "Don't leave me. Help me," she panted like a wounded animal.

"Honey, let go so I can help you. It's almost over."

A chilling shriek pierced the still night as she strained with the effort to expel the child. He pried his hand out of hers and moved to the foot of the bed to receive the infant. She grabbed the wooden spindles in the headboard and pushed.

A moment later, he held a baby in his hands. A sound no louder than a mewing kitten came from the delicate body. *His* daughter, regardless of who fathered her. A love so protective and so fierce took possession of his heart that he thought he would die of it. He bathed her gently, as he didn't want her first moments on earth to be harsh and frightening. Then he wrapped her in a soft blanket and took her to Cora Lee's bedside.

"She's beautiful," he muttered through a throat constricted with emotion.

Cora Lee opened her swollen eyelids and stared at the child Jubal laid in her arms. "What have I done?" Eyes wide, Cora Lee looked up in alarm at Jubal. "I've hated this child for something she didn't do, and she looks so beautiful and innocent. She's just a baby, not a monster." She groaned and laid her head back on the pillow, misery etched on her face. "I can't raise this baby on my own. Can you look past your feelings and help me?"

"Listen to me." Jubal sat down on the bed. "This is my daughter. Our daughter. And, she's beautiful, and she'll grow up to be the woman we make her. I love you, Cora Lee. I wouldn't want a million acres with a woman I didn't love. We can be a family. It's up to us, you and me." He looked at her face, with lines of exhaustion marring her features.

"You mean that, don't you?" Her voice was raspy and tired.

"I've loved you almost from the beginning. That's why I stayed. Not for the land. I've seen how valiant and courageous you are." He squeezed her hand while he caressed the baby's head. "Cora Lee, the South will rise again. I want to be part of it, with you by my side. I want to add brothers and sisters to this little one's life, if you're willing."

A flush stole across her face, and she looked away.

Jubal held his breath. Had he frightened her? Maybe he was going too fast. She had just gone through the pain of childbirth and he was asking her to go through it again and again with a man she didn't love, or even know well. Why couldn't he have just kept his mouth shut and worked on her a little at a time? She turned back and looked at him.

"I want to." She reached for his hand.

"You do?" He swallowed hard, surprised by her words.

"Yes." She placed her free hand in his and smiled. "Jubal, you're a good man. How could I not love you? You've been patient and kind, while I was awful. I know I can trust you with my heart. And with the baby's too. I was thinking, maybe we should name her Hope."

"Hope sounds right," he said in a husky voice. Then he leaned over and placed his lips gently on Cora Lee's. He wrapped his arms around her neck and kissed her hard, as if promising to love her forever.

When they caught a breath, he gazed at Hope. A tiny fist wrapped around his finger and filled his heart with hope. He decided then and there that she had his ears, and no one would ever be able to tell him she didn't.

Jan Brand is a freelance writer from Arlington, Texas. She is the former Assistant Director of North Texas Christian Writers, a consortium of twenty-two writers' groups, with a membership exceeding three hundred. She has been published in *Victoria Magazine, Chicken Soup for the Soul,* the *Christian Communicator* and others.

Opposites Attract

MaKayla Martinez

Sienna's wings twinged at the impact with the cold metal. They shivered from where they rested deep in her back. Suppressing a grimace, she steadied herself on her feet.

Toby kept walking like he hadn't just tossed her into a wall of lockers with zero effort. Sienna heard him laughing with his buddies. If this didn't happen every day at 8:25, the other students might be concerned.

281

Most of them were. The first time.

It seemed the bully liked the way her weightless body flew across the hall. Of course, he didn't know why he found it so easy to throw her. He must have assumed it was his own strength, not her hollow bones.

Heat rose in her stomach, and Sienna swallowed hard to calm it. If she opened her mouth she might burn something.

Still gulping, she began to move, joining the throng of students jostling each other to get to class on time. It always took too long to control herself after encountering Toby. She'd have to calm down in pre-calc. She sped her pace.

When she began to jog, her backpack was torn from the crook of her arm. Books, paper, and pens clattered to the floor.

Sienna looked behind her to identify the perpetrator. A tall boy in a plaid button-up and a blue t-shirt was halfway down the hall already, running to his next class. He didn't seem to notice he had just dumped her belongings on the floor.

The heat stuck to her throat, and sizzled. She opened her mouth and one puff of steam escaped.

Seven periods passed without further incident. Sienna took things from her locker in preparation to leave. Homework weighed down her backpack.

She heard loud banging from farther down the hall. Lockers being jostled. What was the commotion about? Two boys wrestled in the center of the hall.

Toby and the guy who had knocked down her backpack this morning.

Curious, Sienna closed her locker and got closer. The boys shouted at each other, their voices carrying down the hall, but the small crowd that had gathered around them kept silent.

"I'll beat on whoever I please!" Toby threw the other boy into the lockers on Sienna's left.

The second boy did nothing. He just stood there and let Toby whale on him. "Really? Even a girl?"

"Any girl I want." Toby hit him so hard, the other boy fell to the dirty floor.

He said nothing. Looking up at Sienna, he caught her gaze and held it.

Then it hit her. This boy was fighting for her. Well, no one had asked him to do that.

Nevertheless, this guy was getting beaten to a pulp because he'd asked Toby to stop throwing her into the lockers. She should help him, but she couldn't do much. At least, not without revealing her secret. That she would never do for some guy.

Maybe she could blow on Toby, apply a little heat. She tried to summon the warmth in her stomach. But it wasn't there. She stood paralyzed. The fire in her belly had been there for so long she didn't remember a time without it. She battled it every day. And now all of a sudden it was gone?

Sienna lost interest in the fight and sought refuge in the bathroom. Holding herself up at the sink, she breathed hard, trying to force her gut to combust.

"Come on, come back." She searched for the familiar warmth until at last it returned. The law dictated that she take a deep breath and let it go. But by then she felt more frustrated than she had in a long time. She needed to let off some steam.

She scanned the stalls, then let a stream of fire flow, relishing the searing sensation in her mouth as her flesh hardened.

The same guy who had been fighting with Toby stumbled in the doorway. Toby must have beat him good for him to have been confused enough to waltz into

the girls bathroom. But he walked right into the flames.
His mouth opened to scream before he was engulfed.

And just like that, the flame in Sienna's gut went out.

The boy collapsed to the floor, his skin red and charred, oozing.

"Ugh!" No matter how many times she saw it, it would never cease to gross her out.

She hurried to peek into the hallway. It was empty. She dragged the boy outside, and unfurled her wings. Another t-shirt destroyed. They peeled themselves from her back, which in any other situation would have been smooth, a thin, red line the only outward evidence of any non-human anatomy. Sienna's wingspan spread over 20 feet wide. Leathery skin, red like a brick, stretched over four finger bones.

She wrapped her arms around the blistered young man. He was heavy but it wouldn't matter for long. As long as her wings were open, Sienna was a slave to the wind. Her body-to-wing ratio couldn't compete. Keeping a grip on the body was the hard part.

The wind was good, so the journey was short. From the rear, they approached the single floor residence surrounded by a chain link fence that Sienna called home. At least, for now. All the houses on the block faced the same direction so it was safe enough to land in the backyard. She knocked on the kitchen door. Two raps, six and then three. Uncle Sheridan opened the door and groaned, taking the body in one hand and throwing him on the couch.

Then he rounded on her. "What have you done now?"

Sienna pulled her long, dark hair free from a fresh

shirt. "I was just letting off a little steam, and he stumbled into the girl's bathroom." She joined her uncle at a table in their small kitchen.

Uncle Sheridan's eyes narrowed. "Why would you need to blow off steam just then?"

She shifted her weight a little. "It's confusing."

Uncle Sheridan gave her the 'no nonsense' look.

"Okay, look Uncle Sher, my flame was gone. Just like that, it was gone. I panicked. So when it came back, I had to be sure."

Uncle Sheridan looked confused. "It was gone and then it was back. What's that all about?"

"I'm a pixie." In the living room next door, the boy on the couch stood up and looked at them through the hallway. "And I extinguished your flame."

Her mouth fell open and she gawked at the stranger. His skin looked perfect, if a little pink. Words stuck in her throat.

He stepped forward, and extended his hand to shake Uncle Sheridan's. "Hi, my name is Ryan."

Sienna's first instinct was to roast him, but her gut came up empty. She looked to Uncle Sheridan. He seemed to come to the same conclusion. So he punched Ryan in the nose instead.

Sometime later, Ryan sat at the dining table, guzzling a glass of milk. No one had said a word or even moved until he had pulled himself off the floor, holding his face.

Uncle Sheridan couldn't handle the silence any longer. "Pixie?" He cleared his voice to keep it from cracking. "Why exactly are you..." The question hung in the air, unfinished and unanswered.

Ryan tilted his head back to finish off the milk and rubbed his nose one more time. Then he took a deep breath. "Whew! That was a doozy."

Sienna scoffed. As if now was the time to joke.

Uncle Sheridan leaned forward and raised an eyebrow. Sienna knew from experience that Uncle Sheridan could burn more with a glare than the fire breathing.

"I told you I was a pixie. Still am actually." Ryan smiled like he cracked himself up.

Both Uncle Sheridan and Sienna leaned back in their chairs and waited for a better explanation.

"How are you still alive?" Sienna pointed at his arm. Not even the hair was singed.

Ryan shrugged as if giving up the attempt at humor. "Pixies are creatures of life. Creatures of destruction, like dragons"—He gestured around the table. —"cannot lethally wound us. And whenever we're close to you, your fire goes out. It's the law of nature." He made a gesture like he was throwing a ball from one hand to the other. "Life cannot eradicate death, and death cannot beat life. Just the way it is."

Sienna stared at him, speechless. None of that made any sense.

But Uncle Sheridan nodded. "This is dragon territory. You can't be here."

Ryan shrugged. "It's the border of dragon territory. My home and the school I just transferred to, are within pixie territory. Just barely, but still. I never actually crossed the border until about three blocks west."

Uncle Sheridan growled, which failed to move Ryan. "But even if you knew about Sienna, you aren't supposed to reveal yourself, or even approach her."

The boy shifted in his chair for the first time. "I did everything I could to avoid her. I sensed her heat the first time we passed in the hallway." He threw a glance my way. "But I saw Toby pushing her around every morning. I had to say something."

Uncle Sheridan glowered in her direction, but continued talking to Ryan. "Sienna told me the rest. Now the only question is, will you report us to the Mythosium?"

Sienna struggled to keep her mouth shut. Another snitch telling the council of mythological creatures where they were? That was the last thing they needed. She couldn't hold her tongue. "Uncle Sher, what are we going to do now?"

Uncle Sheridan sighed. "Relax, Si. Right now, we need to send Mr. Ryan home so his mother won't worry. But I can't do that until he gives us his word that neither he nor his parents will report our border violation to the Mythosium." Uncle Sheridan stared at Ryan and waited.

The pixie stood and shifted a lock of his brown hair to reveal a leaf, a maple leaf, pressed into his skin. Sienna almost gagged.

Uncle Sheridan seemed pleased. In fact, he stood up and spread his wings. They hunched in the meager space, but were magnificent nonetheless. They spanned an impressive 30 feet and sported same light brown color as Uncle Sheridan's skin, now exposed as his shirt fell away. Despite the last five feet missing, leaving the ends of his wings in an ugly scar, they were still impressive. Ryan eyed them with awe.

The end of Uncle Sheridan's right wing touched the leaf in Ryan's neck.

Ryan placed a hand on Uncle Sheridan's wing and repeated Uncle Sheridan's request. "Neither I or my parents will report the border violation of Sienna Humphrey or her uncle."

Then both of them nodded. The whole thing was very melodramatic.

But it satisfied Uncle Sheridan. "Do you need a ride home?"

Ryan shook his head. "I've got a bus pass. I'll be fine." His chair screeched on the linoleum when he pushed back from the table.

"Sienna, see him to the stop." Uncle Sheridan waved her toward the kitchen door.

Her shoulders slumped. The bus stop was a block away, and this time she couldn't fly. She walked over and held the door open for Ryan. "Come on. I don't have all day."

The afternoon sun warmed the back of her neck as they started down the street. How annoying. She glanced at Ryan. He extinguished her flame. What did that mean? And did he do it on purpose or was it a genetic thing that happened independent of his thought or control?

"You don't have to let Toby push you around like that. Just FYI." Ryan kept pace with her, and managed to give his voice a firm edge, even while panting for breath. "There are other ways to stand up for yourself."

She flapped a hand at him. "It's not worth talking about."

He stopped, forcing her to follow suit, albeit several steps later. "I think you're worth talking about."

Ryan stood there in his baggy jeans that weren't *too* baggy, hair that fell in front of his face just right, and a hand in his back pocket.

Sienna fought the urge to walk over and kick him. "What?"

He looked her in the eye, and never wavered once. "I've been watching you for almost a month. In order to avoid you properly, you understand." He winked at her. "From what I've seen, I think you're pretty amazing."

He took a step closer.

Sienna stared at him for a moment. Was he crazy or just crazy forward? She pointed down the block. "The bus stop is that way. Good luck, buddy." She turned and walked back to the house.

Uncle Sheridan didn't say anything when she entered, but his eyes had glazed over and he'd aged ten years while she was gone. Sienna had ruined their situation again, and they were both tired of moving.

The next morning, Ryan waited for Sienna at her locker, and that annoying icy feeling in her gut returned.

"What are you doing here?"

Ryan didn't say anything but tilted his head behind him. Toby glared at her from the water fountain, but he didn't move to approach her.

She rolled her eyes. "What did you do to that guy yesterday?"

"Not much, that's for sure." He leaned on the locker beside Sienna's, hands in his pockets. "But he's gonna have to give you a rain check on the locker smashing thing, today."

She grabbed her history textbook and slammed the door. "I never asked for your help." She walked away.

Ryan followed. "Listen, I need to talk to you about something."

She sped her pace. History class sounded like a better idea than dawdling in halls until the very last minute.

"Sienna?" Ryan caught her elbow. "I really need to talk to you."

The wrinkle in his forehead convinced her to give him half a second. "What?"

He looked from side to side, which seemed pointless being in a hallway full of people. He put a hand on her shoulder and pushed her against the wall between the lockers and the door to the girl's bathroom. The yellow tape that 'cautioned' them from entering, crinkled when she moved.

She didn't quite fit in the space. "Gracious! I thought Toby was taking the day off."

"I'm sorry. But if I got caught telling you about this, it would be the end of both of us." He leaned in closer. "I have to show you something."

Sienna crossed her arms. "I have class in like two minutes, you know."

Ryan ignored her and pulled a wrinkled piece of paper from his back pocket. "Take a look at this."

Using the tips of her fingers she smoothed out the creases. Uncle Sheridan's face peered up at her from a poster. Beneath the photo in bold letters were instructions for 'making your approach' and 'where to deliver the perpetrator'.

Her breath caught in her throat. "What is this?"

"I did a little research when I got home last night. I couldn't figure out why your uncle would enroll you in a school over the border. This is what I found." He ducked so he could catch her eye. "Your uncle is a wanted man."

"How did you get this?" Sienna's voice squeaked. "Where did you find it?"

"My dad is..." He cleared his throat, and leaned on the wall behind her with an outstretched arm. "Well, he might be a bounty hunter."

Sienna brought up both hands and slammed them into his chest as hard as she could. "And you didn't mention this yesterday? You made an oath!"

"And I intend to keep that oath." He locked his gaze with hers. "I mean that."

She studied him. "Why? Why would you keep us and our... situation, from your father?"

He placed his other hand on the wall near her cheek, boxing her in with both arms. "Am I really that subtle?"

Sienna swallowed. "I hardly think a crush is worth—

" She glanced at the poster in her hand. "—50,000 dollars."

He stepped back and stared at the ground, giving Sienna space to breathe again. He started to shake his head as he pulled something else out of his pocket. Two somethings. "Is it worth two tickets to Homecoming this weekend?"

She laughed out loud. "I can't tell if that was smooth, or the dorkiest thing I've ever heard."

"Why can't it be both?" He grinned, revealing a dimple that formed a pit in her stomach. "And of course, if you go with me, I would continue to have motivation to keep your secret."

She pressed her lips together. "Uh-huh, there it is."

"Why are you going again?" Uncle Sheridan hadn't taken the news well. He sat in the recliner trying to read a book, and failing. "With the bounty hunter's son?"

Sienna walked across the living room throwing pillows off the couch as she went. "Because if I go, he won't tell his dad that you're the missing intelligence expert, hiding your niece from the Mythosium because you didn't want her wings clipped." She gave her Uncle a significant look. "Have you seen my clutch?"

"You know, we could just move. Solve two problems at once." He picked up a purple sequined bag from the table beside him and held it out to her.

"That's more trouble than it's worth yet." She took the bag, and threw it on the coffee table in the center of the room. "And that's a change purse." Going back to her search, she put a hand under one of the cushions.

"You were never supposed to have to pay for this." Uncle Sheridan's voice conveyed sincerity.

Sienna pulled a denim, snap-closed clutch out of the couch. "It's not the worst thing in the world. And I

291

can handle myself with that pixie." She crossed to her Uncle and gave him a hug. "If worse comes to worse, I'll deck him, fly home, and then we can move. Okay?"

He patted her hand, and tried to smile. "Deal."

"How do I look?" She took a step back and twirled. The white halter top dress, and the way her hair twisted at the nape of her neck, left her shoulders bare to the small of her back. The purple irises on the skirt flared as she turned, then answered the call of gravity to drape over her hips and fall just below her knees. She pointed her toes, graceful in her four inch wedges.

If she didn't know better, she'd have thought she saw a tear in Uncle Sheridan's eye. "You look great, Si."

The doorbell rang.

She leaned over and kissed his forehead. "Wait up if you want."

Ryan took her hand as they approached the gymnasium. Sienna fought the urge to take it back.

White and blue streamers decorated the gym. A disco ball hung from the ceiling to cast flickering reflections over everything. Tables lined the walls, leaving the center of the room clear for a crowd of couples dancing to a pop song in the dim light. The back of the room offered a variety of beverages, and hors d'oeuvres.

"Would you like to dance?" Ryan held her hand out in front of them and put his other arm behind his back.

"Not really." She attempted to plant her feet. But with the fire in her belly gone every time she was near Ryan, she found herself without willpower. Like the ice in her veins was so heavy she couldn't fight back.

As they stepped onto the dance floor, the song changed. Soft piano mingled with slow guitar to form a ballad. Without hesitation, he took her waist and pulled her close. A tingling feeling started to climb Sienna's throat.

"Why did you ask me to the dance?" Her hand twitched on his arm.

A question appeared in his eyes. "I'm not sure how much more obvious I can be."

"I know you think you like me." She brushed a stray hair behind her ear. "But what makes you think you want to hang out with me?"

He stepped closer and continued leading her across the floor. "That's a stupid question."

It didn't feel stupid to Sienna. She pried his hand off her waist. "I have a headache. Can you get me something to drink?"

Ryan bit his lip, but she couldn't tell what he was thinking. "Sure."

Sienna watched him walk away. Why did he get on her nerves so much? Comforting heat from within warmed her spine. But when Ryan was close, all bets were off.

Finding an empty table, she sat and tried to forge through her doubts with the searing feeling in her gut. One night was only one night, right?

Her stomach froze. Ryan had come back with the drinks. She turned and looked for him, but she couldn't see him. He had to be close. She twisted in her seat.

A hand closed over her shoulder. "Don't make a fuss. Just walk with me."

A man. Sienna didn't recognize the voice. His hand slid around her neck. A thought occurred to her—not a bad idea to let him lead her away from all the people. So she got up and with careful steps she walked out of the gym, scanning the room for Ryan as she left.

The hand on her neck tightened. "Your boyfriend isn't coming to save you, girlie. Just keep walking."

Cold air chilled her exposed skin in the parking lot.

She hadn't noticed when she'd arrived with Ryan, but now it felt like she was getting frostbite in her knees.

Her accoster twisted her around and pushed her down on the curb. His face came into view as he took up a position on her left. She didn't recognize him and his weird, scruffy beard, and long, ragged hair.

"What do you think you're doing?" Sienna used her most forceful voice.

His chuckled made her skin crawl. "You don't need to know."

Sienna sighed. What a waste of time, sitting here and listening to all this useless posturing. "Where's the pixie?"

The hairy man's lips parted in surprise at her question. "I already told you, your boyfriend isn't coming to help you."

She glared at him. "Let's get one thing straight. He's not my boyfriend. And I was talking about your pixie."

He raised his gaze and spoke to something behind her. "You told me she didn't know."

Another man appeared from behind on her right, and Sienna almost lost her breath. This man was an exact copy of Ryan, only taller, and with a few more wrinkles around the eyes.

Ryan's dad.

Pain shot through her chest. She'd known this was going to happen, somewhere deep inside. So why did it hurt so much to realize that Ryan had sold her out?

"Sienna?" Ryan ran out of the gymnasium doors.

"I'm here." She poured anger into a scowl. If looks could burn, Ryan would have been a pile of ash, pixie or not.

"Dad? What are you doing?" He sounded sincerely surprised.

Of course, he had to be a good actor. He'd kept her on his hook, and all of this was just a part of the show.

She wrapped her arms around herself. The temperature was getting colder.

"Son." Ryan's dad nodded at him. "I'm getting myself a check, that's what I'm doing."

"You can't get anything for Sienna. She isn't the one on the poster." Ryan came closer. Slow and quiet steps brought him to her side. "Sheridan is the one you want." The hairy man put a hand on Ryan's back. "Yes. But with the little one, we can get the older one to do what we say, even without pixies."

Sienna's gut twisted. It was true. Uncle Sheridan would do anything to rescue her. She was the reason he'd been banished in the first place. He gave up his life rather than let her live through that awful operation.

Ryan knelt behind her, and pressed his lips against her ear. "When I give you the signal, open your wings."

Sienna wrenched her neck away. "Don't touch me."

"Now that you've said your goodbyes, son, perhaps you might like to help." The man moved a step closer.

Ryan shrugged, and circled to stand in front of her. He gave her a small smile. "Wait."

Sienna blinked. Was he serious? He wanted her to knock these guys out? But he was...

The hairy man growled at them, his teeth elongating into fangs. Claws sprouted from his fingers. If ever there was a time to trust a guy who confused her as much as Ryan, now would be it.

She stared at him, trying to ignore the men. Forcing herself to trust his judgement. Every fiber of her being told her this was a bad idea, but what choice did she have? She had no fire, no plan, and nowhere to run.

Ryan held her gaze. His eyes were green, the color of summer grass. Why hadn't she noticed before? He reached down and took her hand, his touch warm. "Now."

Sienna closed her eyes and leaned forward to give

her wings room to unfold into their full glory. They crashed into the men, throwing them halfway across the parking lot. With a sickening jolt, the pointed bone at the end of each wing tore through flesh. The bone she wasn't supposed to have.

When she opened her eyes, Sienna found herself falling backward. A tiny breeze got caught in her wings and tossed her over. The tough skin and sparse scales made contact with the concrete sidewalk, as she lay half on the asphalt, and half on the walkway. Ryan appeared and offered a hand. Taking it, she let him haul her to her feet.

His gaze locked on her wings. "They're so beautiful."

Sienna held on to Ryan as they folded back into her shoulder blades. She didn't let go until she was stable. And maybe a little longer than that.

With a nod, she indicated the injured men. "And destructive."

Ryan approached the wolfman. "Dad will be fine. He's a pixie, after all. But this guy..." He felt for a pulse. "This guy might need a medic."

Sienna stood glued to the spot. "So you didn't tell your dad? About us?"

Ryan looked up from where he knelt beside the wounded canine. "No. I didn't. He must have followed me when I picked you up earlier and recognized your uncle." He shrugged. "I guess I've been acting a little suspicious."

Sneaking around with a dragon, and keeping secrets about who he was going to homecoming with could be classified as suspicious. Yes.

She widened her eyes. "What about Uncle Sheridan? They'll be going after him too." She patted her hips and realized she still wore the dress. "I left my phone inside." She started to run, but Ryan caught her arm.

"We can't go back in there. We gotta bolt."

"But what about my uncle?" Sienna threw a glance at the man lying in a puddle on the asphalt, ratting his long, ragged hair. "And that guy. We need help." Ryan grabbed her other elbow and held her still. "Relax, I already called your uncle when I noticed you were missing. I was afraid something like this would happen. You can't exactly burn up the ladies room and not expect the Mythic community to notice." He pulled a cell phone out of his slacks pocket. "I'll call 911, but we gotta go."

He pushed her around the back of the building.

By the time Ryan had finished his phone call, Sienna shivered with a cold that had nothing to do with temperature. He slipped out of his suit jacket and draped it over her. "Are you okay?"

She avoided making eye contact. "I've never been cold before."

"I'm sorry. I wish my nature wasn't at odds with yours. I'm not doing it on purpose." He rubbed his hands over his arms.

She tapped a toe in a small puddle. "You never asked me why Uncle Sheridan and I didn't want my wings clipped."

He sat down on a cinder block beside her. "That's because I already know."

What did he think he knew? She eyed him through narrowed lids.

"You asked me earlier why I wanted to hang out with you. It's because I saw you."

Sienna snorted. "Now is not the time for unending flattery, all right. Just give me the truth."

"That is the truth." He raised his hands in a show of surrender. "I saw you when Toby smashed you against the wall every day." He moved his knee until it touched hers. "I saw you at your most vulnerable, and I felt your fire. You were ready to fight back, but you didn't."

"Yeah, so?"

"So... it taught me something." He put his arm around her shoulder and squeezed. "You are beautiful." He held up a finger before she could protest. "And not just on the outside. For years, you and your uncle have been oppressed because of who you are. Because you're 'dangerous'." He made air quotes with his free hand. "No one should have the power to force you to do anything you want to do. Once upon a time, dragons were a magnificent and free race. My dad just doesn't get it." He smiled at her. "And I would do anything to put a smile on your face."

Sienna nudged him and tried not to smirk.

"Besides." He leaned his forehead against hers and lowered his voice to a whisper. "I kinda like that little claw thing you got going on."

She punched him in the kidney. "Not funny."

His hand slid down her back, causing her heart to beat faster than it ever had before. "Oh, come on, the wolfman's going to be fine, and he deserved a few scars anyway. And you've gotta admit." He brought his face very close to hers. "The wings are kinda cool."

He leaned in and kissed her.

Against her better judgement, Sienna let him. Her back tingled where his fingers pressed into her spine. His breath on her cheek lit a fire in her chest. Her fingers curled around his bicep without her permission.

Then he let go, and she realized she'd closed her eyes, breath bursting in her lungs.

Ryan stood, and held out a hand to help her up. "Come on, your uncle is meeting us at the bus station."

She stood on wobbly knees and struggled to regain control. "What about you? If you go home your dad will skin you alive. And he isn't technically a creature of destruction."

He threaded his fingers through hers. "Yeah, I guess I'm coming with you." He squeezed her hand. "You okay with that?"

She looked him in the eye as she shivered in the cool night wind. Her lips pulled back in a smirk. "Only if I can keep the jacket."

MaKayla Martinez has had a passion for writing since she was six years old. In thirteen years, she's come all the way from bedtime stories for her little sister, to currently working on her fifth novel. MaKayla lives in Northern Utah with her family and two cats who often like to give their two cents.

One of the things I enjoy most in fiction is meeting a likable character who has no idea that her world is about to change. If we were reading a thriller, that would be the moment when we shout, "Don't open that door!" In a romance, it might be when a grocery bag tears, cans go flying, and a handsome guy steps in to help. Anna Zogg's second contribution to our collection is a (pardon the pun) sweet story about a young woman who isn't happy to find herself in need of help. – VS

Sweeter than Strawberry Jam

Anna Zogg

"Nana, would you *please* stop trying to help." Annoyance laced Zoe's voice. "I've got this."

"You can't carry all these yourself." Her grandmother grabbed the bag of bread and crackers. As she trudged up the long flight of stairs, her thin fingers clutched the railing.

Zoe groaned. All morning Nana had insisted on "helping," from the strawberry harvesting at a U-pick farm to the grocery shopping.

So much for my day off.

Squelching frustration, Zoe grabbed the last five sacks out of the car. The soup and mini juice cans weighed a ton. Arms full, she struggled to shut the trunk. Turning, she contemplated the concrete stairs up to the landing and additional steps to the open second floor.

She shifted the heavy load. "I can do this." If she didn't, Nana would totter down again to lend a hand. Every time Zoe watched her frail grandmother negotiate the concrete stairs, her heart leaped into her throat.

The old gripes replayed in her mind. *I wish the agency hadn't given us a second-floor apartment. I wish I'd verified our Oregon housing before signing a four-month contract.*

Halfway up the steps, Zoe paused to watch a couple cars zip away from the apartment complex. Jealousy bit as she imagined where they headed.

Clothes shopping? Early dinner with friends? Maybe a movie.

A vehicle squeezed next to hers. Zoe squinted at the driver.

Please let it not be that guy from across the hall!

Six weeks before, he had moved in and immediately latched onto Nana. Somehow, her grandmother had a knack for attracting his type—the charming kind who liked to take advantage of elderly, vulnerable women. That had happened several times already as Zoe traveled across the country. Her previous scrub-tech assignment had ended with her and Nana moving to a nearby hotel to escape a wannabe moocher.

The driver climbed out of his car.

Great. It was the neighbor—same paint-splattered clothing, unshaven face and tousled black hair. Up close he looked even scruffier than through the blinds of her apartment window.

She whipped around to run up the steps. The bags of canned goods flew in a graceful arc, smacked the metal handrail and ripped apart. "No!" Escapees bounced down the steps.

"Whoa." Her neighbor flung up his hands as a cascade of tin ricocheted on the concrete.

After dumping the remaining groceries on the landing, she ran down. "I'm so sorry." She scooped up the nearest can and shoved it into the crook of her arm.

"Allow me."

To her dismay, he pulled a battered milk crate from his car and loaded wayward cans into it.

"You really don't..." She dropped soup and juice at the bottom of the steps before running for more. Some cans rested by the carport and others rolled back and forth hypnotically on the uneven blacktop. How many more were there? As she gathered them, she spied a small gleaming disk under the carport.

Her neighbor beelined to it at the same time.

"I win." He snatched up the prune juice, eyebrows rising as he read the label. "You must really like this stuff. I've counted at least ten."

Her face flamed. "They're for my grandmother." She juggled the other items and reached for the juice.

"I'll add it to my stash."

"No, really, I—" Something slipped in her arms. Though Zoe scrambled to keep hold, the whole mass broke loose. Cans flew everywhere. Again.

Her blood pressure escalated when he laughed.

It took forever to corral all the groceries. Finally, a pile of dented cans sat at her feet as she and the neighbor stood by her apartment door.

Avoiding eye contact, she noted flecks of paint on his face and grime on his neck. On the inside of one forearm she glimpsed part of a questionable tattoo. "Thanks for the help."

"Happy to." He set the half-filled crate next to her welcome mat.

With her hand on the doorknob, she waited for him to walk away. *I am not going to ask him in.* Nana would most likely invite him to dinner, and then Zoe would never get rid of him.

Several awkward moments dragged by before he backed toward his door, jingling his keys. "By the way, I'm Greg. Nice to finally meet you."

"Mm-hm." Measuring out a half smile, she ducked inside and firmly shut her door.

So what if the groceries sat in the hallway? She'd get them later. *After* he was gone.

I don't mean to be rude, but...

Nana had an agenda, which was to fix up Zoe with every friendly and available man in the vicinity. Clearly Greg was next on her grandmother's radar. But not hers. A certain handsome physician's assistant had filled her radar screen for three months, but she didn't dare confess that to her matchmaker-minded grandmother.

Nope. Not happening.

Zoe awakened early the next morning. Was Nana up yet? All was quiet.

So why am I awake?

They'd been up late the night before, preparing fruit for jam. Strawberry was her favorite. Zoe liked to sit on her balcony with a cup of Irish Breakfast tea and toast smothered with sweet, red preserves, talking to God.

Usually Nana made enough homemade jam for Zoe

303

to hand out as gifts for her coworkers. Despite the clutter and mess, she liked her grandmother to keep busy while she worked at the hospital. That was preferable to Nana napping all day or worse—wandering around the neighborhood, getting lost or being taken advantage of by who-knew-whom.

Snuggling under her blankets, Zoe rolled on her side. At the sound of an engine, she popped upright. Was that Greg? She leaped out of bed and glimpsed his car disappear from the lot. *Perfect.* Now would be the time to leave the emptied milk crate by his door.

After throwing on a plaid robe, she grabbed the container from the foyer. She'd just stepped into the hallway when his door flew open. He stopped and gaped.

"Oh," she squeaked. The heat that flooded her cheeks could start a campfire.

Where was the scruffy guy from yesterday? Showered and shaved, he appeared spotless in gray slacks and a pristine cream shirt. The delightful scent of a wood-tone aftershave tickled her nose.

He looked downright handsome.

"Good morning." He grinned.

She clutched the neck of her robe and forced her voice to cooperate. "I wanted to return this." *Before you knocked on my door and asked for it.* "Before you missed it."

His eyes were dark blue, not brown as she'd first thought. And was that a Celtic cross on the inside of his forearm? Not so questionable after all.

He stepped closer to take the crate. "Appreciate it." However, he didn't put it into his apartment but continued to grin. His gaze, flickering downward, reminded her of what she wore. And what a disaster she must look like.

"I'd better..." She jabbed a thumb in the direction of her living room.

"I'm curious. Do you go to church anywhere?"

"Um, no." Everywhere she had lived, she never found a congregation that pleased both herself and Nana. After several tries, Nana finally announced that she didn't care for church at all. Though Zoe missed the fellowship, she decided to stay home Sunday mornings for her grandmother's sake.

"If you like, you could come to mine. Not today, obviously." His head tilted to one side. "The music might be a bit loud for your grandmother, though."

"She could turn down her hearing aids." Zoe stiffened. *Why'd I say that?*

"Awesome." He set the crate in his apartment before locking the door. "Gotta run. Hope your day is better than yesterday."

Before she could say another word, he bounded down the steps.

She stared after him, the scent of his aftershave lingering in the air.

❧

"Nana, what are we going to do with this much jam?" She counted fifteen half pints. "We've used only half the strawberries." Even if Zoe gave her coworkers two jars each, they'd have plenty leftover. More than she could eat in two years. She would end up hauling them to her next assignment.

"I'm sure we'll think of something, dear." Nana's hazel eyes twinkled in obvious satisfaction as she pushed back fluffy white hair.

Of course, that wasn't her worry. Never was. Zoe was the one who stressed over details.

She stretched backwards, muscles still protesting from the berry picking. "Can we be done for today?"

"Certainly. I'll take care of the rest while you're at work."

After they cleaned up the kitchen, Nana flipped on the TV.

"I'm going to shoot off an email to Mom." In her bedroom, Zoe booted up her computer and typed, "Hey, Mom. Ready for some news?" Her mother always loved to hear the weird things that happened at work, so she described a recent case. Then she relayed some of the frustrations of the day before, knowing Mom didn't mind the complaining. After all, Nana wasn't her mother.

Dad had been an only child. Before his passing, Zoe promised to watch over Nana. While Zoe attended school, she moved into her grandmother's house. Mom couldn't assume the responsibility for her mother-in-law because she was still raising three teens from a second marriage. When Zoe started working with an agency for traveling scrub techs, her grandmother was delighted to tag along. The last four years had been great.

Except for days like yesterday when everything seemed to take ten times longer.

"I love her dearly, Mom," she typed. "But sometimes...well, you know."

She was just signing off when Nana's voice caught her ear. Was she on the phone?

After listening a moment longer, Zoe rose and peeked out her bedroom.

There, at the front door, stood Greg What's-His-Name. He raised a hand in greeting as he continued speaking to Nana.

Great.

A quick glance in the dresser mirror revealed she looked as dreadful as she had earlier that morning. Her wavy brown hair still appeared uncombed, she wore no makeup and a smear of jam marred her white t-shirt. With Greg in her line of sight, she couldn't gracefully slip into the bathroom and repair her looks.

And why would I want to anyway?

He grinned at her as she walked down the hallway. "How's it going?"

"Good." She managed a stiff smile.

"Look, Zoe." Nana held a glossy brochure. "Greg invited us to his church. I'm so excited to go."

She stared at her grandmother. Now wasn't a good time to remind Nana what she'd said about church.

"I'll provide the ride." Greg flashed a grin at them both. "Eight work?"

Before she could say anything, Nana piped up. "Oh, eight would be perfect. We're always up at the crack of dawn."

Zoe resisted rolling her eyes. The "crack of dawn" for Nana usually meant between nine and noon.

"Eight's fine." Her tone sounded barely tolerable, even to her own ears.

"Okay, next Sunday we've got a date." With a nod, Greg left.

She bristled. *Date?* After she closed the door, she bit her lip to keep from berating her grandmother. *Please, oh, please, God, make Nana forget about church by next Sunday.*

"This certainly looks interesting." The older woman fingered the colorful brochure.

"Let me see." Zoe held out her hand.

Pursing her lips, she looked over the information. A community church? That sounded pretty innocuous. However, she hardened her resolve. One visit and she'd excuse herself *and* Nana from going again.

Zoe yawned as she parked the car. Before she headed up to her apartment, she took a few moments to contemplate her conversation with the Director of

Nursing. The offer of a contract extension hadn't come as a surprise, but the other offer did. Profuse in her compliments, the director had mentioned a possibility of hiring Zoe permanently.

Am I ready to settle in one place? She planned to travel for a few more years, then return to Colorado. But in the time she'd been away, Denver no longer felt like home. Though Zoe loved this hospital in Keizer, she always got the itch to move on when her contract drew to a close. Not long ago her agency mentioned a promising position in Montana. With summer approaching, even Alaska might be fun.

Or am I waffling because of Dr. D?

Zoe leaned her head back. Earlier he lingered in the OR while she cleaned up, giving them a chance to talk. Was he finally warming to her?

He was tall, good looking, smart and obviously going somewhere. Okay, he was a bit arrogant and used language she didn't care for, but he could change. Though he technically wasn't an MD, the female staff dubbed him Doctor Dreamier because he was cuter than the TV character. Zoe agreed. He was nothing like...

Abruptly, she straightened. *Why am I comparing him to Greg?*

Greg was, well, shorter. Five eight maybe? Blue-collar worker obviously, since he always arrived home in filthy clothing and drove a beat-up car. Any education beyond high school? Hard to tell. Nana once mentioned that Keizer, Oregon was his hometown. And he was a little older than Zoe. Twenty-eight? Twenty-nine?

I hate to be judgmental, but...

Greg appeared to be floating through life. No goals, no ambitions. His loud friends came and went at all hours during the week. Because they'd been partying?

Definitely not my cup of tea.

Slowly, she got out of the car and headed up the stairs. Keys poised, she heard voices inside her apartment.

Someone was chatting with Nana. Greg again? Though Zoe leaned into the door, she couldn't understand what they were saying. She fought her rising irritation. Why was he there?

When his voice drew closer, she bolted up the next flight of steps. She would not be able to muster one ounce of politeness. Not tonight. And definitely not after her encounter with Doctor Dreamier.

"Thanks again for the jam." Greg's voice floated up to Zoe. "I'm sure everyone will love them."

"You're welcome. Have a good night."

Both apartment doors shut.

Who would love the jam? Zoe gritted her teeth, wondering what her grandmother had promised.

She waited a minute longer before deciding the coast was clear.

"Guess what?" Nana's eyes danced as Zoe entered the apartment. "Greg is going to sell my jam at his church."

She dropped her purse and keys on a pile of envelopes. "Is that legal?"

"It's for a fund raiser. The money will go to Africa."

Whatever. Hiding her irritation, Zoe ducked her head to study the mail. Why was everything Greg suggested automatically a great idea?

"I need to make coverings for the lids. Do you know where my calico material is? Can you get it right away? I have so much to do."

Zoe groaned. More than anything, she wanted to soak in a hot bath, not look for fabric. She hauled that stuff all over because Nana couldn't live without it.

As she tramped into her walk-in closet, her grandmother trotted along. "Greg thinks we can get five dollars apiece. Isn't that wonderful? Greg said they're sure to be a hit. And that they'll probably sell out in minutes."

While Nana sat on the bed and chattered, Zoe dug through several cardboard boxes. By the time she found the material, her closet was in disarray.

Zoe plopped on the carpet. "And when is all this happening?"

"Sunday. Do you think Saturday we can pick strawberries?"

"No." The word came out more sharply than she intended. After taking a deep breath, she softened her voice. "We wouldn't have time to pick more and make jam before Sunday."

"True." Her grandmother didn't seem rebuffed by the harsh tone.

She clenched her jaw. "Nana, do you think it wise to invite strange men into the apartment while I'm away? Remember our agreement?"

"Of course I remember, dear. But Greg isn't a stranger. We've chatted lots. He always carries the trash out for me."

Zoe blinked. "He does?"

"Thursdays, after you leave, I put the bag by the front door. Greg takes it as he heads off to work."

"But—"

"And he's the one who changed the light bulbs above the vanity. Remember the two you couldn't unscrew?"

"I thought maintenance took care of that."

"Greg had it done long before they came."

"Oh." She slumped.

"So you see, dear, he's not a stranger. He's a nice young man. And a good neighbor." With that, Nana rose and left the room.

As Zoe stretched out on the carpeted floor, a long sigh escaped. Now she recalled some pertinent facts from her grandmother's ramblings. The mention of a nice neighbor. The kindness of an unnamed man. All along, Nana had been talking about Greg.

When had Zoe developed the habit of dismissing everything her grandmother said?

What else have I been wrong about, Lord?

༺ஐ༻

"What do you think so far?" Greg leaned across Nana to ask Zoe.

The praise band was so loud that she merely gave the thumbs up. That would have to do because she refused to yell in church—even though this place looked more like a warehouse than a traditional building.

His smile and nodding head told her the answer sufficed.

Crowds packed the place. How many people were there? Two hundred? The décor was nothing to speak of and certainly didn't have the usual hushed church feel. A platform with no lectern, no organ, no piano? Stage center, one lone stool waited for the speaker while the band clustered on both sides. And Nana liked this?

Swaying to the beat, she grinned like a Cheshire cat. Zoe merely mouthed the words to a popular Christian song displayed on two massive screens.

When the service ended, Greg ushered them into the aisle. "We need to clear out before the next service."

"There's another one?"

He grinned. "Yep. Two on Sunday mornings, one at night."

"And this many people come?"

He nodded.

Okay, the sermon had been great. And the music. And the enthusiasm of the congregants, but... Zoe resisted capitulating so easily.

"Hey, Greg, who're your friends?" A pretty blonde

woman stopped them in the foyer.

"My neighbors, Phoebe and Zoe Johnson."

She focused on Nana. "Oh, isn't she the one who had a real bad cold?" She gripped Greg's arm. "About a month ago?"

"As a matter of fact, yes." He glanced down at her hand, then at Zoe. His mouth tightened. Was he embarrassed?

Still hanging on his arm, the woman smiled. "We prayed for you."

"Thank you." Nana beamed. "God answered your prayers."

"Could you give us a second?" The woman stepped closer to speak to Greg. "Group tonight at your place? Then Ryan's on Tuesday and Thursday?"

He nodded, but again threw Zoe a glance.

Group? Were those Greg's loud visitors Zoe so often heard?

As soon as the blonde bid them goodbye, he blew out a breath. As though relieved?

Again, they moved toward the exit, his protective arm keeping Nana from being jostled.

"Before we leave, I need to make one stop." She pointed to a restroom.

Zoe leaned closer. "Want me to go with you?"

Nana waved her off. "I'll be right back."

That left them to find a spot out of the streams of people that flowed both directions through the foyer. Zoe again studied the large banner above the sanctuary doors. *The mission field begins in our own hearts.* What did that mean exactly? She resisted the temptation to ask Greg. Besides, conversation was nearly impossible with all the commotion.

She slouched against a wall. What was that woman's comment all about? And why had Greg talked to other people about Nana?

He leaned toward Zoe. "Everything okay?"

"Yeah. Great." Her head bobbed.

"You seem a bit subdued."

She scrambled for a topic. "Nana apparently liked the service."

"But you didn't?"

"No, I loved it. Really."

"But?" he prodded.

"I'm shocked Nana did. I thought she hated this kind of church."

"She told me you did."

"What?" She straightened. "She..." Zoe stammered to a halt. Nana!

He chuckled, then grew quiet. "I hope you don't mind my asking prayer for Phoeb. I was really worried when she had that bad cold."

Phoeb? Usually Nana reserved that name for her closest friends.

Greg leaned closer. "You probably think I'm a nosy neighbor, but I really care for her."

"Why?" Then Zoe amended her abrupt question. "I mean, it's unusual for—well, a guy your age to worry about an old lady. Especially someone who's not related."

He took his time answering as he scanned the crowds, acknowledging several people who waved. "She reminds me of my grandmother who passed ten months ago. Granddad died not long after. They both went so quickly. For the last several weeks, I've spent all my spare time fixing up their farmhouse. Makes me miss them both."

Before she could respond, his face lit up. "There's Phoeb." He moved toward Nana when she paused outside the restroom. Zoe followed more slowly, sobered by all he'd said.

Clearly she'd misjudged her neighbor.

❦

"Can you believe he stayed at her place all night?" The circulator in the operating room made a face. "Obviously taking advantage of her husband being out of town."

The floater, an RN, tittered.

Only half listening to the gossip, Zoe opened the room for the upcoming surgery. She had no interest in the OR trash talk. Besides, she was there to work, not stand around and gab.

However, her ears pricked up when one woman said under her breath, "Yeah, Doctor Dreamier's making his rounds again."

What? Her stomach soured at the tittle-tattle as the women melted into giggles.

Zoe concentrated on the back table, glad when quiet eventually settled on the room. "Can we do the initial count please?" She needed at least one of them to verify everything before the patient was wheeled in for surgery.

"Sure." The circulator came over, gaze flickering between the instruments and her. "Heard you and Doctor D are getting kind of chummy."

Zoe's head shot up. "We've only chatted a couple of times."

"Uh, huh." She threw a meaningful glance at the RN. "That's how it all starts, ya know. He's used the same technique ever since he hired on."

The nurse added, "You wouldn't know since you're kind of new. But watch out. He's got his eye on you."

Zoe set her jaw. "That's all he'll ever get on me."

"Whatever." Snickering, the RN breezed out of the room.

Zoe continued to ready the room. Could the gossip be true? She shuddered.

I do not want to know.

However, everything made sense now. The flirting between Dr. D and the pediatric nurse. The suggestive remarks. Since the nurse was married, Zoe had thought it innocent.

How naïve of me.

Before the rest of the staff showed up, Doctor D popped in. He smiled in his oh-so-charming way. "Hey there."

"Hello." Zoe cooled her tone.

He glanced around. To make certain they were alone? "What'd you think about catching a bite to eat after work? You off at 3:15?"

"Won't that upset your girlfriend?"

He appeared genuinely puzzled. "What girlfriend?"

When Zoe named the pediatric nurse, his face grew stony. He didn't have a chance to respond because the anesthesiologist arrived.

The dweeb didn't need to explain. His expression said it all.

"Nana. Are you really going to use all these strawberries?" Zoe looked over the mountain of fruit on the kitchen counter.

"Yep. My jam sold out last Sunday. Greg said they wanted more."

If he hadn't talked to Zoe the night before, she would have been irate at the amount of berries he'd purchased, along with sugar, pectin and glass jars.

Nana smiled at the collection. "And tomorrow he said he would help me."

"Doesn't he have to work?"

"He's going to take time off."

"He did, did he?" Zoe tried to muster annoyance, but couldn't. Not since Greg demonstrated his care for

Nana.

And I believe him.

Seeing her grandmother through his eyes made her more appreciative. Yes, Nana was slow. And Zoe had to remind her constantly to take her medication. And she was stubborn. Sometimes sneaky.

But Zoe's heart hurt to think of Nana suddenly gone.

She leaned on the counter while her grandmother sorted the fruit. "Where did you say he works?"

"At the auto repair store. Down the street." Nana's hazel eyes met hers. "He's the manager, you know. His shop got some big customer service award. Three years in a row."

"Mm-hmm." Zoe yawned, pretending disinterest. If she asked too many questions, Nana was sure to tell Greg. "Want me to change so I can help?"

Nana's lips pursed. "You look tired. Long day?"

"Yes." She yawned again. "We had three add-on cases. Seven total. My feet are killing me."

"Thank goodness tomorrow's Friday. You'll have the weekend to rest."

"Not if all this fruit goes unprocessed." But at least they wouldn't have to go berry picking.

"Oh, I'll get it made. This is nothing compared to what I used to do."

Zoe chuckled at her determined tone. "Mind if I go soak in the bath?"

"Not at all, dear."

Ten minutes later she was up to her neck in frothy bubbles, vanilla candles burning. She dozed to the sound of dripping water.

By the time she emerged from the bathroom, she felt refreshed. When she heard voices in the kitchen, she froze. Greg? Here? She tucked damp hair behind one ear.

"I think she's out now." Nana's voice floated down the hallway. "Zoe?"

"Just a sec." She slipped into the bathroom and yanked a comb through her shoulder-length hair, which had gone from wavy to curly. Now she wished she'd chosen to wear something other than pink sweats. In the mirror, her brown eyes looked huge and her cheeks flushed.

She strolled toward the kitchen and stopped as though surprised. "Oh, hi Greg."

"Hey." His smile revealed genuine pleasure. Sleeves rolled up, he paused from hulling strawberries. "You look pretty..." He quickly added, "Um, relaxed."

"Thanks. I feel it."

He cleared his throat. "I was telling Phoeb that I'm about finished with the farmhouse's remodel."

"And I said we should go see it." Mischievousness danced in Nana's grin.

"Maybe." She slid onto a barstool to stay out of their way. The kitchen had barely enough room for two. Three would be tight.

"He mentioned arched doorways and hardwood floors. Reminds me of my old place."

Zoe focused on Greg. "Do you plan to sell it?"

"Nope. I bought it from my grandparents' estate. Sank most of my savings in it. But it's mine now, free and clear."

"Really." His answer surprised her. "You planning to farm?"

"No." He chuckled. "Maybe rent out some of the land. And plant a huge garden."

Nana piped up. "I love to garden."

So do I. Zoe had many fond memories of being elbow deep in dirt, working alongside Pops.

Greg glanced between the two of them. "I'll save you a plot. You can garden to your heart's content."

"Does this mean you'll be moving soon?" Zoe wondered aloud. The twinge of worry surprised her.

But then, my contract's up in a month. Maybe it's better this way. Cut ties now rather than later.

"Yeah." He studied the fruit in his hand. "Couple weeks anyway."

"Hungry, Zoe?" Her grandmother peered at her. "You didn't eat anything after work."

"I'll make a peanut butter sandwich."

Greg grinned as he pointed to the jars she and Nana had processed the weekend before. "You have no shortage of jam if you want that too."

She squeezed through them to grab bread from the cupboard, but couldn't find the peanut butter.

"I used it up," Nana said. "You'll have to get a new jar out of the laundry room."

The tiny space off the kitchen also served as their pantry. Two shelves perched high above the washer. Zoe stood on tiptoes, but her awkward swipes only succeeded in pushing the peanut butter farther out of reach.

"Here, let me." Greg's voice, close by, startled her. The three-inch height difference gave him enough advantage to grab the jar.

Smiling, he held it out to her.

The blue of his eyes is amazing. As well as his smile.

When her fingers contacted his, Zoe's breath caught. Heat flashed across her cheeks.

Looking stunned, Greg seemed frozen. Several moments passed before he released the jar and backed away.

Had he felt it too? Whatever *it* was.

"Thanks," she stammered.

He nodded, only once, before turning back to the strawberries.

Hands shaking, she made a sandwich and returned

to the safety of the barstool without making a fool of herself.

Nana chatted happily, apparently oblivious to the exchange between them.

As Zoe nibbled, her grandmother announced, "Did you know Greg went to China?"

She regarded him. "No. When?"

"A couple years back." He shrugged like it was no big deal. "Six-month mission trip."

"Zoe always wanted to go to China." Nana put more fruit on the cutting board for Greg. "To tell people about God. Or something."

He shot Zoe a smile. "That's awesome. I wouldn't mind going back someday. I fell in love with the people."

"And *I'd* love to stowaway in your suitcase." Nana gathered sliced fruit into a large container. "Think you'd have room for both me and Zoe?"

Nana! She shot her grandmother a hard look, which she quickly wiped out of existence when Greg looked her way.

"Absolutely." His lips pressed together as he ducked his head. Had he seen Zoe's glare?

Nana grinned. "Then it's all arranged."

As they worked, Zoe squelched chuckles several times at how Nana bossed Greg around. When she sternly instructed him about the right way to properly seal jars, he merely nodded as though eating every word. His patience appeared inexhaustible.

In no time, they packed the strawberries in containers in preparation for the jam making on the morrow.

"I have to put in a few hours at the shop, but I'll go in early." Greg glanced between them. "Can I come over at ten?"

"Perfect. Zoe will be at work so she won't be in our way." Nana stood by the door and patted his arm.

"Thanks so much for your help."

"And thank *you*." He nodded at Zoe. "Have a good night."

"You too." At his piercing look, warmth rose to her face.

After Nana shut the door, a grin nearly split her face. Zoe couldn't remember the last time she looked so happy.

"I'm going to hit the sack, Nana." She slid off the stool. "It's past my bedtime."

Yet despite the late hour, she couldn't sleep. *Greg is nothing like I'd imagined.* Every time they were together, he surprised her anew.

Then she recalled that in a month, her initial contract would end and they would move.

Or will we?

"Zoe, I'm here to replace you." A scrub tech entered the OR in the middle of a bowel resection.

She straightened. "What's going on?"

"Your grandmother had an emergency. Someone called."

In moments, Zoe broke scrub and left the room to hunt up the charge nurse. Her heart pounded as though she'd run a mile. "What's going on? What happened?"

"Stay calm." The woman's voice sounded cool and professional. "Your grandmother fell and cut her head. A neighbor is bringing her to the ER. Don't worry about the rest of your shift—it's covered."

"Thanks." Too impatient for the elevator, Zoe flew through the halls and down the stairs.

Nana! Tears stung her eyes. She finally found Greg in a hallway. Face white, he stopped pacing when he saw her.

"They took her back a few minutes ago." He grabbed her arm. "Zoe, I'm so sorry. I should've—"

"It's okay. Let me find out what's going on."

"I'll wait right here."

After a brief search, she located her grandmother in an exam room. Nana lay on a table, eyes closed. A large square of gauze covered her forehead. Though her torso was draped, Zoe glimpsed her blood-splattered shirt. She gulped.

An RN intercepted Zoe and spoke in low tones. "We just numbed her. Giving the local time to work before the doc stitches her up."

"Thanks."

"Her vitals are good, but we've ordered an MRI to rule out a concussion."

Zoe nodded. "Okay."

The nurse hugged her. "Your grandmother's tough. Everything'll be okay."

She's so kind. Everyone has been.

As Zoe approached her grandmother, she noted her hearing aids on a side tray.

"Nana?" Raising her voice, she took her hand. "How are you doing?"

Her grandmother cracked an eye. "Can't complain."

She smiled at the matter-of-fact tone. Then she gulped again. Hard. "What happened?"

"Oh, I spilled water and slipped. I'm still mad about this whole thing."

"Were you knocked out?"

"Nah. But I bled like a stuck pig. The kitchen's a mess."

"Don't worry. I'll clean it up."

Zoe turned when she heard a sound by the door.

"That the doctor?" Nana raised her head.

"Yes."

"I want you to leave. Now."

"But—"

"No buts." Her grandmother's voice grew stern. "Other sick folks is one thing. I know you wouldn't like seeing me getting stitched."

So true.

"I'll be right outside." After she kissed Nana's cheek, she returned to where Greg waited.

He clenched and unclenched his hands. "How is she?"

"She'll be okay." Strange how calm and detached she sounded, like Nana was merely getting a haircut. Zoe sat on the edge of a chair, back ramrod straight while he took a seat beside her.

"I left her for only a few minutes." He shook his head.

"It wasn't your fault." Zoe rested her hand on his. "She's going to be fine."

His mouth tightened. "I can't get over how much blood there was." His glance took in her scrubs. "I suppose that's all in a day's work for you."

"Usually." Her voice caught. "But not when it comes to Nana."

He gently squeezed her shoulder.

The longer they chatted, the more Greg appeared to relax. However, she felt like a spring coiled inside, more and more tightly. What if Nana had been seriously injured? Or worse?

Zoe refused to dwell on that possibility.

"Tell me if you need anything." Zoe caressed her grandmother's arm. "And I mean *anything.*"

"I second that." Greg stood nearby.

For some reason, seeing Nana in her own bed lessened some anxiety. That and the kitchen restored to spotlessness. The hospital staff had sent them home with a beautiful bouquet of flowers, which Zoe placed on the dresser.

They've been so kind to me. And Nana.

"You're making an awful fuss." Her voice grew sleepy. "But it's good to be home."

Zoe straightened the blanket. "I was going to warn the hospital to get handcuffs if they wanted to keep you overnight."

A ghost of a smile passed over her lips. "Fat chance."

"I would have backed Zoe on this." Greg gripped the footboard. "Head wounds can be serious."

"Serious, shmeerious." Nana blinked and sighed.

Zoe turned the light down until it cast a muted glow. "I'm going to stay up. Just in case."

"I'm fine." The large bandage above one eyebrow softened her grandmother's glare. "You need your sleep."

"Not happening." Zoe shook her head.

Greg cleared his throat. "How about I take a part of tonight's watch?"

She pressed her lips together. "No, Nana's my responsibility."

"Why not let me help?"

"It's okay." Zoe held up one hand. "Really."

His jaw tightened, but he said nothing more.

They remained silent as Nana slowly slipped into sleep. Frown etching his forehead, Greg glanced between them. Was he still worried about Nana? Or irritated Zoe wouldn't let him help?

"I'm going to make some tea and toast." She brushed past him.

He followed hard on her heels. "Zoe, wait."

When she didn't stop, he grabbed her arm in the dim hallway.

"Why won't you let me sit up with Phoeb?" He kept his voice low. "I want to help." When she didn't respond, his grip tightened. "I really care for her. You know that. Why does it threaten you?"

"I'm not—I don't..."

The lamp from the living room lit his features. His expression showed only genuine concern. Yes, he did care for Nana.

More than I do, Lord. I'm always so self-centered. So unkind.

One minute she was stunned by her silent confession and the next tears spilled down her cheeks.

I'm a terrible granddaughter. Always impatient, ungrateful, sharp-tongued. When was the last time she told Nana she loved her?

Zoe didn't know how it happened, but she found herself in Greg's arms, crying.

What if Nana had died? Zoe would have felt guilty the rest of her life. Every day she would have beaten herself up with all the things she should have said or done.

The realization made her sob all the harder.

Murmuring soft words, Greg stroked her back. Eventually, her tears subsided into giant gulps of air. Unwilling to leave the comfort of his embrace, she kept her face pressed to his shoulder.

What a kind man he was. At every turn, he demonstrated thoughtfulness. And now, in his gentle hold, she realized she could easily fall in love with him.

Or had that already happened?

Yes. The realization rocked her. *I have fallen in love.*

Her heart thumped harder as she reveled in the strength of his arms and the tenderness of his voice. The dozens of ways she admired him raced through her mind. The longer Greg held her, the more she rested against him. This felt so right. *He* felt so right.

As though aware something had changed in her, his breathing slowed, growing deeper. Shifting his weight, he leaned into her. His head lowered. Inviting.

Zoe turned her face until his breath tickled her cheek.

Very softly, his lips touched hers and lingered. Wanting the kiss to go on, she tilted her head even more.

He suddenly pulled back. "I shouldn't have—wow. That was unforgiveable."

She blinked. "What was?"

"I took advantage while you were crying." Looking away, he ran a hand through his hair. "I'm sorry."

"I'm not." Aghast at her bold confession, she gulped. His eyebrows shot up. "You aren't?"

"No." She gripped the doorframe. "It was really nice." Actually the sweetest kiss she'd ever gotten.

"I thought so too." His mouth tightened. "Before deciding I was a total jerk."

"You're not." She shook her head. "I'm the jerk. Believe me."

Forgive me, God. I've been so wrong. Not just about Greg, but about so much.

A bemused expression crossed his face. "Does this mean I can sit up with Phoeb?"

"If you don't mind my company. We need to talk." She ducked her head. "Greg, I've been so wrong. About so many things."

"I'm willing to listen as long as you like." He took both her hands in his.

Managing a tremulous smile, she gazed up at him. *Forget Montana or Alaska. This is where I need to be.* "I would like that. More than anything."

Except his kisses, which were sweeter than strawberry jam.

Anna Zogg is a romantic who believes in happy endings. (After all, isn't the greatest love story about God's love for humankind?) Author of many articles and two books, she finds herself drawn to love stories again and again. Ms. Zogg and her husband, John (of 35 years) currently live in Utah. www.annazogg.com

From author Kathleen Fuller comes a charming regency romance that hooked me from the first line. I can see the cobbled walkways, the blossoming gardens, the manor house's grand entry hall. Not to mention that sly smile on the hero's face when he steals the kiss that sends us on a delightful journey to a more stately period of time than our own. This story will leave you with a smile on your face, and I can't think of a better way to end this book. – VS

Love's True Kiss

Kathleen Fuller

It was a beautiful summer day when Helena Davies kissed her arch nemesis.

The heavens should be weeping instead, she thought bitterly as her lips parted from Graham Pembleton's sly mouth. She stepped back, her well-worn day slipper nearly catching on one of the courtyard cobblestones. "That, my lord," she said, wiping her mouth with the back of her hand, "was appalling."

His grin grew cheekier, which intensified her foul mood. "You, my lady, were the one waxing rather non-poetically about your lack of kissing experience."

"Those words had nothing to do with my *personal* experience." She lifted her chin, barely able to meet his gaze. Her skin flushed with a heat not caused by the warmth of the day or the layers of garments her mother insisted she wear to protect her pale, delicate skin. "I thought I was alone. I am practicing for a play."

"A play," he said, not looking the least bit convinced.

"Yes."

"And when will you be performing this play? I must make sure to get a front row seat."

Bother. Not only had he caught her voicing a small prayer out loud that she would please, please, *please* at least experience one kiss before she was firmly on the shelf, he knew she was lying. "The date has yet to be firmed."

"I see. Pray tell, what is the name of this play? *A Desperate Woman*, perhaps?"

She chose to ignore his insult. "You shouldn't be sneaking around my garden, catching me unawares."

"My garden," he reminded her. To his credit, some of the mirth slipped from his expression. "Although you are welcome to visit any time you like."

"I'm only here out of courtesy to my mother and yours." She picked up the parasol she'd dropped when he unexpectedly appeared from nowhere and—and rather delightfully—kissed her. *Bother again.* Her lips still tingled from his surprising move.

When she and her mother arrived at Sparrow Hill in response to Lady Pembleton's invitation, Helena had been relieved to find Graham wasn't present. Unable to take the idle chatter between the two older women in the tearoom, she'd escaped to the garden, walking the familiar paths, her heart aching with longing to be back in her country home. When her father decided to sell the property to pay off his debts, she had begged him not to. Her pleadings fell on deaf ears, and now she and her parents lived on a smaller, less quaint estate an hour south.

Why would her mother want to come back here? Didn't she long to live in this home again as much as Helena did? Wasn't she galled that Graham had bought the place only a day after her father announced he was selling it?

No, her mother was actually quite pleased by the purchase. Their families had been friends for years. Helena practically knew Graham from the cradle, and her parents had been relieved that the estate was now in good hands—with Graham ensconced as the head of the household.

She turned from him, unable to meet his eye. It had been over three years since they last saw each other— longer if she'd had her way. He'd left for service in the war, and her mother had informed her that he sustained a serious wound in his arm at the Battle of Waterloo. He must be completely healed from that wound, since his embrace had been both gentle and fierce. She shivered from the recent memory.

Graham's boots made deliberate sounds against the cobblestones as he came round to face her. "I must say, I'm surprised to see you here. I thought Sparrow Hill would be the last place you'd want to be."

"You are correct," she said, with a lift of her chin. "But I cannot refuse my mother. She insisted I come. However, if I'd known you were here I would have feigned a headache." She put her fingertips to her temple. "I believe I have a real one now."

He lifted his upper lip in an unpleasant smirk. "Glad

to see nothing has changed between us."

"It never will."

"Never?" His eyebrow arched.

To her infernal consternation she noticed that despite their acrimonious relationship staying the course, Graham himself had indeed changed. At twenty-five he was broader at the shoulder, the cut of his dark jacket emphasizing the size of his chest and the trimness of his waist. He wore long pants, which had recently come into fashion, but she could imagine that he turned an elegant calf on the dance floor nevertheless. Oh, now her temples were definitely throbbing. Why would she be thinking about Graham's calves, for heaven's sake?

"Never is a long time, my lady."

"Stop calling me that." She scowled. "You may mock my station now, my lord. However, there may come a time when you will defer to me."

His expression lost all humor at that point. "Will that purge you of your bitterness toward me, Helena? Would marrying a viscount, or, daresay, a *duke*, make you feel better about yourself?"

"My *self* is perfectly fine," she said, although his words brought another flush to her face, this time one filled with embarrassment. She didn't have a single suitor, much less a noble one. Graham, upon the death of his father two years ago, had inherited his earldom. Yet another thing to hold over her head, a constant reminder that he was better than her. Even the kiss had been demeaning, despite the brief thrilling moment when she forgot who she was kissing and let the spark that ignited between them flow through her. She shivered again.

"Have you an illness, Miss Helena?" He dropped the teasing moniker of *my lady* he'd given to her when they were eight years old. "You have shivered twice during our conversation."

"I feel a chill, that is all."

"I see. That explains the sheen of perspiration on your brow as we stand underneath a blazing sun." His gray eyes danced. "Perhaps you should go inside and borrow one of Mother's winter overcoats, if the July air is so bitterly cold."

She wanted to stamp her foot and walk away from him, but refused to give into childish behavior. That would only provide him more ammunition. "I would like to be alone, please." She turned her back on him and pretended to be thoroughly interested in a nearby yellow rosebush. She heard him release a heavy sigh behind her.

"Helena," he said, his voice serious. "Will you never forgive me that one indiscretion when we were both mere youths? Will you hold it against me until I am cold in my grave?"

Her fingers stilled on the petal of one of the delicate roses. "Perhaps not as long as that."

"Then only long enough to dance in front of my headstone."

She whirled around. "You really see me as that cold?"

"You, my dear Helena, could make the sun itself freeze over."

His words stopped any further protest. In fact, they cut her deeply. She had been accused over the years, even by her own mother who had tried in vain to match her with one of the very lowest members of the *ton*, of being a frigid fish. What no one knew was that her heart was bruised and battered—specifically by the very man standing before her. She refused to let anyone else rip it to shreds.

"I'm sorry." Graham averted his gaze, his back stiffening as he put his hands behind him. "That was uncalled for."

But she couldn't reply. She turned from him, the sting of tears in her eyes. They had been the best of friends once, he her confidant, as she found most of the women in her circle of acquaintances to not only be without intellectual depth, but also incessant gossips. So when she confided her interest in Pierce, the Duke of Hansberry's very eligible, very handsome, and very desired son, she had told him in the strictest confidence.

Graham had taken that information straight to Pierce, which ended up making her a laughing stock for the better part of the Season.

Because, as she painfully discovered, she was not only unacceptable to Pierce in temperament, she didn't possess a single physical feature to recommend her. She discovered that knowledge the night of the Hansberry's first ball of the Season. Standing near a column, a group of insipid girls had loudly discussed Pierce's assertions within Helena's earshot.

"As if she thought she had a chance with him," Tabitha Kitteridge said, only partially hiding her large mouth behind a bejeweled fan.

Katherine Cotter giggled delicately. "Everyone knows he's keen on beautiful pale skin."

"Helena's looks like a small pox victim," Doris Todhunter added.

"Not to mention," Beatrice Scott said, "Her figure is...less than becoming, shall we say?"

At that point Tabitha must have noticed Helena's presence, because she hushed the rest of the young women. That didn't stop the merriment in their eyes when they glanced her way. Or the fear in Helena's breast when she saw them disperse among the large crowd, whispering to other ladies of the *ton*, each of them casting her a variety of looks designed to take her down a peg at a time until the climb back up to regain her self-esteem seemed impossible.

That nasty business happened when she was eighteen. Since then she had lost a stone, so her figure wasn't as heavy, but was still considered a bit too voluptuous. Her complexion had also sorted itself out, thus her mother's insistence that Helena keep her skin protected at all times. Despite this, she still wasn't a beauty and never would be.

With age did come one benefit, however. She now understood the true underpinnings of all that gossip—every eligible woman had wanted Pierce, and they would slash each other to ribbons to get him. In the end, he never got to choose his wife, as his marriage was arranged by his father to further their family's political fortunes. Pierce's wife was neither petite nor extremely pale, but she was very sweet. Their marriage, from all accounts, was a good one.

While it was all well and fine that Pierce got his happy ending, Helena was still searching for hers. It certainly wouldn't be found with the man who stood behind her, waiting for her to acknowledge his pitiful apology.

"If you'll excuse me." She fled the garden before he saw how, with a mere kiss, he had opened a wound she thought had healed long ago.

If it were possible for the ground to swallow him whole, Graham would have welcomed it. Yet again, he had bumbled things with Helena. Since his return from France he had wanted to see her, but held off, knowing she would refuse his card. Today he had kept himself hidden from sight until he saw her sneak off to the garden, which he knew she would do eventually. She loved it here, and loved Sparrow Hill. That was the chief reason he bought the property—he couldn't imagine her never being able to walk the garden paths or ride in the fields again.

He sat down on a stone bench near a cluster of rose bushes. She was more beautiful than ever, and when he'd overheard her praying about a simple kiss, he couldn't help himself. She wasn't rehearsing a play. She was pouring out her deepest secret, and he had taken advantage of the opportunity. No wonder she was angry with him, and since he couldn't stop himself from mucking everything up whenever he was around her, she probably would always hold him in the lowest esteem.

Graham rubbed his elbow, more out of force of habit than pain. On warm days like this, the war wound didn't bother him. Yet on cold winter nights the joint would ache, reminding him of the agony he experienced when the musket ball had shattered the bone.

However, a much bigger problem than his elbow loomed over him. What was he going to do about Helena? Or rather, how was he to dispel his affection for her? Because it was plain that she felt nothing but contempt for him.

Or did she? His mouth turned up in a small smile as he remembered the kiss, the way her mouth formed a shocked O when he had pressed his lips to hers. And how, for the briefest of moments, she melted into him, returning the kiss in a way he had only experienced in his dreams.

Then she had reverted to her typical form...and he to his, which as usual had her fleeing and him baffled. Why did he waste his time with her? How many profuse apologies for spilling her confidence about her feelings for Pierce must he offer? She refused to let the grudge go. Maybe if she knew why he did it...

He shot up from the bench and began to pace.

Helena worried about being on the shelf, and at nearly twenty-six, she should. But he had worries of his own. Primarily about the state of his own future. He wanted a wife and children. He wanted to settle down at Sparrow Hill, indulge in his interest in horticulture and live a quiet, content life. He'd had enough adventure on the continent to last four lifetimes. During the war he'd met plenty of lovely women, and interest in his own suit had been renewed when he inherited the earldom from his father. Not to be immodest, but he could take his pick of eligible ladies. Why then did his heart insist on being tied to a bull headed, prickly, too-intelligent-for-her-own-good woman who refused to bend to current fashion? She not only enjoyed long rides in the countryside, but wasn't afraid to eat more than a few dainty cucumber sandwiches. His feelings were beyond his understanding and he would give away a goodly portion of his well-stocked coffers to forget about her.

But he couldn't. Her face had been the one foremost in his mind during battle, when the thought of her helped press down his fear. When the pain from his wound became unbearable, her visage calmed the agony. He loved her keen intellect, her devotion to her parents, her passion for the outdoors, her ability to carry on a witty conversation. He loved her, and had for most of his life.

However, his poor judgment and her animosity toward him had ruined everything—and he was at a loss to know how to fix it.

Helena handed her parasol to the Pembleton's butler as she entered through the front door of Sparrow Hill. She barely had her wits in check after her encounter with Graham when she entered the much cooler great hall.

"Shall I bring you some lemonade?" The butler swept her head-to-toe with a gaze. "Your mother and Lady Pembleton are still in the drawing room taking tea.

"That would be lovely, thank you." Helena headed for the drawing room as the butler excused himself. She tried not to think of this as her home, but it was difficult. Lady Pembleton had redecorated it beautifully, but the essence of the house remained. Helena took a deep breath, put both her longing to return to Sparrow Hill and her encounter with Graham out of her mind, and headed for the drawing room.

She stopped when she heard the conversation between her mother and Graham's.

"Honestly, Damara, something must be done." Lady Pembleton's normally composed voice sounded definitely perturbed.

"I fear there may be nothing we can do," Mother replied. "My daughter is far too headstrong for her own good."

Helena bristled at her mother's assessment. Did no one hold her in esteem any more? And why were they discussing her behind her back?

"There's naught to be done with my Graham, either." The clink of china accompanied Lady Pembleton's sigh. "Despite our children's vast intelligence, they are certainly blind to what is in plain sight."

Frowning, Helena leaned closer to the door, which was cracked open. What was in plain sight?

She jumped as a hand gripped her shoulder. Glancing up, her mouth gaped wide as she saw Graham standing behind her. He put his finger over his lips and leaned forward, almost close enough that his chest touched her upper back.

Helena would have promptly set him to rights at that moment if she weren't so blatantly curious to find out what their mothers were discussing.

"Perhaps we should have intervened earlier," Lady Pembleton said. "When they were younger."

"We agreed to let them figure things out, remember?" A pause. "I'll admit I didn't expect your Graham to join the service."

"Neither did I. I begged him not to, but he felt duty bound. I can say that I'm proud of him, however. He is an honorable man."

Helena resisted the urge to look at Graham, who no doubt was basking in the glory of his mother's praise. If she only knew how her son couldn't be trusted with the simplest of secrets.

"That he is," Mother said. "Yet another thing to recommend him."

This time Helena did look at Graham, fully expecting him to be eating her mother's words with a proverbial silver spoon. Instead he looked thoughtful...even a bit humbled by the compliment. A spark kindled inside Helena...an ember she had extinguished the day Graham had betrayed her confidence.

"I have done what I could," her mother continued. "My attempts at setting up Helena with some of the most irritating men in London have been for naught. She not only dismisses them, she refuses to see how perfect Graham is in comparison."

"What?" Helena nearly burst into the room, but Graham's hand clamped over her mouth and held her in place.

"And I expected Graham to seek Helena out when he returned from war," Lady Pembleton added. "Instead, he mopes around the house, mired in melancholy. Those who have tried to pay him visits have been sent away posthaste. I thought when he suggested I invite you and Helena over for tea he would have at least put in an appearance, but I have yet to see him since breakfast."

Helena wriggled out of Graham's grasp and turned around, practically in his arms. He was several inches taller than she, and with their close proximity to the door and each other, her eye line was at the center of his chest. She looked up at him and noted the flush in his cheeks, the confusion in his eyes.

"I guess there's nothing to be done for them," Mother said. "Unless we come right out and meddle."

"We haven't been meddling so far?"

Her mother chuckled. "Oh, I believe we both know that we could meddle much further."

"That's it." Graham moved Helena aside—gently, she noticed—and entered the drawing room. "What the devil is going on here?"

Helena followed, taking in their mothers' shocked expressions.

"Graham, I—" Lady Pembleton said.

"Helena, I—" her mother said.

"You what?" Graham exclaimed, with more anger than Helena had ever seen him display. He was normally so affable, barely becoming ruffled even when sharply provoked. His steadiness was one of his many appealing factors.

"We were just discussing..." Lady Pembleton looked to Helena's mother for help.

Graham scowled. "Discussing what?"

"Oh, there's no use being coy about it." Helena's mother looked directly at Graham. "We were discussing you and Helena."

"We know," he said, sounding like he was chewing on glass.

"You were eavesdropping?" Lady Pembleton looked aghast. "How impertinent of you."

"Don't change the subject, Mother."

Helena watched this exchange, eager to let Graham deal with their mothers, especially since she was still thinking about the conversation they'd overheard. Graham suggested that she and her mother come for tea? Why would he have instigated that? He wasn't here when they arrived. Or was he?

And what about the kiss in the garden? She thought he had done it to mock her, the way he had mocked her feelings for Pierce by telling him. What if...

"Mine and Helena's relationship—not that there is one," he said pointedly, giving Helena an arch look, "is our business only."

"Right," Helena said, returning his arch expression now that he had clarified that they indeed did not have a relationship. Bother, but the man was confusing and irritating.

"We will not be discussed, nor will we be meddled with." Graham folded his arms over his chest. Strong biceps bulged beneath his jacket. *Double bother.*

The mothers exchanged an amused look. "Of course, darling," Lady Pembleton said. "Your intense protestations have been heard."

"You're trifling with us," he muttered, unfolding his arms.

Lady Pembleton rose and elegantly crossed the room to her son. "Neither I nor Damara would ever trifle with either of your feelings." She looked at Helena. "We love both of you very much."

"We just wish..." her mother said, trailing off.

"Wish what?" Helena asked, joining the conversation for the first time.

"For some honesty. That is all."

Lady Pembleton nodded, returned to her seat, picked up her teacup and said, "Lovely summer day, isn't it Damara?"

"Why yes," her mother responded, selecting a small sandwich from the silver tray. "Despite the heat."

"I rather enjoy warm weather." Lady Pembleton

sipped her tea. "Much better than the London chill we get in winter."

"Ah. But we don't feel it as acutely here in the country. Or at least, it seems more bearable for some reason."

"For the love of..." Graham turned on his heel and left the room, not sparing a glance at Helena.

Which left her feeling keenly alone. Their mothers continued the banal weather conversation as if Helena wasn't there and as if they weren't concerned about Graham's abrupt disappearance. Helena had to admit she *was* concerned. She hurried from the drawing room, only to remember when she was outside that she had neglected to give a by your leave as well.

"Graham?" She lifted the skirt of her day dress and rushed to the back of the house. He loved the garden as much as she did. When she found him sitting on a stone bench, his head hanging and his hands clasped loosely between his long legs, her concern intensified. She could handle an acerbic Graham, a teasing Graham, even a loose-lipped Graham, but she couldn't stand to see him distressed.

He didn't look up as she walked toward him and stopped a few steps away from the bench. He must have known she was there, and she waited for him to acknowledge her. When he didn't, she said, "My lord," with the utmost respect.

"Don't." He glanced up at her, his gray eyes devoid of their usual liveliness. "This is not the time for kindness."

"I don't understand."

Shoving his hand through his black hair, he sat up. "Our mothers want honesty, and I was anything but honest a few moment ago."

She frowned. "Graham, what are you on about?"

He rose from the bench. "Helena, I wronged you

years ago, and I'm sorry about that. But when I did, I had..." he swallowed. "I had good intentions."

"How could making me the laughing stock of the Season be a part of any good intention?"

"Because I didn't want Pierce anywhere near you."

Helena's mouth opened, then closed again. Her brow furrowed as she digested this bit of news. "Why?"

"Because I wanted you." He looked at her, his gray eyes darkening to storm clouds. "I thought if I told Pierce that you were an unsuitable prospect, that would clear the way for me."

The words settled over her like a thunderhead. If he thought this revelation would soothe her injury, he was mistaken. She drew herself up. "So you were the one who told him I was fat and ugly?"

"No!" Shock registered on his face and he went to her. "You have never been fat and ugly. Ever! Any disparaging of your appearance never came from me. I don't believe Pierce was the source of that gossip, either."

She bit the inside of her lip, struggling to maintain her temper while butterflies flitted around in her stomach.

"You, Helena Davies, are the most beautiful creature I've ever known." His hand trembled slightly as he touched one of the blonde curls framing her face.

"Even with wide hips and a pockmarked face?" She couldn't keep the words from slipping out, or the tear that ran down her cheek. The harsh words about her appearance uttered many years ago had done so much damage. She turned away from Graham, unable to look at him, not wanting him witness her vanity.

He touched her chin, tilting her face toward him. "All I've ever seen was my lovely Helena." He dropped his hand. "And all I could think about was how I ruined everything between us."

She could barely breathe. The intensity of his gaze, the grief in his tone, along with the fact that he was only inches away left her gasping for air.

"I'm so very, very sorry Helena. I should have never broken your confidence. I should have been honest with you about my feelings. Then perhaps..." He looked away. "Never mind."

Her heart squeezed in her chest. Truths long hidden, even from herself, struggled to surface. "If you are honest with me, then I must be honest with you. I never liked Pierce."

His gaze darted to her. "What?"

"He's pompous, stuffy, and not that handsome." She sighed. "I told you I liked him to make you jealous."

"You did?"

Her cheeks burned. "Yes. And if I had been honest with you, then the insidious gossip never would have happened." She sighed. "I have only myself to blame."

"No." He inched closer to her, until the space between them was minimal. "You trusted me."

"With a lie."

"Nevertheless, it is my fault—"

She pressed a fingertip to his soft lips. The contact sent a delightful ripple coursing up her arm. "Let us agree that we are both at fault, shall we?"

Smiling beneath her touch, he took her hand and clasped it to his heart. "Perhaps now would be a good time to tell the truth?"

Could he hear her heart thrumming in her chest? "I believe it might be."

"Do you care about me, Helena?"

"No," she said.

The hope in his eyes dimmed. "I see."

With more courage than she knew she possessed, she cupped his cheek with her hand. "Honesty, remember? I don't just care for you Graham—I love you."

Joy ignited in his eyes. "And I love you." He smiled and drew her in his arms. "We should try kissing again. Methinks it will be better this time."

As he bent to kiss her, she whispered, "Methinks you're right."

Louisa and Damara smiled at each other, then turned to look out the window again. If their children thought the garden gave them privacy, they were quite wrong. From the vantage point of the drawing room, the two mothers watched Graham and Helena exchange a tender, and rather lengthy, kiss.

"Finally," Louisa said. "I feared they would both be near thirty before they sorted themselves out."

"Agreed," Damara said. "I wonder what finally brought them together."

The women looked at each other and laughed.

Kathleen Fuller is the author of over thirty books, including the best-selling Hearts of Middlefield series. She and her husband James have three children and divide their time between Ohio and Arkansas. Kathleen loves to travel, spend time with her family, and consume ridiculous amounts of caffeine and chocolate on a daily basis. Visit her website at www.kathleenfuller.com.

Do you enjoy fiction with a touch of romance?
Look for these novels by Next Step Books authors.
Visit www.nextstepbooks.org

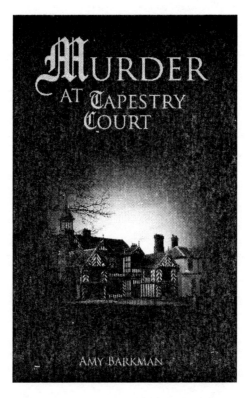

Psychologist Elizabeth Daily flees to the gated community of
Tapestry Court for a sabbatical to untangle parts of her own
life, both professional and romantic. But the shadows of
decades old secrets interwoven with present day mysteries
there are distracting - and may be dangerous. Among the old
world setting and charming neighbors, does a decade old
murderer hide behind a tapestry of lies? And can Elizabeth
discover the truth in time?

Time is on his side - but has hers run out?

During a late-evening run, Lindsey Hayden is nearly killed
along the Oregon coastal highway. She cannot explain the
mysterious doorway that appears in the middle of the road,
or the stranger who steps through the lighted entryway to
save her life.

Alex Northam cannot deny that Lindsey's letters reached
across time and changed him. Though he was sent to rescue
a child, surely saving Lindsey's life won't have an adverse
effect on his mission. Letting her die is not an option. But
Alex soon discovers that the fate of the woman he cares for
becomes the epicenter of his assignment. His selfless—some
say reckless—act may have drastic consequences. Not only
for Lindsey, but for all of humanity.

Belief in the One God is dangerous in the ancient city of
Cainlan. But when the daughter of a pagan priestess meets
the son of a religious fanatic, she is drawn to Shem's caring
manner and deep faith. Eliana believes his assertion that the
One God will wipe the earth clean of the corruption that fills
it, especially when she discovers a terrifying secret known
only to those high in the government's ruling council.

Though desperate to escape her destiny, Eliana's life has
been preordained. Not even Shem's God can rescue her from
the fate for which she was born—to become the next high
priestess to the pagan god Cain.